LAST TO FOLD

LAST TO FOLD

★ DAVID DUFFY ★

THOMAS DUNNE BOOKS
ST. MARTIN'S PRESS
NEW YORK

THOMAS DUNNE BOOKS.
An imprint of St. Martin's Press.

LAST TO FOLD. Copyright © 2011 by David Duffy. All rights reserved. Printed in the United States of America. For information, address St. Martin's Press, 175 Fifth Avenue, New York, N.Y. 10010.

www.thomasdunnebooks.com
www.stmartins.com

Library of Congress Cataloging-in-Publication Data

Duffy, David L.
    Last to fold / David Duffy. — 1st ed.
        p. cm.
    ISBN 978-0-312-62190-2
    1. Espionage, Soviet—Fiction.   2. Spy stories. gsafd   I. Title.
    PS3604.U377L37 2011
    813'.6—dc22

                                        2010042129

First Edition: April 2011

10 9 8 7 6 5 4 3 2 1

For Marcelline,
who makes everything possible

★ CHAPTER 1 ★

The news broke first on Ibansk.com, as it often does these days, the hyperbolic blog having filled the void left by the Kremlin-controlled media for informative, if overheated, news of the New Russia. They say even Putin reads it—secretly, of course. Citizen Ivan Ivanovich Ivanov, the anonymous impresario behind Ibansk, was digging in the Cheka's graveyard again, a favorite spot of his and a dangerous place to be found with a shovel. No one's caught on to Ivanov yet, but plenty of people would happily see him buried. I know because I know a lot of them. As I read his latest post, I had the feeling the list just got longer.

OLIGARCH FOUND?

Has a final chapter been written in one of Ibansk's more sordid tales—that's saying something, no?—the greed-driven life and none-too-early death of one of New Russia's most notorious oligarchs? Or is this the first entry in a new book of mystery and deceit?

Anatoly Kosokov. Even longtime denizens of Ibansk will be scratching their heads, pulling at the cords of memory. Kosokov? Who the hell, pray tell, is Kosokov? Abramovich, Berezovsky, Gusinsky, Khodorkovsky—sure, all well-known names, although two live in

London, one in Tel Aviv, and one in solitary confinement in Siberia. But Kosokov?

Ivanov asks, how soon we forget? Patience. He will explain all.

Kosokov wasn't as flamboyant as his fellow thieves. He didn't buy yachts, estates in England or France, or football clubs. Still, he was just as ruthless and made himself almost as rich—until the end.

An accountant by training, Kosokov worked in the vast *aparat* of the Soviet Finance Ministry. His sister married one of Yeltsin's chief aides. Sounding more familiar? In the early years of transition, he acquired a series of banks and built them into Rosnobank, Russia's third largest. He was worth billions. Then came the financial crisis of 1998, the collapse of the GKOs (an Ibanskian version of a financial guarantee if there ever was one), and the devaluation of the ruble. Fortunes evaporated overnight, including Kosokov's. Or did it?

I remembered Kosokov. A short, coarse, ambitious man, too sure of himself by half. He made a point of telling you how well he knew everyone from Yeltsin on down. Exactly the kind of guy to make a killing in Russia's train-wreck transition to capitalism. He wasn't one of us—us being the Cheka, Lenin's original and still my preferred name for the ChK/GPU/OGPU/KVD/NKVD/MVD/MGB/KGB/SVR/FKB/FSB. Most know it as the KGB, or today's acronym, FSB. The secret police by any label you choose.

Kosokov was always around, acting as if he belonged. I didn't think much about it at the time, but it seemed odd, looking back. The Cheka has always taken care of itself first, and we were under attack from all sides back then, following the failed Gorbachev coup and the collapse of the Party. Kosokov was one who argued loud and long for putting us out of business. Our paths might have become intertwined later on, but I was long gone by then, and he, of course, had disappeared. Or had he?

I went back to Ibansk.com.

Rosnobank didn't fail until a year later, October 1999. Rumors abounded—embezzlement, money laundering, financing ties to Chechen terrorists. The answers went up in smoke—literally, along with the depositors' funds—in a spectacular fire that gutted the headquarters tower in central Moscow. Arson, certainly, but as with so many such investigations in Ibansk, the perpetrators were never found, even though this was without doubt a sophisticated crime involving much preparation and many hands. Nine dead, the life savings of millions—gone. Depositors queued for weeks to find they had nothing left. But this is Ibansk—who gives a damn about them?

The authorities went looking for Kosokov, although just what they planned to do if they found him is still a question. The case foundered, and in due course fell onto the slag heap of forgotten offenses.

Until now. A charred corpse has been unearthed—a decade old!—in an old Soviet shelter beneath the burned-out barn at Kosokov's dacha in the Valdai Hills. And Ivanov is told—sssshhhhh!—in strictest confidence, by sources too well placed not to know, that DNA tests will prove it to be the body of Anatoly Kosokov.

Ivanov will neither waste bandwidth nor insult intelligence by listing the myriad questions this discovery raises. He *will*, however, go looking for answers. Keep your browsers open to Ibansk. Ivanov is on the case!

Even as an ex-Chekist, I don't try to defend the Soviet system. I lived it on all sides, experienced everything it could inflict, for forty years. I still have the scars. I moved to New York to get away from my past and to keep some distance from the cauldron of Wild West capitalism, pseudo-democracy, and Cheka control we now refer to as the New Russia. Ivanov's more direct. He calls it Ibansk, which translates roughly as Fucktown. Making a clean break is never easy, though, especially in this global age, even forty-seven hundred miles and an ocean away.

We have a saying in Russia. If a pig comes to your table, he will put his feet on it. Trouble is, no one tells you how to spot the pig.

★ CHAPTER 2 ★

I found a parking place, legit, on East Eighty-third, just off Fifth. Good till eleven thirty, when the street cleaners come, but I expected to be on my way by then.

I'd driven uptown, Ivanov's florid prose filling my head. He takes great pleasure in it, but it's a far cry from the hard, flat, biting satire of the original Soviet-era creator of Ivanov and Ibansk, Alexander Zinoviev. He was a master wordsmith. Fucktown was his moniker then, when it was even more apt.

My destination was two blocks south, and that's all it took to work up a sweat. We were entering the second week of a mid-June heat wave. The thermometer hadn't seen the seventies in six days. Not the dry heat of Chandler's Santa Anas, the kind that made meek wives thumb carving knives while eying their husbands' necks. This was heavy, soaking New York heat. The air clung to your body like a wet black garbage bag, and everybody on the street looked like he carried a meat-ax. Yesterday topped out at ninety-nine, and Con Ed blew a transformer. Most of Midtown lost power. Office buildings emptied, and bars swelled—the former had lost air-conditioning, but the latter still had ice. The city seemed evenly divided between those fuming at the disruption and those determined to turn calamity into a good time. I had one foot in each camp.

The aftereffects were still being felt this morning, including on the subway, which was one reason I drove uptown. I enjoy heat, most of the time. Where I grew up, there was precious little of it. Even so, like everyone else, I was hoping this would end soon.

The weather wasn't the only thing aggravating New York. A credit crunch, not too different from the one that wiped out Kosokov, was jerking the financial markets around like a sadist with a dog on a leash. The previous week, on Wednesday, the stock market dived three hundred points. On Thursday it lost another two twenty. It tried to rally Friday morning, before the bottom fell out and the Dow lost five percent. Yesterday was a shaky day, but flat, a relief to everyone. Nobody was predicting what would happen next. I keep a little money in the market, but I'm enough of a Marxist not to bet too much on the cornerstone of capitalism. Like Chekhov said, when you live on cash, you understand the limits of the world around you. That's a minority point of view in this town.

I was early, so I crossed the street to get a better look at 998 Fifth Avenue from the plaza in front of the Metropolitan Museum. Twelve stories of Italian Renaissance–style limestone evoked wealth and solidity—a lot of wealth and solidity. The building's exterior was newly cleaned, and the stone shone bright white. Panels of green and gold marble, set into the walls at the eighth and twelfth floors, sparkled. One of the first apartment buildings that was designed to coax New York's wealthy out of their town houses into a uniquely American residential experiment—communal living for millionaires. The facade reminded me, as the stolid prewar co-ops on Fifth and Park often do, of the massive Stalinist apartment blocks that line several of Moscow's main boulevards. They have the same solidity, the same anonymity, the same imposing mass, the same we'll-be-here-long-after-you're-gone attitude. Not that astonishing, given that many were built around the same time. The Moscow buildings, however, were constructed for a completely different kind of communal living, every room jammed with multiple families. No workingmen (other than servants) ever lived at 998 Fifth, and the men who did were unlikely to appreciate the comparison.

I knew from the real estate columns that apartments in buildings like this rarely came on the market, and when they did, the prices ran into tens of millions. A broker I'd dated once told me, with more than a little breathless reverence, you needed three times the purchase price in liquid assets—stocks, bonds, cash—before the co-op boards that ruled these residential fiefs would even think of letting you in the door. The ratio was even higher in "the best" buildings. That relationship didn't last, probably because she figured out I wasn't Avenue material. The man I was going to see, Rory P. Mulholland, had no problem making the cut—or hadn't when he bought the apartment. Today, if the *Wall Street Journal* and the *New York Post* were to be believed, he was feeling the pinch.

I pictured Mulholland as an American Kosokov—plump, arrogant, imperious. The little research I'd done supported that impression. A second-generation Irish immigrant, he'd also made his fortune as a banker, turning a sleepy New England credit union into America's sixth-largest lender, mainly by catering to people with credit ratings others wouldn't touch. FirstTrustBank was the country's most aggressive marketer of credit cards and a major player in the subprime mortgage market. Mulholland preyed on the poor, charging a healthy premium for providing them access to credit the rest of us take for granted. He was the kind of man Marx blamed for the world's problems. Lenin would have had him arrested, Stalin—shot. Now maybe the markets were going to mete out their own brand of punishment. It was becoming more and more clear that Mulholland had borrowed long and lent short, which even an ex-socialist knows is a form of Russian roulette. Wall Street sharks, sensing one of their own wounded in the water, were circling. FTB's stock had almost halved since Wednesday.

I didn't expect to like Mulholland much, I'd already told Bernie that, and I was ninety percent sure I didn't want to work for him. I also had business in Moscow I was eager to attend to, a big breakthrough in a decade-long project. Bernie asked me to meet with him at least, and Bernie and I go way back, to the days when he was on one side and I was on the other. He's also my best source of business. One reason being he has much higher tolerance for self-important men like Mulholland than I do.

I took a deep breath and started to cross the street. I stopped, choking on wet air caught in my throat. Three identical SUVs, windows tinted black, paraded down Fifth Avenue and halted, double-parked at the corner. Police vehicles of some kind. I waited, but no one got out. Probably part of a motorcade, getting ready to form. Plenty of diplomats and dignitaries in this part of town. I continued across and approached the entrance of the building under a heavy iron awning. The door opened before I got there. The limestone lobby was cool and dark, a welcome change from the sidewalk. A uniformed doorman looked me up and down without giving any indication of the impression formed. I said I was there to see Mr. Mulholland. The doorman looked over to another uniformed man behind a desk, who lifted a receiver.

"Who shall I say is here?"

I told him. He punched a button, waited, said, "Mr. Turbo," into the receiver, hung up, and nodded toward the elevator in the back. Yet another man in uniform drove silently to the ninth floor. Expensive place to live at Christmas.

The elevator man pulled back the gate. I stepped out of the walnut cab into a small vestibule. A pair of mahogany double doors opened before I could knock. A man in a dark suit, white shirt, and silver tie gestured that I should enter.

"Wait here, please."

He left me in an entrance hall that would not have been out of place in an English manor house. No windows, a half-dozen doors, and a large curved staircase in one corner ascending to the heavens. Plenty of pictures, all Old Masters, some better than others, biblical themes. I was trying to divine the message an arrow-riddled St. Sebastian conveyed to arriving guests when the man in the silver tie returned.

"This way, please."

He led me to a door at the far end of the hall, knocked once, and stood aside. I went in.

The room was dark and cool, like the lobby. No light from the windows, only lamps. Geography said we were on the side of the building overlooking Central Park, where most people would want to show off the view, but the curtains were drawn. Too bad—sunlight was a short-lived visitor where I come from and never to be shut out entirely, even in a heat wave. Another manor house room, double height, paneled, bookshelves all around, with what looked to be a family crest plastered onto the vaulted ceiling. An outsized marble fireplace took up one end, counterbalanced by an enormous partners' desk at the other. The desktop was clean except for two computer flat-screens. Over the fireplace was a large Virgin Mary holding the Christ Child. Early Italian Renaissance, unless I missed my guess. Mary was lovely, but I've never gotten used to the adult features Renaissance painters give the baby Jesus. A carved balustrade circumnavigated the bookshelves at the second level. The books were leather bound, and some looked as though they'd actually been read, but not, I was willing to wager, by their current owner.

Two men rose from chairs by the fireplace. Bernie Kordlite came across an acre of Oriental carpet, hand outstretched, smiling. He was medium height, five-ten, two inches shorter than I am. In his sixties, he was losing the baldness battle and showing some paunch. He had a round face, wide mouth, and small nose, on which was perched a pair of circular horn-rimmed glasses. He was dressed in a three-button sack suit and striped tie. Bernie is perpetually dressed in a three-button sack suit and striped tie. I've always wanted to ask Barbara, his wife, if that's what he sleeps in.

"Hello, Turbo," Bernie said, grabbing my hand. "Thanks for coming uptown. Let me introduce Rory Mulholland. Rory, this is Turbo Vlost."

Mulholland stood by his chair, waiting for me to come to him. I thought about standing my ground, too, forcing him to take the first step, but I'd come here because Bernie asked me to, and it was pointless to pick a fight, especially a petty one, as soon as I walked through the door. I was tempted though.

"How do you do, Mr. Vlost," Mulholland said.

I took his hand. Fleshy, his grip neither firm nor limp.

"Call me Turbo."

He didn't say, *Call me Rory.* He sat and gave me the once-over, not intently, but as if he were vaguely curious how someone like me came to be in his library. His face was as expressionless as the doorman's downstairs.

Mulholland wore a suit as well, but his was tailored. Double-breasted, dark gray with a heavy white stripe that stated without question Savile Row. His white shirt had a blue *RPM* monogram on the French cuff. Woven blue and gold silk tie that probably cost more than my car. Tied in a Windsor knot. I've never trusted men who use Windsor knots. The entire Brezhnev Politburo wore them, and they were all hard-asses. I shouldn't talk—I haven't worn a tie in years.

Mulholland was shorter than I expected—about five foot eight—

and rounder, too. He looked younger than his sixty-eight years. His dark curly hair was still full—no gray. His face was without wrinkles, his complexion Irish-pale with round red cheeks—an aging Pillsbury Doughboy, except for one thing. He had hard, dark eyes behind round tortoiseshell glasses that tried to soften them but didn't stand a chance. A predator's eyes. I knew them from the Gulag and the Cheka, and I've always made a point of keeping my distance.

I turned to Bernie with a look in my eyes that said, *I want out,* but he either didn't get the message or ignored me. "Sit down, Turbo. Coffee?"

"No, thanks. Had my fill."

"Excuse me a moment," Mulholland said, walking to the desk at the far end. Just after nine thirty, I had a pretty good idea what he was doing. He pushed a couple of keys on his computer. "Market opened down fifty, we're down two. Not an auspicious start to the day." "We" would be FirstTrustBankCorp, of which he owned twelve percent.

I took off my jacket, probably a breach of etiquette, and sat next to Bernie. I was wearing the same thing I always wear, gray linen jacket, black T-shirt, beige linen trousers. In winter, I substitute leather and flannel for the linen and a turtleneck for the T-shirt. Saves a lot of time in the morning, not thinking about what to wear.

Mulholland came back down the long room and reclaimed his seat. He straightened his cuffs, then his tie, looked at Bernie, and turned toward me. He was trying to decide between more small talk and getting down to business. Once he started telling his story, he was vulnerable. By the time he finished, I'd own some piece of him. Men like Mulholland didn't get where they got by exposing themselves. He was instinctively uneasy, trying to delay the inevitable. I waited patiently. Given the mindset I'd brought with me, I was somewhat enjoying the moment.

Bernie, however, was in a hurry, or just uncomfortable with the silence. "Right," he said, "Rory, perhaps you'd like to tell Turbo—"

Mulholland held up a pudgy finger. It showed his age more accurately than his face. "I have a few questions for Mr. Vlost first."

He wanted to run the meeting, maintain control for as long as he could. I turned and tried to look attentive—for Bernie's sake.

"You were in the KGB," he said. A statement, not a question.

I nodded.

"How did you come to choose that career?"

"Beat being a prisoner."

That got a reaction. Usually does.

"I don't understand."

"Limited career choices. Could've been a criminal. Had most of the necessary training, but prison and I didn't agree. KGB looked pretty good by comparison."

"I still don't follow."

I wondered how much Bernie had told him and, not for the first time, how much he knew.

"Law, crime, and punishment were ill-defined concepts in the Soviet Union. The line moved around. A lot of people started out on one side and ended up on the other. I was lucky, I have some skills that were useful."

This was the truth, as far as it went, which wasn't very far. The rest of the story was something I, along with millions of other Russians, don't discuss. Shame is the most insidious of human emotions—worse than death, as another of our proverbs puts it.

"It didn't bother you to enforce the same law that victimized you?"

"Who said I was victimized?"

Bernie said, "Rory, I—"

Mulholland said, "You were a member of the Party." Another statement.

"Had to be."

"You believe all that Marxist-Leninist claptrap?"

"Marx was a pretty good historian but a poor student of human nature. Even in its pure form, before the Bolsheviks got hold of it, Communism is a flawed ideology. People don't want to share. They want to keep everything they can get."

I looked around the paneled room. Mulholland frowned, and Bernie winced.

"Why did the KGB want you?"

"Languages. I speak seven."

"You were well trained. I don't hear any accent."

"*Mes amis français me disent la même chose.* I don't hear any Boston brogue either."

"That would be the nuns. Another kind of police." He smiled at his joke. "What did you do in the KGB?"

"Started out in the Second Chief Directorate, counterintelligence. Spent most of my career in the First Department of the First Chief Directorate. That's the part that spies on you." I gave him a friendly grin to let him know it was nothing personal, which he did not return. "Retired with the rank of colonel. That's about all I can say."

"Can or want to?"

I shook my head. The look on his face said people didn't do that to him very often. The look went away.

"How long have you been here?"

"Since '93."

"Why'd you leave?"

"Everything about Russia was changing. Except the KGB. When Primakov took over, he offered an early retirement program. I took him up on it."

He looked as if I'd finally said something sensible.

"Married?"

"Used to be."

"Divorced?"

I nodded.

"That's unfortunate."

"Not according to my ex-wife."

"That's not what I mean. Marriage is a sacrament. Divorce is something that shouldn't . . . Children?"

"One son. Grown now."

"No thoughts of marrying again?"

"I don't see—"

"Not queer, are you?"

I considered whether that was any of his damned business, which was a waste of time because of course it wasn't. Bernie stopped me before I could say so.

"Rory—"

Mulholland held up the fleshy hand again. "These questions may seem impertinent, Mr. Vlost, but I need to assure myself that I can trust you. The matter that brings you here involves my family, which is the most important thing in my life, after God. Bernie tells me you are smart, honest, and competent. That's all to the good. But you are not an American. In fact, you were a sworn enemy of our country for your entire career. Your divorce indicates a certain lack of faith in one of the institutions that holds our society together. I'm wondering if there are other moral lapses."

Moral lapses. From a guy who practiced legal loan-sharking. I turned to Bernie again, but he'd acquired a powerful interest in the carpet. I swung back to Mulholland, who was watching me intently. Might as well put an end to this now.

"I drink vodka. Beer, too. I play cards, for money. Tried dope, did inhale, didn't like it, went back to vodka. My childhood friends were all what you'd call juvenile delinquents. Some went on to become full-fledged criminals. I chase tail from time to time, female, if that makes a difference to you. I've covered most of the seven deadly sins at one point or another—except maybe greed, but only because guys like you cornered the market. I don't expect to change my ways. Perhaps I'm not your man, Mr. Mulholland. I'd certainly understand if you felt that way." I stood and picked up my jacket.

"Sit down," he barked. The hard, dark eyes got darker. "We're not finished yet."

That surprised me—I would have bet the dacha on being thrown out. I did as he asked, perhaps because my curiosity—an eighth mortal sin, if there ever was one—was kicking in. We sat silently for a good several minutes, which didn't seem to bother Mulholland or me. Bernie bent forward and rubbed his hands between his knees. Eventually Mulholland got up, walked to the desk, announced the market was now down ninety and FTB two and a half, returned to his chair, and said, "Tell me about your company."

"No company, just me. I get paid to find things. Sometimes people. Sometimes valuables. Sometimes information. I work for all kinds of clients—individuals, corporations, insurance companies. Even, when I have to, for lawyers like Bernie."

Nobody laughed at my attempt at levity. I reached into my jacket and found a business card, which I handed across. He looked it over and scowled.

"'Vlost and Found?' What's that—a joke?"

"A lot of Russian humor is based on wordplay."

His expression indicated Russian humor was a waste of time. Dislike was winning the war with curiosity. I'd just about had enough of him.

"Tell me about some of your clients," he said.

"I don't talk about them."

"Surely you have references."

"Bernie here will vouch for me. At least, I think he will."

I looked at Bernie, who clearly was not happy with the way things were going.

"I cannot proceed on this basis," Mulholland said.

"Fine by me." I picked up my jacket again.

"Wait," Bernie said. "Rory, be reasonable. You wouldn't want Turbo to talk about you. He's done work for a number of clients of the firm. They all speak highly. No one has ever complained."

I suspected few people got away with telling Rory Mulholland to "be reasonable," but there were plenty of reasons Bernie had a successful second career as one of the top lawyers in New York, not least among them was he knew how to play his clients.

Mulholland made a show of thinking it over. The whole morning so far had been for show—I wouldn't have been there if he hadn't already decided to talk about his problem—but the playacting had gone on long enough.

"Please sit, Mr. Vlost," Mulholland said. "Tell me this. Turbo doesn't sound Russian—is it really your given name?"

"Some of it," I said. Mulholland waited for me to continue, but I'd said all I planned to. I saw irritation in his eyes and exasperation in Bernie's—with me this time. I got ready again to leave.

"All right, Mr. Vlost, have it your way," Mulholland said. "I take it that what we discuss here will remain between us."

"That's right." I still didn't like him. I was now ninety-eight percent sure I didn't want to work for him, but he'd still get the same deal I gave everybody.

He made one more show of thinking it over, rose and walked to the desk again. "Dow's down two fifty. We're off four. Screen's solid red." He reached in a drawer and returned holding a photograph and a piece of paper. He handed both to me.

"Our daughter. Eva."

The photo showed a blue-eyed, auburn-haired young woman. A crude snapshot, printed on a home printer, but her beauty was hard to obscure. She was seated on a chair, against a dark brown wall, chest forward, hands behind her back, as if tied there. A *New York Times* covered her lap. The front page was from a few days before. She stared straight at the camera. A man's hand held a gun to the girl's left temple. Glock 9 mm. She didn't look scared or worried or in pain, but there's always a surreal quality to hostage photos that makes them hard to judge. The picture did capture a funny look in her eyes that took me a minute to place. The look kids in the orphanage got, the orphanage I spent my childhood in, on the rare day when another child's parents miraculously appeared. A look of longing mixed with hopelessness. A look that said, *Why can't that be me?* and knew it never would. Not a look you'd expect on a beautiful young woman, daughter of Rory Mulholland, even if she did have a gun to her head.

The note read,

DAUGHTER VERY PRETTY. I VERY HORNY. FRIENDS TOO. WE ALL FUCK HER SOON.
$100,000. USED MONEY—$10 AND $20. WE CALL, BE READY.
NO POLICE. NO TRICKS.
OR WE ALL FUCK HER, THEN KILL HER.
ASSHOLE.

The "asshole" didn't ring right somehow, but I often have thoughts like that. I ignored this one.

"When did you get this?" I asked.

"Yesterday."

"You haven't heard from them since?"

"No."

"You will soon. They won't give you much time to think about options. When was the last time you saw your daughter?"

"I . . . I'm not sure. A few weeks ago. She has her own apartment."

"How old?"

"Nineteen."

"Student?"

"Marymount Manhattan. She's in their theater program."

The way he said "theater program" indicated he thought it a waste of time and money. He was fidgeting now.

"Any idea why they'd pick on her—or you?"

"None. Eva . . . she's my wife's daughter, from her first marriage. Her husband died." He had to add that, I suppose, to protect his moral purity. "I adopted her, and . . . I feel about her as if she were my own."

That sounded sincere, as much as I didn't like to admit it. I didn't doubt his concern—Even so, nothing about this felt right. "What exactly do you want me to do?"

"I thought that was obvious. Find the kidnappers. Bring Eva home. How do you work? Hourly like Bernie? Lower rate, I hope." He laughed at his second attempt at a joke.

I shook my head. "I charge a percentage—thirty-three percent of what I recover. Plus expenses." Bernie winced. He knew "plus expenses" meant I didn't want the job.

The financier came to the fore. "Thirty-three percent—that's aggressive."

"Same as a headhunter."

"But how . . . In a case like this . . . How do you put a value on . . . Eva?"

"I don't. You do."

He looked at me squarely for the first time since we'd started talking. I had a mental image of an old-fashioned adding machine in his brain, the kind with rows of buttons and a big arm on the side, toting up sums, calculating how much he could get away with.

"They want a hundred thousand," he said after a while.

"They're testing the waters."

He nodded, as though he hadn't expected that gambit to work. "I like round numbers. Let's say a million."

"If she was my daughter, I'd say two."

He was halfway out of his chair, sputtering. "That's six hundred sixty—"

"Plus expenses."

"That's . . ." He searched for the word he wanted as he eased back into his chair. "Usurious."

I shrugged. Bernie looked pained. "The eighteen percent your bank charges on credit card debt is usurious—especially when the money costs you three—but people pay it."

"That's completely different. That's . . ."

"The market economy?"

He was scowling again. Bernie was pretending to look out the window—through the drawn curtains.

"I may have been raised on Marxist-Leninist claptrap, as you call it, but I understand the market economy as well as the next guy, including the law of supply and demand. There's only one of me. I don't have partners or associates or employees. What you see is what you get, but that by definition limits the supply. I also have one-of-a-kind technology that's not cheap. On the other hand, people lose things all the time. You're the first one today. Could be a half-dozen more by sundown. I choose the cases I take on. Usually because they interest me or they pay well."

"I gather I'm in the second category," he said.

"You're not in either category yet."

A new look came over Mulholland's face, one that said I'd finally hit home. "All right, Mr. Vlost, have it your way. Good day."

He stood and walked to his desk. He had the same look on his face when I left, but I didn't know if it was for me or the sea of red on his computer screen.

★ CHAPTER 3 ★

Bernie caught up as I was waiting for the elevator, his round face several shades of red and purple.

"God damn it, Turbo, what the hell's got into you?"

"I told you I didn't want to work for him."

"You did a hell of a job telling him, too."

"He doesn't want to pay the freight."

"Can you blame him? Six hundred sixty-six thousand dollars?"

"Plus expenses."

"Yes, I know. Plus the goddamned expenses."

"I don't work cheap."

"Unless you choose to."

I'd done a job once for a friend of Bernie's wife, an artist with a small trust fund whose husband had taken her money and decamped to Las Vegas. I found him before he lost it all, but there wasn't much left, and it was pretty clear that was what she'd have to live on. I refused payment. She gave me a painting that I like a lot. It hangs in my office. Barbara Kordlite never misses an opportunity to remind her husband what a great guy I am. One reason he puts up with me.

"I'm not working cheap for a man like Mulholland."

The elevator door slid open. Bernie put out a hand. "Sorry, we're not leaving just yet." The door closed again.

"Look, Turbo, Rory's a proud man, like you. You ought to recognize that. Stubborn, too, just like you. Yes, he's got people around him all day telling him how brilliant he is, a problem you don't have, but that goes along with being the kind of guy he is. Cut him some slack. His bank's on the ropes. His daughter's been kidnapped. He's worried. Since he's the largest client of Hayes & Franklin, when he has worries, I get ulcers. And you, my friend, are supposed to be the solution to his problem and the tonic for my gut, but you have to decide you're not going to like the guy and then you have to prove to yourself that he really is an asshole so you can tell yourself how you were right all along. You're the one who's acting like a stubborn ass."

I laughed. That's the thing I love about Bernie. He gets right to the heart of the matter, and he isn't afraid to tell you exactly what he thinks.

"Stubborn Russian asses turned the course of the Great Patriotic War."

"So you've told me—a dozen times. It's still World War II to me, and D-day the turning point. Come on, Turbo. If I can fix it with Rory, will you at least finish hearing him out?"

I made a small show of thinking it over. Moscow was tugging hard, but those ghosts could wait another few days. I wasn't going to turn Bernie down. "Okay."

"Good. Be right back."

I waited in the small vestibule, half hoping Mulholland proved as stubborn as Bernie said he was and half wondering what about the man made me dislike him. The sanctimonious questioning made it easy to find him objectionable. Half a lifetime under Soviet rule led me to distrust anyone who takes overt pride in his or her beliefs, be they religious, political, or whatever. Then there were those eyes. I was thinking about them and getting ready to call the elevator again when Bernie returned, smiling.

"All set," he said, leading the way back inside. "Watch your step, though. I think he kind of likes you."

Mulholland came across the carpet this time, hand extended. I took it, and we all went back to the same chairs we were sitting in before.

"This may sound like impertinence," he said. "I don't mean it that way. Your son—how do you get on with him?"

That wasn't any of his damned business, but I sensed he was either sincerely curious or looking for some common ground between us. Anyway, I was on my good behavior now.

"I haven't seen him since he was two."

I expected a look of exasperation, even hostility, but I swear the black eyes softened, then dampened, in sympathy, perhaps even sorrow. Maybe Bernie was right and I was being stubborn.

"My fault entirely," I said quickly. "I made mistakes. I won't bore you with the details. A lot of them don't make much sense anymore. A day doesn't go by when I don't think about the things that happened and what I could've—should've—done differently."

I definitely saw black kindness now. I looked for sincerity behind it. That's the toughest thing to fake. To my surprise, that was there, too. Another point for Bernie.

Mulholland sensed my investigation and misread it. "I'm sorry," he said quickly. "I didn't mean to pry. We all make mistakes, I . . . Being a good parent is . . ."

I waited for him to finish one sentence or the other, but he stared off into the dark room, lost in his own thoughts. I kept thinking about that look and why I'd told him as much as I had. Maybe underneath it all, I liked him, too?

After a moment, Bernie cleared his throat, and Mulholland seemed to return to the present. The black eyes regained their hardness.

"I apologize for my earlier outburst, Mr. Vlost. This has been a difficult day—one of many. Of course your fee is not an issue. I must ask, however, that you keep this matter entirely between us. I believe what the kidnappers say—about the police. No one must know, including my wife. She's been under tremendous strain, for which I feel responsible. My business problems. She and Eva had a huge fight the last time Eva was here, which is why we haven't seen her. I'm very afraid Felix will think she's to blame for what's happened."

"Felix?"

"Her given name's Felicity. She won't use it."

"What did they fight over?"

"It's not important. Felix and Eva . . . they have a complicated relationship, like many mothers and daughters, I suppose. Theirs has a tendency to erupt from time to time."

"You're sure it has no bearing? It's possible Eva could—"

He cut me off. "I know what you're going to say, and I don't believe it. She may have her issues, but she's not that kind of girl."

I tried to remember when the word "issue" replaced "problem" in the American branch of the English language. As if nomenclature could make either go away. Not enough Americans read Orwell. I let it go—I could find out plenty about whatever problems Eva had in due course and make my own assessment as to what kind of girl she was.

"You need anything else from me?" Mulholland said.

"I'll need to borrow the picture."

"I don't see—"

"I'm only interested in where and when it was taken. I'll make no copies, and I'll return it as soon as I'm finished."

"I'm going to assume you're a man of your word."

Mulholland had a way of ending every sentence with a grimace as if he expected you to take issue with what he'd just said. He didn't make it easy to get along.

A knock on the door made us all turn. The man in the silver tie entered and crossed the big carpet, looking left and right and wringing his hands. He whispered a few words in his employer's ear and hurried back the way he'd come. Black turned to midnight as Mulholland swung toward Bernie.

"You said we had a deal with her."

"Victoria? We did. We do."

"Not anymore. The FBI is on its way up."

"That can't be. I—"

Mulholland started issuing orders, the anger in his voice replaced by cool efficiency. Bernie nodded, making a mental list, as he searched his pockets until he found his cell phone. A plan was being put into motion.

"Get hold of Coughlin and O'Neal at the office," Mulholland said. "They'll know what to do."

Bernie was punching a number into the phone. "We'll have to put out an announcement. No question this is a disclosable event."

"I know. We have a crisis plan. Supposed to be for the plane going down or something like that, but it'll serve the purpose."

"I'll get Alan and his team downtown ASAP," Bernie said. "You won't be there any longer than necessary."

Another knock. We all stood as the door opened and six men in suits came in, all looking this way and that before their eyes settled on the three of us.

"Rory Mulholland?" the largest of the men in suits said.

"That's right."

"You're under arrest. Come with us, please. Taylor, read him his rights."

I'd heard Mulholland say "FBI," but it hadn't registered he meant *that* FBI. The idea of him being hauled away in handcuffs was too incongruous. These men clearly belonged to the SUVs downstairs, though, and they were here on official business. I looked at my watch. Almost ten thirty. What had they been waiting for? The Cheka would have hauled Mulholland out of bed in the middle of the night, locked him in Lubyanka or Lefortovo, and not let him sleep again until he confessed to whatever crime they were convinced he had committed. But this was America. Perhaps the Justice Department had its rules of etiquette. *Bankers should not be busted prior to ten o'clock in the morning.*

Taylor took a pair of handcuffs from his pocket. Mulholland crossed the big carpet at his own pace, head high. I had to give him credit. He probably never in his life expected to be arrested, certainly not in his own home, and he was doing his damnedest to carry it off dignity intact. I had an unkind thought about how long he'd maintain the decorum once he got fingerprinted, mug-shotted, and stripped, then reminded myself that his impending humiliation was something millions of innocents had been put through—and worse. It was nothing to gloat over.

Mulholland stopped at the desk to check the computer screen. He might have slumped a little then but recovered quickly. Bernie's phone buzzed as the FBI men led Mulholland outside. He looked at the screen and grunted. The gears of his brain upshifted a speed as he opened the phone. Bernie doesn't get angry often. This morning, he was seriously pissed off.

"Goddammit, Victoria, what the hell is going on? . . . You can skip the goddamned pleasantries . . . I can see that, I'm right here with him. I thought we had a deal . . . What do you mean, changed? What the hell changed?"

He listened for a few minutes, almost breaking in a few times, but thinking better of it. Finally he said, "Victoria, if you weren't my former partner, I'd tell you exactly what I think of you. As it is, I'll just say you're full of shit, and we'll prove it—to your embarrassment."

He listened again. Then, "Okay, do me a favor, huh? Take him in the back, skip the perp walk. He doesn't deserve . . . Oh, come on, Victoria, you can make . . . What happened to innocent before proven . . . Goddammit!"

He jammed the cell phone into his pocket, muttered, "Bitch," and followed his client out the door.

I hesitated. I'm no stranger to sudden arrests—no Russian of my generation is. Still, I was now an unwanted observer—no one had invited me to watch this. The last time I'd been witness to the authorities arriving unannounced, I'd been on the other side. I was the instigator then, but fate plays nasty tricks, and what I ended up instigating was the unraveling of my career, my marriage, and my family. I thought I'd locked that memory away, in the cell of unwanted reminiscences, but Mulholland and the FBI had set it loose. I had the unpleasant feeling fate was about to intervene again. If I'd had the slightest premonition of how, I'd have stayed right there and barred the door.

Out in the entrance hall, Mulholland stood surrounded by the men in suits. Bernie pushed his way through.

"Victoria says something changed, won't say what. I tried to get her to forgo the perp walk, but—"

"I understand," Mulholland said. "We'll beat this thing. They've got nothing because there's nothing to have. This is just a feeble attempt at intimidation."

"I'll call Tom and Walter," Bernie said.

"Let's go," one of the suits said.

Having waited as long as they'd waited, the Feds now seemed in quite a hurry to drag Mulholland downtown. They were working to some kind of schedule. Had someone tipped off a local TV news crew or two to be ready outside Police Plaza at eleven o'clock or thereabouts? Bernie thought so, and he'd said as much on the phone. No question Mulholland in his Savile Row suit, tie, and handcuffs, being led inside for booking, would make a good clip for the evening news.

Survivors learn early in the camps never to let anything occupy their full attention. Trouble was all around, and it could come from any direction, take any form—a malevolent guard, another prisoner with a grudge, a new arrival who coveted the patch of straw on the floor you slept on, a lifelong jailbird who coveted you. Staying alert was one way to stay alive. You developed a sixth sense. Mine was sending signals before I heard her voice—but the FBI suits and Mulholland blocked the door. Nowhere to run.

The voice came from above, halfway up the curved staircase. Its steely sharp edge sliced down my spine. I never expected to hear it again. I certainly never expected to hear it here. I'd spent a decade and a half building a new life. It had its faults, but it was mine by design, and I was largely content with it. It took only an instant for her to cut it to shreds.

"Rory? What's going on? Who are these men? Rory! Are those handcuffs?"

★ CHAPTER 4 ★

They teach you in spy school how to keep control, never show emotion, especially surprise, regardless of circumstance. I'd actually learned that lesson years before, playing cards with the *urki* scum in the Gulag, where losing the game could mean losing a pound of flesh—literally, of the winner's choosing. I don't think anyone saw the double, triple, or quadruple take I did as she came down the curved stairs. My head didn't move. At least I don't believe it did. Just my eyes—and my brain, which started vibrating as if plugged into an electric socket.

Mulholland took a step in her direction, but two suited arms held him back. Bernie hurried across the hall instead.

"Don't worry, Felix. Everything'll be fine. There's been . . . There's been a misunderstanding. It's all going to be worked out."

"Misunderstanding? I'm not a fool, Bernie, don't treat me like one. These men are police, aren't they?"

Bernie nodded as she brushed past until she was a few feet from the group of suits. She moved with purpose. She hadn't seen me yet. I was out of her field of vision, standing by the library door.

"I'd like to see some identification, please," she said.

The big man took a wallet with an ID card from his breast pocket and held it in front of her face.

"What's the charge against my husband?"

"Mail fraud, wire fraud, securities fraud, obstruction, lying to federal officers in pursuit of an investigation. And money laundering. So far."

I could have been imagining things, but her face changed at the words "money laundering." Something—surprise? fear?—passed through, and she all but stepped back as if shoved. Whatever it was vanished as quickly as it appeared.

"Where are you taking him?" she said.

"Downtown. Foley Square."

"What about bail?"

"Not my department, ma'am. You'll have to talk to the judge."

"Rory . . ."

He took her hands in his. She wore two rings—a gold wedding band and a rock the size of an onion dome. "Don't worry. It'll be okay, like Bernie says. I'll be home for dinner."

"But . . ."

"Bernie's already got lawyers on the way. They'll take care of everything."

"Let's go, Mulholland," the FBI man said. "People are waiting to talk to you."

Mulholland nodded and let go of his wife's hands. She stood aside.

The FBI man took a long look around the manor hall room. "Nice shack," he said as he pushed Mulholland toward the elevator.

I stayed in my spot, waiting for the inevitable, thinking I'd gladly change places with Mulholland if it got me out of here. She turned toward the library and froze when her eyes got around to me. Twenty-plus years hadn't changed her at all.

It's a little-known fact, because it's such a little-known country, but Lithuania produces way more than its share of the world's most beautiful women. Polina was Exhibit A, maybe even more beautiful because she was a Russian-Lithuanian mix. Tall, blond, and slender in a pale violet sleeveless dress, tucked at the waist, that set off her eyes, which were deep indigo. Red lips that didn't need the gloss she'd applied. Hair, cut to look like it hadn't been touched, fell well below her shoulders. They were square, her back straight, and her legs ended up near her neck. White skin, the hue and texture of a marble sculpture, with the features to match, like the sculptures of goddesses in the museum across Fifth Avenue. In another time or place she might have been named Hera, Aphrodite, or Athena and tormented the souls of ancient man. I'd experienced the torment firsthand. I knew for a fact she was twenty years younger than her husband.

Her stare intensified as she made sure she was seeing what her eyes told her she was seeing. I had to hand it to her as well—two life-changing shocks in as many minutes, and she barely blinked.

"Hello, Polya," I said.

"What the fuck do you want here, you loathsome shit?" she said in Russian. One question answered—the years hadn't softened her temper or tempered her language. The wounds of the Great Disintegration, as I've come to think of it, still festered.

"I'll let Bernie explain," I said in English. "You might believe him." I switched to Russian. "I'll tell you this much—had I known you were here, I wouldn't have come. You can bet whatever happiness we had on that."

She stayed with Russian. "There was no happiness, you prick, just a long string of lies. You're lying now. Get out! Get away from me!"

The strain was beginning to show. I went back to English. "You both have a lot to do. I'll be on my way."

I crossed the hall and called the elevator. I could feel her eyes burning into my back. Bernie swung back and forth between the two of us, one of the few times I'd seen him unsure of how to proceed. I felt bad about leaving him to explain, but he got paid a lot of money to deal with difficult situations. I turned around in the elevator as the door closed. She was still glowering. If she'd had anything in her hands, she would have thrown it.

The uniformed driver didn't say a word as he took me to the lobby.

Outside, it was easily over ninety. Waves of heat rose from the asphalt, shimmering in the sunlight. A mime worked the thin crowd on the museum's steps, but he was hot, too, and his heart wasn't in it. I had time before I needed to move my car, so I took off my jacket and walked into Central Park. The flowering trees were over for the season, but everything was in full leaf, which made it feel a little cooler. Mulholland paid a fortune to live across the street from one of New York's great treasures, yet he closed himself off from its beauty. He'd never spent a winter in northern Siberia, where cold and dark stretch on so long you wonder if the sun will ever rise again.

I sat on the wall behind the museum and stretched my arms and legs while I watched a few masochistic joggers on Park Drive and contemplated fate and irony. Russians have a great appreciation for the latter, one reason we haven't given up entirely on the former, with everything our history has served up. I would've paid a good part of Mulholland's fee to know what the woman calling herself Felix Mulholland was telling Bernie, perhaps this very minute, and what Bernie was telling her—especially if he was respecting his client's restriction. I'd have given more to know what she was doing here in New York, other than apparently being married to Mulholland, but I didn't have to pay for that. I could get a pretty good idea by the time I returned to the office.

The more immediate question was whether I'd go forward with the assignment, if I was allowed to. Try as I might, I felt only a little sympathy for Mulholland. He was a loan shark and a bully. But how much of that assessment was now tinged by . . . by what—jealousy? That wasn't right. Not after everything that happened, not after all these years. What then? Envy? No—I'd done my time. Polina wasn't wholly responsible for the Disintegration—I played my part, too—but I wouldn't want to go through that again. Maybe just good old suspicion. Was I being set up? If so, why? By whom? And to what end, after all these years? Polina and I had twisted pasts—jointly and each on his or her own. We weren't the only people tied up in them. She could be an instrument of someone else as easily as she could be acting on her own. There were plenty of scenarios. I couldn't see one that made sense, but that didn't mean it wasn't there.

First step—more information. I took out my cell phone and punched in a number. A machine answered with no message, just the electronic beep. "You won't like this, but I can explain. Wake up the Basilisk. Mulholland, yes, that Mulholland, Rory P., and his wife, Felicity, known as Felix, although that's not her real name, and their daughter, Eva. Also a woman named Polina Barsukova. You'll be pleased to hear the man himself is on his way to the Tombs as I speak. Back in an hour."

A pretty girl smiled at me as she ran by. Her tanned torso was shiny-wet and her athletic bra soaked with sweat, but she breathed easily and kept up a quick pace. Women fall into two camps, pretty evenly divided, on the subject of men with shaved heads like mine. Yea or nay—no one is ambivalent. My hair, which was once bushy and black, started to fall out when I was in my late twenties, probably the result of malnourishment when I was young. That's what I blame any malady on—a time when I was powerless to control my life, which I go to extremes to do now. Rather than watch the thatch thin and recede, I shaved my scalp. I have no idea what would grow back if I stopped. The rest of me is in good shape, although I work hard to keep it that way. I tell myself I can make up for a half-starved youth with an overexercised middle age. I'm not thin—"stocky" would be the newspaper description—but I don't carry any extra weight on my six-foot, two-hundred-pound frame. Staying in shape is one of my vanities, and one payoff is having your work appreciated by a good-looking babe on a hot summer day. There was a time when one of them was the woman now calling herself Felix Mulholland.

When I got back to my car, four teenaged boys were eying it appreciatively from the sidewalk. I grinned at them as I unlocked the door, and they grinned back, elbowing each other and pointing, before heading off to wherever they were going. I got in, undid the roof latches, and pushed the button to retract the top. The thirty-year-old engine started on the turn of the key. I closed the door. The *Potemkin* was ready to cast off.

The car gets a lot of attention. A bright red Cadillac Eldorado, built in 1975, the last year before emission controls, it has a white ragtop, red leather interior, and the largest V8 Detroit ever squeezed into a production-line chassis. It puts out 365 horses at 4,400 RPM. Gas mileage approaches single digits, but I don't drive that much, so I tell myself that my carbon footprint is still smaller than most SUV owners'.

I love the Eldo because of its size and swagger. America's persona at the height of the Cold War, when Nixon and Brezhnev tried to one-up each other in the eyes of the rest of the world and demonstrate that their system was the Chosen One. The Eldo was one way America stated, with emphasis, *We are winning.* I was on the other side at the time, a sworn enemy of the Main Adversary and everything it stood for, but I had been captivated by the pure ostentation of the car ever since I first saw its picture in a magazine. Then, as now, I'm easily intrigued by things American.

Buying one the first time I lived here, in 1977 as a junior officer in the KGB's New York *rezindentura,* was both impractical and a quick way to end my career. When I returned in 1993 as a private citizen, I had no such constraints. I found one in Florida, with low mileage and no rust, flew to Tampa that afternoon, and drove it home. On the way, I christened it *Potemkin,* after the mutinous battleship made famous by Eisenstein's classic film. More Russian humor.

I took the FDR downtown, got off at Water Street, and was immediately mired in traffic. Driving any car in New York is silly, but driving a boat the size of the *Potemkin* is a juvenile indulgence, one that almost makes up for a childhood without toys. I crawled the three blocks to my garage, raised the top, and reluctantly turned the Eldo over to José, the day manager, who takes care of it as if it were his own. Then I went up to the office to learn what my ex-wife had been up to for the last twenty years.

★ CHAPTER 5 ★

Everything was quiet except for the hum of air-conditioning and computer fans, and Pig Pen. We rent the twenty-eighth floor of a nondescript steel-and-glass tower at Pine and Water. It's about twenty times more space than I need, but Foos and the Basilisk require room, mainly the Basilisk.

The space is actually cheap. We got a great deal on a long-term lease in the wake of 9/11 when no one wanted to work downtown. I already lived on South Street, so I looked at the location as a plus. Foos lives in Brooklyn and never goes above Fourteenth Street, unless it's an emergency. We've got million-dollar views of Wall Street, New York Harbor, the Brooklyn Bridge, and the Statue of Liberty as a bonus.

I made my way through the banks of computer servers that separate the reception area from the rest of the space. Twelve floor-to-ceiling rows, each forty feet long with four-foot aisles in between. They sit on a raised floor under which run miles of cable and supplemental cooling ducts. Sometimes, when I want to lose myself in a problem, I pace the aisles in the dim light and the white noise of the fans. It's a kind of alternative reality, a desert canyon of electronic intelligence. When I sense the machines trying to speak to me, I turn on the lights or leave.

Behind the server farm is a large open area with two seating arrangements—one organized like a living room, the other a big conference table and a dozen chairs. Around the perimeter are a dozen glassed-in offices and conference rooms, one each for me, Foos, and Pig Pen, and the rest for visitors we rarely have. Foos has converted a second office into sleeping quarters. He says he likes to work nights, but I wouldn't be surprised if he moved in permanently. I prefer to leave work behind at the end of the day.

"Hello, Russky," a large African gray parrot squawked from the office he calls home. "Pizza?"

His favorite food, which Foos indulges him, and he thinks everyone else should follow suit. He primarily likes the crust, but lately he's developed a taste for anchovies. Lombardi's in SoHo is his favorite.

"No dice. You're already overweight, Pig Pen," I said. "Not good for a parrot. Makes you look like a vulture with a dye job."

He considered that for a moment, realization dawning that I wasn't carrying the flat cardboard box that contains culinary nirvana. He muttered something I couldn't catch, maybe a new word he was working on, and kept one eye on me while he gnawed, if that's what parrots do, on the metal mesh of the cage that encloses his office.

"Pizza!" he tried again. He's nothing if not persistent. Parrots don't have lips, of course, which makes *p* a difficult letter to pronounce, something Foos didn't consider when he named Pig Pen after the late drummer of his favorite rock band. "Pizza" comes out more like "rizza," but we have no trouble understanding what he wants.

"Pig Pen Parrot picks a peck of pickled parrot pizza?" I said.

That got me an angry one-eyed glare. He can't wrap his beak around the tongue twister, and it annoys him no end. I feel guilty teasing him, but it does serve to get him off the subject.

"Where's the boss?" I asked.

"Boss Man. Pizza." Pig Pen has a vocabulary approaching a hundred fifty words, to which he adds about a word every other week. He's efficient. "Pizza" does double-duty for lunch and dinner. "Pancakes"—"rancakes"—serves for breakfast.

"Anything going on?"

"Twenty minutes, Lincoln, forty minutes, Holland."

"GWB?"

"Flat tire, upper deck."

"Mass transit?"

He gave me his "who cares?" look and went back to chewing the cage.

Foos furnished Pig Pen's office with two large Ficus trees, some potted plants, three perches, a swing, and an electric fountain that burbles water over a copper plate and some rocks. He has a view of the Manhattan and Brooklyn bridges. He also has a radio. It took him a day to learn how to work it and a week to determine his favorite station—1010 WINS. He pays special attention to "Traffic and Transit on the Ones," although for reasons he's yet to confide, he's much more concerned with the state of bridges and tunnels than subways and buses. The day he learns to pronounce Kosciuszko, I'm putting him up for auction on eBay.

"Thanks for the update," I said, heading for my office. *"Do svidaniya."*

"Ciao . . ."

Language skills are my contribution to his education.

". . . cheapskate."

"What?" I turned back.

"No pizza—cheapskate," he said, the feathers on the back of his neck ruffling as his head nodded up and down. I swear he grins when he knows he's come out with a zinger. I left him to his self-congratulation.

My office is in the northeast corner, with a view up the East River and out to the Verrazano-Narrows Bridge (Pig Pen knows that one). I can also see the roof of the building I live in two blocks away, where sometimes my well-endowed upstairs neighbor, Tina, sunbathes topless on her roof deck, oblivious to the walls of windows that surround her. Unfortunately, she's happily married to a former backup linebacker for the New York Giants, so the best I can do is look on from afar, with the help of a pair of Steiner 20×80 military binoculars.

Tina wasn't out, so I checked my e-mail. A message from Foos with the subject "SLUMMING?" It contained a link to a series of pages containing the information the Basilisk had generated on the Mulhollands. I went to the kitchen and made a grilled cheese sandwich from the cheddar and multigrain bread I found there. I grabbed a beer and returned to my office, ignoring the parrot's imploring calls for sustenance. One of the things I miss about Russia is the beer, which may not be the best in the world, but it has a distinctive flavor I got used to. Most American beer is tasteless. I buy the occasional microbrew, but mostly I drink Czech pilsners—Pilsner Urquell or Budweiser Budvar, sold as Chechvar in the United States because of a trademark dispute with the Busch behemoth in St. Louis. They're dry, they have a lot of flavor without being too hop-heavy, and they taste something like home.

I looked at the Basilisk's work while I ate. Plenty of information on Mulholland himself, but mostly what you'd expect—houses (New York, Oyster Bay, Palm Beach), investments, although most of his wealth was in FTB stock, memberships, charitable boards, and so on. He and his wife had a housekeeper, Marisa Cabarillas, living with them. The butler must live elsewhere. He garaged a Maybach limousine and a Range Rover down the block, to the tune of more than two grand a month. He traveled to Europe three times in the last year on a Gulfstream V leased by FirstTrust, stopping in London, Frankfurt, and Zurich each trip. In January, he'd used his black American Express card to purchase two suits at Huntsman, six shirts at Turnbull & Asser, a bracelet for the missus at Asprey, and a Mantegna drawing at Conalghi. The Basilisk told me where he stayed and where he ate. I could've had a record of his phone calls, but it didn't seem necessary. One interesting fact—in the last two months, he'd moved several million dollars into a brokerage account at Morgan Stanley. He'd been a big—make that very big—buyer of FTB stock. Those purchases were all badly under water now, and if he'd been buying on margin, he was almost certainly suffering a credit squeeze of his own.

Eva Mulholland lived at 211 East Seventieth Street, in an apartment that set someone back $5,250 a month—Dad, no doubt. Her occupation was student. She had $1,489 in her checking account. Her credit card charges indicated an affinity for the restaurants of Tribeca and the boutiques of SoHo and the Meatpacking District. She'd spent Christmas in the Caribbean and spring break in London and Moscow. Being a Mulholland wasn't all bad.

Not all good, either. Eva had a record—a guilty plea to a marijuana possession charge two years earlier and another to shoplifting three months ago. Two suspended sentences—and two stints in rehab. Before the first bust, she had three thousand dollars deposited into her checking account every month. Electronic transfer from her father's account. Since she got out of the detox center on Riverside Drive that had set her folks back sixty-five thousand dollars (for the first visit), her allowance had been cut by two-thirds. Dad's idea of a tight leash.

The thing most of us don't think about—or don't want to think about—is how much information we generate on ourselves every day. Our appetites, our preferences, our habits and routines, our families, jobs, and finances. Most everything we do leaves a trail. Every phone call, e-mail, Web search, cash withdrawal, purchase, bill payment, trip, car rental, insurance claim, you name it. The trick is connecting up all those data points, among the billions and billions of others permanently stored in data-miners' databases, to put together a profile of a person or tell you what someone is up to. That's what the Basilisk does better than anything out there. I know. I use everything out there.

Having dispensed with the warm-up acts, I turned to the main event. The file on Felicity Mulholland was illuminating—up to a point. She'd married Rory in 2004. If I were being spiteful, I might have expected her to have led the Upper East Side trophy-wife life since then. I was wrong. No charges at Madison Avenue boutiques. No lunches at overpriced French restaurants where nobody pays attention to the food. A few evenings out—concerts at Carnegie Hall and Lincoln Center—but not many. She paid regular, not overly frequent, attention to her hair, face, and nails. She'd taken a Christmas trip to London, flying coach, but stayed only one night at an innocuous hotel in Hammersmith, and flown home the next day. Paid cash for the airline ticket. No shopping, no theater, no restaurants. She made a similar trip in February. Polina and I had lived in London. My first foreign posting with the KGB. She'd never shown any interest in Hammersmith.

Before she married Mulholland, Felicity used the last name Kendall and lived in a rental on West Fifty-eighth Street for two years. Before that, she didn't appear to live anywhere for three. Before *that,* she lived in a studio apartment in Queens, near LaGuardia Airport—a single woman, no Eva, no kids of any kind. All of which was accounted for by the fact that the real Felicity Kendall died when she was struck by a drunk driver on Queens Boulevard in 1997. Polina picked up her identity in 2000. The Basilisk came up empty on Polina Barsukova, which suggested she was already using another name when she arrived here. Hard to avoid concluding that Polina had something to hide. Question was, from whom? My leading candidate would be husband number two. Jealousy was part of his makeup, he believed firmly in getting even, and he had a reputation for cruelty and ruthlessness that I knew to be one hundred percent well deserved.

I'd heard they'd split, but that was ten years ago. I'd also heard she'd been carrying on an affair with Kosokov. They both dropped from sight after 1999. Guess I'd assumed they'd gone off together, to the extent I'd thought about it. I'd been exiled, after all, partly by her, partly by the Cheka, partly self-imposed. I might not even be thinking about any of this today without Ivanov's item on Kosokov this morning. *That* was another factor to be considered.

A loud *arrrr-oooo-gahhhh* reverberated through the space. Our doorbell—Foos's contribution to office ambience. He likes to hit it on the way in. Pig Pen called out "Pizza!" in response. A few moments later, the hulk of a six-foot-five mountain man dressed in black filled my door, holding a half-chewed slice.

"Man, you are definitely hangin' in the wrong 'hood," the boom-box voice boomed.

The first time you meet him—maybe a few times after that—Foos is an intimidating sight. For openers, he's two hundred sixty pounds big. The weight is evenly distributed. He's not fat, but no one would call him muscled either. His preferred form of exercise is walking to his next meal. He's in his midforties, with a sharp face and black eyes—but unlike Mulholland's, his sparkle with curiosity and humor. A large, pointed nose runs left to right as you look at him. His mouth opens mostly on the right side, adding to his lopsided appearance. He wears heavy black rectangular glasses with chunky lenses and carries a thick mane of black curly hair that cascades around his shoulders, arms, and chest. If he ever cut it, the barber would need a pickup to haul away the clippings. Everything about him shouts eccentric, if not downright strange, and in his case, you can judge a book by its cover. Some people march to their own drummer—Foos has his own rock group. The thing I can never figure is, whenever he shows up with a new girlfriend—roughly every other month—she looks like she stepped out of a Ralph Lauren ad. He, of course, treats this like it's perfectly natural. As Artie Shaw once observed, women aren't attracted to Mick Jagger by his looks. Artie should know—he married Ava Gardner *and* Lana Turner.

"Didn't see many of your friends up there, that's true," I said. "Bernie asked me to help. Mulholland's his biggest client."

"Ah, the Cardinal Consigliere. That explains it. He knows all the best people."

"He helps pay the rent."

"True enough, much as I don't like to admit it. But you and Bernie have all you're getting from me. If there's any justice, that scumbag will do at least five years."

I hadn't been completely honest with Mulholland about my business. I do have a partner. We have a handshake deal that I'll never disclose his involvement. In fact, our entire partnership is based on a handshake, which can be nerve-racking since Foos is unpredictable, to put it mildly. "Scumbag" is the moniker he applies to most of our clients, especially the successful ones, his views unmitigated by his own fortune. But he has special reason to dislike Mulholland.

Foos, or Foster Klaus Helix as his birth certificate says, is a certified genius and certainly paranoid. Maybe all geniuses are a little wacko, I don't know, he's the only one I've ever met. He grew up in Palo Alto and dropped out of high school, but by the time he was twenty, he had a Ph.D. in mathematics and computer science from Stanford. He came east to take a position at the Institute for Advanced Study in Princeton, the place Einstein hung his hat for thirty years. He got interested in relational data, as he calls it—what one thing can tell you about another, what two things can tell you about a third, what three things can tell you about a thousand. That led him to the work being done by companies like ChoicePoint and Seisint and Lexis-Nexis, which maintain some fifty billion data files on virtually every American—people in other countries, too—which they make available to marketers looking for new ways to sell people things they don't need and government agencies looking for new ways to keep an eye on the body politic under the pretext of fighting crime, terrorism, or whatever evil comes along to supplant terrorism. State security by another name.

Fifty billion is a lot of files to organize, search, correlate, and compare, and Foos found each company's software lacking in some respect.

He set out to write a program that would do better than any one of them—or all three combined. He succeeded. He started his own company and soon had a client list that included half the Fortune 500 and several hundred federal, state, and local law enforcement agencies—and FirstTrustBank.

Foos was more naive in those days. He was horrified to discover FTB was using his technology to determine whom to bombard with junk mail and telephone marketing offers for new "free credit cards with special introductory interest rates" that jumped to eighteen percent after the first six months. He cut them off. FTB, which had a contract, took him to court—and won. At which point, Foos—I thought the nickname referred to the foosball game every dot-com company had to have, but he swears he's never played—had an epiphany, not unlike the men who worked on the Manhattan Project. He'd invented his software because it could solve problems better than what came before. In the right hands, it could be used for a lot of beneficial purposes—catching a serial killer, for example, or shutting down a financial scam before it sucked in too many victims. In the wrong hands, it was downright, deeply, totally invasive. Of course, it was impossible to keep it out of the wrong hands—those belonging to men like Mulholland. Foos sold his business, pocketing $100 million on the deal. Then he went to work on a new and improved version—on the grounds that he needed to keep track of what the bastards were up to—which he dubbed Basilisk after the mythological beast, the most poisonous creature on the planet. There's a painting of one in our reception area—rooster's head and legs, body of a hawk, a dragon's scaly wings, and a serpent's pointed tail. It's damned ugly. He also started a foundation, endowed with half the proceeds from the sale. STOP, or Stop Terrorizing Our Privacy, has the self-appointed mission of monitoring, exposing, and thwarting the data-mining activities of marketers, advertisers, data collectors, cops, spies, lawyers, bureaucrats, and anyone else Foos sets his sights on.

"I'm not sticking up for Mulholland," I said. "Especially since he's married to my ex-wife."

He was raising the pizza to his mouth. It stopped in midair. He stood for a minute, mouth open. "You shitting me?!" Sometimes I can surprise even him.

"Wish I was. She's the one calling herself Felicity, or Felix, these days. Her daughter's been kidnapped. He wants our help, but he hasn't told her. And I'm betting he doesn't know anything about her past."

I held out the photo. He finished off the slice and took it. Behind the thick lenses, the eyes worked over the picture like a scanner as the brain put the power of multiple workstations through the paces of considering and rejecting a series of scenarios—all the ones I'd thought of and only he knew how many myriad more.

Eventually he said, "Could be real. Could be she's into some kinky scene and needs dough."

"She may have a drug problem."

"That could explain it, too." He dropped his bulk into a chair. "How do you and the ex get on?"

"Haven't seen her in twenty years. We got married young—for all the wrong reasons. She was what you'd call high maintenance. I thought I could conquer that, and I needed a wife to get a foreign posting. The KGB didn't send single men abroad for fear they'd fall into the clutches of some capitalist vixen."

"Good thinking."

"We made it eight years. One son—Aleksei, I've mentioned him once or twice."

He nodded. "The kid you haven't seen since he was two."

"That's right. When the breakup came, it was characterized by betrayal, violence, and retribution—all on her part. On the other hand, she felt I'd deceived her for as long as I'd known her, and she wasn't wrong about that, although there were extenuating circumstances. You want details?"

He shook his head. "Not unless they're relevant."

"Only to us. So imagine my surprise when Bernie asks me to meet with his client Mulholland who's got a kidnap problem and she waltzes down the stairs."

He nodded with understanding. "Kinda broke your flow."

"One way of putting it. Mulholland's her third husband, so far as I know."

He considered that for a moment. I'd given him the name of the second in my phone message. Even geniuses get tripped up by the conventions of Russian naming, the feminization of Barsukov, for example, to Barsukova.

"Dame got a commitment problem or just lousy taste?" he asked.

"Maybe both—man in the middle's Lachko Barsukov."

"The mobster?"

"One and the same."

"No shit?"

"No shit."

"*That's* why I let you hang out—entertainment value. You can't make this stuff up."

"Me and Pig Pen."

"I doubt that's the way Pig Pen sees it. Mulholland really get busted?"

"Uh-huh. I was there. I got the impression from Bernie the Feds have had him in their sights for a while."

"Goddamned government moves with the speed of cold molasses. They should've nailed that bastard years ago. Still, I may volunteer my services—they can use the Basilisk for free. Make sure they get him this time."

"Don't be rash. We get six hundred sixty-six K, if we find the girl—and he's around to write the check."

"Huh. What price getting even? There's an ethical dilemma that bears consideration. You definitely going ahead with this thing?"

I shrugged in ambivalence I didn't necessarily feel. I knew where I was leaning. "I wouldn't mind clipping Mulholland for that six sixty-six."

"Uh-huh. You and I both know the probability gods didn't put Mulholland, your ex-wife, and Lachko Barsukov in your path for their own amusement."

"That's the problem with you mathematicians. No room for luck—good or bad."

"You gonna operate on luck, let's get a deck of cards. You'll need Mulholland's fee to cover your losses."

I laughed. He grinned a lopsided grin. "Look," he said, "any competent bookmaker would give two-to-one odds that photo's faked and the kidnapping thing's bull. He wouldn't even want to calculate the chances of your ex-wife showing up married to your new client after . . . how many years has it been?"

"A lot bigger number than the odds. But you're not figuring in the intangibles."

"Pain and death are pretty damned tangible."

"I'm talking about curiosity—mine."

"Do I remember something about a dead cat?"

"We both know there's another shoe that's going to drop. Maybe I want to see what it is."

"You ask me, it's gonna be a steel-toed boot swinging toward your face."

"I'll remember to duck."

He shrugged. "They're your teeth."

He pushed himself to his feet and headed off to his office. A minute later, I could hear him banging away on his keyboard. He types with the same subtle touch that characterizes the rest of his approach to life.

I was about to call Bernie to see if I still had a client when the phone rang and a young male voice announced itself as Malcolm Watkins from Hayes & Franklin. The kidnappers wanted their money—tonight.

Decision time now for real.

Mulholland apparently considered me still in his employ. Polina would have tried to get me fired, but her husband's prison problems doubtless complicated her efforts, and maybe she hadn't tried too hard. With all the trouble she'd gone to to cover her tracks—not just one but two new identities (maybe more, for all I knew)—the last thing she wanted was exposure. She'd have to give Bernie a convincing reason to overrule his client. While she probably trusted him as much as anyone, she didn't trust anyone very far. She definitely wouldn't have told him the truth.

Her surprise this morning had seemed genuine. She still despised me, she'd made that clear, but her anger also covered fear, fear that she'd been recognized, fear that someone now knew who she'd become. I was a threat, but the far bigger threat was Lachko, who was almost certainly unaware that his ex-wife and daughter were living in the same city he was. That explained her marriage to Mulholland (I'd already eliminated love as a reason, however unfairly) and her low profile since. Polina had always sought protection. As a child, she'd witnessed her father, a general in the GRU, cashiered out of the army, tried for treason, and sent to the Gulag. Her family and her life had disintegrated around her, and she carried a constant terror that it would happen again. It did, with me, one root of her hatred. She sought refuge in Lachko. Kosokov, too. But Kosokov ended up dead in 1999, according to Ivanov. For whatever reason, she hadn't gone back to Lachko, she'd run, come here. She'd brought Eva with her and become Felicity Kendall. But what about Aleksei? Had she left him behind in Russia? Or . . .

I didn't want to think about *or*.

Polina was resourceful. She'd had enough money and know-how to acquire a new identity. She knew her way around New York. She'd lived here twice before, with me. Even so, alone, in a foreign city, with Eva to worry about, she wouldn't have felt safe. Especially if she thought Lachko was looking for her. So she'd married Mulholland and his money and settled down. Then—bang! bang! bang!—her cover's blown, her husband's jailed, and his fortune's shrinking faster than an ice cube on the sidewalk outside. Unless I badly missed my guess, she'd be petrified. If this was a setup, it seemed doubtful she was part of it, unless someone was setting both of us up, together. That someone could be Lachko, but I still had the same questions—why and why now and what for?

Lachko hated me, of course. He'd played his part in the Disintegration. He'd destroyed my marriage and my career, and he'd walked off with the prize he coveted in Polina. If he'd wanted me dead, it wouldn't have been difficult to arrange. At the time, back in Moscow, I'd waited for the late-night knock at the door presaging the trip to the cells of Lubyanka, but it never came. I'd often wondered if Lachko had tried but his father had vetoed the plan. As time passed, I more or less ceased worrying, although the alarm bells jangled in my head when I learned Lachko had moved to New York. He hadn't looked me up, and I stayed away from Brighton Beach, where he lived. He might not even know I lived in the same city—he had bigger fish to fry these days.

Lachko ran Russian organized crime in New York. In the post-Soviet chaos, he and his twin brother, Vasily, used their positions to build a highly successful criminal organization in Moscow whose core businesses were protection and extortion, but which had expanded into all manner of related rackets—drugs, smuggling, money laundering, prostitution, contract killing, and more recently cyber-crime. A few years before, they'd gone international, and Lachko moved here to oversee the U.S. interests of the Badger brothers—Barsukov translates to Badger. I followed their progress from a safe distance via Ibansk.com. After the Cheka, the Badgers are Ivanov's favorite subject, probably because it's impossible to separate the two. As I'd told Mulholland, the line between criminals and those charged with catching them was never clear in Soviet times. In the New Russia, it disappeared entirely.

Try as I might, I couldn't see why Lachko would bother with me, or even with Polina, for that matter, after all this time. The flaw in that logic was, I was assuming he had matured into a rational human being since I saw him last, when there was no reason to believe he wasn't the same brutal, vindictive, destructive bastard I knew him to be—from painful firsthand experience.

The card player in me said I couldn't yet see enough of the cards on the rest of the table to fold my hand. The Chekist in me said, if this was Lachko at work, I could walk away but he'd follow. Better to play on, eyes open. Besides, having put socialism solidly in my past, there was still that six sixty-six, plus expenses.

I should have been mindful of another Russian proverb. The only free cheese is in the mousetrap.

★ CHAPTER 6 ★

Hayes & Franklin rents twelve floors of One New York Plaza, a big, ugly, waffle-walled tower at the southeast tip of Manhattan, five minutes' walk from my office. Almost six o'clock, but the thermometer was still into the nineties, the air as solid as concrete. I could feel the heat of the sidewalk through my shoes.

The building's modern, but Hayes & Franklin's offices are decorated right out of the Thomas Chippendale catalog, if Thomas Chippendale had a catalog, which maybe he did. Lots of reproduction mahogany furniture, nautical pictures, and prints of birds and botanicals. Bernie occupied a corner office overlooking the South Ferry Terminal. Documents were stacked on every available surface, including the floor. I took two piles off the chair across from his desk and sat down. He didn't look up, just muttered, "Fuck it," to something he was reading, pencil in hand. He put a blunt black line across the page.

Despite his harried appearance, Bernie's a cool customer. Almost never raises his voice. I'd been surprised by his swearing this morning, and it didn't appear his temperament had improved. Mulholland and FTB had him under a lot of strain. Maybe other clients, too. Or he'd spent too much of the day with Polina. I didn't want to make a bad day worse, but there was no way around it.

"How's Mulholland?" I asked.

He raised one eye. "They're keeping him overnight. Arraignment and bail in the morning. Totally fucking unnecessary. He could've been out this afternoon. Except that the goddamned U.S. attorney feels she has to make a show of how tough she can be on white-collar defendants because she spent most of her career defending them. It's all bullshit, starting with the charges. Bullshit politics, bullshit playing to the media, more bullshit. Meanwhile Rory's still in the Tombs—for no good goddamned reason. She's busting my balls over bail, too. To think I got that woman made partner. No good deed goes unpunished."

His voice had risen through most of his rant, almost to a yell, then softened again at the end until he sounded remorseful. He was having a worse day than I thought. I hesitated to ask a question, for fear of setting him off again, but I wasn't clear I was following.

"What woman?" I said.

He looked at me like I'd just stepped off the boat from some country permanently mired in the Middle Ages. "This is a federal case, you Cossack. That means it's run by the Justice Department and the Justice Department's designated representative in this judicial district, so we're talking about the U.S. fucking attorney for the Southern District of New York!"

"And she was your partner?"

"Before she ascended to her current lofty heights of public service, yes, she toiled here in the fields of Hayes & Franklin, where, thanks in part to me, she became a very well paid partner. Bitch."

"Sorry I asked. Let's drop it."

He pushed his chair back from the desk, put down the pencil, and rubbed his eyes behind his glasses.

"Sorry, Turbo. Been a long day, so far. I need to vent, I guess—but I do feel like I've got a knife in my back. Victoria was a partner here before she got her current appointment. She came to us in a merger, a firm in Atlanta. She put in to move to New York. I took her under my wing since I came in as an outsider, too. She's a white-collar crime specialist, like I said. She worked her ass off, developed quite a reputation. When she came up for partner, I shoved it through. No question she deserved it, but it was still a fight with the old stiffs who think they run this place. Woman, Dixie accent, criminal law—not the Hayes & Franklin mold. She got the U.S. attorney post six months ago. Big-time appointment. Now the bitch wants two mil bail. No good deed . . ."

"That was her on the phone this morning, at Mulholland's apartment?"

"Courtesy call. Some frigging courtesy. We had an understanding. She's been looking into FTB for months. Predatory lending makes good press. Sorry, that's unfair. Not at all clear she could've made a case, but between you, me, and the microphone in the wall, some of FTB's practices were close to the line. Anyway, when the credit crunch hit, we talked, and I thought we agreed, absent compelling evidence, she'd leave Rory alone so he could focus on saving the bank. There are jobs at stake, among other things."

"Maybe she found the compelling evidence."

"Rory says there's nothing to find. Our own investigation—Hayes & Franklin, I mean—backs him up."

"Not the first time a client's lied to his lawyer."

"Thanks, Turbo. I can always count on you to cheer me up."

"What about the money laundering?"

"This morning's the first time I heard anything about that. We're looking into it."

"Surprised Felix Mulholland, too."

He pulled his chair back to the desk and leaned forward. "What do you mean?"

"I was watching. Something about that spooked her."

"You sure?"

"The first job of a good spy . . ."

"Don't give me the assess-human-nature speech. I've heard it as many times as the Russians winning World War II. So what's the deal between the two of you?"

"What'd she tell you?"

"She's a client, Turbo. What she tells me is between us."

"Be careful how much stock you put in your clients, Bernie. Felix Mulholland was no more born Felicity Kendall in Jackson Heights, Queens, than I was born Richard Nixon in Yorba Linda, California. She's a client with a past. Colorful is one adjective. I'm sure the *Post* will find others."

That got him out of the chair, half standing, leaning forward. "The *Post*? What the hell are you talking about?"

Since I arrived, Bernie had been talking at me, sometimes to me. He was preoccupied with other problems, I understood that, but I wanted his full attention for the next few minutes—partly for his own good and partly because I needed him to appreciate I was coming clean. However this thing played later tonight, Bernie had to believe my judgment was unclouded by emotional connections rooted in ancient history. The threat of more unwanted media coverage—from an always unwanted source—did the trick. I chose my words carefully.

"I take it Mulholland didn't have you guys check her out before he popped the question?"

"No! Of course not. Why . . ."

Bernie sat down and pushed back from the desk again, putting distance between himself and whatever he feared I was about to say. The look on his face was the one of a well-dressed pedestrian as he jumps back from the curb, knowing he's too late to avoid the muddy splash from the taxi accelerating through a great big puddle.

"Prenup?" I asked.

"None of your damned business," he growled.

Careful. Bernie took confidentiality seriously. Appearing to pry wasn't going to help. "True enough. You know she was married before?"

"No. Why is that relevant in this day and age?"

"Mulholland's her third, at least."

"So?"

"Second's named Barsukov."

The chair slid forward in a flash and Bernie leaned into my face. *"Lachko Barsukov?"*

"Yep."

"Jesus Christ. How do you know this?" He was fully in my face now.

"I'm the first."

★ CHAPTER 7 ★

I watched all five Kübler-Ross stages pass through his eyes—denial, anger, bargaining, depression, acceptance—in the time it took him to slump back into his chair. Then anger returned.

"Goddammit!" He banged the desk with both fists. "Why the hell didn't you tell me?"

"Didn't know until I saw her this morning. First time since 1989."

Bernie and I have done business together for nearly a decade. I have always been straight with him, not least because he's the one who gets me hired, but also because when he was with the CIA, he had the rep as the most astute analyst the Americans had. I'm not sure I could put one over on him if I tried. Since we were on opposite sides for two decades, I assume there's some little lingering doubt in his mind about where I'm coming from at moments like these. He also doesn't like surprises. He was taking his time before deciding how to proceed.

"Straight up?" he said.

"Straight up. Our split was anything but amicable, on both sides. That's what I told her, when I spoke Russian, this morning. If I'd known she was married to Mulholland, I never would have set foot in that apartment."

He thought about that a few minutes more, and anger was replaced by acceptance. It looked as though I'd come through clean, at least for the time being.

"I need this like another ulcer," he said.

"What did she tell you, if it's okay to ask?"

His look said it wasn't okay.

"Let me guess, then. Something like, she knew me years ago, back before the beginning of recorded time, when she was just an innocent child, ignorant of the ways of the world, and I pulled dark, evil wool over those innocent eyes until the day she found out, to her total shock and horror, that I'm a lying, deceitful, no-good son of a bitch. She probably worked in dead babies' blood dripping from my teeth for good measure."

He chuckled, a little. "That's close. Her description was more robust."

"So how come I'm still here?"

He sighed. "Too many problems. This was one I could hand off, or so I thought. I figured Rory had hired you, it was his call to fire you. But now . . ." He took off his glasses and rubbed his eyes again. I could see the red from across the desk. "I don't know, Turbo, to tell you the truth. This complicates everything, and I don't have time to deal with more complications. I guess I could send one of our associates with the money . . ."

I hadn't come through so clean after all. He was really reaching. I said, "And explain to his/her wife/husband, girlfriend/boyfriend, mother/father what happened when things go bad. You don't need that. This whole thing smells bad. You know that as well as I do. Even money Eva's in on the scam, but I'm not sure that explains it. That's why I told you what I told you. I'll handle it, but I may have to improvise if things go wrong."

He replaced his glasses. "You think Barsukov's tied up in this?"

"That's the question I've been asking myself all day. Truth is, I don't know. He hates me, and it's clear Polina—I mean Felix—is hiding from something or someone, and I'd have to guess that's him. I haven't spoken to him in years, and I have no idea if he knows who she's become."

"Jesus. It gets better and better. You got any good news?"

I decided not to tell him about Foos's offer to help the government with its case against Mulholland.

"It could be this isn't about Felix," I said, "at least not in the way you think."

He raised an eyebrow. "What's that supposed to mean?"

"This wouldn't be the first time she and Lachko Barsukov teamed up against me."

The eyebrow stayed up. "There were a lot of rumors running around Langley back in the eighties about how you and Barsukov got cross-wired. Details were hard to come by. KGB put the lid on. She was part of that?"

"Tangentially. Collateral damage morphed into collateral assault."

The glasses came off again. "Tell me straight—your willingness to help, this has nothing to do on your part with getting even or anything like that?"

"It was all over long ago."

"For real?"

"Cheka honor."

"Cheka honor." He shook his head. "That's supposed to make me believe you?"

I shrugged. "We didn't have Boy Scouts."

He put his glasses on, stood, and went to the window and looked out, most likely without seeing anything. He was trying to make up his mind about something. I let him take his time.

"I don't think this has anything to do with you," he said when he turned back to face me.

"Because?"

"What do you know about whaling?"

"Phishing for big fish. Send bogus e-mail, try to get the recipient to open an attachment that installs a keyboarding bug, phisher can see everything on your computer. It's one of Lachko's businesses, but he's got plenty of competition. Did Mulholland . . ."

He nodded. "About three months ago. We've had other clients get scammed, too. Bait in his instance was a fake letter from the U.S. attorney, Southern District. Most people know better than to open unsolicited attachments, but since this looked exactly like the real deal, he didn't think twice."

"He get keyboarded?"

He nodded. "Didn't tell us until ten days ago. Whoever it was copied a lot of computer activity. Of course, we informed Victoria right away, since it was her fake paper. Could be one reason she felt she had to move on Rory before anything else happened."

"You think there's a connection?"

"Don't know. That's why I bring it up. Could've been Barsukov."

"Could've been, but we don't know enough." I looked at my watch. "Still want me to make the drop?"

He nodded. "I don't have a lot of options, as you point out. But I want to be clear on priorities—girl, money, kidnappers, in that order."

"What about explanation?"

"Girl, money, kidnappers, in that order."

"You don't want to know what's going on?"

"I want to know your efforts are focused where they should be—especially, as you say, if you have to improvise."

He wasn't in a mood to argue, and his priorities were the ones I'd focus on first in any event—then I'd find out what was going on.

"Okay," I said, "but here's one more piece of information you may want to factor in. Mulholland's been buying FTB stock with every dime he can raise for the last two months."

He'd started for the door, but his head whipped around. "Buying? You sure?"

"Uh-huh. Basilisk told me."

"That monster ought to be illegal. I didn't know. Thanks. I don't know what it means, other than Rory's a man of his convictions. He believes in himself and his bank."

"Knowing that changes everything I thought about him," I said with a grin.

"Keep your opinions to yourself. He's your client."

"I know. I'm looking forward to collecting that six sixty-six. Plus—"

"I know. Plus the goddamned expenses. Sometimes I wonder how we won the Cold War. I spent the better part of three decades analyzing Russians, and I still have no idea what makes you tick."

"You didn't win." He'd heard this speech before, too. Maybe it was national pride, but I never tired of making the point, especially to Americans. "We lost."

★ CHAPTER 8 ★

Girl, money, kidnappers.

Bernie's priorities were fine as far as they went, but they didn't go far enough. I had a plan for the money. The same plan would lead me to the kidnappers, if there were any kidnappers, and I'd figure out what to do with them once I saw them in the flesh. Neither worried me much. The girl was a different issue. Priority one, of course, as she should be. Only problem was, she wouldn't be anywhere near the drop site tonight, no matter what the supposed kidnappers said. That much I was reasonably certain of, and that moved explanation up on the priority list. No point in pushing the point now. Bernie's hands were tied, as were mine, by the same client—or the same client's wife.

Bernie led me down the hall to a small conference room. A red backpack sat on a table surrounded by leather chairs. A clean-cut young man in a suit stood as we came in.

Bernie said, "This is Malcolm Watkins. You spoke on the phone."

I shook hands with the kid and pointed to the backpack. "That the money?"

"Yes, sir. They specified a red backpack."

"What did they sound like?"

"What do you mean?"

"The voice on the phone—man, woman, American, foreign, young, old?"

"Oh, sorry. I have no idea—Mrs. Mulholland talked to them."

I looked at Bernie. "Mulholland said—"

"I know. No way around telling her. I'll deal with Rory."

I didn't point out she almost certainly already knew. I'd caused enough trouble. Instead, I asked, "What's the drill?"

Franklin looked down at a yellow legal pad. "Bring the money to the Sheraton at Newark Airport tonight at ten. Alone. She said they repeated that. Go to the front door with the backpack, wait. You'll be searched. No guns. Then you go to the room they tell you. The door will be ajar. Put the backpack on the bed and leave. The girl will be in the lobby. They said if anything goes wrong, they'll kill her first, then you."

He said the last part awkwardly, clearly uncomfortable. This wasn't what he'd been trained for. I nodded and smiled.

"Don't worry. These guys probably learned that watching TV. Let's see what we have." I picked up the backpack. It was full of bills, tens and twenties, banded into packs of a thousand dollars each. I looked up at Watkins. "All here, right?"

"Yes, sir. Counted it twice."

I took the box of small electronic devices from my messenger bag and selected one about the size and shape of a Wheat Thins cracker. Then I reached around in the backpack until I felt an inside pocket, and used some Super Glue to stick the RFID tag to the nylon. Bernie and Watkins watched while I rezipped the pocket, the latter with some suspicion.

"Radio frequency identification transponder," I said. "RFID. Everybody's using them. Casinos, Walmart, car rental companies—it's the big new thing. Sends a signal to my laptop. GPS software communicates with the satellite, tells me where the backpack is."

Watkins looked at Bernie, then back at me. "She said they said no tricks. They said—"

I cut him off. Whatever they said wasn't important. "These guys have any brains at all, they'll expect us to try something. Hundred grand's too much money to just piss away—that's how they'll look at it. This is an older radio tag. I want them to find it. So they won't look for this one." I held up a piece of plastic about the size of a grain of rice. "New generation, just out. Japanese, of course."

I removed a pack of bills from the bag and slid a twenty from the middle. A tiny drop of glue stuck the transponder to the currency, which I reinserted into the pack. "If they take the money and leave the bag, we'll still know where they are."

Bernie said, "What will you do when you find them?"

"Don't know. Depends in part on who they are. I'll think of something." I picked up the red backpack along with my bag. "Better get going. Might be traffic in the tunnel. Where do you want me to call?"

"We'll be here," Bernie said. "Good luck."

I walked north through the all but empty, muggy streets. I keep the *Potemkin* in a garage on Pearl Street. I keep the Vlost and Found company car—a black 2003 Ford Crown Victoria, Police Interceptor model—in an open lot on Water Street. I call it the *Valdez,* after the ill-fated tanker, not the Madison Avenue coffee character. It has seventy-five thousand miles on the odometer, dents in the front fender and back door, and cost $9,800. It's essentially a Crown Vic with a bunch of extra features and equipment and drives like its namesake, but it'll move when you ask it to, and I couldn't care less if it gets nicked, dinged, or totaled. A perfect New York City car.

I tossed the bags in back and headed for the Holland Tunnel, where it was still rush hour. I wanted to arrive early, get the lay of the land. The dashboard clock read 8:33 when I left. At 9:02, I pulled into the Sheraton's parking lot. I found a space near the entrance and sat in the dusk. It felt a little like the old days, when I'd been stationed here before—meeting an agent when exposure for either of us had dire consequences. This time, though, I hadn't chosen the venue, and the dire consequences would all fall on me.

I watched the parking lot in the failing light. If I were doing this, I'd have a man in the lot, two in the lobby, and two upstairs, in the room next door or, better, across the hall, all connected with earphone radios. Their first concern would be the money, their second, me. No reason for them to do anything so long as I followed instructions. Which I fully intended to do. Up to a point.

At 9:42, a car drove in, its headlights sweeping across the *Valdez* and the front of the hotel. It parked on the other side of the entrance. A man in a rumpled sports coat got out and unloaded a wheeler suitcase from the trunk. It was red. Shit. Nothing I could do. I held my breath as he pulled it to the front door. He stopped in the lighted entranceway to search his pockets. It took forever before he found what he was looking for—his cell phone. I almost got out and yelled at him to keep moving, but nobody attacked him. Nobody came out to greet him. From what I could see, there was nobody to pay him any attention whatsoever. He finally continued inside. The parking lot returned to emptiness. I waited several more minutes before exhaling slowly. They knew who they were waiting for.

At 9:55, I slid a SIG Pro 9 mm handgun, a compact, double-action autoloader with a polymer frame and a ten-round magazine, into the backpack with the bills, working it down almost to the bottom. I don't like guns. The result of having them pointed at me in my youth. I don't carry one as a rule, but I wasn't sure what I was in for tonight, so better safe than sorry. I figured the guy at the door, if there was a guy at the door, would search me and make sure the backpack contained the money, but he was unlikely to dump it out in the parking lot. Or so I hoped.

I locked the car, hoisted the backpack, and walked toward the entrance. The bright lights of the covered doorway cast everything around it in shadow. No doorman, no bellhop, no other guests, just a big, empty, well-lighted space. To walk into that, like the guy with the suitcase, was to present a target a blind man couldn't miss from a quarter mile away. I stopped fifteen feet short, still in the shadows. Growing up in a Marxist bureaucracy teaches many things, and one of them is patience. I could stand there all night if need be. I was disobeying instructions, but if they meant me harm, I might get a half second of warning. I waited, stock-still, one eye on the door, peripheral vision searching the parking lot for any sign of movement among the cars.

Newark is known as a tough town, but it's not Moscow. Nobody shot me from the shadows. After two long minutes, a man in a dark-colored shirt pushed his way out the door and straight in my direction.

"Back to car," he said without breaking stride.

He followed me to the *Valdez*. When we got there, he had a gun in his hand.

"Bag on car. Hands on car." Ukrainian accent.

I put the backpack on the hood and my hands on the roof. He ran his free hand over my arms, legs, and torso. He opened the backpack, looked inside, shook it once, pulled out a pack of bills, fanned it, and replaced it. The one flaw in my plan was that he'd try to accompany me upstairs, but he put the backpack on the car, walked around to the other side, and said, "Go. Three twelve."

I took the money and walked to the hotel without looking back.

The lobby was empty, but the cocktail lounge, on an open, raised floor to one side, was a third full. Could be another one there. I didn't look but walked straight to the elevators, the backpack over my shoulder for all to see, and punched 3. I transferred the SIG to my waistband during the ride.

The door opened in a small waiting area. Empty corridors ran in both directions. Room 312 was to the right. Door ajar, as promised. I pushed it open and stopped. No movement. No sound, other than the hum of hotel machinery and a TV somewhere down the hall.

Inside the door, a narrow hall extended past a closet and bathroom on the left into the room itself, which was filled with a king-sized bed, a desk, and a chair. Standard hotel design.

I had just put the backpack on the bed when I heard a noise. I started to turn, but a blow landed on the back of my head. Something hard, knocking me forward, onto the bed. I held myself up, which was a mistake because it got me another crack on the skull. I fell to the floor, woozy but conscious and alert enough to pretend I was out cold. A foot poked my side a couple of times. I refused to move and tried to keep my breathing slow and steady.

A male voice, speaking Ukrainian, said, "Watch him while I get the money."

I heard the sounds of the backpack being emptied. The same voice spoke again.

"Jerk-fuck thinks he smart. Look at this."

The other man said, "Shit. You think that's—"

"Not now, fool! Search him. Get his keys—and anything else."

The other man bent over me. Vodka on his breath. I felt his hands in my jacket pocket. When he tried to push me over, I pulled the SIG from my back and stuck it in his face.

"Back off."

The man pulled away fast, afraid. The other man said, "Shit!" and bolted for the door, carrying a blue backpack.

"Looks like it's you and me, pal." I made a show of raising the gun.

"No . . . I . . . Please . . ."

He backed slowly away, as if any sudden movement would cause me to fire.

"Get out," I hissed.

He was gone in an instant, leaving a Raven MP-25, a true junk gun, on the bed.

I hefted the pistol and ejected the clip. Full, but the safety was on. He'd probably hit me with the butt. I felt the back of my head. Some swelling near the base of the skull, a little blood, not too much. These guys were amateurs, and incompetent ones at that, but the fact that they were Ukrainians was one more coincidence I didn't like.

The red backpack was on the floor, empty. The transponder was next to it. I sat on the bed long enough for my head to clear, then took the plastic liner from the ice bucket and filled it at the ice machine on my way downstairs. The lobby bar was still busy. No Eva. No one under the age of thirty. I wasn't surprised, but I wanted to be able to tell Bernie I was thorough.

I returned to the elevator. The Sheraton had ten floors, eight with guest rooms. The top two were labeled CLUB LEVEL and required a special key. I assumed the Ukrainians wouldn't have sprung for those. Thirty-eight rooms to a floor, two hundred thirty to check. I started on eight and worked my way down, knocking on every door. Business was slow, and fewer than a hundred rooms were occupied. I asked for Eva wherever someone answered. Most responded, "Wrong room" or "Not here." I interrupted two couples in the throes of passion. The first woman screamed, "My husband!" The second man told me to "Fuck off!" Three other women threatened to call security. One guy invited me to join the poker game he was running in his suite. The whole process took just over half an hour.

Eva wasn't there, just as I'd expected. Never had been. Time for Plan B. The Ukrainians might know where she was. More likely, I'd have to find a way to get them to spill who they were working for. Along the way, of course, I'd retrieve the money and discourage whoever needed discouraging from trying to put another bite on the Mulhollands. Priorities.

No one near my car. The Ukrainians were long gone—or so they thought. I wedged the melting ice bag against the headrest and leaned against it. The cold felt good. I turned on my laptop, took out my cell phone, and dialed Bernie's number. He answered on the first ring.

"Turbo! Where are you?"

"Hotel parking lot. We had a little scuffle, but everything's okay now."

"What? Are you all right? Have you got Eva? What about the money?"

At least he asked about me first. "I'm okay. Bump on the head, that's all. No Eva. Not here. Never was. I searched the whole hotel. I should know about the money in a minute."

"What should I tell Rory? And Felix?"

"I wouldn't tell them anything yet. Bear with me." I put down the phone and picked up the laptop. A few clicks of the cursor and a map filled the screen. An arrow pointed to a block in Jersey City, not far from the Holland Tunnel. I picked up the phone.

"Looks like they didn't go far. Jersey City. I'm on my way. I'll call later, but it could be a while."

I closed the phone before he could argue, pulled out of the lot, and found my way onto I-78 East. When I was through the tolls and climbing the ramp onto the Pulaski Skyway, I made two more calls. The first was to Foos, with the Jersey City address. I woke him up, but he's used to that. The second was to Gayeff, a former Soviet Olympic discus thrower. He and his twin brother, Maks, who competed in the shot put, did contract work for the Cheka after they retired from athletics. They now run a numbers operation in Brighton Beach and moonlight as muscle for hire, mainly, I think, because they enjoy it.

Gayeff was awake, but I probably interrupted something—he didn't sound happy to hear from me. He agreed to round up Maks and meet me in an hour.

When I got to Jersey City, I found a parking place, adjusted what was left of the ice in the bag, and settled in to wait. It was going to be a long night. Not least for the men holed up at 145 Montgomery Street.

★ CHAPTER 9 ★

Montgomery Street was in the process of gentrification. About half the three-story brick row houses in the block containing 145 looked like they'd had significant money put into them. The other half did not. Number 145 was in the latter group.

I'd been there ten minutes when Foos called. "Three apartments. Two tenants have lived there several years—Sanchez and Rodriguez. Third place is empty, or rented off the books, Apartment 1A. Need anything else?"

"Don't know yet. I'm waiting for reinforcements."

"Track and Field?" His nickname for Gayeff and Maks. He thinks it's hilarious. "Don't let those boys get out of hand. I'm going for pizza. Back in twenty." Foos likes to smoke a little dope from time to time, which invariably gives him the munchies.

I rested my head against the melting ice, which was having a generally therapeutic effect. At twelve fifty-five, a green Econoline van rolled down the street and pulled into a parking space across from mine. Reinforcements had arrived.

Gayeff came around to my passenger side and got in. He was a large muscular man who looked every inch a large muscular man. The years away from professional competition hadn't added any fat. He had a square face, round nose, small eyes, and a buzz cut. When he grinned, as he did now in greeting, pencil-thin lips extended a half inch at either end in a flat line.

"What's the deal?" he said.

"Take a pass by 145. We want apartment 1A, ground floor."

"Huh." He shut the door quietly and walked down the block. A minute later he returned on the other side of the street and climbed back in the car.

"Can't tell much. Bars on the windows and air conditioners. Double door, double locked on the front. Apartment's in the back, on the right. We can do it, but they'll know we're coming."

"Let's wait. Anyone comes out who doesn't look Hispanic, grab him."

"Huh." He went back to the van.

We didn't have to wait long. The door opened fifteen minutes later, and a man stood on the stoop long enough to light a cigarette before coming down the stairs and turning away from where I was parked. The same guy who hit me. Gayeff followed on foot. The van pulled out and followed him. I followed the van. We all turned right at the corner and stopped briefly midblock while the van's sliding door opened and Gayeff hustled the man inside. I followed a few more blocks until we reached a commercial neighborhood and the van pulled over. The door slid open, and Maks looked out, wearing the same thin grin as his twin. He moved aside, and I climbed in.

Gayeff held the Ukrainian with two clamplike hands. He was dark-haired, unshaven. A knife, a wallet, and some keys sat on the floor of the van. I took the Raven from my pocket and put it against his forehead.

"You forgot this."

He whimpered and tried to slide away. Gayeff held firm. I put away the gun and picked up the wallet. A driver's license bore the name Ilarion Nedelenko and an address in Brooklyn, Manhattan Beach. Pictures of an overweight, unattractive woman and an equally overweight, unattractive young girl. I nodded to Maks, stepped outside, and called Foos. He confirmed the address, adding a phone number, immigration information, the make, model, and registration number of an

59

old Ford Taurus, and the names of the wife and child. First thing was to find out if these guys were operating with protection. They were on Lachko's turf, but they weren't the kind of men he'd have confidence in. If they were freelancing, it shouldn't be difficult to terrify them into cooperating—they were already living on borrowed time.

I told Maks what I had in mind, and we climbed back in the van. I made a show of pocketing my cell phone before I said to Maks in Russian, "Lachko says he's a useless *pizda staraya*—old cunt. Kill him. Use his gun."

Maks grinned and rummaged through a toolbox. He held up a screwdriver. The man's eyes bounced in their sockets. The Badger's calling card was a screwdriver in the right eye.

Maks said, "What about the wife and kid?"

"He doesn't care. That's up to you."

Maks grinned again. "Gayeff likes fat broads."

The man began babbling in Ukrainian. He hadn't done anything, please let him explain, we had the wrong guy, please don't hurt his wife and daughter, and so on. I let him beg for a while, then ordered him in Russian to shut up. I was right about freelancing. I knelt in front of him and held out my old KGB identity card.

"The Cheka never goes away, you know. We're everywhere. We see everything. We know everything. Even here. Tell me why I shouldn't kill you now and let my friends spend the rest of the night enjoying themselves with Katerina and Pavla."

I don't know whether it was the card or the Christian names, but the terror overwhelmed him. Howls of fear intermingled with meaningless ramblings.

"Shut up and listen to me! You have one chance. One chance to save your family and your own worthless skin. You give me the wrong answer, I will know, and I will turn you over to these two."

Maks waggled the screwdriver. The man sobbed, "Noooo."

"How many men in the house?"

He hesitated. He wasn't as terrified as I thought. Turn up the heat. I rationalized that psychological terror was preferable to its physical cousin, but the truth was I'd also been trained by some nasty motherfuckers.

"Kill him."

I handed Maks the Raven, which he put to Nedelenko's temple.

"No! No! Wait!" Nedelenko was screaming. "Two, there are two."

"Names," I said, putting as much cold as I could into my voice.

"Dolnak, Kalynych."

"First names?"

"Marko, Diodor."

"Armed?"

"Revolvers."

"Layout?"

He described a two-room apartment with a small kitchen and bath.

"Money there?"

He nodded.

"Maybe I'm going to give you another chance. Maybe."

I went outside and called Foos again, with Nedelenko's names. It took him less than ten minutes to come up with addresses and phone numbers, also in Manhattan Beach. One of the men, Marko, had a family. I got back in the van.

"We're going back to the house. You're going to take us in. Anything goes wrong, you die first. Understand?"

He nodded.

We left my car and drove the van back to Montgomery Street. Nedelenko had keys for the front door. He led us down a hallway with a dirty linoleum floor and yellowed, peeling paint to a single door in the back. The three of us stood to one side. He knocked twice and said his name before he put his key in the lock. As soon as he turned it, I pulled him back, Gayeff kicked open the door, and the brothers burst in. There were shouts of surprise and the pop of a silencer. After a minute, Maks said, "Okay."

I brought in Nedelenko, which probably didn't add any years to his life expectancy, but he should have chosen his business associates more wisely. Like he said, there were two men in the room, one on an old couch, the man from the parking lot, and one at a table with money on it. Next to the money was a revolver and a BlackBerry. The room was hardly any cooler than outside. An old air conditioner chugged away in the window, but to little effect. The man at the table, the other man in the hotel room, wore a tank top and held his bleeding shoulder. His skin was covered in tattoos. His eyes were darker and tougher than Nedelenko's. They showed pain but not fear. The ringleader. The other man was scared. His eyes darted around the room. Sweat stained his shirt halfway down his rib cage.

Momentum was an ally. Don't give them time to think. I went straight to the man at the table, picked up the gun, and poked the wound. He tried not to show the pain, but it was too much.

"Which one are you? Marko? Diodor?"

His eyes widened, but he said nothing. I nodded at Maks, who put his gun against the man's cheek.

"Which?"

"Mar . . . Marko."

"Good. Let me explain the situation. You are clumsy and you are stupid. You are operating on the Badger's turf, which means you also have a death wish." I took out my cell phone. "One call and—"

"No! Ratko said—" Marko caught himself. That name rang a vague bell, but I wanted to keep the pressure on.

"Ratko said what?"

Marko shook his head. I poked his wound again and he grimaced. I pushed harder and he cried out.

"Okay, okay, please. We know rules. We no break. Ratko said everything okay with the Badger. I swear."

"You can swear to Barsukov. See if he believes you. Personally, I think you're full of shit."

"No! It's truth!"

"Shut up. Listen. You have two problems. One is the Badger. The other is me. He already has men on their way to your home on Amherst Street. I can call them off—if you give me reason to."

Marko started out of the chair. He was scared now. "No! You wouldn't—"

I shoved him back, hitting his wounded shoulder. His face was filled with pain.

"You don't think so? You are wrong. Listen to me. Where's the girl?"

"Girl? What girl?"

I only had to feint in the direction of his shoulder before he screamed.

"No! Stop! Please! I . . . I don't know girl. Ratko say pick up money. That's all."

"And he'd take care of Barsukov?"

"Yes! I told you . . ."

"I still think you're full of shit. Let's see what Lachko thinks."

I took out my cell phone and walked into the bedroom. Marko wailed as I shut the door. I was all but certain they knew nothing of Eva. As expected, they were working for someone else—Ratko—and he might. I waited a few minutes, returned to the living room, and spoke quietly to Gayeff and Maks. I surveyed the three men, all of whom looked terrified.

"You," I said, pointing to the man I hadn't spoken with yet. "In there."

I followed him to the bedroom, Raven in hand.

"Take off your clothes. Kneel on the bed, face forward."

"Wait," he cried. "Please . . ."

"Now!"

He did as he was told. I put the muzzle to the back of his head. "One chance. Where's the girl?"

"No know! No girl! Please!"

"All right, where's Ratko?"

"No know! No know! Marko—"

I moved the gun to the right and fired past his ear into the mattress. The crack was loud in the small space. The man fell forward sobbing. The room smelled of shit. I believed him.

The door opened, and Gayeff came in quickly. He leaned over the man on the bed and said in Russian, "My friend is kind. I am not. You make one noise, I will kill you." He raked the man's cheek with his pistol to make sure he understood. The man sobbed quietly.

I returned to the living room.

"You two! Clothes off! On your knees. Now! I gave your friend a chance to live. He didn't take it." I shrugged. "Maybe you are smarter."

They looked at each other wide-eyed and then at me. I raised my gun hand as if to strike Marko, and he started to undress quickly. Nedelenko followed.

"Down, now!"

They dropped to their knees facing the wall.

I put the barrel of the gun to the back of Marko's neck. "You've probably gathered by now the Badger doesn't give a fuck what happens to you. Where do I find Ratko?"

Marko turned slightly to look at Nedelenko.

"You're next, Nedelenko. Tell him to answer."

"All right," Marko said. "Don't shoot. We only pick up money."

"Where is he?"

"He has apartment. New York. Sixth Avenue, Twenty-first Street, new building."

"What name?"

"What?"

"What name does he rent the apartment under?"

"His name. Rislyakov."

"What do you think?" I said to Maks.

He spat on the floor.

"No! It's truth! I swear. We no lie!"

I knocked on the bedroom door, and Gayeff came out.

"Get in there," I said to the Ukrainians. "Don't even think about coming out that door for an hour. My friend will shoot the first one who tries."

Marko and Nedelenko shuffled into the bedroom. Cries of surprise turned to anger as Gayeff closed the door behind them. I put the money in the bag as Maks gathered up the clothes. I pocketed Marko's BlackBerry and signaled the twins outside.

"Wait until they make a run for it. Forget Kalynych. Follow the other two and let me know where they go."

I drove back to Manhattan, keeping the car at the speed limit while my mind raced. This was still America—New York, New Jersey— but the last few hours felt like I was back in Russia, more specifically the old Soviet Union. Terror, intimidation, fear know no boundaries. I'd used that to my advantage, thanks to the power of the Basilisk and the stupidity of the Ukrainians, but I wasn't happy about it. I'd meant to leave that life behind. I slid back to it all too easily, and in a way, this was worse. In the old days, the law, however oppressive and corrupt, gave me the right. Tonight, I'd acted on my own—no law, no right, just a fake ID, a little information, and the ability to terrify.

I could tell myself it was the only way to find the girl, she could be in danger. Priorities.

That was a lie. I'd done what I'd done because I could. A bad habit to fall back into.

I pushed guilt aside and tried to focus on facts. The probability that Eva Mulholland had actually been kidnapped, never high, had fallen to near zero. The note was real, the photo faked, both most likely concocted by Ratko Rislyakov—I was still trying to place where I'd heard that name—and Eva Mulholland. The delivery instructions were accurate, except for the part about Eva. The Ukrainians were working for Ratko. Eva probably needed money for drugs, Ratko could have his own high-cost vices. It all made sense, except that the Ukrainians expected Ratko to clear things with Barsukov. That meant he had pull with the Badger. *That* opened up a host of other questions. Was Ratko aware of Eva's real identity? Did Eva know Ratko was connected to her biological father? Did Eva know her biological father was in New York City? Was Polina aware of any of this? I could guess at the answers, but they'd be only that—guesses.

One good thing—nobody was after me, or they hadn't been before tonight. Somebody—Ratko Rislyakov?—was now out a hundred K. So I still had a terrified Polina and a pissed-off kidnapper/extortionist to worry about. Maybe the head of the Russian mob, too. Who already hated me more than anyone else on earth. Not a game I would have chosen to sit in on, had I had the chance to preview the other players. Like it or not, I was in it now, and I still couldn't see enough cards to get a feel for the game. First order of business tomorrow was to introduce myself to one guy at the table I hadn't met.

I called Bernie as I came out of the tunnel on the Manhattan side.

No answer—he'd gone home after all. I left a message that I'd drop off the money later that day. I put the *Valdez* in its lot and stopped by the office to put the gun, bag, and BlackBerry in the safe.

The smell of marijuana hung in the air. Foos was asleep in his office-bedroom. It would take a small explosion to wake him. Pig Pen was another matter.

"Nighttime, Russky," he said as I passed his door.

"I know, Pig Pen. Sorry. Go back to sleep."

"Wacky weed."

"That's the boss, right, Pig Pen? Not you?"

Through the dark I could just make out a half-open eye with a look that said, *Don't be too sure*. Great. A stoned parrot.

"Good night, Pig Pen."

"Good night, cheapskate."

I took some comfort in the fact that he latches on to his latest word only until someone teaches him a new one.

I drank a small glass of vodka in the kitchen while I tried to remember why Ratko's name sounded familiar. I didn't get very far, and the vodka didn't help. Maybe sleep would. My watch read 3:37 as I walked home through the empty streets. It was still hot.

★ CHAPTER 10 ★

The Chekist coughed, put his lighter to another cigarette, and clicked PLAY. The decade-old tape, digitally transferred to a laptop, crackled to life. Poor sound quality, plenty of background hiss, but the voices were clear. Not that it mattered—he'd listened enough times over the years to memorize the contents. Still, he took some pride in the job his technicians had done wiring the dacha. Neither of them had ever known. Not that that mattered either.

A nurse stopped at his door, wrinkling her nose. He hadn't seen her before. She frowned at him, the cigarette, and the NO SMOKING sign above his head. She started to speak, but his hard stare drew her eyes to the name on the end of the hospital bed. She gave a small shriek and scurried away. He went back to the tape.

A TV played. The disembodied voice of the news reader described the carnage in central Moscow as firefighters fought to bring the blaze at Rosnobank under control. It would take them another fifteen hours, by which time the office tower would be only a charred shell. The death toll would just miss double digits. *Could've been much worse,* the Chekist thought, not for the first time. He'd taken all the precautions he could.

Over the TV came the sounds of drawers being opened and closed, papers ruffled, the occasional curse, vodka poured into a glass. Kosokov was getting drunk while he got ready to run. He didn't know he was already dead.

Gorbenko's voice. *"You'll never make it, you know. They'll have men at every border crossing. They will have anticipated this."*

"I'll worry about making it," Kosokov said. *"If the Cheka's as smart as everyone says it is, we'd all still be working for the Party."*

"Don't be a fool, Anatoly Andreivich. Look what they did to your bank. They're shutting everything down, erasing all the tracks, eliminating all the links. You're a very big link. You and I, we're the only two who could expose everything."

"I'm counting on that fact to keep me alive. You made your deal, Boris. You're on your own with it. I'll take my chances by myself."

"You're crazy! The CPS can provide protection. We can bring the Cheka down. Yeltsin will have no choice but to purge the entire organization when people see what they've done. It's their one big weakness. No one will have difficulty believing they murdered innocent Russians to pursue their own ends. Especially once you and I lay out the evidence. Like the Katyn massacre. There will be national outrage."

"National outrage? Russia today? Hah! Don't make me laugh. Neither of us will live to see it, in any event. Like I said, you made your deal. Good luck to you. I'm taking my evidence with me. My life insurance policy."

The crash of a door thrown open. Her voice. *"Tolik, I came as soon as I could. What the hell is going on? What are you doing here? Oh . . . Who the hell are you?"*

Gorbenko said, *"No names. Better that way. Call me Leo. I'll be in the kitchen."*

"Tolik, what the hell is happening?"

"Look at the TV. Your fucking husband is destroying everything. You, too. You didn't tell him, did you?"

"Lachko? What are you talking about?"

"Look."

More TV noise for a minute, then Polina. *"Jesus! That's . . ."*

"That's right. The bank. Maybe you'd prefer I was there."

"Don't be an ass. What . . ."

"The Cheka, you fool, that's what. Covering their evil tracks." A grunt as Kosokov pushed himself to his feet.

"The fire, how did it start?" she said.

"Start? It was set. The whole building, all at once, early this morning. WHOOSH!"

"And you think the FSB . . ."

"Think? Think? Polya, I know."

"But why?"

"Polya, did it ever enter that beautiful, egocentric, self-centered, narcissistic head of yours that all your success, all those big property deals you engineered, all the money we made, in reality have nothing, as in not one fucking thing, to do with you?"

"You're drunk. This is nonsense."

"Nonsense? Nonsense, she says. Let me explain something, something that should be obvious, if you ever stopped to think about it. We're the Cheka's bank, Polya. We have been since 1992. We've financed more operations than I can count. I kept a record. It's all on these CDs. I knew one day they wouldn't need us anymore, that this is what would happen. These CDs might just keep us alive. Take a look if you don't believe me."

Another stretch of silence, punctuated by periodic sounds from Kosokov.

Some ten years earlier, in October 1999, the Chekist was already in his car, cursing snow and Moscow traffic and berating his driver to go faster toward Kosokov's dacha. Now, listening for the hundredth—two hundredth?—time, he had no difficulty remembering each of the participants and every piece of bad luck he stumbled over that day. He fished out another cigarette as he waited for the moment Polina learned the truth.

The tape rolled. Kosokov was pouring more vodka. Goddamned fool, the Chekist thought. You should have run. Right now. But you thought you could outsmart the Cheka. If you'd just run, maybe none of this would've happened.

There it was, the quick intake of breath, followed by the curse. Then, *"Jesus Christ, Tolik, what the hell have you done?"*

"Keep going, Polya. The best part's at the end."

The Chekist stopped the tape and reached for the phone. Time to move. He wasn't in the best shape for it—he was tired, and his chest ached. The doctors said he needed another couple of days, but he had no choice. To wait was to risk everything. Fucking Kosokov. Fucking Gorbenko. Fucking Rislyakov. Fucking Polina.

He'd been sloppy ten years ago. Uncharacteristically so. Now he was paying for his negligence. He wouldn't make the same mistake twice.

★ CHAPTER 11 ★

Six fifteen A.M., eighty-five degrees, the air heavy enough to hold in my hands. I wake up at six, no matter what—a habit I've never been able to break. I live on South Street in what was once a warehouse serving the seaport two blocks north. The seaport is now a tourist attraction, and the warehouse had long fallen into disuse when enterprising artists converted its big, open floors into studios and residences. Initially they were illegal, but as with hundreds of loft buildings in New York, that eventually got sorted out, thanks to a lot of hard work, some legal wrangling, and a few envelopes filled with cash. In 1996, I moved in two years after it became kosher. In recent years, my neighbors who've been there since the beginning have started to acknowledge me.

I own half the sixth floor in the back, away from the noise of the elevated FDR Drive, which passes outside our door. My windows face south and west into the canyons of Wall Street. I've kept the space mostly open—living area, bedroom, guest room, and baths in twenty-two hundred square feet—a reaction to the cramped quarters of my childhood. It's still more a commercial neighborhood than a residential one, but that doesn't bother me. I like the solitude, especially at night. Another reaction.

I stretched outside the building in my running clothes and an old painter's hat. I took off to the south, picking up speed for the first half mile before settling into my normal gait, thinking about Polina, Ratko Rislyakov, and whether Marko and company had figured a way out of Jersey City.

I did one of my five-mile loops, this one down through Battery Park at the tip of Manhattan and up the west side along the Hudson to Greenwich Village, where I turned east through the quiet cobbled streets all the way across the island before heading south again and home. I try to run at least five days a week, regardless of weather, although days like this make me question my resolve if not my sanity. On alternate mornings I take a shorter route and stop at the gym to work the weights.

I arrived back in the neighborhood hot, soaked, and possibly enlightened—I had an idea where I'd seen Rislyakov's name. I used to cool off strolling the Fulton Fish Market down the street, taking in the seafood and the characters who worked there, but the market's moved up to the Bronx, and only a lingering fishy smell remains. They'll have to tear up the asphalt to get rid of that. Today, I just walked around the block a couple of times and bought a bagel at the deli. I met Tina in the lobby, filling out her top beautifully, as she always did.

"Off to work," she chirped. Too bad. Well, it was a lousy day for sunbathing.

I showered quickly, poured some coffee, and logged on to Ibansk. com. I paused to read Ivanov's latest post. It started with his signature rant about how the Cheka, "the state within a state," had taken over the state itself, along with everything else, as Vladimir Putin and Iakov Barsukov "dispatched Cheka operatives throughout the government, industrial, and criminal structures of Ibansk with the mission of throttling democracy, corrupting free enterprise, and coddling crooks. Most important, wrapping Cheka hands tight around any strings worth pulling."

Ivanov's keyboard spews acid—he makes no attempt to be balanced. That's one reason he's as popular as he is. Power run amok—especially Cheka power—is unmitigated evil, in his single-minded opinion, and the only defense left is holding it up to the bright light of the blog. I don't always agree, but it's hard to argue with his basic premise. The fact is, the Cheka does pull about every string worth pulling in Russia these days, and has since the fall of the Yeltsin government. One of these strings is the regular media, all but entirely state controlled. Ivanov and a few others are lone voices trying to tell what they see as the truth in a thoroughly hostile environment. Truth, even imperfect truth, gave Ivanov a voice of authority. In a land where the official voice lied with impunity—confident that no one would notice or care—Ivanov shouted, "Pay attention!" as loud and long as he could. He screamed the truth as he saw it, just as Zinoviev, his Soviet-era predecessor, had done.

Where Ivanov and I part company is the subject of Iakov Barsukov. To Ivanov, he's the personification of Cheka malfeasance, Putin's chief henchman in the inexorable extension of Cheka control. He may not be totally wrong about that—but to me, Iakov's the man who plucked me from the living hell of my adolescence, recognized a talent, and gave me a chance for a career and a real life. Without him, I doubt I'd have made twenty. Even with everything that happened later—to me, to him, to our families, to our friendship—it's hard to turn against a man like that.

Ivanov had news.

DIVINE JUSTICE . . . NOT A MOMENT TOO SOON?

We hear that illness stalks the Barsukov clan—although confederation might be a more accurate term these days, as time, disagreement, and even accusations of disloyalty have driven the various members of the ferret family in diverse directions. Will the threat of mortality heal old wounds as it opens new ones?

Iakov, *père,* of course, suffers from advanced age—something few Russians experience—and perennial bronchitis. Now son Lachko has been laid low with cancer of the esophagus. The result of a lifelong love of *papirosi*—or a sign from heaven that enough is enough? Ivanov is not privy to the thinking of the celestial authorities, but he can always hope.

The Badger brothers, Lachko and Vasily, are Ibansk's leading criminals. Vasily runs the rackets here in the old country with sharp claws and bloody teeth. Lachko was dispatched to New York when his checkered

Cheka career—once destined for the pinnacle of Lubyanka—came to its ignominious end. Even those less cynical than Ivanov could question the wisdom of installing an officer once accused of smuggling, theft, and embezzlement as chief of the FSB's Investigations Directorate, but consistency and common sense have never been Cheka hallmarks. Nepotism, on the other hand . . .

Ivanov digresses. One thing is certain. Even the most powerful Chekist cannot outrun the clock. Time numbers their days. How many more does Lachko have? Ivanov has the best sources in Ibansk, but that has yet to be confided.

He can hope, however.

I scrolled back through Ivanov's blog, looking for an old post. I stopped here and there to skim diatribes on the Cheka and the Barsukovs, making sure they added nothing to my current knowledge. Ibansk .com was a way to check in on a world I'd left behind and planned to continue to leave behind. Now, thanks in part to Ivanov himself, that world had jumped years of time, a continent, and an ocean to land here, today. Polina, Lachko, even the Cheka, all seemed to be chasing me down. How long before Ivanov started calling the race? After last night, on another sweaty New York morning, the world I was living in was feeling more and more like Fucktown.

I kept scrolling and found what I was looking for, back in early May.

WHERE'S RATKO?

One of Ibansk's more colorful, up-and-coming criminals (God knows, we have up-and-comers aplenty) has suddenly dropped from the scene.

In the all-night-world all over Ibansk, from Moscow's chanson clubs to Mayfair's casinos to New York's oh-so-hip (or should that be SoHo hip?) city-that-never-sleeps nightspots, the young and the reckless, feckless but rarely checkless, are asking the same question—Where's Ratko?

He cut—still cuts? (in Ibansk one must always ask)—a wide swath, does/did young Rad Rislyakov, who goes by *nom de guerre* Ratko

I remembered that scheme. It had been the first really big heist of identity information—the one that put large-scale ID theft on the map. At least forty million accounts, maybe as many as a hundred million, as Ivanov claimed. Front-page news at the time. Front-page news again a few years later when one of the hackers heisted another hundred million credit card numbers, demonstrating the old fool-me-once/ fool-me-twice adage was as apt as ever. Foos was bemused by the brazenness—the hackers literally reeled in their prey with a laptop and some wireless equipment readily purchasable on the Internet, sitting in a car in a strip mall parking lot. He was more appalled by the near total lack of security on the part of major retailing chains. Most of all, he wondered what the thieves planned to do with all those names and numbers.

It appeared Rad Rislyakov—Ratko Risly—was a big-time player, which didn't mesh on any of a number of levels with the lowlifes supposedly working for him, and certainly not with the three Ukrainians I'd met last night in Jersey City.

Ivanov had more to add.

Ratko burns the candle at both ends—on three continents. For the last few months, he's been seen in the company of an auburn-haired, blue-eyed creature, as gorgeous as any beauty in Ibansk—no exaggeration, Ivanov swears!—but then he and she dropped out of sight. Ivanov is doubly curious because heretofore Ratko has been seen mainly in the company of pretty young men. A foot in each camp, perhaps.

Did the Badger Brothers rein in their wayward genius, fearing he could flame out? Ivanov hears he's been busy building a new profit center for the Barsukov empire—a high-tech, hush-hush money laundry capable of making billions vanish into the international ether. Perhaps he was attracting the wrong kind of attention to his own exploits. Many avenues for Ivanov to explore. Stay tuned!

Could there be two Rad Rislyakovs? Unlikely. The photo in my pocket of Eva Mulholland—an "auburn-haired, blue-eyed beauty" if there ever was one—made it more so. But if Ratko was such a bigshot, globe-trotting, jet-setting, high-tech crook, why was he pretending to screw around with penny-ante kidnapping?

One more manifestation of Fucktown?

One way to find out—ask.

It was still early, but Chelsea bustles at all hours, especially along Sixth Avenue, where the big discount emporia have reclaimed the elegant limestone buildings constructed originally as department stores for the carriage trade. Times change. In New York, commerce adapts and carries on. Yet Mother Nature can work her will, even in the concrete jungle, and this morning, the heat sucked life from the street. A cab dropped me outside Rislyakov's luxury loft conversion. (New York is still waiting for its first nonluxury conversion.)

The lobby was all blond wood and stainless steel. A uniformed doorman, Hispanic, early thirties, sat behind a circular counter. I told him who I was there to see.

He shook his head. "Not home."

"When was the last time he was home?"

"Can't say. We're not allowed—"

I slid a Department of Homeland Security ID card across the blond wood. A forgery, a good one, a gift from a Russian FSB officer for whom I did a favor. The man looked down at the card and up at me.

"You'll be helping your country. Rislyakov runs with a suspicious crowd, Middle East connections, if you know what I mean."

"I had no idea. He's . . . He's always been polite to me."

"Of course he has. No way you could know. When did you last see him?"

The man thought for a moment. "Couple months, now that I think about it. He didn't say anything about going away. But that's not unusual."

"Anyone else asking for him?"

He hesitated. I tapped the card on the counter. "Couple of guys—foreign guys, Russian maybe, I'm not sure. Big men, thick accents. They come by every few days. Gave me . . . They wanted me to call them when Mr. Rislyakov returns. I wouldn't, of course."

"Of course. You have the key to the apartment?"

"I can't—"

"You heard of the Patriot Act?"

"Yes, sir."

"Gives us the power to prosecute people who prevent us from stopping a terrorist incident before it occurs."

"Hey! I never—"

"Of course you didn't. Key?"

He opened a drawer and handed across a ring. "You want 7B. Left off the elevator."

"Thanks." I put a fifty on the counter.

"That's not necessary, sir. I didn't realize . . . I'm glad to help."

"Don't worry. The Patriot Act created a special fund for situations like this. Consider it a thank-you from a grateful government."

I headed for the elevator before he could think too much. One reason I chose to live in America is that I agree with Churchill. Democracy is the worst form of government yet invented—except for all the others that have been tried. Proof point—the Patriot Act is exactly the kind of law that could've been enacted by the Communist Party Central Committee. I assuaged the mild guilt I felt over the Homeland Security ruse with the argument that it was a lot less harmful than the fear I'd instilled in Jersey City last night.

The elevator opened onto a small hallway with five doors. I rang the bell for 7B and waited. Nothing. I rang again. No sound from within. I unlocked the door and entered.

The air was hot, still, and stale. No one had been here in weeks, if not months, as the doorman said. A large, open, modern space that resembled the lobby in its use of wood and steel. A lot of Sheetrock painted white, big windows out to Sixth Avenue. Double glass muffled the noise from the street.

The space was neat and clean. No clutter. I spent a short hour going through it. At the end, I had a portrait of a young man with expensive taste in design, clothes, furniture, toiletries, and sex toys, but not much else. A lot of things were missing—a computer, for one, for a reputed geek, but maybe he had a laptop he took with him. Also photographs, mementos, notes, files—all the things that accumulate in life, even a young one. Remove the clothes and toiletries and it was as if no one lived here; the apartment could have been a sale model. Nothing here for me. On the way out, I noted a stack of books next to an easy chair. Ross Macdonald and Graham Greene, *Travels with My Aunt* on top. At least Ratko had good taste in writers.

I went back to the lobby and gave the keys to the doorman. His eyes traveled to two large men sitting on black leather chairs. They were as broad and coarse as the decor was sleek and trendy. Pasty faces, cheap suits, unfriendly eyes. One of them stood and came toward me.

"*Dobrya utro,*" I said. "Good morning."

"*Yeb vas,*" he replied. "Fuck off."

"Thought so."

"Thought what, asshole?"

"*Urki* muscle. You work for Lachko?"

"Don't fuck with us."

"Fine. See ya."

As I turned I started a count in my head. I got to eight.

"Wait." He wasn't quick, but the dimwit's brain was starting to function. "What do you want here?"

"See Ratko."

"What for?"

"Friend of friend."

"He ain't here."

"So I'm told. But if he's not, why are you?"

"Fuck off."

The brain had apparently maxed out. He went back to his seat and took out a pack of cigarettes before remembering he couldn't light up inside. He put them back in his pocket with a curse. These weren't the Badger's best men. One more try wouldn't do any harm.

"Hey, I've been trying to call Ratko, but nobody answers. When's the last time anyone saw him?"

"Fuck off."

That seemed to be the extent of his conversational repertoire. They would certainly report my presence. Question was, did I want to make it easy for Lachko to know I was interested.

Couldn't hurt.

Bullshit.

It could hurt in the extreme.

That didn't stop me from saying, "Tell Lachko, Turbo sends his regards."

Neither man looked up as I walked out the door.

Five phone messages from Bernie at the office, two from last night and three this morning. One from Gayeff, curt but informative.

"Guys left at six. One went out to a shelter, came back with clothes. The two we followed went straight to SoHo, 32 Greene. Couldn't see the buzzer, but there was no one home. Followed them to Manhattan Beach. Same addresses you had. One more thing. Somebody followed us following them. Blue Chevy Impala. Probably a rental. New York plates but couldn't get the number without getting spotted. Car stayed at Greene Street when we went back to Brooklyn."

Who the hell could that have been? And where did they pick us up? The hotel? Montgomery Street? Maybe Marko and his friends were sharper than I thought. But I still had the money. I checked the safe, just to make sure.

I gave Foos and Pig Pen a rundown on the night's activities. The parrot gets obstreperous if he's left out of the loop.

"Wait a minute," Foos said. "You telling me this guy Risly pulled off the T.J. Maxx job?"

"That's right."

"Shrewd dude. That was one ballsy hack."

"See what the Basilisk can find on him. He goes by Risly and Rislyakov. His apartment is 663 Sixth. SoHo address is 32 Greene."

"Sure."

I had gotten some coffee and a traffic update from Pig Pen when Foos's baritone rumbled through the office like close-by thunder. The last bites of a bacon-egg-cheese-grease-on-a-roll concoction sat on tinfoil on his desk. My doctor is constantly on my case about blood pressure and cholesterol. He has me on statins, and I watch what I eat. I tried to compare notes once with Foos, but he just grinned and said he had no issues. I think he was swallowing a cheeseburger at the time. Like the Ralph Lauren girlfriends—life just isn't fair.

"No Rislys or Rislyakovs at 32 Greene. But there is a Goncharov. Number 6A."

"Goncharov?"

"Alexander." He banged on the keyboard.

"Ratko has a sense of humor. The Russian poet Pushkin's first name was Alexander, and his wife's name was Goncharova."

"Hilarious. The Rislyakov side of his personality has a gambling problem. Accounts at four online casinos. Down about eight hundred grand, all told."

"You don't say?"

"I also say he's three months behind on the rent in Chelsea. Eighty-five hundred a month. Sold the car in May—Audi TT—for eighteen grand. Stiffed the garage for two months before that. Prepaid Con Ed and Time Warner. Eight hundred and change. That covers Internet and phone."

"Huh. Sounds like he was getting ready to run."

"Yep. Goncharov's up to date on the financial basics of life, but he's accumulating credit cards and bank accounts. Eight Visas, five Master-Cards, five Amex. Only just started using them, though. Been running up a Visa bill in Moscow the last eight days—six grand and change. Hotel, restaurants, a few shops. Huh, he used a Rislyakov Visa. Can you tell what this is?"

I leaned over his shoulder. "Looks like an undertaker."

"We all gotta go sometime. Let's see. He's got bank accounts at Chase, Citi, B of A, and some locals. Twenty-two in all. Nothing much in them. Few hundred each. I'd say he's getting ready to leave Rislyakov and his debts hanging, and switch to the Goncharov identity. Maybe he was arranging for Rislyakov's funeral."

"Funny. Phone calls?"

"Patience. On to those next."

"Think I'll pay a visit to Greene Street. Order another breakfast delight. On me."

I went next door and called Bernie.

"I've got Mulholland's money. And a possible line on the so-called kidnapper. Unless I miss my guess, he's sleeping with Eva. Although he might be gay—or AC/DC."

"Turbo! It's already been a long day. Make sense. What happened last night?"

"The less you know, in your current capacity of practicing attorney, the better."

"Just give me the basics." Bernie's twenty-five years in the CIA were spent mostly behind a desk. Sometimes he can't contain his curiosity.

"Three Ukrainians, small-time hoods. I used some contract muscle. We shot one of them so they'd know we were serious, then faked killing another so his pals would talk. Oh, and we threatened to hunt down their families, kill them or worse. The last time I saw the Ukrainians, they were naked in bed together in a Jersey City rent-a-flop."

"Okay, you made your point."

"The Ukrainians are working for a guy named Rislyakov. He works for Barsukov."

"That's not good."

"Yeah, but Rislyakov's not where he's supposed to be. Lachko's got men out looking for him."

"That's supposed to make me feel better?"

"Rislyakov's a geek playboy. Geek as in Gates, not Onassis. He probably has a gambling problem, and rumor is, he's dropped from sight. Before he dropped he was seen a lot with an auburn-haired, blue-eyed beauty on his arm. Sound familiar?"

"I really don't need this."

"She's still priority one, right?"

"Right."

"I've got an idea where Rislyakov and Eva might be. I'll be by later with the dough. Mulholland sprung?"

"Arraignment's in an hour."

"Good luck."

Pig Pen was watching as I headed for the door.

"*Au revoir*, parrot."

"*Adios,* cheapskate."

The Basilisk was humming as I passed through its core.

★ CHAPTER 12 ★

Lower Greene Street was quiet in the late-morning haze. The bazaars of Canal Street bustled at the far end of the block, but only a few cars and fewer pedestrians passed 32 Greene. A gray eight-story loft building with a cast-iron facade that needed paint. The hand-lettered sign by the buzzer for 6A read GONCHAROV. I pushed the button, waited, pushed again, waited and pushed again. I pushed the other buzzers to see if I could at least get into the building. That didn't work either.

I crossed the street and looked up. The windows on the sixth floor needed washing even more than the facade needed paint. I took out my cell phone and found the number I wanted.

"Gina," the clipped voice answered immediately.

"I know that. I called you."

"Turbo!"

"Want a job?"

"Does it involve running around sweating buckets in this fucking heat?"

"Involves watching a building. From the street. No shade."

"And the hottest friggin' day of the year."

"You want the job or not?"

"Yeah. I need the bread. But I'm only good till six. I've got a job at the library for the summer. It's air-conditioned."

"That's fine. I'll spell you then. Thirty-two Greene. We're interested in 6A. I just want to know who comes and goes. I'll wait across the street."

"I'll be there in fifteen, twenty tops."

I often use college students for simple research or observation jobs. They're good at blending into the background. I know because I was trained to be, and I recognize the talent. Gina's a junior at NYU and one of the best—smart, quick, intuitive, tenacious. All attitude with a mouth attached, but she doesn't have the two annoying habits that afflict three-quarters of America's youth: ending every sentence as a question (I'm told that's called "uptalk") and injecting the word "like" into every third phrase she speaks, the San Fernando Valley's most pronounced contribution to the culture. Fascism isn't good for much, but a dictatorial approach to language has its merits. One of the few things the French and I agree on.

I leaned against the brick, but it was too hot. As I straightened, a Town Car parked down the block. A man got out and came in my direction. Same breed as the thugs at Ratko's apartment building. My message had traveled fast. Did he know about Goncharov's studio, or had he followed me?

He opened his coat to show the automatic in his waistband. "Let's go," he said. "We're already late. Fucking traffic."

"No good. Tell Lachko—"

"Get in the fucking car. Now!"

He had the gun halfway out when I said, "Okay. Quick call first." Who knew how many men Lachko had here. I wanted to warn off Gina.

"No calls. In the car."

He climbed into the Lincoln after me. Another side of Russian beef was behind the wheel. He smelled of sweat and tobacco in equal measure.

"Move," the man said. The car took off, rattling as it accelerated on the cobblestones. I didn't ask where we were going. At the corner, the driver turned east across the bricks of Grand Street toward Brighton Beach.

Don't buy the house, buy the neighborhood—another Russian proverb. Exactly what Lachko Barsukov did.

Lachko owned a full square block in Brighton Beach. On two sides, he left the existing houses. The other two blocks he demolished and constructed a replica of the Beloselsky-Belozersky Palace, an enormous baroque-neoclassical pile of pink stone, gilded columns, and marble statuary that must have a hundred rooms. The original stands on Nevsky Prospekt, St. Petersburg's main drag, a bigger-than-life billboard advertising excessive opulence and reminding us why the tsars had to go. The Badger's reproduction was evidence that both the wealth and ostentation of the New Russians were on a scale with their predecessors'.

Two guards approached the car while it idled outside a massive iron gate. The driver put down the window, and one of them signaled someone somewhere. The gates swung open. The Lincoln pulled into a courtyard and parked to one side. It looked out of place next to a refurbished ZiL limousine, doubtless belonging once to a Politburo boss, a red Bentley, and a white stretch Hummer. Another two men approached as we got out of the car. One held a gun while the other patted me down. Then he pointed to a door across the courtyard.

Yet another man waited at the door and took me up a flight of marble stairs and down a long marble corridor to a reception room furnished entirely in Biedermeier. He knocked once on a paneled door, entered briefly, then stepped back. In I went. I wasn't ready for the sight.

Lachko and I had once been close, as close as two men can be who don't like each other. His father, Iakov, the man who had guided my early career in the Cheka, also welcomed me into his family. I loved him like the father I never knew and tried to love Lachko and his brother, Vasily, too, but affection doesn't necessarily pass down generations. Iakov was the glue, and over time, Lachko and I moved apart, old planks separating with age and wear. Then events intervened, and whatever glue was left was burned—scorched would be more accurate. Ivanov said he was sick. Ivanov had a spy.

Lachko was about my size and build—or had been the last time I saw him. Disease had taken sixty or seventy pounds, and overfed muscles were now starved and atrophied. He was wearing a silk polo shirt, warm-up jacket, and track pants that probably cost more than one of Mulholland's suits. They couldn't disguise the devastation. His cheeks and lips, once plump and heavy, now pulled against the bone. Two enormous dark black eyebrows hung over what was left of the face, thunderclouds ready to erupt. The withdrawal of flesh made them all the more pronounced. The eyes beneath hadn't changed—they were as cold and gray as ever. He had a plastic oxygen tube in his nostrils and a Belomorkanal smoking in his right hand.

The room was all white—walls, carpet, furniture, marble mantelpiece. The sole exceptions were a bright red lacquered desk and the pile of pillows on his white leather daybed—an array of red, green, and gold, too many to count. The effect was quite striking and very Russian, in its gaudy kind of way. We've never been known for subtlety.

"Greetings, Electrifikady Turbanevich, you shit-eating son of a whore fucked up the ass by her pederast father," Lachko wheezed in Russian, smoke floating from his mouth. "I hope you don't mind paying a visit to an old, sick friend." He stopped to cough.

Russians excel at vocal vitriol. The language facilitates improbable, attention-grabbing slurs, and Lachko was well practiced at the verbal body slam. To respond was simply to invite more.

"Lachko, I am sorry. I heard about your illness. I hoped it wasn't true."

"Bullshit. You'd dance on my grave naked. These fucking doctors. They say I have cancer. They may be right. They say it can be treated, maybe. They may be right about that, too. They tell me to stop smoking. Fuck what they say. What can I offer you? Coffee, beer, vodka?"

"Nothing," I said.

"Vodka, Sergei," Lachko said to a large, well-built man in a silk suit and wraparound mirrored sunglasses. "Two glasses. You will drink with me, Electrifikady Turbanevich. We have not had many opportunities recently, and who knows how many we have left."

I thought he was referring to his disease, but the grim grin on his withered lips told me to think again.

Lachko picked up a couple of cashews from the crystal bowl on the table beside the bed and dropped them, one by one, into his mouth. He chewed slowly. He'd eaten the nuts for years—in a small way, they were part of the reason for our rift. He used to smuggle them by the bushel, intended for a store serving the *nomenklatura,* the privileged class, but diverted to the Barsukov private stock.

"How long has it been, Turbo? Twenty years, twenty-five?"

"That's how you wanted it."

"That is correct. I still do. I had hoped to finish my days without ever setting sight on your piss-ugly face. Do you like my home?"

"Magnificent," I lied. "I recognized it immediately, of course."

"Of course." The withered lips turned ever so slightly upward beneath the pointed nose, as close as Lachko ever came to a real smile.

He did not offer me a seat, so I remained standing. I didn't try to make small talk or fill in the years. If he was interested, he'd know what I've been up to.

Sergei returned with a chilled bottle and two glasses. He poured Lachko's first, then mine. Lachko held his up.

"*Za vashe zdorovye*—to health, Electrifikady Turbanevich. Mine, that is. You can rot from your maggot-infested insides out for all I care." He tossed back the drink. I skipped the return toast and took a sip. Lachko was watching my every move. The scrawny paw scooped up more nuts. He hacked twice, spat in a silver bucket on the floor and fired up another Belomorkanal.

Lachko chain-smoked a vicious brand of *papirosa,* an unfiltered Russian cigarette made by stuffing the cheapest possible tobacco into a cardboard tube. They were introduced in the 1930s to commemorate the completion of the Belomorsko-Baltiyskiy Kanal, the White Sea–Baltic Canal, which runs from St. Petersburg through a hundred and forty miles of rock to the White Sea. One of Stalin's showpiece projects, built entirely by prison labor from the Gulag—170,000 laborers to be precise—using only handmade picks, shovels, wheelbarrows, and such. No machines. No explosives. No technology. Tens of thousands died of starvation, exposure, exhaustion, and illness. Of course, the cigarettes have killed many times more. The irony is, when it was completed, the canal was too shallow and too poorly constructed to be of much use. Still, it *was* completed, and therefore it needed to be commemorated.

"I'm told you've been asking after an associate of mine," he said.

"If I'd known he worked for you, I would have come here first," I lied again.

He appeared to consider that, weighing its truthfulness, deciding whether he cared. "What do you want with him?"

There was a question requiring a delicate answer. What did he know? It rarely paid to underestimate Lachko.

"He kidnapped a young woman. Or he and the young woman pretended she was kidnapped. I was hired to deal with the problem."

"Kidnapping? Ratko? Don't make me laugh."

"Why would I make up such a stupid story?"

"Who's the girl?"

"Not your concern."

Mistake, I knew it as I said it. The fist came down on the table, and the crystal bowl jumped. Cashews spilled over the top. He still had strength.

"I decide what concerns me, Electrifikady Turbanevich. Look around you. Have no doubt, I alone decide. You concern me now, you and this bullshit kidnapping. Who hired you?"

I was treading on cracking ice around a gaping hole. "A rich American. I didn't know it had anything to do with Ratko until his associates told me last night. He hires stupid people."

"How much was he after?"

"Hundred grand."

That came as a surprise. The storm-cloud eyebrows wobbled slightly. He reached for some more cashews.

"Who are these associates?"

"Three Ukrainians."

"Names?"

"They don't matter."

Another mistake. The thunderclouds shook until he brought his anger under control. "You understand as well as I, it will be easier for everyone, including these stupid Ukrainians, if you tell me who they are. If I have to find out myself . . ."

Sergei grinned and flexed his fist. I did understand. This was the way the Cheka worked. Pressure, squeeze, exploit. The only *modus* he knew. Here he was a criminal, but he was a Chekist at heart, and I was on his turf. His rules ruled, and I wouldn't do Marko and Company any favors by bucking them. I told him their names. The thunderclouds twitched and Sergei took out his cell phone. The Ukrainians would soon be receiving visitors.

"You're not drinking, Turbo. How's Aleksei?"

"Why?"

"You show such an interest in my affairs after all these years, I thought I should return the favor. Still working for those shit-sucking faggots at the CPS?"

Not sure where he was going, or whether he was just needling me, I stayed silent.

"He and some other pea-brained bunglers have been sniffing around Rislyakov, too. I was curious if there's a connection. Perhaps you're trying to help out."

"I haven't talked to my son in years, Lachko."

"You blame me, of course."

"I didn't say that. How's Iakov?"

He didn't answer, just glowered.

"Ivanov says his bronchitis—"

"Ivanov. Hah!" He practically spat the words. "We should have shot that bastard Zinoviev when we had the chance. Filthy liar."

This time he did spit.

"This new bastard's no better, maybe worse. Ibansk-dot-com! Thinks he's funny. He's arrogant, they all are. He'll make a mistake and the Cheka's axe will chop his balls into farina. I hope I live to see it."

He spat again and lighted another *papirosa*. The air-conditioning was working fine, but the room smelled like damp cardboard.

Sergei closed his cell phone as he returned to his boss's side. Lachko nodded, and he went to the desk and brought me a thick manila envelope.

"Like your son, you're sticking that ugly nose up a lot of assholes that aren't yours," Lachko said. "Open it. It's what you've been looking for."

I undid the clasp and looked inside, but I already knew what I'd find. Lachko wheezed again, or maybe it was a laugh. "You thought you were so smart, you and your little faggot helper, snooping. You thought you could fool the Cheka. Hah! Sasha's in a cell, Turbo, and it's your fault. There'll be an interrogation, and he'll confess. They always do, as you know. What happens next is up to you."

I lunged toward Lachko. Strong arms wrapped around me from behind. I could feel Sergei's breath on my neck. I couldn't move. I could barely breathe.

"Sasha didn't do . . ." Sergei squeezed. I couldn't finish.

"What? Sasha didn't what?" Lachko said, smiling. He was enjoying himself.

Sergei loosed his grip—a little. "He didn't do anything. You know that. He was helping me with information about my family."

"Selling state secrets, Turbo. That's twenty years."

"State secrets? My mother's—"

"Gulag secrets are Cheka secrets, Turbo. You, of all people, should know that. You're not the only one, by the way, he was assisting. He had a long list of clients, I'm told. Maybe enough to hang for."

Sergei tightened his hold. My chest ached.

"What do you want with Rislyakov?" Lachko said.

"Kid . . . nap. I told you the truth."

"You haven't become any more cooperative with age, Electrifikady Turbanevich."

"Tell Sergei he can let go," I managed to hiss. "I'll stay right here. I'd like some vodka."

Lachko nodded, and the arms released me. He pulled himself upright on the daybed.

"Do you know why you're still alive, Turbo?"

There was no good answer to that.

"What my father saw in you, I'll never fucking understand. Once a shitty little *zek,* always a shitty *zek.* You had no place in the Cheka, you have no place in the world. No one wants to know you, not when they discover that's what you really are. Polina fucked half the officers at Yasenevo when she found out. She even fucked me. You didn't have the balls to tell her yourself."

I threw my glass, but missed, before Sergei's arms clamped on again. Shame and hatred filled my veins—shame for myself, hatred for him, more hatred for myself and where I came from. I pulled against Sergei, but he held on. The rage passed, but the humiliation remained, as it always does, razor wire wrapped tight around the soul. For the millionth time, I told myself to ignore it, it meant nothing. For the millionth time, I had no chance.

Lachko didn't budge, the cold gray eyes staring at me, filled with loathing, waiting. "You haven't had the balls to tell your own son either, have you, *zek* coward?" he said.

The rage came roaring back. I couldn't have responded if I wanted to.

"Maybe I'll take care of that, too. If I don't have him killed first. Like you, he's getting too close to things that don't concern him."

I lunged again—or tried. Sergei squeezed. My ribs felt like they were cracking.

Lachko said, "I will happily drink vodka while I rip your dead eyes from their sockets with the strength I have left. Here's a deal, your lifeline, more than you deserve. Stay away from Rislyakov. And tell that mouse-eyed son of yours to do the same. That goes for the other leprous whores at CPS, too. He's none of their fucking business. He's no longer any of yours."

"I just told you—we haven't spoken since Aleksei was two." My voice came out as a wheeze almost as weak as his.

"*BULLSHIT!*" The fist landed on the table again, and the cashews danced across the glass. "Russian sons obey their fathers, even when the fathers are pathetic, pointless piss-colored *zeks*. If either of you try to do something stupid, it will be the last mistake both of you make. And your faggot friend might just rot in his cell forever. Now get out."

Sergei shoved me back down the long hall. He didn't need to push—I went willingly.

I spent the first half of the ride back to Manhattan thinking about how easily Lachko could inflict pain and self-loathing, not just with his threats toward Sasha and Aleksei, but with his bigoted reminders of my background. He struck every chance he got. The fact that he'd been committing crimes against the state, the Party, and the Cheka, to which we'd all sworn oaths, was irrelevant. I'd undermined his rise to the top, and he was going to spend the rest of his life getting even. Polina was one way. Another was my past. Once I let him see how much he could hurt, he attacked with relish.

Millions of Russians are just like me. The fact that we're all victims of a calculated, state-sanctioned system of betrayal does nothing to relieve our shame and disgust. We can't even feel any kinship with our fellow *zeks*. None of us wants to recognize a fellow traveler—if we do, we admit our complicity in the horrors of our Gulag pasts. The complicit victim. The Soviets' greatest irony. Stalin's enduring legacy.

I spent two decades running from my childhood inside the very organization that did so much to shape it. I've spent another trying to find freedom in a foreign land where we're all told, repeatedly, we can be anything we want to be. Even so, like anyone, I'm a prisoner of the past, as surely as I was born an inmate of the Gulag. I've yet to find freedom from either.

Bemoaning fate was getting me nowhere, as usual, so I spent the rest of the ride making a mental list of things out of whack—right here, right now, today. Polina/Felix hiding out on Fifth Avenue. Ratko Risly kidnapping Eva Mulholland. Eva's cooperation. Barsukov's fear about Ratko. Sasha, a low-level FSB archivist, whose only crime was helping people like me find out what happened to their families, locked in a cell, serving as leverage for something Lachko knew I couldn't deliver. As we came out of the tunnel, I thought about my options. The only one that made any sense was going back to Greene Street.

★ CHAPTER 13 ★

Sergei left me outside the office at 6:30. He hadn't said a word. I walked around to the sidewalk. His window slid down. He dropped the manila envelope on the pavement.

"Boss said you forgot this. He also said, '*Oo ti bya, galava, kak, oon a bizyanie jopuh*—your face looks like a monkey's ass.'"

The window rose as he sped away. I took the envelope upstairs. Foos was nowhere to be seen. Pig Pen was sleeping. I dialed Gina's number.

"Sorry I stood you up."

"What happened to you? I waited as long as I could, but I had to split at six twenty. I was late as it was."

"Thanks. Not your fault. You see anyone?"

"Guy, girl, and an older guy."

"Together?"

"No. Guy came first, at four fifteen. Girl at ten to six, and the older guy just before I left, six ten."

"Describe them."

"Girl's tall and thin, about five-nine. Probably eighteen, nineteen years old. Reddish-brown hair, real blue eyes. Great skin, you see that, even across the street. Hot figure, could be a model."

I'd seen a picture of someone who looked like that, tied up with a gun to her head. Eva Mulholland.

"She looked kind of nervous," Gina said.

"Strung out?"

"Maybe. More furtive, jumpy. Like she's afraid someone's gonna take something away from her."

"The guy?"

"Medium height. Medium build. Brown hair, expensive cut. Good-looking, slightly pudgy, big nose. Dressed in black. Had a suitcase, one of those rollers, and a messenger bag."

"Look like Dustin Hoffman?"

"Yeah, when he was younger."

"The older guy?"

"Seventy, maybe seventy-five. White hair, tall, maybe six-four. Thin as can be. Wearing a suit—you don't see many of those in SoHo. Looked like he was checking numbers as he came down the block. He rang the bell and got buzzed in. Girl, too. First guy had keys."

That description sounded all too familiar. I would have dismissed it as coincidence, even though my Cheka training didn't believe in coincidence, except that I'd just spent an unpleasant hour with his son. This was turning into a family reunion.

"You want me to go back when I get off here?" Gina said.

"Send me a bill and forget you were ever there."

"You're the boss."

I went downstairs, hailed a cab, and told the driver Franklin and Broadway, where there's a building with an entrance on each street. I watched out the back window the entire ride but saw nothing. I got out on Franklin, went inside, came out on Broadway, walked a block south, then east to City Hall subway station, stopping along the way to look in shop windows, tie my shoe, buy the *Post* at a newsstand. Nobody appeared to be following me. At City Hall, I caught a crowded uptown train to Fourteenth Street, where I waited until the doors started to close to step out. Up and down the platform, nobody followed. I crossed over to the downtown side and repeated the trick back at City Hall. I returned to the street and hailed a cab. This time I said Greene and Grand. I was sure I was clean of tails.

The block was still quiet. Almost eight o'clock now, but no cool to the evening air. Just to be sure, I waited in a door across from number 32 for fifteen minutes, watching for any activity on the street. A few people walked by, carrying briefcases, backpacks, and shopping bags. Locals on their way home. This was a daytime block. SoHo nightlife was Prince, Spring, and West Broadway.

I crossed and rang Goncharov's buzzer once, twice, three times. No answer. I returned to my watching post and called a Russian locksmith I know. Forty minutes later a van pulled up with AAA-ACE-ACME LOCKSMITHS painted on the side. A wiry man got out and grinned.

I met him at the front door. Three minutes later we were climbing a stifling stairwell to the sixth floor. Two doors, marked A and B. I pointed to the former, and he went to work. It took twelve minutes before the door swung open on oiled hinges. Glad that I'd insisted on expenses from the Mulhollands, I gave the man five hundred dollars. He nodded his thanks and left. I stepped into the cool, dry, air-conditioned air of Alexander Goncharov's loft.

The lights were on. A dozen halogen cans shone like high noon from the twelve-foot ceiling. If Ratko's Chelsea apartment was minimalist-chic, this was neoclassical color run amuck—greens, reds, and golds everywhere. A pair of enormous matching sofas faced each other in the center of the room—each could seat six—covered in embroidered gold fabric folded over on itself in a way that defied both physics and finance. Maroon upholstered chairs bookended the sofas. Ebony coffee table with mother-of-pearl inlay in the center. The full-length curtains shimmered avocado and orange. Green paint on the walls, the kind of green and the kind of paint you hire a guy who doesn't advertise in the Yellow Pages to spend weeks applying. Carpeting picked up all those colors and worked them against red and sky blue in a chain-link pattern. Too much—too much of everything. Before the blood.

A ragged streak marred the carpet, nearly a foot wide, winding from the door, where I stood, through the furniture to a pillared archway at the back of the room. I put a finger to the pile. It came away red and wet. I stood rock still, listening for sounds of life and wishing I had brought a gun. Nothing to hear except the low rush of air being pushed through vents in the ceiling. I followed the trail as quietly as I could, but the old floor creaked under the carpeting. Nothing I could do about that, except stop every few feet to listen. Still no human sounds other than my own.

Through the archway, a kitchen on the right and dining area on the left. I followed the blood down the middle to more pillars and a closed door. Painted steel. I put my ear to the metal. Silence. The knob turned easily in my hand. I gave a gentle push. It didn't budge. I pushed harder, and the hinges moved without squeaking. Movement to my right. I jumped. Nowhere to go. A big water bug skittered across the stainless steel counter, probing for somewhere to disappear. Exposed like me, until he ran down the leg to the floor and under the baseboard. The door swung softly shut. Some kind of automatic closer. I took a minute to regain my breathing before pushing it open again.

A large, square windowless hall with three more doors, one straight ahead and one on each side. Light shone through four ragged holes in the one straight ahead. Below the holes was a body. Beside the body was another.

They lay backs toward me. The closest was dressed in black. The other had white hair. I put a finger to the neck of the man in black. Not cold, but no pulse. I pulled at the shoulder. He fell over backward, wide still eyes staring at the ceiling, the front of his black shirt covered in dark red. The late Ratko Risly, unless I missed my guess. The other body was breathing. I rolled him over softly.

Iakov! I found the light switch. His eyes were closed, his right shoulder was soaked in blood. I patted his face gently. The eyes opened.

"Iakov?"

Crack!

The bullet passed over my back. Another hole in the door, this one a few inches higher than the others.

I hit the door low and hard. It pulled away from hinges and latch, and I fell into the room with splintering wood, rolling fast until I banged into a wall. I pushed back one revolution and came up in a crouch. Eva Mulholland, naked on a bed, lined up another shot.

Crack!

Wide. I grabbed her wrist, and the gun fell on the sheets. She looked straight at me, but what she saw, if anything, was anyone's guess. I picked up the gun and slapped her, not hard, but not gently either.

"Eva!"

She stared straight ahead.

"Turbo. Friend of your parents."

More stare.

I passed a hand a few inches in front of her face.

No reaction.

"That Ratko outside?"

No response.

"You shoot him?"

Nothing.

I pushed her gently, and she fell backward on the pillows. Like Gina said, a model's figure, inherited from her mother. Fine shoulders, small, round breasts, tucked waist, narrow hips, long, slender legs. Under other circumstances, she'd be beautiful to gaze upon, except the beauty was marred by ugly scars and discolored skin covering both thighs from knees to hips. Burns, or bad medical treatment. Circumstances, as well as decorum, vetoed closer examination. I pulled the sheet over her nakedness and ejected the clip from the automatic, a Glock 9 mm. The same one in the photograph? Four gone. Two at me, one in Iakov, one in Ratko? For whatever reason, that didn't feel right. I put the gun in my pocket and went back to Iakov.

His eyes were still open. He blinked once as I knelt beside him.

"Turbo?" His voice was just above a whisper.

"It's me. How bad are you hurt?"

"He who's destined to hang won't drown."

I smiled. If his humor was intact, the rest of him couldn't be too badly injured. I exhaled. I hadn't realized I was holding my breath.

"Who shot you?" I said.

"Don't know. Didn't see."

"I'll get help. You want an ambulance or Lachko?"

He closed his eyes for the better part of a minute before he said, "Lachko."

I'd never known for sure how deep the split between them ran. Since I was part of the cause—the whole cause, in their eyes—I'd never asked, but it had to be serious if it took that long to choose the lesser of two evils when he had a bullet in the chest. At least the brain was functioning. That was a good sign.

"I'll call him. The girl in the bedroom—she's your granddaughter, isn't she?"

He looked surprised. "Eva?"

"That's right. She's drugged. I'm going to get her help."

He waved his good hand and closed his eyes, as if trying to think. "She's Lachko's child, Turbo," he said after another minute. "He'll take care of her."

It was clear from my visit that afternoon, Lachko didn't know about Polina. A good guess he didn't know Eva was here either. Getting between them was a true fool's errand, but I'd been hired to find the girl. I went back to the bedroom. Eva lay as I left her, sheet around her shoulders, eyes staring into space. King-sized bed, four-poster. Mahogany. Two bullet holes in the wall behind. They hadn't missed by much. T-shirt and jeans tossed on the floor. A can of Diet Coke on the bedside table, half drunk. I sniffed the top. Smelled like Coke. Another door led to a bathroom-spa bigger than the bedroom. Whirlpool twice the size of the gold sofas, steam shower, sauna, two sinks, racks of multicolored towels.

Back in the hall, Iakov had worked himself up against the wall. He watched as I went through the dead man's pockets. Keys, change, eight hundred twenty-four dollars, and a U.S. passport in the name of Alexander Goncharov. In the last pocket, a shiny new BlackBerry. The message light blinked. I pocketed the BlackBerry and replaced everything else.

"I want that," Iakov said.

"What?"

"BlackBerry—I want it."

"Okay, later."

A rolling suitcase by the bed was packed full of men's clothes, mostly worn, mostly black. The luggage tag read GONCHAROV with the Greene Street address. The used boarding pass indicated he'd just flown in from Moscow. Beside the suitcase was a messenger bag with a laptop inside. I put it to one side.

"That, too."

Iakov had pulled himself to the open door. He was cataloging my every move. The caution of an old spymaster? More than that. Why should I be surprised?

"Stay still, Iakov. You're losing blood. I'm calling Lachko now."

"That computer is mine, Turbo."

"Okay."

I went out to the kitchen-dining area, where he couldn't follow, and weighed the merits of my cell phone versus Ratko's landline. Both would leave a trail, but going out to a pay phone would take too much time. I decided on the latter for the first call—to Brighton Beach. When a man's voice answered I said, "Tell Lachko it's Turbo."

It didn't take long before Lachko said, "Nothing in twenty years, twice in twelve hours. To what do I owe this misfortune?"

"I'm with Iakov. He's okay, but he needs a hospital. He's been shot."

"Turbo, what the fuck are you talking about?"

I repeated myself.

"You fucking with me? Let me speak to him."

Lachko didn't know his father was in New York. I shouldn't have been surprised by that either. I carried the phone back to the hall.

"I told Lachko you need help. He wants to hear you say it."

"Listen to Turbo, Lachko," Iakov said into the phone. "I'll explain later."

He handed it back. I went back through the door as Lachko wheezed, "Where the fuck are you and what the fuck are you doing there?"

"Thirty-two Greene, between Grand and Canal, 6A. Belongs to Rislyakov, although here he goes by Goncharov. He's here, too, but he's dead."

"What the fuck?!"

"I'm playing it straight, Lachko. Rislyakov was dead when I got here. He was shot, too, from the looks of it. I found him and Iakov and called you."

I could hear him barking orders in Russian. I looked at my watch. I figured I had at least forty minutes before they got here, but I'd be gone in thirty to be sure.

Lachko said, "I thought we agreed—stay the fuck away from Rislyakov."

"I didn't know he would be here. Iakov neither."

"Bullshit. What else is there?"

I hesitated. He was going to find out soon enough from Iakov. "Eva. Stoned silly. She might have shot Iakov, without knowing what she was doing. She tried to shoot me. I don't think she shot Ratko."

"Eva? What the hell? Turbo, I am personally going to—"

"Shut up, Lachko. You're not going to do anything. I'm taking Eva to get help."

"You stay right the fuck where you are. My men are on their way."

"I'll be gone by the time they get here. She can't wait. Could be an overdose."

"Turbo, do exactly as I fucking say."

"Lachko, I could have called the cops. I still can."

Silence. I thought I could hear the scratch of a lighter and the faint crackle of burning tobacco.

"I'm telling you one more time . . ."

"Don't bother. I'll tell Iakov help is on the way."

My second call was to Bernie. I used my phone for that. He wouldn't like it, but he was going to have to get his hands dirty. He was at the office.

"Mulholland sprung?" I asked.

"Million dollars bond."

"He's got more trouble."

"I don't need this, Turbo."

"You don't begin to know the truth of that. I'm with Eva. The least of her problems is she's *non compos*—totally zonked on something. She can't talk, but she can shoot, which she did, at me."

"Christ! Are you all right?"

"Fine. The drugs didn't help her aim."

"Least of her problems?"

"Yeah. I'm not going to tell you about the worst. You won't approve of how I'm handling them. I need someone to take Eva to a hospital—someone you can trust. She might have overdosed, and have her checked out thoroughly, including STDs."

"STDs?"

"Sexually transmitted diseases."

"Turbo!"

"She's naked in a bachelor pad, Bernie. Just being prudent."

Sharp intake. "You got any good news?"

"She's alive. That's not a universal truth here."

That stopped him. "Turbo, have you called the police?"

"Not yet."

"Do you intend to?"

"If anyone asks, Bernie, I called you about Eva, that's all. How long do you need to get someone to SoHo?"

"Give me half an hour. I'll set it up at NYU Hospital. Rory's on the board. Where are you?"

I looked at my watch. "We'll be at Grand and Mercer, southeast corner, at ten fifteen."

"Turbo, I—"

"I'll need to talk to Eva when she comes out of it. Before anyone else—including her parents. Got it?"

"Turbo, I can't—"

"You have to. Unless you want Mulholland and his daughter to have adjoining cells."

Silence. Then, "Okay."

"Ten fifteen."

Iakov hadn't moved. His eyes were closed, but his breathing was slow and easy. The other doors in the hall opened to a bathroom and a den. A quick check found nothing of interest in either.

I knelt by Iakov and put my hand on his hair. His eyes opened, and he smiled.

"Lachko's men should be here in fifteen minutes. They'll get you to a hospital."

"Are you . . ."

"It'll be better if I'm not here. Lachko and I . . . Well, you know better than most. I'll come see you tomorrow."

"Okay."

I went to get Eva. "We're going to get you some help, okay?"

I wasn't expecting a reply, and I didn't get one. It took a long five minutes to get her dressed. Iakov was nodding again when I took the messenger bag and put it by the front door. I went through the drawers in the kitchen until I found masking tape to hold the latch of the door and the front door downstairs. I spent five more minutes carefully removing all evidence of my presence from the loft.

Eva had little interest in walking, so I leaned her body against mine and held her upright with my right arm under hers. We'd gotten as far as the hall when I felt her stiffen suddenly and start to shake. Her eyes grew wide as she looked down at Iakov. Then she screamed—a long piercing wail. *"NOOOOOOOOOOOOOO . . ."*

I picked her up and carried her to the gold sofa in the living room. She stopped screaming, but her eyes stayed wide with terror.

"Eva!"

She didn't move or speak.

"That's your grandfather."

No response. Eyes still wide. Terrified. I backed away. She didn't move.

I returned to the hall. "What was that about?"

"No idea. My condition?"

This was no time to argue, but we both knew Eva's scream wasn't one of surprise. It was a wail of terror, deep-rooted terror. "She needs help," I said.

He was trying to push himself up with his good arm. "Where's the computer?"

"I've got it. Lie still, Iakov. Lachko won't be long."

"No! Leave it. It's . . . mine."

"It's Rislyakov's."

"Goddammit, Turbo! This is Cheka business."

I was halfway out the door. His eyes were wide open now, his injury all but forgotten. He looked as determined as I'd ever seen him.

"Cheka business?"

"You heard me. I want that computer."

"I'll bring it to you tomorrow."

"Turbo . . ."

I left, before he could argue further, carrying Eva down the stairs and most of the way to Grand and Mercer, Iakov's assertion, angry, defiant— *This is Cheka business*—filling my head. A Town Car idled at the corner. The window slid down, and young Malcolm Watkins peered out.

"Didn't tell you about this in law school, did they?" I said.

"Not at Harvard. My father wanted me to go to Chicago."

I made a mental note to tell Bernie the kid was okay. He helped me load Eva in the backseat and crawled in after her.

"She's high on something. Not sure if she took it or it was slipped into her drink. She's also terrified, but I have no idea of what. Sorry I can't be more specific."

He nodded and spoke to the driver. The car pulled away. I gave a wide berth to Greene Street as I walked south out of SoHo and through what's left of Little Italy and Chinatown back to the office.

Cheka business?

Foos was sipping Kalashnikov vodka and banging away at his keyboard. I picked up the bottle and examined the label, eyebrow raised.

"He's entitled to make a buck," Foos said.

I fetched a glass from the kitchen. General Mikhail Timofeyevich Kalashnikov invented the most successful weapon in the history of weaponry, the AK-47 rifle. More than a hundred million in circulation. Unfortunately, since he'd done it in service of the Soviet state, he hadn't earned a kopek, and two Hero of Socialist Labor medals won't get you on the Moscow Metro these days. So he was cashing in, any way he could, like everyone else in the great Russian rush to capitalism. As Foos said, who could blame him? I took a sip. The bottle had been out too long, so the vodka had lost its chill, but it still tasted good. I made a silent toast to the general while I took Ratko's laptop from the messenger bag.

"I need to copy a hard drive. Pronto."

"Everybody's in a hurry. Let's see."

I handed it across. He opened the top, pushed the power button, and sipped his vodka.

"Problem," he said.

"Encrypted?"

"Yep. Where'd you find it?"

"Belonged to Ratko Risly."

"Belonged?"

"He doesn't need it anymore."

"Whose fault is that?"

I told him how I'd spent my evening.

"Who shot Risly?"

"No idea. Then again, I have no idea what the whole thing is about. I'm hoping something on the computer will tell me. I'm going to have to hand it over to one Barsukov or another, probably tomorrow."

"Okay. We'll try brute force. See how good the late Mr. Risly was. Once we get in, copying is no big deal."

"Can you do it so no one knows? Ratko probably has some tech-savvy associates."

"You're talking to the maestro."

"How about a keyboarding bug, one that can't be found if someone looks?"

"No problemo."

"I owe you."

"You're working on a lifetime tab."

"In that case, the next bottle of Kalashnikov is on me."

I put the Glock and the BlackBerry in the safe, next to the payoff money I'd forgotten to return to Bernie. I'd take care of that first thing tomorrow.

Or so I thought.

★ CHAPTER 14 ★

The Chekist moved the indicator on the computer forward. He knew the exact spot.

Polina said, *"Jesus Christ, Tolik, have you gone mad? They'll kill us for this."*

"I didn't plant the bombs, Polya. But we did provide the money. That's why they burned the bank. To kill us, they have to find us. We're leaving, within the hour. I can get us into Latvia, and from there—"

"Who's that man—Leo?"

"Gorbenko. Boris Gorbenko. FSB colonel. Point man on the whole operation. He determined the targets, recruited the others, acquired the explosive, oversaw the whole thing. The money moved through him."

"Jesus Christ, Tolik. He's a mass murderer. What's he doing here?"

"He's had an epiphany, a little late in the game. He's concluded that the people he did all this for—the real mass murderers—plan to kill him, too. He made a deal with the CPS, told them his story. They want him to bring me in, too."

"And?"

"I told him no deal, of course. Our only choice is to run, disappear, buy new identities abroad and make sure the Cheka knows that we've hidden those CDs in a safe place."

"Who else knows?"

"No one."

"And Leo?"

"Forget him. He's a dead man."

"No way, Tolik. We don't know him. He's already double-crossed the Cheka. We're nothing." Her voice dropped to a whisper. "He could be listening right now."

The whispers became inaudible, their intensity apparent, individual words impossible to make out. Except at the end. Polina, her anger rising, said, "God damn it, Tolik, if you won't, I will. Come on."

Nothing for a few minutes, then Polina's voice with Gorbenko. They'd moved to the kitchen.

"Leo?" she said.

"What the . . ."

"Move, out the door."

"Kosokov, what the fuck is this? I have no time for—"

The shotgun roar drowned the rest of the sentence.

Polina spoke again. "One barrel left. Move!"

The door creaked open and banged shut a few seconds later.

Silence on the tape.

It came back to life with a rumble. As the Chekist found out when he got there, they'd taken Gorbenko to the barn.

"Over there," Polina said.

"What do you want?" Gorbenko said, his voice betraying panic.

"We'll get to that. Open that trapdoor."

A grunt as he pulled at the concrete slab covering the hatch in the back of the barn.

"Look, Kosokov, I can—"

The blast from the shotgun cut him off. The Chekist would see later she'd hit him square in the chest. The force knocked him through the opening and down the cement stairs to his grave.

Kosokov said, "Jesus Christ, Polya. You didn't have to—"

"Where's Eva?"

"But you just—"

"Where's Eva, God damn it?"

"I don't know. Around somewhere. She was playing with her doll an hour ago."

"Find her. Finish getting ready. I have to go to our dacha. That'll take an hour, it's already snowing, but I have money there, and jewelry we can sell."

"What about . . . What about him?"

"Leave him. He was the Cheka's stooge, let them worry about it. And stop drinking. We've got a long night."

The barn door rolled closed. Silence on the tape again until they were back in the house.

"I put Eva's stuff in this bag," Polina said. *"She must be outside. I'll leave it by the front door. I'll be back in an hour."*

Kosokov belched. The Chekist stopped the tape. Timing, they say, is everything. His, that day, had been a little off. Today it was better.

★ CHAPTER 15 ★

I checked e-mail as soon as I got up. Foos's message, timed at 3:42 A.M., said, "Risly was good, but not as good as he probably thought he was. I'm in. Gonna grab some shut-eye. I'll have whatever there is to have in the morning."

I called Brighton Beach. I didn't worry about the hour.

"What the fuck do you want now?" Lachko said.

"How's Iakov?"

"In the fucking hospital."

"He's alive."

"I suppose you take credit for that."

"He was lucky. Which hospital?"

"Why?"

"I want to visit."

"Stay the fuck away, Turbo. We've had enough of you."

"I've got Rislyakov's computer."

That stopped him. "What computer?"

"Laptop. He had it with him yesterday." Iakov hadn't said anything to Lachko about the computer.

"It belongs to me. I want it back."

"That's why I'm calling. As soon as I hear that Sasha is out of jail, all charges dropped, back at his job, you can have it."

"Turbo, you dick-sucking son of—"

"That's the deal. Tell Sasha to contact me in the usual way. I'll call back when I hear from him. Which hospital?"

"Fuck your mother. Mount Sinai."

"I'll drop by later this morning."

The line went dead. I wiped away the sweat on my forehead. The air-conditioning was working, but the temperature had risen ten degrees in two minutes.

He hadn't asked about Eva. One more thing out of whack.

I ran three miles at a good clip, legs loose, body ready to do whatever I asked, despite the heat. I pumped iron for half an hour. When I got home at seven fifteen, a black Suburban with tinted windows was idling out of place in front of my building. Two men in suits got out. I recognized the big one—he'd been with the group that arrested Mulholland. He wasn't quite as large as a refrigerator, but he had the same boxy build.

"Your name Vlost?" he said.

"Who wants to know?" I replied, smiling to signal I wasn't being obstinate, just cautious.

Fridge pulled out a wallet and showed me an ID card that read FBI. "Special Agent Coyle. This is Agent Sawicki. Boss wants to talk to you."

Sawicki grunted. I wondered if he knew I was Russian.

"This a social invitation or you guys strictly business?"

"It'll be better for all concerned if you come along for a chat," Coyle said.

Sawicki grunted again.

I pulled at my sweat-drenched T-shirt. "Can I shower first? Whoever your boss is probably doesn't want to meet me like this."

Sawicki grinned at that. Coyle hesitated.

"You can come upstairs if you like. I'm not going anywhere."

"We'll be in the car," Coyle said. "Make it quick. She doesn't like to be kept waiting—and she's been waiting since last night."

Sawicki grinned again. For whatever reason, Coyle was giving me a heads-up. I smiled. "Appreciate that. I'll be right back. You guys want coffee, there's a deli around the corner."

He nodded. "Already found it."

The three of us drove in silence to an office tower in St. Andrews Plaza, one of a hodgepodge of government, court, and police buildings between City Hall and Chinatown. The area teems from late morning to late afternoon, but at five after eight on another hot day, it was dead quiet. The Suburban's air ran full blast the whole way and almost stopped my sweating by the time we arrived.

A brief walk through the heat, a longer wait to be metal detected, and a still longer ride in a slow government-service elevator. The sign on the glass door read UNITED STATES ATTORNEY, SOUTHERN DISTRICT–NEW YORK. No receptionist at the desk. Coyle left me with Sawicki and went down a hall. A few minutes later, he took me down the same hall to the end. Empty outer office. In the room behind, a raven-haired woman stood at the window, her back toward me. She turned as Coyle left, closing the door.

"I'm told y'all are fuckin' around in not just one but two of my cases. Suppos'n you tell me why and what for before I have your ass deported back to whatever socialist shit-hole you came from in the first place."

★ CHAPTER 16 ★

I listen to what used to be called country music because of, as Charlie Parker once reportedly said, "the stories, man, the stories." It's now known by the nondescriptive "roots" or "Americana," but whatever the term, I was standing in front of the inspiration for countless tunes about the honky-tonk angels who turn otherwise strong-minded men into helpless fools. When I finally told her that, she took it as a compliment—she's a big fan of Loretta Lynn.

Victoria de Millenuits. Victoria of a thousand nights. I realize I'm in no position to say it, but what's in a name? It fits her like a pair of tight jeans.

She's a few inches shorter than I am and built, to use a marvelous metaphor, like a brick shithouse. (Americans, like Russians, can be clever with wordplay, even when it makes no sense.) She has long legs, a full figure, just the right amount of honky-tonk mascara and lipstick, and a pout that turns men—at least this one—to jelly before she gets her lips fully formed. She wears her black hair thick and long, past her shoulders. The eyes—green ellipses that seem descended directly from ancient Egypt—are as deep as the Nile. They laugh when she wants them to and turn sad when she doesn't. Her nose is a touch too small and her mouth—those pouting lips—too large. The overall effect would have driven Botticelli to distraction.

That first meeting, in her U.S. attorney's office, the full package was on subdued display. An Armani suit straightened the shithouse curves, but they still took my mind off worrying whether Agents Coyle and Sawicki knew about Greene Street. The black hair was pulled back and tied up behind her head. Horn-rimmed glasses wrapped the green eyes, but they didn't dull the color. Jade is jade, no matter what it's encased in.

I stuck out my hand. "Pleasure to meet you. Call me Turbo."

That defused her—for a nanosecond.

"I know your damned name. Sit down!"

I kept my hand outstretched. "Then you have the advantage. You are?"

"The goddamned U.S. attorney for the Southern District!"

"Your title is stenciled on the door. I'm asking your name. Courtesy's a starting point in the socialist shit-hole I come from."

The eyes flashed, jade striking iron. I'd pushed it too far. Then they softened, the lips curled up, and she laughed. A big laugh—one that knew something about life. An Armani-clad arm came across the desk. The grip was firm.

"Victoria. Victoria de Millenuits. Thank you for coming to see me on short notice. Apologies for my greeting. You know what they say about litigators."

"No, we didn't have any to talk about."

The flash was back. "Don't push your luck."

"Okay. Doesn't matter. May I sit?"

"Please."

I took my chair, she took hers. We eyed each other across a big, cheap, veneered desk, as feminine as a tractor. The rest of the office had the same feel. Men's club wannabe leather. She read my thoughts.

"I haven't been here long, a few months. My predecessor's decor. No time to redecorate."

"Not a priority."

"I was appointed to do a job. That's my focus. Furniture . . ." She waved a delicate hand in the air.

"The kids I grew up with would've killed for a shit-hole like this."

The flash was back. "All right, goddammit. Y'all made your point."

I was trying to place the accent—Southern, certainly, more bayou than banjo.

"Description wasn't inaccurate, if it makes any difference."

She dropped her eyes as she opened a file on her desk, brought the eyes back up and said, "Small talk's been a pleasure, Mr. Vlost. Let's get down to cases."

"Turbo."

"Where'd you spend last night?"

"Why?"

"My men waited outside your building until after one."

"You work late."

"I work till whenever. Where were you?"

"I work late, too."

"Doing what?"

"I think my lawyer would advise against answering that."

"Because you have something to hide?"

"Because he doesn't approve of fishing expeditions."

"This wouldn't be our mutual friend Bernie Kordlite?"

"Why do you ask?"

"He gave me your name and address."

"Bernie sold me out?"

"I could've looked in the phone book. What's your business, Mr. Vlost?"

"Turbo." I took out a business card and handed it across.

She laughed—another real laugh. "Vlost and Found? Whatever your business is, we know you're not a comedian."

"I help people find things."

"That make you a flatfoot?"

"I believe gumshoe is the correct technical term."

"What's Mulholland looking for?"

I shook my head. "I'm sure Bernie didn't tell you I'd answer that."

She looked down at her desk. "What's your business have to do with Lachko Barsukov?"

"Lachko's an old friend. From the socialist shit-hole."

"And Rad Rislyakov, also known as Ratko Risly?"

Careful now. "You seem to know a lot about my movements."

She took a photograph from the file and turned it toward me. I was looking at myself getting out of the Lincoln in the Badger's Brighton Beach courtyard. The close focus and blurred background said it had been taken with a long telephoto lens. She turned over another picture. I was exiting Ratko's Chelsea apartment building.

She said, "Tuesday, you're at Mulholland's. Coyle saw you there. Yesterday morning, you show up at Risly's building. Later, you pop out to Brighton Beach for a visit with a top member of Russian organized crime, someone who's in business with the someone you went to see that morning. When you get back to Manhattan, you play cute all over downtown, then on the Lexington Avenue IRT, like you want to lose anyone following you. Then you don't come home. Bernie says you're straight, but Bernie used to be a spook, too. What are you up to, Mr. Vlost?"

I gave up on her calling me Turbo, at least temporarily. "Sounds like I was successful."

"Successful? At what?"

"Losing that tail."

She slapped the desk. "Goddammit—"

"Okay, okay. Lachko's an old friend, like I said. We used to work together—in the KGB. I heard he was sick."

"So you were visiting a sick friend?"

"Sure. Is that a crime, even if we are both ex-socialists?"

She ignored me. "Why the shenanigans in the subway?"

"Don't like being followed. Occupational hangover."

"Why did you think you were being followed?"

"I wasn't wrong."

"You're not as smart as you think you are either. Tell me something I don't know."

"Lachko has a couple of guys camped out in Ratko's lobby. You know that. He was asking questions about Ratko yesterday that suggest Ratko has dropped out of sight. And since you'll undoubtedly ask, no, I don't know where he is."

Technically and spiritually true, if factually dubious. Two out of three ain't bad.

"Your powers of deduction knock me over. You know who Risly is?"

"No."

"Why would he want to drop out of sight?"

"Never met the guy. Have you?"

The jade flashed again. "Why did you go to see him?"

"Had something to talk about."

"Something involving Barsukov or Mulholland—or both?"

"I hope you won't hold it against me if I don't answer that. Maybe if you tell me why you're interested in Risly, I could help."

"Just my luck—a socialist with scruples. I'll ask again—what do you want with Risly?"

"I think this is where I came in."

"I can make life difficult."

"You mentioned that earlier. First thing you said. Kind of got us off on the wrong foot. I'll take my chances on whether the different agencies in the federal government have actually started talking to each other."

"You really do think you're clever, don't you? Is Mulholland your client?"

"Suppose I gave you my word that whatever my business, as you put it, with Mulholland, it has nothing to do with predatory lending or anything else at FirstTrustBank."

She doodled on her notepad while she considered that. "Don't take offense, but what's the word of a socialist spook worth?" she asked with a smile.

"Former socialist spook. Now I'm just another small businessman, backbone of the American economy."

"Don't give yourself airs. What about Barsukov and Risly?"

"Straight up—I have no business with Barsukov. He and I had a falling-out back in the eighties. Big one. Yesterday was the first time I'd seen him in more than twenty years. I hope it's the last. He does, too."

"How do you know that?"

"He told me."

"How sick is he?"

"I'm not an oncologist, but he's my age and used to be my size and weight. He looks like he's eighty and weighs one-twenty. He's got cancer and he's still chain-smoking. I wouldn't bet on him being around this time next year. On the other hand, I was recently reminded of a saying we have. He who's destined to hang won't drown."

"Not before I nail his ass. And Risly?"

I shook my head with a grin. "I'll tell you this. I very much doubt that my business with Risly, again as you put it, has anything to do with whatever you're interested in."

"What makes you say that?"

"He was trying a very stupid shakedown. It didn't work."

"What kind of shakedown?"

"Amateur effort. Not even worth talking about."

"That's your opinion."

I shrugged.

"Who was he shaking, Mulholland?"

I shrugged again.

"Somebody phished Mulholland."

"Yeah, I understand Ratko's got quite a rep in those circles. I don't know anything about that."

"Your word as an ex-socialist spook turned law-abiding small businessman?"

"That's right."

"The phisher used a forged letter from my office. That pisses me off. I also infer the phisher knows more about my business than he should. Bernie tells me you know your way around technology crime."

"I met Mulholland for the first time Tuesday morning. I'd hardly heard of him before then. My word as an ex-socialist spook."

She made another note. No jade flash this time.

"All right, Mr. Vlost. Thanks for your time. If you learn anything about Risly, I'd like to know."

"You're counting on a lot of ex-socialist goodwill."

"Very funny. Bernie said you could be a real pain in the ass."

"I'm really very friendly and engaging. Let me buy you dinner."

The green eyes gave me an I-can't-believe-you-just-said-that look over the top of the glasses.

"I think we'll get along better on a strictly business basis."

"That's been a real treat so far."

One more flash. Sooner or later I was bound to get burned, if I got the chance. She closed the file in front of her and stood.

"Good day, Mr. Vlost. If you ask him, Bernie will tell you I can be a pain in the ass, too. He'll also confirm my reputation for periodically crushing neighboring anatomical appendages. Maybe everything you say is true and this has all been one big coincidence. If so, nice meeting you. But feminine intuition and the statistics course I took back in college say bull to that."

"Sometimes, an inside straight fills."

"Maybe. Whatever you're up to, y'all'd be well advised to stay the hell out of my way. If I find out you are fuckin' around in my cases—or if you've been less than one hundred percent straight—I'll make sure you do time in a good old American jail for obstruction, and that's before I get your ass deported. Do I make myself clear?"

The twang was back. She worked hard to cover it, but it came out when she got angry. I found it charming. I was finding everything about her charming.

Before I could say more than "Very clear," a clock chimed 9:00 and the end of the first round. Coyle and Sawicki were nowhere to be seen as I showed myself out of the building. A young man in a white linen suit with black curly hair and an eye patch gave me a quick once-over as I passed through the reception area. He didn't look American, more European, and could've been Russian. I almost spoke to him, to test my hypothesis, but prudence knocked on my skull and said I'd already used up the day's quota of luck.

★ CHAPTER 17 ★

The heat sucked the energy off the street. Traffic—vehicular and pedestrian—moved a beat slow, and the mood was morose. BEARS RULE—DOW DROPS 610, the *Post* cried from a newsstand. I'd lost track of the market gyrations. Maybe I could train Pig Pen to broaden his horizons and provide updates on the Dow Jones.

No cabs in sight. I walked slowly back downtown, replaying the conversation with Victoria as I went. Coyle seeing me at Mulholland's was a coincidence—or bad luck, depending on your point of view—but she had people watching Barsukov's palace and Ratko's building. She didn't know about Greene Street, at least not yet. Lucky for me, or I wouldn't be walking around. Why did she bring me in to show her hand? Maybe Bernie's word was good enough for her. More likely, she didn't have much, so she was reaching for something.

I stopped at the deli and ordered black coffee and a toasted bagel, one half with butter and jam. I chewed that on the way to the office.

"Hello, Russky," Pig Pen said, his eyes fixed on the brown paper bag. "Pizza?" A mix of eternal hope and here-and-now resignation in his voice.

"Good morning, Pig Pen. Bagel," I said, removing his half.

"Cream cheese?"

"No cream cheese for parrots."

"Cream cheese?" he tried again, but he saw the fix was in.

"Cream cheese means cholesterol, and cholesterol makes Pig Pen an ex-parrot." I have no idea how a parrot's cardiovascular system works, but it seemed a reasonable assumption. Besides, Pig Pen thinks he's human like the rest of us.

"Python," he said, his head bobbing up and down. He's a fan of the dead parrot skit, along with everyone else, even if his ancestry is the butt of the joke. I handed over the bagel. He pulled off a piece.

"Onion!" Things were looking up.

"Happy now?"

"Muchas gracias . . ."

"You're welcome."

". . . cheapskate."

The neck feathers ruffled. Maybe I'm mistaken, and twelve is still adolescence in parrot years.

"Where's the boss?"

"Pancakes." Breakfast.

"Pig Pen, what do you know about Wall Street?"

"BQE?"

"No, not traffic. Stock market. Dow Jones. NASDAQ."

"Cross Bronx. Accident cleared."

"Is your life's ambition to be a cab driver?"

"Triborough—two lanes closed."

He went back to the bagel. Morning rush hour was the wrong time for this conversation.

"Tell Foos I said thanks for the hard drive."

"Drive-by."

"Not drive-by, hard drive. Computer."

He nodded as he chewed, but I think he was just pacifying me.

Bernie's secretary confirmed he was in the office. I got the hundred grand from the safe and walked down to Hayes & Franklin. Shirt wrinkled and tie loosened, he was bent over a thick stack of papers. He barely looked up when I dropped the bag on his desk.

"You want to count it?"

He shook his head.

"Do I need a receipt?"

Another shake.

"Who should I talk to about my fee, you or Mulholland?"

He held up the papers he was reading. Bloodshot eyes, exhaustion written all over his face.

"Bankruptcy petition, Turbo. Mulholland's busted."

"Come on, Bernie, this is America. People like Mulholland don't go broke."

"Remember how you told me he was buying FTB? You didn't know the half of it. He was buying on margin—as the stock fell. Best we can figure, he paid north of nine hundred million for shares now worth three." He looked at his computer screen. "Less. Market opened down again."

"Surely he's got other assets."

"Yeah, but looks like he's pledged those, too. We're trying to get a full picture. It's a mess."

"I'm sorry,"

He took off his glasses and wiped them on his tie. "He's not such a bad guy when you get to know him. Rory and I . . . We met at college, Yale, two scholarship kids in a pool of privilege. He was a poor mick from the wrong Boston 'burbs, me a Jew from Brooklyn. We formed a bond of sorts, us against the rest. Went our separate ways afterward but stayed in touch—holiday cards, reunions, that sort of thing. When I started here, he called me up, said he needed a lawyer he could trust. FTB was already a pretty big bank then, and he sealed the deal here for me. I owe him. He's human like the rest of us, he's got his flaws, but . . ."

"I won't argue with you, not today."

"Don't worry about your fee. We'll get it, one way or another."

"I'm not worried," I said, mainly to be polite. "How's the girl?"

He shook his head. "Touch and go. Docs say she was on Rohypnol. Borderline overdose. Still in the ICU."

"The date rape drug?"

"Yeah, but some kids take it recreationally. Roofie, they call it. Amnesiac—she probably won't remember a thing." He shook his head again. "She's been through rehab a couple times already. Didn't take. This stuff with Rory won't help."

"Maybe. Everybody needs a wake-up call. Something that makes you realize it's not all about you—unless you want to piss your life away. In which case, that is all it's about."

"Once more, Turbo, you've found just the right way to cheer me up."

"I met your former partner this morning."

"The piranha?"

"She hauled me in for a talk. Kind of intimated you sold me out."

"No way. You must be getting rusty. She knew who you were, where you'd been, who you'd been with. All she asked for was a character reference, which I'm guessing is why you're not in jail. How'd you make out?"

"All right, under the circumstances. She tried to push me over, I pushed back. No blood spilled."

"Sounds like Victoria. She likes to intimidate first thing out of the box. Thinks she needs even footing with the boys. I've always thought she'd do better using her feminine assets, but who am I to argue? She's done more than all right her way."

"How well do you know her?"

"Like I said, she came here about eight years ago, with that Atlanta firm. She's got brains to match her looks, and she's tenacious as hell. Every guy in the office hit on her with the same result. No soap. Used to be lots of rumors—lesbian, S&M, frigid, you name it. If her time sheets were any indication, not much social life of any kind. She was at the top of billable hours every year she was here.

"We were all surprised by the U.S. attorney appointment, but she networks a lot, she's active in the Bar Association, she's got a great rep in white-collar crime. After all the Wall Street scandals, that's probably what the Justice Department thought they needed. She may be a little out of her depth—organized crime, drugs, and terrorism haven't been her thing—but I bet she figures it out."

"She's trying. Not sure she's there yet."

"Only been a couple of months."

"Okay. I'll get out of your hair."

Bernie went around his desk and closed the door. "How bad was it, when you found Eva last night?"

"Bad as could be. You really want specifics?"

He shook his head. "Why'd you cover? Why not call the cops?"

"Multiple reasons. Eva'd be in jail now, looking at lots worse than a possible drug rap. There was a dead guy in that loft who's tied up with the Russian mob. He ran the kidnap scheme, I'm pretty sure, but no question Eva was in on it. She was walking around the streets of SoHo yesterday afternoon."

"So?"

"This whole thing's screwy, has been since the beginning. Like your former partner pointed out an hour ago, Tuesday, I meet Mulholland, who thinks his daughter's been kidnapped. Then he gets arrested. He's worried about his wife, but he doesn't know who she really is. I go looking for the supposed kidnapper—Rad Rislyakov, a.k.a. Ratko Risly, big-time identity thief, screwing around with a small-time shakedown. Next thing I know, Lachko Barsukov—that's right, that Lachko Barsukov—whom I haven't seen in twenty-plus years, tells me to stay away from Ratko and applies some heavy pressure. But he doesn't know about his ex-wife, now married to Mulholland, or his daughter, who's screwing around with Rislyakov. Then I find Eva in Ratko's hideaway, blotto, along with a corpse that's probably Ratko. I also find Lachko's father—right again, Iakov Barsukov—who has no reason to be there, except he says it's Cheka business. I also find a computer that may tell me what Lachko is worried about and Victoria is looking for. Haven't had a chance to check yet. So maybe I'm in a position to solve the mystery, help Eva, make a deal with Lachko, and possibly help Victoria, although I don't know at the time I want to do that—but not if I call the cops. Make sense now?"

Bernie shook his head and opened the door. "About as much sense as a Russian novel. Sorry I asked."

"Life's not as simple as crossing a field."

"One of your proverbs?"

"One of the more cheerful ones."

Foos was chewing another bacon-egg-cheese-grease-on-a-roll when I got back to the office.

"I'm guessing Pig Pen's jealous."

"He offered to trade his bagel and got all out of sorts when I declined. You could at least get him cream cheese."

"I'm trying to prolong his life, although I'm not sure why."

"Pig Pen said something about a drive-by."

"Pig Pen's a bird brain. I said hard drive."

"You may have grabbed more than you bargained for when you took that computer."

"Lachko and his father are keen to get their hands on it—that tells me something."

"The something is what it's running. I left it asleep last night, but online in case someone wanted to e-mail the late Mr. Risly. This morning, it woke itself up at six, activated e-mail, and received a bunch of messages. Three hundred twelve to be exact. Came in from all over, including overseas. Couple of apps went to work, downloaded the data in the e-mails, sorted them, sent out a bunch of new messages. Those went through zombies, so I can't tell where they ended up."

"All automatically?"

"Yep."

"What's in the e-mails?"

"You'll see. Lists of figures. Code, most likely."

"Lists? You mean like spreadsheets?"

"Yeah, but these aren't calculations, just lists."

"Hold on."

I retrieved both BlackBerrys from the safe. Long list of new messages on Ratko's. Shorter one on Marko's. None of the senders meant anything to me, but I showed them to Foos.

"This one's getting copied on all the e-mails. The other's only receiving a few."

"First one belonged to Ratko. The other to one of his associates."

"Ratko sent himself copies. There's more. You told me Mulholland got phished. Risly was the phisher. They've got three computers on a wireless network. Risly hacked all of them."

"Ratko's got—had—a talent for that kind of thing."

"Yeah, but phishers, as we know, play a percentage game. They phish lots of people, hoping to sucker a few, and they're looking for stuff they can steal—bank accounts, brokerage accounts, hard assets."

"So?"

"The only person Risly phished was Mulholland, and it looks like all he stole was information. Then someone took that information from him."

"How's that work?"

"Ratko removed a big file from one of Mulholland's computers. Removed as in removed—stolen, then erased, permanently. No way to retrieve it. He clearly wanted the only copy. Then someone moved that same file, along with another one, to an external drive and erased them from Ratko's hard drive. Again permanently."

"No way to tell what they were?"

"Uh-uh. Just two big-ass files, two hundred ninety gig and three hundred fifty gig."

"That someone was likely Ratko himself."

"True enough, but where's the hard drive?"

"Good question. He didn't have it with him. It wasn't at the loft or in Chelsea."

"Anyone know you have his computer?"

"The aforementioned Barsukovs."

"I'd watch my step, then—a little more carefully than the late Mr. Risly did."

"I'll do that."

"There's more. E-mail, from Risly's computer through a zombie to felixmulholland@aol.com. Listen to this. 'Greetings, Polina Barsukova. We know who you are, who you were, what you did, what you're trying to do. We know it all. We're thinking a partnership could be attractive for both of us. You get to keep your income stream—or 50% of it. You get to stay alive. We'll be the only ones who know who you are, who you've become. You can't find us. But don't doubt for a second we know exactly where to find you. We'll be in touch soon. In the meantime, if you don't believe us, check your computer. You'll find something missing. We have it now—another reason we think you'll welcome a partnership.' No signature, no return address."

"When did she get that?"

"April eighth."

"Right after the phishing expedition."

"That's right. A week later, she gets another message. Contains a list of bank accounts and instructions for her to transfer money into them. Doesn't make any mention of amounts, just percentages. Take a look."

He spun the laptop around. The message read,

Greetings again, Polina Barsukova.

By now, you've had a chance to consider our offer of partnership and we're certain you find it attractive. Here's what you will do.

Each month, you will receive a list of bank account numbers. On the 10th of the month, you will transfer from the accounts in which you have received payment 50% of those amounts in equal installments to the account numbers we provide.

If you miss a transfer, we will make a call to Brighton Beach. That will cause great pain. If you miss one more, we will make another—to Moscow. You know the price you will pay then.

No margin for error, Polina Barsukova. We trust we understand each other.

Here are the accounts for May:
197663874305-57
170190980928-98
316587686784-96
976223958279-83
737893690837-32
762137263728-53
712635558821-72
863876879297-24
267659876869-66
128763809890-52

I turned the computer back. "Basilisk didn't show any of this activity."

He nodded. "I know. I double-checked. But the e-mail refers to 'the accounts in which you have received payment.' They could be, probably are, under some other name or names."

"Ratko seems to know all about whatever arrangement she has in place for whatever she's up to. When the money's coming in, where it's coming in to, and the fact that he doesn't mention an amount suggests he knows how much. He's working both sides of this deal. But why?"

He spun the computer back. "Hold the phone. She gets another e-mail, couple weeks ago. Thanks her for the May payments. Gives her the account numbers for June. Then it says, 'We're afraid we must make a one-time assessment to cover the partnership start-up costs. Shipping and handling charges. $100,000. This will be a cash payment, small, used bills, please, tens and twenties. You have a week to collect the money. We'll be in touch with delivery instructions.' "

"Hundred grand? That can't be coincidental."

"It's not. That picture you showed me, the kidnap photo? Photoshopped. Four separate images, the girl, the gun, the *Times*, and the background."

"How'd Ratko . . ."

"He didn't. It was Photoshopped on Mulholland's computer. The same computer used to type the kidnap note. Look."

He banged on the keyboard and turned the laptop around. Four images, as he said—Eva, the newspaper, the hand with the gun, and a chair against a brown wall. Foos reached around to the keyboard.

"Voilà."

The four images merged into the picture Mulholland had handed me Tuesday morning.

"And here's your kidnap note."

He hit a few more keys, and the note appeared on the screen.

"I'm not into judgment," he said, "but it looks to me like you've been taken for a ride."

I couldn't argue. "You install the keyboarding bug?"

"Anyone does anything with that computer, you've got a front row seat."

"And no one—especially Lachko Barsukov—is going to know we were in there?"

He raised a bushy black eyebrow, his usual reaction to a question that's beneath response.

"Sorry," I said. "We need to erase all this. I have to hand the computer back to the Barsukovs."

"Already done. You're looking at the copy I put on this hard drive. Figured you'd want to keep your inadequacies to yourself." He clicked some keys, pulled out a cable, closed the laptop, and pushed it across the desk.

"One more thing. I got waylaid this morning by a pissed-off U.S. attorney."

"Uh-oh. He know about your extralegal activities?"

"Fortunately not. But *she* knows more about me than I like. She also turned down my dinner invitation."

"Cause and effect?"

"See what the Basilisk can find on her, starting with a home phone. Victoria de Millenuits is her name."

"Millenuits? Midnight?"

"Close. *Mille*—thousand, *nuits*—nights."

He shrugged. "My dinner invitations are usually accepted. I'll look into it after lunch. Pig Pen and I have a date at Lombardi's."

I took Ratko's laptop and Foos's external drive to my office and woke up my own computer. I plugged in a cable, and an icon for Ratko's hard drive appeared on my desktop waiting to be invaded. Almost like the good old days.

Not. Still, given that the computer now belonged to the Barsukovs, I enjoyed the irony.

I clicked on the icon, and the hard drive opened up. The home page for something called the Slavic Center for Personal Development appeared. I ignored that and began to work through the contents, starting with the spreadsheets. Two hours later, I was less than a quarter done, and my eyes hurt. I felt like a beer but settled for a glass of water and went back to my desk.

If Bill Gates had a dollar for every line of Excel spreadsheet employed by Ratko Risly, he'd have many more millions than he already does. The computer contained workbook after workbook, each titled with a number and all following the same format—a group of three columns on the left, five on the right, but the right columns contained many, many more entries. The first column in each group appeared to be a date. The earliest started six months ago. The most recent were the ones the computer added by itself this morning. The other columns contained what could be account numbers and dollar amounts, but that was pure guesswork on my part. On the other hand, why keep such elaborate records for anything other than financial transactions? Ratko's outgoing mail contained messages similar in content—five columns of numbers—but the messages, which numbered dozens per day, went to an array of addresses. Zombies, Foos said. Sleeping computers, left online, hijacked by cyber-pirates for a host of nefarious purposes, usually to send spam blasts or to corral into botnets, but also to cover tracks. Ratko's BlackBerry received confirming copies of the e-mails issued by Ratko's computer.

My stomach was rumbling, but I kept at it. Another forty minutes and I'd found the contents of several of Marko's e-mails logged into various workbooks. Sure enough, on the five-column side, every entry had a match a day or two later. The three-column entries were singles. I was pretty sure I was looking at the inner workings of the money laundry Ivanov said Ratko was building for Barsukov, but it beat the hell out of me how it worked.

My eyes, head, and stomach were all angry. I checked my e-mail before heading out in search of sustenance and almost cried aloud when I saw Sasha's name in my in-box with the subject "Vacation." That was code—he wasn't writing under any duress. The message read "Weather lousy here. Thinking of a trip. Always wanted to visit Istanbul. Can you recommend hotels?" More code—something had happened (he couldn't know I knew what), and he was going incommunicado for a while. I tapped out, "Try the Four Seasons, in an old prison, you'll like it," to tell him I understood.

Food forgotten for the moment, I placed another call to Brighton Beach. "Tell Lachko I'm going to visit Iakov. I'll leave the computer with him."

★ CHAPTER 18 ★

Iakov had a Central Park view he couldn't use from the top floor of the Guggenheim Pavilion at Mount Sinai. The place felt more like hotel than hospital—carpeted hallways, fancy wallpaper, mahogany doors, private rooms, and, no doubt, room service. No private insurer was footing this tab. Still, all the ersatz luxury couldn't quite excise the commingled smells of illness and death.

Two of Lachko's thugs stood guard. One blocked the door while the other put his pockmarked face a few inches from mine. Tobacco and vodka on his breath. "Lachko said one visit and don't come back, don't call, they don't want to know you exist. I'll take the laptop."

"Iakov asked first." I pushed past them into the room.

Iakov was sleeping, his head lolled over, the back of his bed propped up in a sitting position. His shoulder was wrapped in white gauze under the hospital gown. His color looked good, or as good as a pale-faced Russian's can, and his breathing was slow and even. He had an IV in the back of one hand. A machine beeped electronic indications of life. He hadn't changed much in the twenty-plus years since our last meeting. Permanently thin as well as tall, he'd always looked old for his age, and the years were finally catching up. His bones made their own mountain range beneath the hospital sheet. The face wasn't wrinkled, but it had deep creases I didn't remember from the eyes to the flare of the upturned nose, then down to the corners of his mouth. The white hair flopped over his forehead. It was thinning, patches of scalp beneath. I sat beside the bed and took his hand.

There was a time when I would have walked the length of the Trans-Siberian Railway barefoot if he'd told me to—no questions asked. Even today, I probably wouldn't dismiss the request out of hand. Iakov was at once savior, mentor, guiding light, and surrogate father. Each of us is responsible for our own destiny, but he was the reason I had any destiny at all. I've often wondered whether his father knew mine—they would have been young officers in the Cheka's early days. I've asked the question but never received a satisfactory answer. Nor has he been forthcoming about how he found me among the hundreds of thousands still in the Gulag in the early 1970s. I've never felt in a position to press either point. Find me he did, though, and one day when I was seventeen, a weak, hungry, tired, calloused kid, clad in rags, I was brought to the office of the commandant of the Vorkuta camps and interviewed by a man in a captain's uniform, first in Russian, then in Ukrainian, then Hungarian and Polish, and finally in broken English. His skills were passable. Mine were better. Two days later, still digesting my first real meal in years, I was on a train to Moscow.

I was installed in a small apartment with seven other students at the Foreign Language Institute, where I studied English and French. I didn't know it, but this was a training ground for the Cheka. In time, I was taught the basics of intelligence—building agent networks, surveillance, agent communication, etc. Seems funny looking back, but this would comprise most of my formal training. The rest I had to learn on my own—overseen, sometimes firsthand, others from a distance, but consistently, by Iakov.

The eyelashes flickered once or twice before opening to reveal piercing sky blue. Where Lachko and his brother got their hostile gray, I'll never know.

"Turbo!"

"Hello, Iakov. How do you feel?"

He waited a minute, taking stock. "Pretty fit, for a seventy-four-year-old Russian with bronchitis and a bullet wound."

"You look good."

"They tell me I can probably leave tomorrow. That would never happen in Moscow."

"You wouldn't get this room in Moscow, either. Well, maybe *you* would."

"Don't start. Capitalism has its faults, too."

"I didn't come here to argue. I just wanted to see that you're okay."

"Thanks, if I remember, to you."

"Fate was kind, for once."

He smiled.

"What happened in that loft, Iakov?"

"The American police want to know the same thing. They were here this morning."

"They don't know about me, do they?"

"Turbo, what kind of jackass do you take me for, after all these years?" His eyes sparkled, showing the rebuke was half in jest.

"I've never doubted you. But what were you doing there?"

"I told you—Cheka business."

"Am I permitted to ask what kind?"

He smiled up at me, but he didn't answer.

"I'm guessing it involves this computer you want so badly." I held out the laptop.

He took the machine. "Rislyakov was working on something for me."

"Did that something involve Eva?"

"No!" He spoke too fast. His voice softened again. "I didn't know she was there. How is she?"

"Alive. Near overdose of a bad drug—Rohypnol. Not sure whether she took it or Ratko gave it to her."

"Ratko wouldn't . . ." He stopped. "I shouldn't say. I don't know. Where is she?"

Something told me to be careful. "A friend took her to a hospital. Your Cheka business, does it involve Polina?"

"Polina?" He nearly spat out the name. "I never . . . Why these questions?"

"I'm just trying to figure out what happened."

"This is none of your affair. At least, I don't see how it could be. But perhaps you should tell me what you were doing there last night."

"I wanted to talk to Rislyakov."

"Why? What's he have to do with you?"

I'd thought about this on the way uptown. How much was I willing to give? I decided to stick with the truth—or the truth as I knew it before Foos erased the inner workings of Ratko's computer.

"Rislyakov, and maybe Eva, hatched a stupid fake kidnap scheme.

They were hitting on Eva's father, her adoptive father. He hired me to take care of the kidnappers."

"Kidnapping? What the devil for?"

"Not clear. How well did you know Rislyakov?"

"Not well. He was Lachko's protégé."

"You aware he had a gambling problem?"

That came as a clear surprise. "No."

"Was Lachko?"

"I don't believe so. I don't know. Lachko and I . . . We don't talk much anymore. He doesn't confide in me, hasn't since . . . you know."

"You still blame me for that?"

"At my age, I don't blame anyone, except life and fate."

"Lachko does."

"You ruined his career."

"He hasn't done badly."

"You know what I mean. He was going to run the Cheka."

"Maybe he should've thought about that before he started stealing."

"Everybody stole, Turbo. You know that, too."

"Not true. *You* know that."

"All right, *you* didn't. You still could've looked the other way."

"Like everyone else."

"We've been over this ground before. Is there a reason you're taking us on another tour?"

Good question. No good answer, except that old wounds, when they're deep enough, don't heal.

"What happened last night? Who shot you?"

He shook his head. "Rislyakov and I were talking. Someone buzzed from outside, and he asked me to wait in the back. I heard him yell, and the shot. I wasn't armed—I stayed where I was. I didn't hear anything else, so I thought whoever it was had left. He was just outside that door to the kitchen, waiting. He shot me as soon as I opened it. I must have passed out. The next thing I remember is you."

The blue eyes were thoughtful. I thought about the questions he wasn't asking, like *Why was Eva in that loft? Is Polina living here?* He could already know the answers. Or he could be biding his time. Or some other reason altogether. Iakov taught me to play chess when I was a student at the Foreign Language Institute. I was never much good at it. He always beat me.

He gave up a pawn. "So Polina's remarried?"

"That's right."

"She's still married to Lachko."

"Apparently that hasn't stopped her."

"Who's the new father Eva has?"

Another caution signal. "Does it matter?"

"Turbo!" The voice was sharp. "Remember where your loyalties lie. Lachko will want to see her. He has a right."

"The loyalty question got put through the grinder back then, Iakov."

"Your memory is self-serving, as so many are. You started the grinder."

I stood and went to the wall of the small room.

"Tell me about this kidnapping," Iakov said.

"Not much to tell. Just Ratko—or Ratko and Eva—trying to score a quick hundred grand. I assume he had an impatient casino creditor. Unfortunately for him, he had some associates who were neither bright nor brave, which is how I got to Greene Street. Did he and Lachko have some kind of rift, do you know?"

"Why do you ask that?" The sharpness was back.

"The name on the buzzer was Goncharov. Lachko didn't know that."

"You'll have to talk to Lachko. Rislyakov was only doing a job for me."

He was lying. I could feel it. He'd been tiptoeing around the truth as carefully as I had.

I pointed to the computer on his lap. "Lachko wants that, too."

"You told him you had it?"

"Only way to find out what hospital you were in."

He smiled. "You explore its contents?"

"Of course."

"Of course. Anything interesting?"

"Spreadsheets. I assume they're what Lachko wants."

"What else?"

"Nothing."

"Truth?"

I tried to read what was behind the blue eyes. He was watching me watching him. I gave him the same face I use when I'm holding a full house, although I felt like I had anything but.

"Truth."

He opened the laptop and turned it on, balancing it on his legs and working the keyboard with his one good hand. After a few minutes, he said, "How thoroughly did you check this?"

"Thoroughly."

"Data recovery?"

"Two large files copied and removed—permanently—some time ago."

He nodded, as if that were the answer he expected. "You tell Lachko that?"

"He didn't ask."

He nodded and continued to work the keyboard.

"What happened between Lachko and Polina?" I asked.

"Why do you care?"

"Curiosity."

"She was never loyal to him, just like she was disloyal to you. She was screwing a man called Kosokov the whole time they were married."

"The banker?"

"That's right. Everyone thought she ran away with him."

"You didn't believe it?"

"It was always too cut-and-dried for me. Life isn't that neat."

"You always said there are a million shades of gray, and my job was to get within a hundred of the right one."

He smiled. "You have no idea how much good it does an old man to see you again."

"I feel the same. I've always regretted everything that happened."

"We can't fight fate."

"You didn't answer my question—about Polina and Cheka business."

"What are you looking for, Turbo?"

"Just trying to solve a riddle for a client," I lied. "What are you looking for?"

"Trying to lay a few old ghosts to rest."

He was lying, too.

The door opened, and the pockmarked thug came in. He nodded at Iakov and whispered in my ear. "Fuck off. Lachko's downstairs."

I looked down at Iakov. "Will you be in Brighton Beach?"

"I don't know."

I picked up his hand again and squeezed it. He smiled up at me.

"You know, of all the men I brought into the Cheka, you were the best."

I smiled back. Just like old times. Only thing missing was warmth.

There was a shaded bench across Fifth Avenue, but I walked a few blocks up to the Conservatory Garden in case Lachko should decide to look out his father's window. All manner of flowers in bloom, including a few purple tulips hanging on to their last petals—color so deep they were almost black. I wondered if they were Russian. I sat in the thick shade of the canopied crabapples and almost felt comfortable. My psyche felt anything but.

I was trying to process too much at once—emotions, reactions, suspicions, doubts. Seeing Iakov for the first time in twenty years, and seeing him in that condition, rattled the door to the soul. Polina resurrected her own grave full of memories. Lachko, too. They all brought back the heartache of the Disintegration. I thought I'd succeeded in locking away those feelings, but Lachko knew how to reach in and squeeze, and his father and Polya, without even trying, amplified the pain.

Then there was Iakov, not telling the truth—for the first time I could remember. He'd betrayed me two decades ago, but that had been aboveboard. Put between a rock and a hard place, he'd chosen Lachko, his own flesh and blood. I understood that. The ramifications were going to be dire for one of us, and family won out. The irony was, Iakov couldn't avoid the chasm that would be ripped open whatever he chose to do. He was too close to see that. I was, too, at the time. This afternoon, he had no need to lie that I could fathom. Yet he had.

Motion beside me. I turned fast, ready to face one of Lachko's goons. The man looking down was the same one I'd seen in Victoria's reception area, in his white linen suit and eye patch. He bowed formally from the waist and extended a hand. "My apologies if I startled you," he said in Russian. "Petrovin. Alexander Petrovich Petrovin."

"Call me Turbo," I replied in English, taking the offered hand. His greeting was old-school Russian. Mine was anything but. Nobody's called me the mouthful my mother saddled me with since the orphanage, except Lachko when he wants to piss me off. "I saw you earlier today, if I'm not mistaken."

"That is correct. I apologize again for intruding. I'm told we have a mutual acquaintance in Rad Rislyakov. I was wondering if you've seen him recently."

"Never met him, I'm afraid." Technically true.

He looked me over, taking his time. He was a handsome man in his midtwenties, maybe an inch taller than I am but a good thirty pounds lighter. The linen suit was well tailored and hung stylishly from his slender frame. With the eye patch and full head of black curly hair, it gave him a certain flair. His one brown eye took me in with intelligence, and his easy smile indicated he meant no offense with his examination.

No reason not to be polite. "Please. Have a seat. Are you working with Victoria?"

"We're collaborating, yes."

"You're in law enforcement?"

"In a manner of speaking. I will apologize in advance and tell you that I am necessarily sparing with the facts of my professional pursuits. Even my real name, well . . . Life is extremely inexpensive in Russia these days, as I'm sure you are aware, especially for people in my line of work. I came from Moscow to see Victoria—and Rislyakov. He was supposed to meet me earlier today, but he didn't show up. That's one reason I asked if you've seen him."

The formality of his tone and language seemed out of place for a man of his age in this day and time. He carried it off without affectation.

"I understand," I said, "but I like to know who—and what—I'm dealing with. Your reticence could make it difficult to find a basis for discussion. You with the FSB?"

"Certainly not!" His tone indicated I'd succeeded in insulting him. "CPS?"

"As I just said . . ."

"You working for yourself or the government?"

He shook his head.

"I don't see how I can help you."

"I believe if we continue our conversation, we will find we have interests in common."

He had a card he wasn't ready to play. "What do we have to discuss?"

"Rad Rislyakov."

"We've just exhausted that."

"I'm not so sure. Rislyakov works for the Barsukovs. You've seen two Barsukovs in two days."

How long had he been following me? Why was Rislyakov so important to him?

He read my thoughts. "I was coming to see you earlier today. I saw you leave. You seemed to have a purpose. I decided to tag along."

"My destination surprise you?"

"Not necessarily. You were in Brighton Beach yesterday."

"Victoria told you about my visit?"

"You were spotted there, as you know."

"So?"

"The Cheka sticks together. You were a colonel in the KGB."

He'd also been checking up. "That ceased to be a state secret years ago."

"The Cheka has a long reach."

"Suppose I told you I haven't set foot in Lubyanka or Yasenevo in more than fifteen years."

He considered that. "Yasenevo—First Chief Directorate?"

"That's right."

He adjusted his eye patch and backed down a little. "I apologize if I'm touchy on the subject. My run-ins with your former colleagues have not always ended well."

"My own run-ins have not always gone smoothly either. The wounds just aren't as readily apparent. Consider me an ex-Chekist."

"Putin says there's no such thing."

"Maybe I'm the exception that proves Comrade Putin's rule."

He sat for a moment, watching me with his one eye. He possessed remarkable presence for someone his age.

"Excuse me for pressing the question, but what kind of dealings does a self-proclaimed ex-Chekist have with the Barsukovs?"

"Old friends." I shrugged.

"What do your old friends have to do with Rad Rislyakov?"

"You'll have to ask them."

"That is hardly likely, as you know."

I shrugged again.

"What were you doing with Iakov just now?"

"Visiting an old friend."

"How did you know he was in the hospital? You say you've been out of touch. My understanding is he only just arrived in New York."

I couldn't see what cards he held, but the ones he was playing indicated a strong hand. Good time to get out of the game. I stood and stretched. "I'm afraid this conversation is too one-sided. Good luck in your inquiries—whatever they are."

"Victoria said you can be less than forthcoming. However, she's not as well informed as I am, at least not yet. For example, I happen to know you spent more than an hour last night at 32 Greene Street, in apartment 6A, which is registered to a certain Alexander Goncharov. Witty fellow. When you left said apartment, you taped the door open. You were accompanied by a young woman who's been seen quite often in the company of Rad Rislyakov. The woman appeared the worse for wear, and you had to hold her up. Not long after, Lachko Barsukov arrived with a small army in tow. Iakov appeared injured when they brought him out, and this morning I learn he was admitted to the hospital with a bullet wound. Superficial, too bad. He's one ex-Chekist the world could do without."

His voice took on a bitter edge, but I hardly noticed. My mind was racing. He hadn't followed me to Greene Street, I was certain of that, and he purposely hadn't told Victoria of my whereabouts. He was playing a solo hand.

"Barsukov's men carried a rug out of the loft. Fat enough to have something wrapped inside—a body, for instance. All of this is made more interesting by your reluctance to tell Victoria where you were last night. Leads someone of a suspicious nature to conclude you have something to hide. I'm going to make the wild guess that this something involves Rad Rislyakov. Correct?"

"I thought you and Victoria were collaborating."

"Ahhhh, you are wondering why I haven't told her what I just told you. We are collaborating on some matters, that is true. I am pursuing others on my own. They are not her affair, nor that of the U.S. government. I thought perhaps my knowledge, which I came upon most serendipitously, I must tell you, might present something of a bargaining chip."

"And you're bargaining for?"

"Rislyakov."

I shook my head.

"Was he in that loft?"

"I just told you, I never met him."

"Was he there—dead or alive? Or was he there and you killed him?"

"Why would I do that?"

"The Barsukovs wanted him dead. Chekists—"

"Yeah, I know, we stick together. Even the devil's not as black as he's painted, Petrovin." Time to play a chip of my own. "What are you after? The money laundry?"

"What do you know about that?" he snapped.

"More than I read on Ibansk-dot-com."

He thought for a minute. "The laptop. When you left Greene Street last night, you had the girl in one arm and a laptop in the other. You had the laptop when you arrived at the hospital today. You don't have it now. You just delivered it to Iakov."

He was much too observant.

"As I said, I have yet to discuss your actions with Victoria, but I think she would find them most interesting. Unless . . . Tell me what happened last night at Greene Street."

"Tell me your real name and who you work for."

He shook his head. "I see no reason . . ."

Victoria's threat, wrapped in bayou twang, to put me behind bars echoed in my ears. Petrovin had an even stronger hand than I thought—and he knew it—even if I couldn't see right now how he'd acquired it. But he couldn't play the cards without losing them. A good time for a little *urki* betting.

"Your threat lacks punch unless you are prepared to follow through on it, and if you do, I might suffer, but you don't necessarily gain. We both want information. Neither of us is willing to divulge what we already know. We're not going to get very far that way. So I'll tell you this much. My interest in Rislyakov has nothing to do with the money laundry. However, I could be in a position to provide a great deal of information on the laundry—how it runs, possibly a record of every transaction it executes. If I'm at liberty to pursue my own inquiries."

"You're willing to share the results?"

"So long as there are no adverse consequences for me or my client."

"Who is?"

I shook my head. "Not the Barsukovs."

"You didn't mention this to Victoria."

"As you point out, you are much better informed."

"A generous, if ambiguous, offer. Forgive me if I ask why you make it and why I should believe it."

"Like I said, I'm trying to be the exception to Putin's rule. That good enough?"

He grinned and adjusted his patch once again. "Admirable, but not remotely good enough. Question is, are you a man one can do business with?"

"Careful. That's how Brezhnev described Nixon."

He laughed out loud. "You don't often meet a Chekist with a sense of humor."

"Former Chekist, remember? I need a little time, Alexander Petrovich. Moscow wasn't built in a day. I'll be in touch. If I'm not, you and Victoria both know where to find me. Where are you staying?"

"You'll understand if I don't answer that. I have a local cell phone.

Here's the number." He handed across a piece of paper. "Do you really follow Ibansk?"

"Doesn't everyone?"

I was still thinking about the man in the eye patch an hour later, back downtown. He reminded me of something, or someone, but I couldn't put my finger on it. I wondered if he wore his white suit in Moscow, where his real identity would be known to those who cared. He was almost daring them—here I am, come and get me. Ballsy, especially since they'd already tried once. Courageous, or crazy, or both. Also, as he said, much too damned well informed—about me.

He'd waited for me at Victoria's office, and he'd followed me to the hospital. Okay, but how had he pegged me at Greene Street? And what was he doing there? And why hadn't I seen him?

What had he said—Iakov had only just arrived in New York?

A few minutes later, Expedia.com and the Basilisk supplied the answer. Ratko, traveling as Alexander Goncharov, had flown from Moscow's Sheremetyevo Airport to JFK on Delta flight 31, which had arrived early at 2:15 P.M. Wednesday. Aeroflot flight 315 carried Alexander Petrovin and Y. Andropov, traveling separately, on the same route and also landed early, at 4:45 P.M. Andropov was Iakov's own joke—the former Cheka chief and general secretary of the Communist Party died in 1984. Petrovin must have spotted Iakov—or somehow knew he was on the flight—and followed him to Greene Street. Then I showed up, then the locksmith, then . . . somehow he managed to hang out without getting spotted.

I called Gina.

"When you were at Greene Street Wednesday, did you see a tall guy with black curly hair and an eye patch?"

"Yeah, now that you mention it. He walked up the block and back down a few minutes later. Didn't stop or look around, so I didn't pay any attention. Handsome guy, white suit—looks a little like Mark Twain. Did I screw up, not mentioning him?"

"Nope. I didn't pay him any attention either. Thanks."

One mystery solved—but new questions raised. Most significantly, to me anyway, why had Iakov followed Ratko to New York? Age and illness made travel difficult, and he hated this city—always had. What prevented his Cheka business from being dealt with in Moscow?

I turned on my laptop. Foos had come through. Or had he?

"Three possibilities. 1) Your prosecutor wannabe pal is schizo. 2) There are two Victoria de Millenuits. 3) She's had her ID heisted. Doesn't sound like your type in any event. Proceed with caution—she has a handgun permit."

The data backed him up. In New York City, Victoria Millenuits owned a condo at Sixty-seventh and Third, for which she paid $1.7 million, no mortgage. She shopped at Bergdorf, Bendel's and Grace's Marketplace. She ate at East Side restaurants, especially a place called Trastevere, maintained a five-figure bank balance, and paid off her three credit cards in full every month. In Fayette County, Pennsylvania, she lived at Windy Ridge Home Court, bought kids' clothes, Wonder Bread, house-brand soda, and the occasional flat-screen TV at Walmart, and had no bank account but four credit cards all pushing their limits. There was a gun permit—in New York—but no phone number.

I was about to pound the desk when I saw his PS at the bottom of the screen—"212-517-4667. Thought I forgot, didn't you?" Sometimes he's not as funny as he thinks he is.

I dialed the number, and a machine picked up. Her voice said simply, "Please leave a message."

"This is Turbo. We Russians are stubborn as well as funny. I'm still hoping you'll join me for dinner. Tonight, Trastevere, eight o'clock. If you haven't checked your credit rating recently, I'd advise it. I'm looking forward to seeing you again, I hope under less confrontational circumstances."

The phone rang as soon as I replaced the receiver. A female voice said, "Please hold for Mr. Mulholland."

He didn't make me hold long. "I need your help again."

"What's wrong?"

"It's Eva. She's . . . not well. Quite ill, in fact."

"I know. I found her last night and got her to a hospital."

"Yes. Bernie told me. We're grateful. Now she's run away. She left the hospital this morning. The doorman at her building says she stopped there before noon. Arrived by cab. He lent her the money to pay the fare. Only stayed about half an hour and left on foot."

"Does your wife know you're calling me?"

"Felix? No. I'm at my office. I called her, of course. She was frantic, as you'd expect. I said I'd get help."

"You might want to tell her who the help is."

"What? Why?"

"Better if she explains. Call her back, then meet me at Eva's apartment."

"I can't leave the office. I've got meetings . . . I'll talk to her. Lachlan, my driver, will meet you. He'll have the keys."

"Half an hour. I'll come to your office after."

"Her building's at—"

"I know where it is."

"How . . ."

I hung up before he could finish and headed for the subway.

★ CHAPTER 19 ★

It took more than an hour to get uptown. A block from the Wall Street station, the sky darkened to the point of nightfall or Armageddon—it felt like even odds which. Close cracks of thunder and street-freezing flashes of lightning portended the latter. A fire hose from the heavens let go as I dropped down the stairs. The train stalled for twenty-five minutes after it left Fifty-first Street. Flooding uptown, the conductor said. The air-conditioning was working, but the car was packed. I'd given my seat to an elderly woman at Twenty-third Street and ended up jammed in the scrum near the door. The old lady got off one stop later, and a young Hispanic man took her place, listening to hip-hop on his headphones so loud the whole car could hear. There are days you can only say, *New York—whattayagonnadoaboutit?*

The crowd surged up the stairs at Sixty-eighth Street, eager to get out of the subterranean steam—until it met the force of bodies rushing down, pushing to escape the rain. I went with the breaking waves and emerged, lightly bruised, on Lexington Avenue. The rain had slackened, but everything's relative—still enough to get soaked in short order. I waited under an overhang outside a hair salon until the storm moved on, ignoring the frowns of the black-clad hairdressers who doubtless considered my shaved pate poor advertising. A layer of mist rose from the wet concrete into the waterlogged atmosphere. The temperature hadn't dropped one degree.

Eva's building was a big, brutal, thirty-story concrete bunker, with its own similarities to Soviet architecture—the Khrushchev-era apartment blocks that mar Moscow and most every Eastern European city. The only thing you could say for this hulk was, unlike its Communist counterparts, it wasn't rotting from the outside in and the inside out. The tower ran the full block from Seventieth to Seventy-first Street, flanked by two small parks east and west (probably the price the developer paid for a midblock building this tall) and a covered driveway along the east side. A gray and black Maybach limousine was parked near the door. The driver got out as I approached and ground a cigarette under his heel. He was built like Jimmy Rushing, Mr. Five-by-Five, except this guy was white with a buzz cut so short you couldn't tell the color of his hair, a flat face, slits for eyes, and purple lips permanently pulled back over tobacco-stained teeth. Despite the heat, he was wearing a cheap wool suit and a flat cap. I looked for the bulge under the arm. It was there. He came in my direction, favoring his right leg.

"You be the snoop." The Irish accent was thick as peat. It's often pleasant to listen to. Not on this guy.

"I'm Turbo, if you're Lachlan."

"Don't like fookin' snoops. Don't like fookin' snoops who're late."

"Talk to the MTA."

"Let's go. Gotta get back to Midtown. Traffic sucks today."

I was going to ask when traffic didn't suck, but he might try to answer. I followed him to the door, where he nodded at the doorman and went straight to the elevator on the north side of the building. We rode to the fifteenth floor. A long hallway with lots of doors. He went to the one marked *F* and used two keys to unlock it. I followed him inside. The air was stale and warm.

"Look around, snoop. But make it quick. I gotta get—"

"You told me. Go ahead. I'll lock up when I leave."

He shook his flat face at that idea, shut the door, and leaned against the frame, arms folded. They were half as wide as he was. I tried to ignore that and focus on the apartment.

We stood in what passed for a foyer but was really one end of the living room. Windows at the far end looked east; I could see the river and Queens beyond. Galley kitchen to my right. A short hallway to the left leading to two bedrooms and a bath. I started with the living room, which was furnished traditionally with lots of chintz and flowered fabric. Everything placed just so. Dad had hired a decorator. The kitchen held all the basic appliances but little else. In the fridge, I found a half-drunk bottle of Perrier, some orange juice, a few staples, and two jars of organic peanut butter. That was mildly interesting, but I had no idea why.

Five-by-Five followed me down the hall to the bedrooms. Her room was simple and feminine—queen bed with lots of pillows, dressing table, pair of chairs, TV, closets. A few fancy outfits, but more jeans and tops than anything else. The bathroom had less makeup than I expected until I told myself I had no way of knowing what to expect.

Flat-screen TV, upholstered chair, and desk in the other room. A few books, more magazines—*Back Stage, Variety, Vanity Fair,* and something called *Stage Directions.* A scribbled note on the desk—"You should have left me with Lena." No signature. From Eva? To Eva? Eva to whomever she thought would come looking for her? Five-by-Five reached for the paper, but I picked it up first and put it in my pocket.

"That ain't yours, snoop."

"I'm here to find Eva, remember? This might be a clue."

I think he gave me a nasty look, but it was hard to tell. His normal look was nasty enough.

No datebook, address book, or checkbook. I hit REDIAL on the telephone and got a drugstore. No answering machine. Probably used the phone company's service. The signal light on the iMac flashed slowly, indicating the computer was asleep. I clicked the mouse, and it came to life.

I almost missed it. The screen flashed, and the digital clock in the upper right corner reset to the current time, 4:52. Before that, it read 11:44. I opened the e-mail program. A slew of unread messages. None opened today. I felt Five-by-Five's breath on my neck as I brought up the Safari browser and clicked on "History."

I guess I shouldn't have been surprised—if she'd been hanging out with Ratko, he would have taught her a trick or two. From the way Eva worked her away around UnderTable.com, she'd learned her lessons well.

"Move it, snoop. You're gonna make me late."

I was tempted to point out that under the circumstances, his tardiness was the least of his employer's problems. I went back to the entryway, where I'd left the case I'd brought from the office. Five-by-Five limped behind. Four-room apartment—he wasn't letting me out of his sight. I took an Apple laptop and FireWire cable from the case and plugged the latter into Eva's computer. I shut down the machine, started it again, and began the transfer of its contents.

"Hey, you can't do that!" Five-by-Five said. I ignored him on the grounds he had no idea what I was doing.

A big left hand reached for the laptop. I caught the wrist and twisted counterclockwise until I'd turned his body half around and he grunted with pain. His breath wreaked of tobacco.

"We work for the same guy," I said. "Call him."

I let go of the wrist and handed him the phone. He ignored it, took a cell phone from his pocket, and went out to the hall. He came back and handed it to me.

"He wants to talk to you."

"Lachlan tells me you're doing something with Eva's computer," Mulholland said.

"Copying the contents of its hard drive."

"Is that necessary?"

"Lachlan and I can stay here all afternoon while I do a manual search. Or I can take the contents back to my office, where I have software that'll do it in an hour. I'm working on the assumption time's of the essence."

There was a pause before he said, "Lachlan can be overprotective, but he means well." I doubted that, at least toward me. "If you put him back on the line, I'll tell him to stay out of your way."

"Did you call your wife?"

Another pause. "We'll discuss that when you get here."

I handed the phone back to Five-by-Five. He returned to the hall. When I finished, he was waiting by the front door, slit-eyes narrower than before, pulled-back lips curled in a sneer. The odds on bonding didn't look good.

Neither of us said anything as he locked up and we rode the elevator to the lobby. Outside, he didn't offer me a lift. He lighted a cigarette and blew smoke in my direction.

"We had a fookin' snoop in the village I come from. One day he woke up with his balls in the blender—while they was still attached."

"Hammett was right."

He looked me up and down. "What the fook does that mean, snoop? Who's Hammett?"

" 'The cheaper the crook, the gaudier the patter.' "

He looked me up and down again. "Who you callin' crook? Who's this fookin' Hammett?"

"Nobody you know."

He looked me over one more time, blew more smoke, and dropped the butt at my feet. He climbed into the limousine and pulled away. I exhaled slowly when the car turned into Seventy-first Street. I checked the office for messages. Nothing. As I put away the phone, the Maybach swung back into the driveway from Seventieth Street and drove slowly past. Five-by-Five watched me through the open window. Time to go. The poststorm heat was suffocating. Despite that, I shivered and headed back to Sixty-eighth Street.

She called as I walked through the cool corridors under Rockefeller Center after another slow subway ride across town. The subterranean halls always seem like they belong in some other city, not New York, where life is on the street—four seasons a year—today, however, they were full of commuters, tourists, and others just escaping the heat. Where had she got my number? I was going to have to talk to Bernie.

"What the fuck do you think you're doing?" she said.

"Following your husband's instructions, for the moment. I haven't told him about you yet. Have you informed him about me?"

"I told him I don't want you anywhere near my family. I'm telling you the same thing. Stay the fuck away from me. Stay away from Eva. Stay away from him. You've done enough damage."

I'd done damage? I almost told her all the things Ratko had phished off her computer, but there would be a more productive time for that. Instead, I said, "I got Eva out of a nasty situation last night. I could have handed her over to the police. I could have left her for Lachko to find. I'd accept a thank-you, but I'm unlikely to get one. Your husband called me today, when she ran from the hospital. He asked me to find her. I'm on my way to see him now. I'll just pick up my fee and tell him you said beat it, if that's what you want. Have a nice day."

"Wait! How bad?"

"How bad what?"

"How bad a situation—where you found Eva."

"I've already told Bernie it's best if I keep that to myself."

"Goddammit, Turbo—she's my daughter."

"That might have meant something, once."

"Bastard. Liar."

"I'm not the one pretending to be someone she isn't."

"Hah! You—the biggest deceiver of all."

We'd had this argument many times before—at higher decibel levels and with more vitriol. Try as I might, I couldn't refute the accuracy of what she said. Still, I made my usual lame attempt.

"My passport was clean. You know that."

"You got the *aparat* to say that. You got the *aparat* to say you had no past. You were a *zek,* Turbo. A lying *zek.* You always will be. How bad, dammit?"

"Bad as could be. Drugs, gun, corpse. Glad you asked?"

"The doctors said Rohypnol."

"They didn't know about the gun. Or the corpse."

"Don't mock me."

"I'm telling you straight. I took care of them. You despise me. I understand that. But I don't necessarily live down to your expectations."

Silence. "Turbo, I . . ."

"Yes?"

"I'm sorry. I've been upset. It's been a hard few weeks. I appreciate what you've done. It's just . . ." Her voice was wound tighter than a bale of tin wire—she was trying hard. I should've given her credit, but old wounds, cut deep, still bleed.

"I'm still a lying *zek*."

"*FUCK YOU!* Get the fuck out of my life!"

"Tell me something first. Eva left a note in her apartment. 'You should have left me with Lena.'"

A long pause. "What?"

"'You should have left me with Lena.' No salutation, no signature. Woman's handwriting. I assume hers."

"I have no idea what that means."

I waited.

"I don't."

I almost believed her the first time. "I have to assume she left it for you. Maybe Mulholland will have an idea."

"No! I mean, I'm sure he won't."

"Eva ever mention someone named Rad Rislyakov, possibly Ratko Risly?"

Even on a cell phone, I could sense her tightening, ever so slightly. She didn't recognize Rislyakov's name, but she sensed danger.

"No. Who's he?"

"Friend, perhaps. Lover, maybe. Pusher, I'm not sure. I do know he's the man blackmailing you."

She took her time processing that. "I'm sorry. I don't follow."

"There's not much you don't follow, Polya. Never has been."

"I go by Felix now."

"What's Rislyakov have on you, other than the fact that you didn't always go by Felix?"

Silence.

"He works for Lachko, Polya."

"*SHIT! JESUS! WHY THE FUCK DIDN'T YOU TELL ME THAT? WHAT THE HELL ARE YOU—*"

"I'll call back."

I broke the connection. The phone buzzed as she tried calling me. I shut off the power. I shouldn't have taken any pleasure, leaving her to stew in fear, but victories over Polina have been few and deserve some modicum of savoring.

FirstTrustBank's logo, a three-dimensional, intertwined *FTB*, spun slowly on a granite pedestal outside its shiny, boring building on Sixth Avenue. The lobby was white and gray marble, and the best thing you could say about it was it was well air-conditioned.

I announced my destination to the guard, who looked me over, looked me over again, and called upstairs. He probably didn't think I was properly dressed for a meeting with the CEO. After a short wait, I was given a sticker for my jacket and told to wear it as long as I was in the building. I took a fast elevator to the fortieth floor, which was labeled, helpfully, EXECUTIVE OFFICES. The two floors above were marked EXECUTIVE DINING AND FITNESS and LIMERICK CLUB.

An attractive woman of a certain age in a tight red dress met me at the elevator, introduced herself as Maude Connolly, and led me through the wide, hushed corridors. I alternated between admiring the machinery of her hips and reflecting on the silence of what was billed as a working office for a bank at risk of failure. Felt more like a mausoleum—maybe appropriate. At the end of the hall were a pair of glass doors with OFFICE OF THE CHAIRMAN stenciled on one. Maude Connolly put a plastic security card against a reader on the wall, which generated an electronic click. With a flick of the gluteus maximus, she pushed open the door and admitted me to the inner sanctum.

A large reception room with a seating area furnished by Mies and Breuer, several secretaries' desks occupied by several secretaries, and a half-dozen doors, all open, leading presumably to executives' offices. Still no noise. Five-by-Five leaned back on a white Barcelona chair, looking like a slug on a tablecloth. Maude Connolly paused, eying him with distaste.

I said, "You could've offered me a lift."

Five-by-Five hauled himself out of the deep, low seat. That took effort and exposed the gun in his armpit. A female friend once observed Barcelona chairs are like Ferraris—you don't sit in either one unless you're wearing pants.

"I'll be searchin' you, snoop. Nobody sees the boss who ain't clean."

Maybe it was the call from Polina, maybe it was Five-by-Five, or it could have been Mulholland himself, but I'd had enough of all of them. "No deal."

"Rules is rules."

I said to Maude Connolly, "Please tell Mr. Mulholland he can talk to me now, I can take his thug down, or I can just leave. He has thirty seconds."

She came back in twenty-seven, smiling. Five-by-Five glared at me the whole time but stayed by his chair.

"This way, please," she said. "Mr. Rory says everything's fine, Lachlan."

Mr. Rory? I gave Five-by-Five a thumbs-up and followed her through the open door.

The office was large and airy, with two walls of windows sporting views over the city to the north and west. One wall held bookshelves stuffed with good-citizen awards and Lucite-encased mementos. The fourth was covered with photographs of golf courses, mostly aerial views of individual holes. Mulholland was a golf nut—something else we lacked in common.

He was seated in a group of upholstered chairs. "You took your time getting here."

"Perils of public transportation. And I had to stop to talk to your wife. What'd the market do today?"

I don't know whether it was the mention of Felix, a Marxist asking about the market, or the fact that the Dow had lost another four hundred points, but the question made his surly look more surly until he turned away. Maybe he didn't like insolence that matched his own. I told myself to improve my mood and behavior, but I saw little reason to follow my instruction.

"Sit down," he snarled. He made a faint stab at courtesy. "Coffee, soda?"

"Nothing, thanks."

"Lachlan says you found some kind of note."

"That's right. 'You should have left me with Lena.' Your wife says she has no idea what that means. Do you?"

"None," he answered too quickly. "Did you find anything on her computer?"

"Haven't checked yet," I said, which was half true. "Your wife pretty much told me not to bother. She'd prefer—make that, she insists—I stay away from all of you."

The snarl turned to a frown. "You said she called."

"Half an hour ago. I told her you asked me to help find Eva. She said cease and desist. Perhaps you two should talk."

The frown deepened. "She indicated you know each other."

"Another time, another place. We were two very different people." I didn't add that was literally true in her case. "Hardly seems relevant now. She can explain if she wants to. I'll take payment for the kidnappers. You and she can decide what you want to do about Eva."

"Bernie said you dealt with them, but he wouldn't say how. What happened?"

"They were some unsavory guys, but fortunately for us, stupid unsavory guys. I took care of them. They won't bother you again."

"You seem very confident."

"I guarantee it—or your money back."

"I'll need an invoice."

"Of course," I said. I picked up a pad of lined paper from the coffee table and wrote "Vlost and Found" at the top, "For services rendered . . . $700,000" underneath, and signed my name below that. I added my taxpayer ID number at the bottom. Whatever the system, the government wants its piece of the action.

"This includes expenses. They ran high."

Mulholland looked at the page and frowned again. "This is somewhat unorthodox. I would assume that—"

"I don't use letterhead. Keeps costs down. And I don't think a more detailed description of my services is in anyone's interest."

Still frowning, he went to his desk and took out a big checkbook and a gold pen. He scribbled for a minute and returned holding a check for $700,000, drawn on his account at FTB. I didn't ask about Bernie's bankruptcy petition. I was tempted to inquire about the bank's solvency but minded my admonition to behave. Still, I intended to make a deposit as soon as I got out of here.

Mulholland was looking me over, trying to decide something. He stood behind his chair, his hands on the back. He dropped his eyes to the floor and brought them back up to meet mine. "Eva was part of the so-called kidnapping, wasn't she?"

He wasn't as obtuse as I gave him credit for. Yet he didn't know the half of it—and I didn't want to be the one to tell him. "She could have been. She's been hanging out with some bad people, criminal people."

He nodded, as if I'd confirmed his hypothesis. "She's always been a troubled child." He sat in his chair, and the frown began to ease. After a minute or two, he just looked glum. "You don't think much of me, do you, Mr. Vlost?"

"I don't know you well enough to have an opinion. Bernie speaks highly, and I've never found reason to fault his judgment."

"A good nonanswer. I don't mind telling you, I've spent much of the last few days staring into an abyss. My business, family . . . I learned years ago you can only fight so many fights at one time. You have to prioritize or be overwhelmed. You have to know when to ask for help."

He stopped long enough to take a breath and collect his thoughts. This couldn't be easy. He'd probably never asked for help in his life.

"I have to attend to my legal problems. I haven't done anything wrong, but that doesn't mean I can be lax in my own defense. I have to save my bank. I owe it to our depositors and shareholders. That leaves Eva, where, I'll be honest, I'm at a loss about what to do."

He put his head in his hands.

"That fight Eva had with her mother the last time we saw her, the one I mentioned when we met before," he said, looking at the floor. "I heard things no one should ever say to someone else, especially family."

He freed his head and looked up. "Maybe that's what some families are all about. I'm not sure I'd know."

"What did they fight about, if you don't mind my asking?"

"What didn't they fight about? Life, each other, me, the past, the future . . . No perceived sin or offense omitted."

Sounded like Polina. "This a common occurrence?"

"I've witnessed three or four. There may have been others. What they lack in frequency they more than make up for in intensity."

"What set this one off?"

"You know, I'm not really sure. Some little thing. You don't see it coming. Then, all of a sudden, it's like each of them puts a match to her own gas can of resentment and anger, and . . . boom!"

He shook his head and put it back in his hands.

"Are you sure you don't know what Eva meant by that note?"

He looked up. The black eyes had lost their hardness. They were needy, almost desperate. "She said it that Sunday, the same thing. 'You should have left me with Lena.' Screamed it at Felix, right before she ran out."

"But you don't know who this Lena is?"

He shook his head again. "Eva had some major trauma in her childhood—the full extent of which I do not know. Lena's part of that, I think. She had no father until I attempted to fill the role. Her mother has—how shall I put this?—cared too much and tried too hard to overcome the other issues."

Mulholland kept his voice low and even. "Eva believes—believes very firmly—that she herself is responsible for much of the misfortune that has befallen her. I also believe she feels guilt for her mother, for reasons I don't know. It's clear this guilt eats away at her, that it's responsible for her lack of self-esteem, her erratic behavior, her drug use, her animosity toward us. Even her stutter. I'm very afraid of what she might try to do. I appreciate your not wanting to get between Felix and me. I'll talk to my wife. Right now, though, I need to know we are doing whatever we can to help Eva. So I'm asking you to find her. If it's a matter of money, I'll pay whatever you ask. Will you help me?"

I couldn't picture the man I'd met last week saying what he'd just said. Perhaps looking into the abyss does change a person.

"I'll do what I can. But even if I find her, I can't guarantee she won't take off again."

He nodded. "I know that, of course. Something else I learned— one step at a time."

"Any idea why she would have run from the hospital?"

He shook his head. "Only to avoid being brought home."

"Any idea where she would have gone?"

"None. I'm afraid that for all our concern, we don't know nearly as much about her as we should. That goes for her mother, too."

"You will talk to her? Your wife, I mean," I said.

"Yes. I'm on my way home now."

"I think you'll find her under some stress."

"About Eva?"

"In part. How much do you know about her past?"

He hesitated, surprised by the question. "Not a great deal. She grew up in Queens, Jackson Heights. Went to CCNY. Sold real estate— very successfully. Married once before. Her first husband died. I haven't pried. Not really my business."

"I don't mean to add to your troubles, but her past is a good deal more complicated than that."

"What are you driving at?"

"Just that I think it's about to catch up with her."

★ CHAPTER 20 ★

Trastevere was in the early Eighties. I didn't know it, the Eighties not being my normal neck of the woods. A simple room, in an elegant kind of way, the kind of simplicity that comes at a price. I arrived hot and sticky and was greeted at the door by an old-world Italian gentleman of about fifty with kind eyes and a warm smile.

"Ms. Millenuits just called," he said when I announced myself. He looked around the room as if trying to decide something. "She . . .

she said she is very sorry, but she's been detained. She doesn't know how long she'll be. She suggests that you meet here tomorrow night. She said . . ." He stopped and looked troubled.

"You're being very kind. I'm guessing she isn't sorry, very or otherwise. You can tell me what she really said."

He was clearly uncomfortable. A good host doesn't attack his guest as soon as he walks in the door.

"Don't worry," I said. "I've already been on the receiving end of Ms. Millenuits's temper. Would you like to see the bruise?"

He smiled, but he didn't relax. He unfolded a piece of paper from his jacket.

"She said, 'Tell that bald Bolshevik he can buy me your best bottle of wine tomorrow night if I cool off between now and then. And tell him to bring his body armor. He's going to need it.' Those were her words. She wanted me to repeat them exactly."

"I'll attest you did as requested, if given the chance," I said with a smile. "No hard feelings." I put out my hand, which he took quickly.

"I'm sorry to—"

"Don't think any more about it. Would it be okay if I had a bite at the bar? Since I'm here, and solo."

"Of course. But please, let me give you a table."

"The bar's fine. I'll have a dry martini with Russian vodka, if you have it, followed by whatever pasta you're recommending tonight."

"Right away."

The martini was cold and dry, just like it should be. It went down quickly, so I ordered another. The pasta came coated with a sauce of escargots and mushrooms that was wondrous in its depth and complexity. I found myself looking forward to coming back regardless of whether Victoria showed up.

The place was busy, as was the bartender. With no one to talk to, other than the owner, who came by three times to make sure I wasn't angry at him, I spent the meal musing on intersections of past and present.

I probably shouldn't have warned Mulholland about Polina. It wasn't my business, and he'd made his own bed (with her)—but in spite of myself, I felt bad for him. Perhaps because I knew in ways he'd yet to experience what he was in for. Perhaps because he'd surprised me with his concern for Eva, real and heartfelt. Perhaps because a new snake pit was about to open at his feet, one he wasn't likely to see before he fell in. Bad enough that Polina had been married to me and hadn't told him, but Lachko was a whole different nest of vipers. I had a mental image of Victoria licking her Cajun chops when she heard the news.

Nothing I'd learned in the last thirty-six hours caused me to change my initial belief that Polina was hiding from Lachko. I still couldn't see why. Lachko had expressed less than no interest in her or Eva. I'd half expected him to drag me back to Brighton Beach or at least send Sergei around, but he hadn't even asked which hospital Eva was in. Maybe he'd found out by other means. Iakov expressed more curiosity in Eva and her mother, and he hated Polina. Always had.

Then there was the enigma of Ratko. He knew exactly who Polina was—he was using the information to put the bite on her. How, and why, had he found out in the first place? Why didn't he tell his boss? Why was he getting ready to disappear as Alexander Goncharov? Greed—not wanting to share the spoils—seemed much too simple an answer.

Iakov's Cheka business somehow involved Ratko. How had he put it—*laying old ghosts to rest?* Why did he need Ratko for that? Why didn't Lachko know his resident tech genius was working on the side for his old man? There was a lot Lachko didn't know—a lot that was going on right under those thundercloud eyebrows. Maybe his illness had slowed him down to the point where he was out of touch. Based on our encounter yesterday, I doubted it.

One piece of good information had come from all this. Aleksei was alive and, according to Lachko, working with the CPS—the Criminal Prosecution Service. I hadn't wanted to show it, but that was the first hard news I'd had in years. It appeared Polina had abandoned him following Kosokov's death. Perhaps she'd left him with her sister, or another relative. Had she been in touch since? Did he know about his mother's new identity? Then there was the question I'd been asking myself for two decades—what, if anything, had she told him about me?

My head was starting to spin, and other investigations tugged. I'd had enough vodka to numb whatever pain was in Sasha's envelope.

Tonight was as good a time as any to look into my own old ghosts. I asked for the check. Two martinis and pasta—eighty-five dollars by the time I signed the receipt. There are sound Marxist reasons why the East Eighties aren't my neck of the woods.

I remembered my disabled cell phone and turned it back on. It buzzed half a minute later.

"BASTARD! Tell me right now . . ."

I've never appreciated the opportunity to listen to other people's phone conversations while I'm eating, even when they're friendly, so I told Polina to hold on, thanked the owner and reminded him I looked forward to sampling his fare again tomorrow, and walked out into the heat of Second Avenue. Just after nine thirty, the street was still hot and busy.

"You keep calling me like this, I might think you have ulterior motives," I said.

"Ulterior motives? My only motive is to get you out of my life!"

"You talk to Mulholland?"

"He's a stubborn fool, like all men."

"He's trying to help. Eva, I mean."

"I can take care of her. I always have."

I didn't point out that Mulholland thought that was part of the problem. Or that I agreed with him. "Why'd you pull that scam?"

"What are you talking about?"

"The kidnap picture. You Photoshopped it, sent it to Mulholland with that bullshit kidnap note. Why didn't you just tell him you were being blackmailed?"

"What? What the fuck are you talking about?"

"You know exactly what I'm talking about."

"How do you . . . Nobody's blackmailing me!"

"If you say so, but the only person delusional this time is you."

"You . . . You . . . You haven't changed at all, you son of a bitch."

"Still the same guy, *zek* and all, I always was. What are you afraid of? Lachko?"

Pause. "Yes."

"Why'd you run out on him?"

"Long story."

"You want to tell it? I'm not far away."

"Stay away from me!"

"I'm not the one trying to hurt you, Polya."

"I said, stay the fuck away."

This was getting nowhere. "Where's Aleksei? Did you leave him in Russia?"

"He's all right. That's all you need to know."

"Lachko says he's working for the CPS."

Another pause, longer this time. "That bastard."

"You can't isolate yourself, Polya. Lachko, me, Mulholland. A couple of us might still be on your side, if you let us."

"I don't need your help."

"I think you do. I think that's why you called. What did Rislyakov take from your computer?"

"This conversation is over."

The line went dead. I was at Seventy-first Street. I walked south and tried calling her from Fifty-eighth Street. I tried again at Fifty-second. No answer. I hailed a downtown cab.

The office was dark, but Pig Pen was awake, listening to his radio.

I retrieved Sasha's envelope and stopped to say good night.

"Truck lanes closed. Exit nine. Fuel spill," he said.

"Not on my route. Pig Pen, what do you know about serendipity?"

He gave me his hostile one-eyed stare. He hates words of multiple syllables—he thinks I'm teasing him.

"No joke, seriously, serendipity."

"Pity me?"

"Not pity. Luck. Good luck."

"Lucky Russky."

"Exactly."

The neck feathers ruffled. "Luck. Crap shoot."

"You've been spending too much time with the boss."

"Crap shoot."

"Okay. Maybe. Boss likes statistics and probabilities, but sometimes you gotta go with what's working. If I roll seven on this crap shoot, pizza's on me."

That grabbed him. "Seven—pizza!"

"You got it."

"Seven. Lucky Russky. Pizza!"

One thing about Pig Pen. He doesn't lack focus.

I took my time walking home. The streets were still steaming. I was anticipating a painful evening, vodka-numbed or not.

"Lucky Russky," Pig Pen had said. If he was right, tomorrow night I wouldn't dine alone.

Solovetsky, March 12, 1938
Dearest Tata,
My heart breaks. I cannot believe this is happening. I have to try to tell someone, so someone knows and I keep my sanity.

We were on our way to work in the forests yesterday, Mama and I, in a large group of prisoners. It had snowed overnight. It was cold, below freezing. I remember willing the sun to rise higher in the sky to provide a little warmth.

Our group slowed when we saw the line of men being led toward Sekirka—the ancient church that has become the killing chamber for the monsters that run this hell on earth. We all knew what the queue meant, and we hung our heads in sorrow and shame—sorrow for our comrades, shame for ourselves and our country.

When I looked up, I saw the shock of red hair in the middle of the shuffling group. I didn't want to believe it at first, but then he turned, and despite the distance, there was no doubt. Papa! We had not seen him since the night of our arrest.

I pointed him out to Mama, who broke into tears. She yelled after him, but he could not hear, she was weak from hunger, and he was too far away. A guard told her to shut up, but she yelled again—"Filya! Filya!"

The guard hit her with his rifle. The line of condemned men moved up the hill toward the church. I watched my father disappear through the doors without hearing Mama call him for the last time. I have never felt such helplessness and misery.

The guard poked me with his gun, and I helped poor Mama to her feet. He shoved us back into line with the others.

There was nothing we could do. Our hearts in pieces, we were led off to work.

I can't understand how anyone, Bolsheviks, Stalinists—we're all Russians!—can do this. My grief is my own, but I'm surrounded by thousands of others with stories just like mine.

We are in an unimaginable place run by incomprehensible people. I go to sleep each night asking God to take me to the eternal under-world—it can't be any more sorrowful than this.

I put down the letter and went to the freezer for the vodka. I hadn't had enough to numb the pain after all.

No one can say how many people died in the Gulag. Estimates run into the millions. I now knew for certain one of them was my grand-father. I have the record of his arrest, with his wife and daughter, on November 26, 1937, the first year of Stalin's Great Terror. I have a re-cord of them at Solovetsky—the cradle of the Gulag, a network of is-lands in the White Sea and the Soviet's first forced labor camp—in 1938. I have an old photograph of the sign that welcomed new arrivals—WITH AN IRON FIST, WE WILL LEAD HUMANITY TO HAPPI-NESS. I know Solovetsky's inmates worked and died in its forests, tim-ber mills, fisheries, and factories. When the islands had been largely deforested, the camps were incorporated into the larger Belbaltlag net-work, whose inmates built the White Sea Canal. Those camps were vacated in 1941, ahead of the German advance, and I have documenta-tion of my mother's transfer to Norillag in Siberia, where she stayed until her release in 1946. My grandparents disappeared from the re-cord. Until now.

My mother's name was Anna. She was nineteen, Eva's age, when she was arrested. Her parents were artists, members of the Russian avant-garde, committed revolutionaries, friends of Malevich, Rodchenko, Olga Rozanova, and the rest. She studied music. She was a singer, a soprano, and apparently an accomplished one, even in her teens. There was no legal reason for their arrest, just some trumped-up charge about working to undermine the revolution. Stalin had set quotas, and the NKVD dutifully fulfilled them, just as other agencies produced economic results to meet the five-year plans. The economics were often fiction; the arrests were real—1,575,259 people in 1937 and 1938 alone. The Cheka shot 681,692 of them.

I stopped at the stereo to turn up the volume. I was listening to Mahler, his Ninth Symphony, perhaps his most prayerful piece, which he wrote after discovering his wife was sleeping with Walter Gropius. He was my mother's favorite composer, or so I've been told. I prefer Prokofiev—I like percussion—but tonight it seemed a little prayer couldn't hurt.

I'd done my best to bury my past. When Iakov got me out of the Gulag and into the Cheka, he also procured a new passport, one that bore no record of my birthplace or incarceration. Over time, serving in the Cheka enabled me to shed the fear of rearrest that haunts many former prisoners, even those who were now "clean" and led a normal life, or as normal as was possible in Soviet Russia. That was all blown up during the Disintegration when Lachko extracted his revenge by informing Polina about my time in the camps. Horrified that my taint would rub off on her, terrified that I would return her to the shambles of insecurity that was her childhood, she did everything she could to use my shame against me. She succeeded beyond her greatest expectations.

It took many more years, the dissolution of the Soviet state, and my finally moving away from Russia before I came to realize that I would remain imprisoned by my past, just as sure as I was an inmate of the Gulag, until I confronted it head-on. I also had the vague idea that the one thing I could give Aleksei was the truth about his family. How and when I would pass it on was an open question, but I figured I'd find a way if and when the time came. First I had to unearth the story.

That's not easy. The Gulag doesn't give up its secrets without a fight. You have to know how to dig, and you need help. Even then, many are buried too deep to ever be found. There's also an emotional price. Working on oneself, the early Bolsheviks had called it—trying to rewire human psychology to adapt to new social goals by altering one's identity. "The new structure of political life demands from us a new structure of the soul," the de facto Bolshevik propagandist Maxim Gorky wrote in 1917. Reconstructing the history of my mother's life was the psychological equivalent of dismantling the soul I structured when Iakov plucked me from the Gulag and I entered the Cheka. Lonely work, but maybe someday I'd be able to tell somebody about it.

Mahler faded to silence. Most symphonies rise to great final crescendos. Not Mahler's Ninth. He hints and feints, starts the climb once or twice, but backs off into deeper contemplation. In the end, as Bernstein put it, he simply lets the strands of sound disintegrate. I've always felt that fourth movement comes as close as anything to capturing the tragedy of the human experience—in a few bars of music.

The vodka glass was empty, too. I didn't need more, but I got a refill anyway, stopping on the way to play Miles Davis and Gil Evans's *Sketches of Spain*. I went back to my papers as Miles sounded the first few bars of "Saeta"—literally, "heart pierced by grief."

I never knew the man with the funny name who was my father. I know how he met my mother in Norillag, a few months before she was released for the first time in 1946. He was an NKVD officer, on the staff of Lavrenty Beria, head of the secret police and Stalin's chief executioner. Her beauty was intact. I have a letter he wrote attesting to that fact. He could not approach her there—*zeks* were nonpersons, untouchables—but as soon as she got out, he found her in Moscow.

This was a risk on his part. Release did not mean rehabilitation in the eyes of the state, and fear ruled the populace. Former prisoners were shunned, then as now, even by family and old friends. My father took the chance, and they fell in love. He also paid the price. They had two years together, but when she was taken away again in 1948, in a wave of rearrests, he was picked up, too. She got a second ten-year sentence and a trip to Dalstroy, a complex of camps in Kolyma in far northeastern Siberia. He was sent to Steplag in what is now Kazakhstan. The fact that he was an NKVD officer, the son of a prominent Chekist and friend of Felix Dzerzhinsky, founder of the Cheka, didn't matter. Or maybe it did. He was released after two years, in 1950. By 1951 he was again wearing an NKVD uniform.

None of this was as unusual as it sounds. Naftaly Frenkel, a Stalin favorite who oversaw construction of the White Sea Canal, rose from prisoner to camp commander. The deputy director of the Dmitlag camp, a guy named Barabanov, was arrested in 1935 for drunkenness and escaped the Great Terror because he was already in jail. He emerged some years later, went back to work for the NKVD, and rose through the ranks until, in 1954, he was deputy director of the entire Gulag.

How my parents reconnected in Kolyma in 1952 is another mystery I'm trying to solve. Maybe they didn't—there are other, less savory explanations for how I came into being—but I've been told by three women who knew her that he came to Kolyma that year and they were reunited, however briefly. I also know they wrote each other constantly and a few letters got through. I also know because when I was born, she named me after him. Thanks, Mom.

When Stalin finally died, everybody owned up, at least for a time, to what a disastrous experiment the Gulag had been. Beria made a play for the premiership, but Khrushchev, Molotov, and others on the Politburo stopped that. He was arrested and shot later in 1953, but in one of his last acts, he began emptying the camps. His first amnesty, declared only a few weeks after Stalin's death, included prisoners with less than five-year sentences, pregnant women, women with children, and prisoners under age eighteen. We totaled more than one million people.

It was one thing to be released, another to get home, especially when home was five thousand frozen miles away. Kolyma is a thousand miles north of Vladivostok, a region that the words frigid, barren, and isolated do not begin to describe. I've been back as an adult, and I cannot believe that anyone survived there. It's said that the permafrost still gives up an occasional corpse, even today.

The only transport was Gulag *stolypinski*, rail cars refitted for prisoners, which meant gutted to hold as many *zeks* as could be squeezed in. My mother didn't make it. This is the irony that breaks my heart whenever I think about it. She spent all but a few years of her adult life in concentration camps, somehow keeping starvation, disease, rape, and worse at bay, but she was too weak to make the final journey home. Pneumonia took her somewhere in the Urals.

I flipped through the pages in Sasha's file. Letters, in her hand, stretching from 1937 to 1953, including her two terms in the Gulag, 1937–46 and 1948–53. They were what I'd been planning to go to Moscow to pick up before the Mulhollands intervened. "Your mother had a cousin who kept every letter she received from her," Sasha e-mailed me. "22! A stroke of luck—I found them in the cousin's file." That Sasha had discovered them was miraculous, but no more so than her finding the means to write in the first place—or that the letters had reached their recipient. Prisoners went to great lengths to record life in the camps and to communicate with those outside, and written records do remain, but not that many.

I skipped though the stack of paper, looking for letters from 1952–53, the time of my birth. Somewhere, I hoped against hope, she might have mentioned my father. A note in a different hand, shaky script drawn by heavy black marker, stopped me cold.

I KEPT THIS ONE, SHIT-SUCKER. MORE TOO. THEY MAKE GOOD READING, IF YOU GIVE A SHIT ABOUT A SHIT-SUCKING ZEK. THE OUTCOME OF THIS POINTLESS STORY SURPRISED EVEN ME. YOU'LL GET A KICK OUT OF IT. IF YOU LIVE TO SEE IT.

Lachko. I thumbed through the pages. The same message had been inserted in place of a half-dozen letters. I had the feeling they all mentioned my father. Lachko had found another way of toying with me.

I turned on my computer and began the laborious process of entering dates, names, and places. I got halfway through the correspondence, but my mind kept going back to that first letter. I couldn't shake the image of the girl and her mother in the cold new snow, watching her red-haired father being led to his execution.

I can remember each of the times in my life when I've cried. At fourteen, when I was sent back to the Gulag. At thirty-six, when I made the choice that would change everything. A few months later when I saw my son for the last time. Now, two-thirds of a century after the fact, I wept for three people whose suffering ceased long ago. Their fate—no different from that of millions of others—made me wonder whether God should have locked the gates to the Garden of Eden when he had the chance and put an end to his experiment with humanity there and then.

I fell asleep, as I often do on such nights, a hollow feeling in my soul, pondering the unanswerable, while the pillows soaked up my tears.

★ CHAPTER 21 ★

The Chekist leaned back and closed his eyes. He didn't need the transferred tape to remember what happened next. It was imprinted on his memory, as permanent and precise as any digital code.

Snow falling heavily as he drove through the birch forest. Three or four inches already on the dirt road. He could see an earlier set of tire tracks, covered by an inch at least. Telling his driver to stop, he knelt in the snow, brushing away the newly fallen flakes with his gloved hand. Outbound tread. Someone had left since he started here ninety minutes ago. Was he too late?

He told the driver to move on. He'd chosen the man just for this job. He knew what to do when they got there.

The headlights of the limousine swept the buildings in the clearing—caretaker's cottage, barn, main house—illuminating their silhouettes in the snowfall. Two Mercedeses parked on the side. He recognized them as Gorbenko's and Kosokov's. Polina's BMW was nowhere in sight. Hers was the tread on the road.

A rectangle of light framed the caretaker as he came out his door, waving in greeting and bending forward, sludging through the wind. The driver leaned across the roof of the car, waiting until the man came close. The caretaker fell backward as the driver shot him, the crack of his pistol muffled by the snow. The driver was halfway to the door of the cottage before the man hit the ground.

The front door to the house was unlocked. The Chekist didn't stop to shake the snow from his suit but turned left toward the study. That's where he'd be. That's where he was, pulling files from a desk drawer.

"I warned you, Anatoly Andreivich," he said.

"Whaaaa!" Kosokov dropped a pile of papers and turned.

"Who were you expecting?"

"I . . . I . . ."

"The Cheka knows. The Cheka always knows. Where's Gorbenko?"

"He . . . I . . ."

The Chekist hit Kosokov in the side of the face with his automatic. Blood spurted from the banker's nose. *"Where's Gorbenko?"*

"He's . . . dead."

"Dead? How?"

"Polina . . ."

That didn't surprise him. Chivalrous to the last. *"God knows what she ever saw in you,"* the Chekist said. *"Just a small greedy coward. Where is she?"*

"Not here."

"I can see that, you fool. Where?" He raised his gun hand to swing at the banker again.

"Stop! She . . . She went back to Moscow."

"Coming back?"

"No."

"Bullshit." With one eye and the gun on Kosokov, the Chekist searched the room. The CDs Kosokov had told Polina about weren't there. *"Let's go,"* he said.

"No! I—"

The Chekist hit him again. *"Show me Gorbenko."* He pushed him to the door and grabbed the half-full vodka bottle on the way out.

The driver was waiting. The Chekist told him to search the house and put the banker's computer and files in the car. Then he followed Kosokov to the barn. The lights were on. The Chekist felt more than saw movement from the right, near a row of horse stalls. When he turned there was nothing there. Probably just a rat. Kosokov led him across the big empty floor to a trapdoor in the back. Cement stairs led down into the hole. An old bomb shelter. The Chekist shone his flashlight through the hatch. The beam caught Gorbenko's lifeless eyes staring up at him from eight feet below. A perfectly serviceable grave.

"Have a drink, Anatoly." He held out the bottle.

Kosokov shook his head.

"I said, have a drink." He raised his gun hand.

Kosokov cowered and put the bottle to his lips.

"That's better," said the Chekist. *"Have another."*

Kosokov did as he was told.

"Good," said the Chekist. *"Now, tell me where you hid the CDs."*

★ CHAPTER 22 ★

I was moving more slowly than usual at 6:00 A.M., thanks to the vodka that helped ease last night's pain. Mornings after evenings with Anna are often like that.

It had rained again overnight, and I ran through the warm, wet streets, thinking about my mother and grandfather, Polina, Lachko, and Ratko Risly. By the time I got home I was wishing I'd stayed in bed.

I brought up Ibansk.com while I drank my coffee.

HAS RATKO BEEN BADGER HUNTING?

The increasingly secretive, but still globe-trotting, Ratko Risly has been spotted, back in his home base of New York—in strange circumstances. Ivanov's international network reports Risly was seen just Wednesday with none other than Papa Badger, Iakov Barsukov, father of gangsters and architect of the resurrection of the modern-day Cheka. The meeting resulted in Iakov recuperating in a Manhattan hospital from a bullet wound in the chest. And Ratko? Ibanskians won't be surprised that no one has heard from him. Ivanov wonders if anyone will, ever again.

Unless I missed my guess, my new friend Petrovin had a direct line to Ivanov. *I* wondered which one was jumping to conclusions, albeit correct conclusions. More immediately, I wondered whether Lachko and his father were reading Ibansk this morning.

"Ratko's computer's online," Foos said when I stopped by his door a half hour later. "Did its self-wake-up–e-mail–data-processing–more-e-mail thing again this morning. Its new owner also did a full data recovery to see what he's got. He found the two files that were removed, just like I did."

"Uh-huh." No doubt now a clock was ticking somewhere in Lachko's fake palace. I went to the kitchen to get coffee. Pig Pen called as I passed his office.

"Lucky Russky?"

"Don't know yet, Pig Pen."

"Crap shoot. Seven?"

"Later. Maybe."

"Cheapskate."

"Don't give up hope."

"Cheapskate."

I took my coffee and the hard drive with Eva's computer contents back to Foos's office.

"What've you got this time?" he asked.

"Eva Mulholland's computer. She did a runner from the hospital yesterday. Went straight home, logged on to UnderTable, bought a bunch of ID info, and split."

"Kid's got an UnderTable account?"

"I'm guessing she's using Ratko's. By the way, all those spreadsheets on Ratko's computer—seems he's running a money laundry."

"I figured that."

"How the hell—"

"Has to be. Numbers tell stories, just like words. You give the computer to Barsukov?"

"Yeah. His father."

"Good work. You delivered maybe the best money laundry in history back to the Russian mob. That lady prosecutor should toss your ass in the hoosegow."

"She would, if she knew. I had my reasons. It was Barsukov's anyway."

"Oh. That's okay, then."

"You know how it works?"

"Pretty good idea." He leaned back in his chair, which was hardly big enough to hold his bulk, and put his feet on the desk. He was warming up for one of his professorial lectures on the way the world functions—which, of course, only he understands. Once he gets up a head of steam, he's hard to stop. On the other hand, he's rarely wrong. I hoped this would be short.

"Got to thinking yesterday. What would require all those transactions, hundreds every day? I went back to the data. Looks like Rislyakov wrote a program that moves money from overseas banks into U.S. accounts, or from the U.S. banks overseas, every morning, in amounts below the reporting requirements. Before you can say wash and dry, the dough is moved again, in smaller amounts, small enough not to attract attention into new accounts—eight hundred fifty, nine hundred bucks a pop. People go around and withdraw equally small amounts in cash from ATMs and redeposit the bread into other accounts and voilà, clean cash. No trail."

"That takes a ton of accounts—thousands, more."

"Sure. Remember all those Social Security numbers he ripped off from T.J. Maxx—maybe a hundred million, right? Not worth jack on the market. Competition's killed identity theft. Check UnderTable—prices are in the crapper. But put a new name with an existing Social Security number, open a bank account, and you've got an untraceable vehicle to move money through. The perfect washing machine. Automate the process and a computer drives the whole thing—orders the electronic transfers and sends out e-mails with instructions for the cash transfers. You recruit the labor and sit back and watch the money move. Even if a courier gets busted, or a bank's security catches on, the accounts are pure fiction. Nothing to trace. Only a few hundred bucks in them at any given time. The potential loss is next to nothing."

"Need a lot of people working ATMs."

"True—but one guy can hit what, six an hour, doing five transactions each. That's two hundred forty transactions in an eight-hour day. Say the average transfer is eight hundred bucks. Hundred ninety thousand dollars a day. One guy. Hundred guys—nineteen million two. Charge five percent, seven, maybe. Move three, four hundred mil a month. You do the math. Gotta hand it to him. Fucking brilliant."

"Except he's dead."

He shrugged. "So Barsukov doesn't run one of the hundred best companies to work for. Still a great scheme."

"Can Barsukov run it without Ratko?"

"It's automated. The computer's the main thing. Barsukov's got that, thanks again to you. It'll run for a while on its own, but sooner or later, he's gonna need two pieces that he's missing."

"The database—to create new accounts."

"Very astute. And the code. There's one piece of the app that's missing, the one that turns all those numbers into transaction records. I'm assuming that's one of the files Ratko removed—for security. It's the right size. The way these things work—"

I held up my free hand. "This is all still guesswork, right?"

"Theory of relativity started out as guesswork."

"Excuse me, Dr. Einstein. I suppose it's my job to come up with the empirical proof."

"You're the one who wants to impress the hot U.S. attorney."

"Yeah. Right now, though, I've got to find the girl. Promised her father, which was probably a mistake."

"Given your recent track record and her old man, I'd agree."

I could've thrown my coffee, but he had a point. "I need a list of calls to and from a cell phone. It's a disposable." I gave him Petrovin's number.

"Anybody we know?"

I shook my head. "Russian mystery cop. Working with the hot U.S. attorney. Knows too damned much about me. I need to level the playing field."

"On it."

I brought up Eva's computer and backtracked through her transactions at UnderTable, one of several Web-based identity exchanges in the Badgers' criminal empire. Used to be, as Foos said, UnderTable and its sister exchanges, Cardshark and ID Warehouse, turned tidy profits. Identity thieves would put the fruits of their labors up for sale, other kinds of crooks would pay the going rate for credit card, bank account, Social Security, and phone numbers, and the Badgers would take a cut of every transaction—eBay for bad guys, complete with its own version of PayPal. But as some wise capitalist once observed, there hasn't been a business invented yet whose profitability wasn't eventually eroded by competition. Over time the going rate has declined from thousands to hundreds to tens of dollars. A few years ago, the forty accounts Eva purchased could've cost two hundred grand. She probably got them for ten, not that she cared, since, as I suspected, she used Ratko's account for payment.

Eva wanted cash, not credit—she bought accounts with bank information and PINs included. If she knew someone who made cards, she could hit a dozen ATMs on the way to her dealer.

I plugged the names and account numbers into the Basilisk. It took a few minutes to troll the financial world before it confirmed my suspicion. Eva had checked into room 604 at the W Hotel on Union Square last night at seven forty-two under the name Elizabeth Long. So far this morning, she'd withdrawn nearly $7,700 from ten accounts at ten different ATMs, eight of which were clustered along lower Second and Third avenues, between Fourth and Fourteenth streets. Lots of young people gravitate toward the East Village, but Second Avenue in the single digits is also the longtime center of Ukrainian New York. I put Eva's computer aside and opened Ratko's. The home page for the Slavic Center for Personal Development came up again, as it had yesterday. Its mission was to "further the growth of Slavic communities worldwide" by "facilitating the social, cultural, and financial development of individuals of Slavic descent." To this end, the center sponsored a wide array of "theoretical and practical programs on all aspects of Slavic life." The center had offices in the major Slavic capitals, as well as Berlin, Frankfurt, Paris, Zurich, London, New York, Chicago, Los Angeles, Dallas, and a half-dozen Asian cities. Slavs get around. Or Slav money. Laundered Slav money. New York's "Slav House" was on Second Avenue between Eighth and Ninth. Multiple reasons for a visit.

Foos called as I passed his office. "That cell phone. Not many incoming calls. Mostly outgoing, to a number in Moscow."

"And?"

"Basilisk has more trouble overseas. Europeans, including Russians, guard their data. So I used some old-fashioned technology and put the number into Google. Belongs to the Criminal Prosecution Service of the Russian Federation."

First stop was the W. I dialed room 604 on the house phone and listened to the electronic ring until it clicked over to voice mail. I took the elevator to six, found her door, and knocked. No answer. She could be asleep. I knocked again—louder. She could be stoned. The Basilisk said she hadn't checked out, but it wouldn't know if she had simply split.

Next stop, Slav House.

The heat was having no apparent impact on lower Second Avenue. The sun-soaked late-morning sidewalks were crowded with people of all types and ages—tattooed students (no nontattooed students that I could see), moms driving baby carriages as if competing in a demolition derby, middle-aged men with guts stretching their wife-beaters, grandmothers carrying more shopping bags than age and physics said they should be able to lift. There had to be a score of ethnicities on the street—Slavs, Latinos, West Indians, African Americans, Chinese, Japanese, Koreans, Indians, Pakistanis, Southeast Asians, Europeans of all origins, American white guys. Polyglot—one big reason I moved to New York. Lots of neighborhoods in this city have forfeited their personalities over the years to chain stores, outsized condo developments, and gentrification led by aptly named yuppies and dinks. Character still spilled out onto the street here from every crack and crevice of the brickwork. Except for the heat and the task at hand, I gladly would have found a sidewalk table, opened a beer, and spent a pleasant hour taking it all in.

The facade of Slav House, on the east side of the avenue one door off the corner of Eighth Street, was as run-down as the Slavic Center's Web site was glossy. Dull green paint peeled off a cheap metal shell pasted to the brick of a four-story tenement sandwiched between an Indian restaurant and a cell phone store. The rest of the block was taken up with a deli, a newsstand, another restaurant (this was also one of New York's Indian culinary centers), a dry cleaner, a pharmacy, two nail salons, and a hairdresser. Similar mix of businesses on the west side, also with apartments above, including one of the bank branches where Eva Mulholland had withdrawn somebody else's money.

I held the door to Slav House for two young women on their way in. They flashed some kind of ID at the muscled guard in the shallow lobby, passed through a turnstile, and disappeared behind a curtained doorway beyond. Only one other door, in the wall behind the guard. Steel, with a big, reinforced lock. Beside the door, high up, was a window fitted with one-way glass.

The guard got off his stool as I approached. "You got ID?"

He spoke English with a heavy accent. I replied in Russian. "I just moved here. Friend told me you got lots of programs that can help."

He switched languages. "What friend?"

"Nedelenko. Ilarion Nedelenko." I wondered if he was still alive.

"Never heard of him."

"I'm from Belarus, Minsk. Nedelenko said you can help people get started here. Jobs, contacts, networking . . ."

"I told you. Don't know no Nedelenko. You want to come here, you have to apply. On the Web site."

"Web site?"

"That's right."

"Nedelenko didn't say . . ."

Three men in their thirties came in. Like the women, they flashed IDs to the guard and proceeded through the turnstile.

"Maybe I could talk to someone else. I was told—"

He shook his head. "No one here to talk to. I told you—"

"Yeah, I heard—Web site."

"That's right."

"But you do run programs, right? Programs to help Slavic people."

"Check out the Web site, pal. Everything we do is there. We don't take in every Ivan off the street."

"Okay."

I returned to the hot sidewalk. No point pushing it—this time.

I went up the block showing the photo of Eva, asking if anyone had seen her. It was slow going. People were busy and not necessarily open to helping. Fair enough. They didn't know who I was or what I was about. At one time, I could terrify anyone into talking just by flashing my KGB card. I don't have that ability anymore (except with the occasional Nedelenko)—and I'm not sorry.

I canvassed the block between Ninth and Tenth, then crossed the street and worked the west side back down. Most of the people I talked to were immigrants with varying knowledge of English, but some also hid behind the pretense of not understanding. As much as I wanted their help, I couldn't fault their reticence.

A salesman stood outside a mattress store across from Slav House smoking a cigarette, a white guy with a bad hairpiece about my age. He looked at the photo, furrowed his brow, looked at me, and said, "What'd she do?"

"Ran away, maybe. Drugs, maybe. Parents are worried."

"They should be, *maybe*. See that over there?" He nodded at Slav House. "Opened a year and a half ago, maybe two. Folks go in and out all day. Funny thing, though. Lot of those folks ain't Slavs, unless they got black Slavs, Puerto Rican Slavs, Asian Slavs I ain't heard about. Lot of 'em are kids."

"So?"

"They got those kids doin' somethin'.'"

"Like what?"

"Don't know. I do know they come and go in teams—three or four at a time. I live in Hoboken. Quiet neighborhood, working class, not a lot of strangers. Four times now, on my day off, I've seen these kids. I know 'cause I recognize them. They're going through my neighborhood, doin' somethin', I just don't know what."

"You're sure?"

"Sure I'm sure. Not a lot to do here all day when business is slow 'cept watch the street. I know most of them kids by sight."

"You know this girl?"

"Yeah. Been seein' her a couple months now."

He spoke with a quiet certainty, not like a man with anything to prove.

"Remember when you last saw her?"

He started to reply but stopped all of a sudden and looked beyond me. His face changed, his voice, too. "Who'd you say you are again?"

"Just a guy looking for that girl."

"Who's that?"

I followed his line of sight to a man a few doors down, fumbling in his pockets like he was looking for something—or he'd just been caught looking. His white shirt and dark suit could not have stood out more against the street of T-shirts and tank tops.

I turned back to the salesman. "Probably FBI. They're looking for the girl, too. She's dating a Russian. Maybe a mobster. They think he might be with her."

"You got lots of stories, pal. Selling mattresses sucks, but it's got benefits, and my wife's sick. I don't need trouble."

"There won't be," I said, pressing a couple of twenties into his hand. "You were just telling me the best Indian place around. That one, three doors down."

The first voice came back. "You got that right. Enjoy your lunch. By the way, the girl came 'bout four o'clock yesterday and again this morning. I remember 'cause she's one of the prettier ones. Saw her go into Slav House, but then I had a customer. Don't know if she came out."

He pocketed the money, crushed the cigarette under his heel, and went inside. I walked down the block toward the FBI man. He saw me coming and looked left and right, nowhere to run.

"I'm Turbo," I said, extending my hand. He pretended to ignore me, studying the display of vacuum cleaners in the window of a housewares store.

"They say you shouldn't buy anything but Electrolux. Just so you know, I'm going to grab some lunch in that Indian joint down the block. Then I'm meeting a friend, young woman I'm tutoring in Russian history, at the coffee shop. Then, depending on the time, I'll either go back to the office or head uptown. Tell your boss I'm looking forward to seeing her again."

He was still trying to ignore me as I walked away.

I got a table in the window and ordered lunch and punched Gina's number on my cell phone. She answered right away.

"How'd you like another job?"

"Sure. I'm still broke."

I gave her the address of the coffee shop. "Meet me there in half an hour."

People came and went in groups of threes and fours from the Slavic Center as I ate. I mopped up the last of the sauce from a pretty good chicken tikka masala with an excellent nan, paid the check, and moved next door. Gina arrived five minutes later and, predictably, turned up her nose as soon as she walked in the door.

"Jesus, Turbo, what's with this dump? There's a Starbucks a block away."

Gina's a bright kid, smarter than most, but like much of her generation she's been brainwashed by the Brand. Having grown up in a society where uniformity was imposed from on high—and any manifestation of individuality, no matter how minor, systematically crushed—I've never understood why Americans seek out, not to mention happily pay a premium for, sameness. I do my best to avoid chains of any kind. Scowling, she gave me a peck on the cheek and sat down.

"Coffee?"

"Don't suppose they have cappuccino?"

I signaled the waitress and ordered a black coffee and a cappuccino. She wrote on her pad and left. I smiled at Gina. She didn't look any happier.

I said, "Remember the girl on Greene Street?"

"Sure."

"Her name's Eva. Her boyfriend's Ratko. Go over to the place across the street, Slav House. There's a big guard just inside the door. Ask for Eva. Tell him she was supposed to meet you there."

"Okay. What gives?"

"I'm looking for the girl. She was seen going in there."

The waitress brought the coffee. Mine was hot and freshly brewed. Hers had a big mound of foamed milk on top. She sipped it carefully.

"Hey, not bad!" She smiled for the first time since she arrived. But she'd be back at Starbucks tomorrow. "Think it's a drug den?"

"Possible, but more likely a front for something else. They threw me out, but I could've used the wrong name. I mean this—don't go beyond the lobby. See what he says about Eva and beat it. If you're not back on the street in ten, I'm coming in after you."

"Got it. Let me finish this first." I checked the street for the FBI while she sipped her coffee, using a spoon to make sure she got all the foamed milk, but he'd given up.

"Okay, I'm off," she said.

"Walk around the block, so no one sees you come straight from here. Same thing on the way back."

"Turbo, you're paranoid."

"Humor me." Where I grew up, paranoia was one way you stayed alive.

She gave me a look that said paranoia was only one of my problems and headed for the door. She turned right and disappeared toward Eighth Street. Almost five minutes passed before I saw her again, on the far sidewalk, approaching Slav House from the north.

When she'd come to the coffee shop, Gina was simply but neatly dressed in a T-shirt and skirt, with her hair tied at the back of her head. Now the T-shirt was askew and hung loosely over her hips, and her hair was a mess. She walked slowly up the block, looking this way and that, unsure of herself and her surroundings. Before I started using college students, I'd hired out-of-work actors, but casting calls kept getting in the way of my assignments. Gina could have taught them a thing or two about conveying vulnerability. She stopped outside Slav House's door, hesitant. She'd decided to improvise. I cursed silently.

She gathered herself up and went inside.

She took the full ten minutes. While I waited, I entertained myself with thoughts of all the bad things that could happen to her, how they were all my fault, and what I would tell her parents in Toledo. I was checking my watch for the fourth time when she reappeared. She held the door for a moment, then walked toward Eighth Street, tucking her shirt in as she went. I left money on the table and went up the block and across to meet her at the corner. She followed me to a Starbucks at Thirteenth Street.

"And what was wrong with the other place?" she said as I held the door. Sometimes you can't win.

She had another cappuccino, I had another black coffee, and we sat at a table in the corner. She said, "I'm not sure what they're up to, but that place is pretty creepy. The girl's not there, or so they say, but they know her. Don't like her, either."

"They?"

"Two guys. The big guard and another guy, short, oily, black hair, mustache, accent from Eastern Europe somewhere. The guard got him when I asked about Eva. He's in the room with the steel door."

"What'd they say?"

"I told the guard I was supposed to meet Eva, like you said. He asked, 'Eva who?' I said, 'Eva, friend of Ratko.' That's when he got the other guy, who wanted to know how I knew Eva, and I said we were friends. Then he said, 'You tell that pretty girl she wants to come around here, bring her boyfriend. Otherwise, fuck off and don't come back. Same goes for you.' Then he went back to his room and I split."

"Huh." Word of Ratko's demise hadn't made it to Slav House.

Four young women came into Starbucks and went to the counter. I'd held the Slav House door for two of them. They'd been empty-handed then, I was almost certain, but now all four carried big shoulder bags, and one consulted a BlackBerry while she waited for her coffee. They spoke quietly among themselves. I couldn't make out what they said.

I took a roll of bills from my pocket and gave Gina five twenties.

"Don't turn around, but four women are about to walk out of here. I saw two at Slav House. Follow them and call me when you get a fix on what they're up to. Don't get too close. They might be looking for tails."

"What if they split up?"

"Stick with the striped T-shirt or the white skirt. Here they come."

Gina and I studied our cups. As soon as the door closed behind them, Gina gave me a quick peck on the cheek and followed. I finished my coffee and went to check the W once more.

★ CHAPTER 23 ★

Gina called as I entered the hotel.

"I'm at Grand Central. They're taking a train. What do you want me to do?"

"Stay with them. Buy a ticket on board. Keep in touch."

I skipped the house phone and went straight to room 604 and knocked. I wasn't prepared when a tentative, female voice said, "Y . . . y . . . yes?"

I could've bluffed my way in—"Maintenance, miss, here to check a leak"—but that wasn't going to encourage her to talk.

"My name's Turbo, Eva. I found you at Ratko's on Wednesday. Got you to the hospital."

A long pause, then the scratch of the security chain being engaged. The door opened a crack, and two blue eyes peered out. A shade lighter than her mother's and as bright, clear, and questioning today as they had been blank and fearful Wednesday night. Blue-black circles underneath, but that easily could have been from lack of sleep.

"I d . . . don't know you. Who's R . . . Ratko?"

That threw me for a moment. "You probably know him as Alexander. Alexander Goncharov."

Recognition. "Wh . . . wh . . . what do you want?"

"I want to talk. That's all."

"Who are y . . . y . . . you again?"

"Turbo. You remember anything about Wednesday?"

She shook her head slowly.

"You tried to shoot me. Remember that?"

"Whaaa?!"

"Twice. Once through the bedroom door, once after I broke it down."

Something registered. Her face scrunched in concentration. "Alexander's pistol . . ."

185

"That's right."

She reached for more but gave up. "Sss . . . sorry. I remember about the gun—the d . . . d . . . drawer where he kept it, that's all."

"That's something."

"Wha . . . what are you doing here? H . . . h . . . how . . . how'd you find me?"

"You used his account at UnderTable."

Surprise, then realization. "Sh . . . shit. My computer. You were in my apartment? *Wh . . . wh . . . who are you?*"

"I get paid to find things. And people."

"But who . . . Oh, I kn . . . know. My mother."

"Actually, your father. He's worried about you. They both are." I gave Polina the benefit of the doubt.

"I don . . . I don't have anything m . . . m . . . more to say." She started to close the door.

"Your dad's in a tough spot, Eva. You know he was arrested?"

That stopped her, for a moment. "What do you m . . . m . . . mean?"

"He's being charged with some heavy crimes—at the bank. He says he can beat them, but the last thing he needs right now is to worry about you."

"Who t . . . told you? My m . . . mother?"

"He did."

She thought about that. She clearly cared for Mulholland, but maybe not enough. She pushed on the door. "Sor . . . sorry."

"Wait." I put my foot in the way. I didn't want to do it like this, but we were going to get to the subject sooner or later, and there was no good way to tell her. "Bad things happened in that loft Wednesday— before I got there."

"What? Wh . . . what are you talking about? Wh . . . wh . . . what kind of things?"

"Alexander."

"Wh . . . wh . . . what about him?"

"I'm sorry, Eva. He's dead. Somebody killed him, Wednesday night. I found the body."

The blue eyes got big with fear and shock, then tears. I had the sense she knew already, on some level, but that didn't make confirmation any easier to take.

I said, "I'll tell you what I know if you let me in."

She shook her head. "I d . . . d . . . don't know you."

"Of course not. You're right. I'll be downstairs, in the lobby. Take your time. I won't make you go home or anywhere else you don't want to. Like I said, I just want to talk. I'm sorry."

I removed my foot, and the door closed softly. I sounded like a fool, but every messenger does, saying they're sorry when they know they can't do a damned thing to help.

I stayed a minute outside the door, listening to the sobs. When they didn't stop, I went downstairs, wondering how long to wait and what to do when I reached whatever deadline I decided on.

Twenty minutes later I hadn't made much progress, and had started thinking about Eva's stutter and whether it was connected to her disfigured thighs, when Gina called again.

"You owe me—big-time. I'm in Stamford."

"What's wrong with Stamford?"

"It's in fucking Connecticut."

"You're from Ohio, what've you got against Connecticut?"

"It's not New York. Anyway, this is weird. One girl got off the train in Mamaroneck. Another in Greenwich. Striped Shirt and the other chick got off here. They split up, I stayed with Stripy. We're doing a tour of ATMs. She's at her third now. I can't get close enough to see for sure what she's doing, but I think she's both taking money out *and* making deposits. Spends about ten minutes at each one. Strange, huh?"

"She choosing them at random?"

"She keeps consulting her BlackBerry. Whoops, we're on the move again. Want me to call you back?"

"I'll hang on."

A few minutes passed before she came back on the line. "Another bank. Chase, second one on this trip. We've hit B of A, a credit union, FirstTrust, and Citi. How can one chick have so many accounts?"

"They're not hers. Stay with her and let me know where she goes when you get back to town. Call whenever, I don't care how late."

"Whenever? Hey, I've got a date tonight. You don't think she's gonna—"

"I think the last stop on that train line is New Haven."

"New Haven! Goddammit, Turbo, I—"

I closed the cell phone before her invective could cross the atmosphere. The elevator door opened. Eva stepped out and looked around until she saw me. She was dressed simply in jeans and a purple T-shirt, no makeup.

"Is this okay?" I asked as she approached. The eyes were puffy but still clear. "We can go somewhere else if you want."

She shook her head and took the seat next to mine. In a few hours, the lobby bar would be a throng of loud music and postworkday revelers, but now it was almost empty.

"Would you like something? Coffee? Cup of tea?"

She shook her head again. "T . . . t . . . tell me about Alexander."

"I will. You tell me something first. You really don't remember anything about Wednesday?'

She shook her head. "I w . . . w . . . went to the loft—I kn . . . knew he was coming home. He'd t . . . tol . . . told me, but n . . . n . . . now I realize he forgot. He's like that sometimes—sp . . . spacey." Tears filled her eyes as she realized she'd used the present tense. She tried to shake them away. I went to the empty bar and returned with a stack of cocktail napkins. She used one to dab her eyes.

"I g . . . g . . . got there, and he was kind of nervous, j . . . jumpy. He said it h . . . h . . . had been a b . . . bad flight. I thought tha . . . that was the reason. Th . . . th . . . then the buzzer rang, and he said it was a g . . . guy he needed to talk to—b . . . business. He said to wait in the b . . . b . . . bedroom. I . . . I thought I'd take a shower, it was so hot and m . . . m . . . muggy. Tha . . . tha . . . that's all I remember."

"Until the hospital."

"Y . . . yeah. I woke up, I didn't know wh . . . wh . . . where I was, how I got there."

"And you didn't take anything? Any drugs?"

"N . . . n . . . n . . . no. I don't do drugs." She stated it as a fact, not a protest.

"You used to, right?"

"N . . . no. I smoke some grass. B . . . b . . . big deal. You've been talking to m . . . my mother. She's got no c . . . clue, n . . . never has."

"What about the rehab?"

She didn't register surprise that I knew. "Tha . . . that's her, too. She p . . . panics over *everything*. Smoke a joint and you're h . . . h . . . hooked on heroin. It's easier to go along, s . . . sometimes."

It might have been the stutter—damned hard to fake—but I believed her. "You were totally out of it when I found you Wednesday. Blotto. Roofies, the doctors said."

"I know. They t . . . told me, too. But I didn't . . . I'd never touch something like that. That's c . . . c . . . crazy."

I still believed her. "Could Ratko, I mean, Alexander have—"

"No! He'd n . . . n . . . never. We w . . . were . . ."

Now she was protesting. I didn't believe her, and she didn't believe herself.

"Did he give you anything to drink? There was a can of Diet Coke by the bed."

She thought for a minute. "Yeah. I w . . . went back to the bedroom, and he c . . . c . . . came back after me, w . . . with the Coke. Said I looked d . . . dehydrated from the heat."

"Did you drink it?"

"I g . . . g . . . guess so, y . . . yeah."

"He drugged you, Eva. I'm sorry to say that, but it's the only way it makes sense."

"B . . . but w . . . w . . . why? We were f . . . friends. We w . . . w . . . w . . . He loved me!"

She all but yelled the last part, another protestation. She caught herself and looked around, afraid to draw attention. No doubt she'd loved him.

"Where'd you meet him?"

She shook her head. "T . . . t . . . tell me what happened. At the l . . . l . . . loft. You s . . . said you would."

"You're right, I did. I got there around eight forty-five. I found two men in the hall outside the bedroom—Alexander and your grandfather, your biological grandfather."

"Wha . . . what?"

"You recognized him. He scared the daylights out of you. Why's that?"

"Grandpa? He was there?"

"That's right."

The fear was back. She pushed her chair away from the table. "I have to go."

"Wait." I took her hand, gently, but ready to hold on if she tried to run. "He's not here now. He can't hurt you. Don't you want to hear the rest of the story?"

She tugged a little, then relaxed and pulled her chair back. "Okay." She started to sit, then straightened again. "W . . . wait. How do you kn . . . know my grandfather?"

"I've known most of your family for years, long before you were born."

"H . . . how?"

"We all used to work together—in Russia."

She backed away. "That m . . . means you w . . . w . . . were . . ."

"Don't worry. Not anymore. I live here now. I work for myself. I took you out of there, remember? I didn't leave you with him."

She sat down slowly, still unsure.

I went on with the story. "Ratko was already dead. Iakov was wounded. There were bullet holes in the bedroom door. I think you heard the shots, got the gun, fired through the door, and someone fired back at you. There were two more bullet holes in the wall behind the bed. I think you must've hit whoever it was, because I could find only one bullet hole in the hall."

She shook her head. "I d . . . don . . . don't remember."

"Don't be hard on yourself. Rohypnol is a powerful amnesiac. You were aware something was going on, something that frightened you. So you got Ratko's gun."

"Why do you keep calling him Ratko?"

"His real name was Rad Rislyakov. People here called him Ratko Risly because he looked like Dustin Hoffman in the movie *Midnight Cowboy*. Any idea who could've shot him? Or your grandfather?"

"No."

"You know he gambled?"

"S . . . sure. B . . . but he said he w . . . was over that."

"You believe him?"

"Y . . . yes." She seemed sincere.

"When you were with him, did he ever seem nervous or afraid? Like someone might hurt him?"

"No. I n . . . n . . . never n . . . noticed anything like that."

I still believed her.

"Did you know he had an apartment in Chelsea?"

She paused, then shook her head. I wasn't sure she was telling the truth.

"When did you meet?" I asked.

"W . . . wait. Wh . . . wh . . . what were you doing there—at the l . . . loft?"

"Looking for Ratko."

She shot me a look just short of "Duh!"

"Sorry—but if I tell you, you're not going to like it."

She didn't hesitate. "You've already d . . . done the w . . . w . . . worst you can d . . . do."

I was trained to keep people talking. Coax, probe, know when to apply pressure. Work the psychology. Take advantage. Manipulate hopes, fears, and insecurities. I used to assuage my conscience with the assertion that it was all in service of a cause. The cause turned out to be bullshit, but at the time it was still a cause. Now? Why was I ripping up this girl's life? She'd already spent most of it a trauma victim. Her boyfriend—that's how she thought of him—had been using her. I'd more or less exposed that part of him. Now I had the chance to show her what a thoroughly nasty shit he was and drag her mother into the muck at the same time. Eva had never done anything to me, at least consciously, probably never done anything to anybody. I could've—should have?—walked away and left her to pick up the pieces. Instead I pushed ahead with the demolition, as I knew I would. If you're afraid of wolves, don't go into the forest, as we say.

"You know what phishing is?"

She nodded slowly.

"Ratko—Alexander—phished your father. About four months ago. He bugged all the computers in the apartment. He found something he was using to blackmail your mother."

"She t . . . t . . . told you this?"

"No. She tried to keep it a secret. She's still trying. You know Ratko was an identity thief. You worked his UnderTable account."

She looked away and back again. "He said . . . he said it was a victimless c . . . crime. Credit cards, b . . . bank accounts, they all have in . . . in . . . insurance."

"So some nameless insurance company is going to pay your hotel bill here."

She looked away again. "Okay. He sh . . . showed me once. He was sh . . . sh . . . showing off. It was the f . . . first time I ever used it. I needed m . . . money, s . . . someplace to go."

"Why not home?"

That got me the "duh" look again.

"Why'd you run from the hospital?"

She hesitated, then looked away. "I was scared."

"Of what?"

She didn't answer and kept her eyes away from mine. "How much tr . . . trouble is my d . . . d . . . dad in?"

"A lot. Yet he's worried about you more than anything. Probably do him a ton of good to see you."

She nodded at that.

"What frightened you at the hospital?"

She looked at the floor.

"What did you mean by that note, the one in your apartment—'You should have left me with Lena'?"

The shriek was muffled by the sob that came right on top of it. "N . . . nothing."

"We both know that's not true. You told your mother the same thing the last time you had a fight."

She turned jittery, fearful. "Who told you that?"

"Your father."

"I w . . . want to g . . . g . . . go now."

She was halfway out of her chair, eyes darting left and right, around me. Her entire demeanor changed—from sorrowful and curious to caged and cornered. I was losing her. I took one more shot.

"Did you know Ratko worked for your father, your real father?"

"Whaaa?!" She swung back toward me, every inch of her trembling.

"What's the matter?"

She shook her head violently as she backed up, knocking over her chair. She was out of my reach before I could stand.

"Eva—"

She bolted, straight out the front door. By the time I got to the street, she was half a block away, up Park Avenue, running fast. I let her go. I wasn't going to catch her, and I'd lost her even if I did. But what was she running from, other than her entire family?

Three people could possibly shed light on that. Two of them hated my guts. A phone call confirmed Iakov was still at Mount Sinai. I caught a cab uptown.

★ CHAPTER 24 ★

Another call. Gina said, "You have no idea how much you owe me."

"He wasn't your type anyway."

"What? How the hell do you know?"

"If he was, he'd go to Stamford, pick you up."

"New Haven, God damn it! Like you said. I follow Stripy back to the station, she gets on a train, joins up with the other chicks, now we're all in fucking New Haven. Same thing there. The group split up, I stick with Stripes. We're at our fifth ATM now."

"Stay on her. She'll head back to New York soon."

"That a promise?"

"Trust me."

Gina was still cursing as the cab pulled up at the Madison Avenue entrance to Mount Sinai. I paid the driver. Lachko's men tried to block Iakov's door, but I pushed through. He was awake, sitting up in bed, reading the *Economist,* looking much the same as yesterday.

"Why didn't they release you?" I asked.

"Tomorrow morning, they say now. Don't ask why, no good answer. One more night. I hate this fucking city."

"How do you feel?"

"Fine. Ready to get out of here."

"Tell me straight this time, what were you doing at Greene Street?"

He closed the magazine and put it on the bed beside him as he looked me up and down. "Is this an interrogation?"

"Not by choice." I took a shot. I might lose a chess piece, but I'd gain information whether I was right or wrong. "You lied the other day. Rislyakov was helping you find Polina. But he crossed you. He found her, but he tried blackmailing her instead."

"I don't know anything about blackmail."

"He gambled. He needed money."

"I had the sense he was up to something. He flew back here before I could get to him, so I came over."

"But you didn't kill him?"

"What I told you Thursday was true. Someone shot both of us. Could have been you."

I ignored that. He was playing his own chess game. "So what business does the Cheka possibly have with Polina?"

He smiled. "Where is she?"

"You first."

He gave me a look I hadn't seen in twenty years. The same look I got the day he called me in after I'd reported that Lachko was stealing. "I don't know where your loyalties lie anymore, Turbo."

"I still owe you everything. That hasn't changed."

"What about the Cheka?"

"I was reminded just the other day, there are no ex-Chekists."

"You prepared to trade?"

"I can't give you Polina."

"Why not?"

"I gave her husband my word. He's my client."

"Why do I care about him?"

"You don't. I do."

He shook his head.

"I'll help you as much as I can, short of that," I said.

His face softened—a little. He didn't like it, but I held the stronger hand.

"Polina stole a great deal of money. Six hundred million dollars—1998 dollars. Must be over a billion now."

"Stole? From the Cheka?"

"She and Kosokov. I told you they were lovers. They had a business, with Lachko. Real estate, buying and selling apartments. Kosokov was the financier. They made a lot of money, but it wasn't enough for her—or him. They were made for each other. Two most venal people I ever met."

I wondered where he'd put his own sons on the venality ladder. "You never stopped watching her, did you?"

He just looked up at me. During the Disintegration, he was the one who told me she was sleeping with my fellow officers at Yasenevo. I never asked how he found out. I didn't need to.

"We used Kosokov's bank. I couldn't stand the bastard, but he had the Yeltsin connection, and in those days, that was useful. He almost went bust in '98, or so we thought. Turns out the bastard was playing a double game, financing the Chechens with our money. Why, I have no idea, except he was making a pretty kopek in the process. He was also moving money abroad as quickly as he could. He had a partner in the Chechen venture, a man named Gorbenko. I'll admit to you now, in the privacy of this room, we covered up a lot about that piece of shit. He was one of ours, a true traitor—drunk, gambler, whoremonger— how he rose so high is an embarrassment. The Chechens turned him. Kosokov killed him, we know now—a falling-out among thieves. But if he hadn't, we would have. I would have pulled the trigger myself."

His voice rose in speed and intensity as well as volume, but he stopped suddenly, as if rethinking. When he continued, he spoke softly.

"We were onto Kosokov, finally, but Gorbenko warned him. A few days before we were ready to move in, Rosnobank Tower burned. Twenty-story steel building, melted. Sophisticated arson. Nothing left, no records, no money."

I remembered that.

"Kosokov disappeared. So did Polina. And Gorbenko. Now we find out he was dead after all. She must have killed him, probably over the money. She's like a praying mantis, master of camouflage, infinite patience, waiting for her prey. She bites the heads off her lovers as soon as they've satisfied her."

I couldn't argue the description.

"We had a lot to deal with, cleaning up the mess. I won't say we did the best job. We had to choose between some lousy options."

"That's another lesson you taught me. Don't look for a good choice in a bad situation, take what will work."

He smiled. "It makes me happy you remember. We dealt with it, but we were still out the six hundred million. I'm responsible. It's a stain on my record, my whole career. I haven't stopped looking for her since. I want to make good while I still can."

It all sounded plausible. It was the way he would think—especially about the stain. Perhaps too plausible. "Why's Eva afraid of you?"

"What?"

"The other night. You terrified her. She recognized you, even through the drugs, and was scared to death. Why?"

"I have no idea. As you say, she was drugged."

"She wasn't drugged when I talked to her earlier today. She was still scared. Of you and Lachko."

"That's her mother's doing. She's poisoned the girl."

"Maybe. Something is wrong with this whole setup, Iakov. How'd Rislyakov identify Polina?"

"As I already observed, he didn't confide in me."

"Here's another thing. I'm pretty sure Polina doesn't have access to anywhere near the kind of money you're talking about."

"How do you know that?"

"She couldn't come up with a hundred grand to buy off Rislyakov."

"She was always miserly as well as venal."

"That's not it."

"Polina's playing with your head again. You, of all people, should know what she's capable of. She's a pathological liar, the ultimate narcissist. Why are you asking me all these questions? Why is this any of your business?"

He was angry. Or his anger, like hers, was covering something else. He was stonewalling about Eva, just as Polina had stonewalled about Ratko. Six hundred million dollars is plenty of reason to stonewall, but despite what Iakov said, Polina had never been greedy—venal, to use his word—in my experience. Self-centered, insecure, needy, narcissistic, volatile, yes. She craved security—emotional security—and attention. Money was part of that, but only part, a means not an end. People change, but not that much. Iakov was wrong about her—or pretending to be. Iakov didn't make many mistakes.

He was watching me. "Get yourself out of here," I said. "I'll see you soon."

I gave his hand a squeeze and exhaled slowly as I went down the carpeted hall. I didn't realize I'd been holding my breath. He probably did.

A black Suburban with tinted windows was parked outside. The driver's window slid down, and Coyle waved me over.

"Visiting another sick friend?" he asked. Hard to say whether he wanted me to hear the sarcasm or just wasn't bothering to cover it.

"That's right. You guys finally twig to the fact he's in town?"

"We get precious little help from the citizenry these days. You have no idea how this particular Barsukov got sick, of course."

"He was shot."

"Thank you for that piece of news. By whom? When? Where?"

"Wednesday night, he says. Didn't see the shooter."

"You in the neighborhood?"

"Nope." Once again, technically true.

"What were you talking about up there?"

"Moscow. The old days."

"What about money? Especially money moving from Moscow here—or vice versa. You talk about that?"

"Not a word. Sorry."

"Bullshit."

"You guys heard of the Slavic Center for Personal Development?"

"This some kind of joke? I'm not feeling funny."

"Serious question."

Coyle looked around inside the SUV. I could see Sawicki in the passenger seat. Maybe one or two more in the back, behind the dark glass. He turned back to me and shook his head. "Okay, so what?"

"Barsukov front. They got branches everywhere they got banks. New York Slav House is down on Second, between Eighth and Ninth."

"So?"

"I was there earlier today. Saw two women go in, empty-handed. They came out with two others, carrying big shoulder bags. They spent the afternoon hitting half the ATMs in Fairfield County."

I couldn't see through the dark lenses of his Ray-Ban aviators, but I'd have bet anything on the eyes narrowing.

"How do you know this?"

"Hold on." I punched Gina's number. "Can you talk?"

"Sure."

"Where are you?"

"Train back to New York, thank God. We just passed Greenwich."

I said to Coyle, "They'll be in Grand Central in half an hour, getting off a New Haven train."

"Descriptions."

I told Gina to describe the four women and handed over the phone. When he gave the phone back, I said to Gina, "You got a list of the banks you and Stripy visited?"

"What the hell you think I've been doing all day, my nails?"

"E-mail it as soon as you can. Enjoy your date."

"Thanks. I meant what I said about owing me."

"Put in for overtime."

"Dammit, Turbo—"

I cut her off. Coyle was talking on his cell phone. When he finished, I said, "I'll send you a list of the banks they hit tomorrow."

He took off the sunglasses. The eyes were indeed narrowed. "How'd you know about the Slavic Center?"

"Private sector legwork."

"Uh-huh. If it were up to me, I'd haul your ass downtown and let Sawicki spend the rest of the night trying to establish a meaningful relationship. His family fled Poland one step ahead of the Red Army. He hates Russians. But you've got a date with the boss."

"My lucky day."

He shook his head. "Don't be too sure. Based on her mood an hour ago, you'd be better off with Sawicki."

★ CHAPTER 25 ★

Once again, I arrived at Trastevere feeling hot and sticky. The owner greeted me with a smile and a handshake. He took me to a table in the front where Victoria was waiting. She looked cool. I felt limp.

She didn't get up. "Giancarlo, I gather y'all have met Mr. Vlost. He's been known to do inappropriate things, so we may not be here long. If I leave, make sure he pays." She turned to me and smiled sweetly, or as sweetly as an alligator can.

I heard her talking, but truth be told, the words didn't register. The Russian language is full of slang, and Russian slang is full of improbable expressions, few of which translate well. They do capture the essence of the situation, however. The one that came to mind was *vafli lovit,* which means, literally, standing around with your mouth open long enough to catch flying dicks. The package Armani had obscured Thursday was on full display tonight. A yellow-gold silk dress came to a V at the top of her chest. Her skin was naturally brown, not acquired at the beach, and smooth. The raven hair fell around her shoulders and shone. A jade pendant and earrings played with the green eyes. No glasses tonight. I could only imagine the hips and legs beneath the table, but by then I realized how long I'd been *vafli lovit,* so I sat down. Victoria had a martini in front of her. I ordered the same, with Russian vodka.

She wasn't finished with me yet. "All right, you fast-talking, ex-socialist son of a bitch, y'all tell me right now how you know what you know."

Coyle wasn't exaggerating. Maybe it was a good thing she hadn't shown up last night.

"Privacy is an elastic concept."

"Don't give me any Russian fast-talking bullshit. How'd you get my number? How'd you know about my bank account? And this restaurant?"

I guess I like to court danger, because I thought briefly about telling her where she lived and how much she paid, but I didn't think Trastevere could withstand the eruption from the Vesuvius across the table if I did.

"I didn't break any laws and I didn't peep through any peepholes, I promise. There's lots of information out there if you know where to look."

She cooled—a little. "My number is unlisted."

"Ever order from a catalog? Call customer service?"

"Sure, but I don't give them my number."

"You don't need to. Computer reads it as soon as it answers the phone."

"You mean . . ."

"Yep. You and thirty million other people who think an unlisted number is a way to buy privacy. Child's play, really. Telephone number's like a digital tag. As good as a Social Security number. Once you have that . . ."

"So what else do you know?"

"Pretty dress. Bergdorf or Bendel's?"

"Fuck you!" She slapped me, hard—and loud.

Giancarlo appeared. "Is everything all right?"

"Fine." I rubbed my cheek. "I said something I shouldn't have. One more bruise. Won't happen again."

He frowned, put down my martini, and left. I turned back to Victoria. The Millenuits pout hit me harder than her hand.

"I'm sorry. That wasn't called for. It's just, this kind of thing really pisses me off."

"Generally or just when it strikes close to home?"

Her hand was in the air again before I could turn. It stopped midway across the table and returned to her lap.

"If you'll excuse me for saying so—and not hit me again—I'm a little surprised this is new to you. Given your job and all."

She sipped her drink and shook her head. "My background is white-collar crime—corporate fraud, accounting cover-ups, insider trading. I'm not an expert on identity theft—as you apparently are."

"In that case, I'm happy to help. What would you like to know?"

"Where you spent Wednesday night. What you want with Rad Rislyakov. And Lachko Barsukov. And Iakov Barsukov. You did say you'd explain over dinner. Here I am—all ears."

She smiled and took another sip. Giancarlo returned, and I let him prolong the truce while he recited the specials.

"You order," I said.

She told him we'd both have the seafood salad and wild mushroom fettuccini. "And bring a good Barolo. Don't worry about cost. He's buying."

I was going to pay for my sins. I steered the conversation toward safer ground.

"Your father was French?"

"Via New Orleans. My mother, Scottish, via east Texas. They lasted about as long as every other Franco-Anglo attempt to get along. My old man lit out for California shortly after I was born."

"*Tu parles français?*"

She shook her head. "Like Loretta says, 'If you're lookin' at me, you're lookin' at country.'"

The designer number she was wearing had as much to do with country as I do with Tanzania. "Loretta?"

"Loretta Lynn. She's kind of a hero for me."

"See, there's something I didn't know."

"Y'all want to keep talkin', you'll . . ."

The twang was pronounced tonight. So was her temper.

Giancarlo brought the first course and the wine. "You'll like this. It's an '89." He poured her a small taste, which she swirled and sipped. She smiled broadly at him, and he grinned back.

"Perfect," she said, and I had the distinct impression she was referring to more than the flavor.

Giancarlo poured. I took a small swallow. I know a little about a lot of things, but wine isn't one of them. I like it fine, but I prefer beer and vodka. I thought that could be about to change as layer after layer of flavor filled my mouth. Victoria was eying me appraisingly.

"I don't think I've ever tasted anything quite like that."

"You're not likely to again." She tucked into her salad.

We ate in silence for a while. The seafood was almost as good as the wine.

"I'm waitin'," she said.

"Petrovin tell you about Iakov?"

She looked up, confused. "Petrovin? Who the hell's Petrovin?"

My turn to be confused. "Russian law enforcement officer? Eye patch? Linen suit? He was in your office yesterday."

"You mean . . . He told you his name's Petrovin?"

"Actually, he told me his name isn't Petrovin, but that's how he introduced himself. He was being cautious."

"Are all Russians crazy?"

"Dostoyevsky would tell you probably. Chekhov would disagree. Zinoviev would blame the system."

"You're all full of horseshit, that's for sure. Give me Hemingway any day."

We weren't going to agree on literature. "What's Petrovin's real name?"

"Uh-uh. He may be crazy, but I'm sure he has reasons, especially when it comes to trusting you. Back to business. Rad Rislyakov."

"You're interested in his money laundry."

"What do you know about that?" she snapped.

"He built it for Barsukov. He uses the information he hacked from T.J. Maxx to create synthetic identities, and he uses those identities to create bank accounts to move money through. He's got an army of couriers working ATMs all over the Tri-State Area. I happened on a few earlier today. Told Coyle an hour ago where to find them and one base of operation."

"You didn't say anything about this the other day."

"Didn't know anything about it the other day."

"You set off my bullshit meter every other time you open your mouth. How do you know what you know?"

"I did some digging. I got lucky. Some of Rislyakov's associates aren't very bright."

"A nonanswer if I ever heard one."

I raised my glass. "Wine's excellent."

"You said your interest in Rislyakov had nothing to do with mine."

"That's true." I debated briefly whether to go on, but I knew I would. You have to give a little to get a little, or perhaps more to the point, I was enjoying myself and her company. Or I do like to live dangerously.

"Rislyakov whaled Mulholland."

"What? He's the one?"

"Uh-huh."

The green eyes grew brighter. "You know that for a fact?"

"Yep. He was blackmailing Mrs. Mulholland."

"How? Why?"

"I'm going to plead privacy on the how. It doesn't have an impact on Mulholland, his bank, or the money laundry. The why I don't know. Except that Ratko had a gambling problem. He might have needed money fast."

"Had?"

Mistake. She was sharp. "He went through rehab. It took."

She eyed me over her fork, uncertain what she believed. "How *do* you know all this?"

"Same way I know about Bergdorf."

That bought me time, at least. She chewed her salad. I took a bite and resolved to be more careful.

"Back to Mulholland. Why'd Rislyakov phish him? Don't tell me he just got lucky."

"That question bothers me, to be candid. I don't have a good answer."

"Have you asked Rislyakov?"

"I told you the other day—we've never met."

"Just checking." She stopped the questions long enough to eat and think. I did the same. The food was every bit as good as last night.

"Tell me about Barsukov—you and Barsukov. Both Barsukovs."

"That's complicated. There's a lot of context."

"We've got half a bottle of wine and the pasta coming. Dessert, too, if we're still talking. Was Wednesday really the first time you'd seen him in twenty years?"

"Scout's honor." Cheka honor wouldn't mean anything to her.

"Not likely. Scout, I mean."

Maybe I should've stuck with it. I thought about what I was going to say. Suppressing my past had blown up one relationship. Would putting it out there, right up front, ignite another? The lifelong need to skip over, to prevaricate, to hide my past, was missing—for the first time. The sense of liberation wasn't jarring—but I think the ground shifted beneath the table.

"My link to the Barsukovs is Iakov, the father. He got me out of the Gulag and into the KGB. I owe him pretty much everything."

"*You* were in the Gulag? Like whatsisname . . . Solzhenitsyn?"

"Born there. My mother was a *zek,* a prisoner. Earned my own ticket back as a teenager. Safe to say I would have died there—years ago—without Iakov."

"This sounds like a good story, for once. Go on."

"You really want to hear it?'

"You have my full attention." The green eyes said she wasn't lying.

"I was born in Dalstroy, a complex of camps in Siberia, the day Stalin died. March fifth, 1953, also the day Prokofiev died, but no one remembers that. My mother spent most of her life in the camps. I never met my father. We were released—she and I—in the amnesty after Stalin's death. She died on the way home. I grew up in an orphanage, got in trouble, got sent back."

"Hold on! You're going too fast. Why was your mother in the Gulag?"

"No real reason. Millions of people were arrested, incarcerated, released, incarcerated again, executed, all for no reason whatsoever. Other than Stalin's insanity. The entire Soviet system was based on betrayal—friend against friend, wife against husband, father against son. We were all complicit, the Soviet people, I mean. One big way the Party kept control. The biggest betrayal of all was the Gulag itself—prisons, work camps, execution chambers, all set up by Russians for Russians who had done nothing, except they'd been betrayed. We've never come to terms with what that means. As a result, I'm a *zek,* and that's a shameful thing to be. In the eyes of other Russians, I'll always be a *zek.* When they see me, they see someone they betrayed. They can't deal with that, so they transfer the betrayal to me. It's my fault. I was a prisoner because I betrayed the Party and the state."

"Jesus! You all are crazy!"

"I won't deny it. It's like when Winston Smith and his lover betray each other at the end of *1984.* They do it because they're forced to by Big Brother. It's not their fault, but once they do, they can no longer look each other in the eye. That was Soviet society, in a nutshell, in fact, not fiction. Still is, to a bigger extent than anyone wants to admit. Solzhenitsyn was one of the few who bucked the system, the culture, the whole deal, by writing about it. Telling the truth for everyone to see. He blew the lid off. But it takes more than one explosion to revolutionize a system that shaped generations. I'll get off my soapbox now."

"No such luck. What about Iakov? And the KGB?"

"I have a facility for languages, and between the orphanage and the camps, I picked up a bunch. That got the attention of the KGB, and they offered me a way out. Iakov was already a fast-rising officer, the Cold War was heating up, and he understood we needed people who could make their way, operate—fit in—overseas. Smartest man I ever met. He ended up the number two man in the whole organization—on merit, not political connections."

"So you went to work for the same people who put your mother in prison?"

"Life's full of ironies, especially if you're Russian."

She shook her head. "Christ. Tell me about the spy part."

A waiter removed our plates and put two bowls of steaming pasta on the table. The mushroom aroma floated upward. Giancarlo offered Parmesan and pepper. I took another sip of wine. The flavors were separating, becoming more distinct—raisins, berries, and something like tar. I didn't know tar could taste good.

"The spy part's pretty mundane. No James Bond. I collected information, a lot of it from newspapers, magazines, TV. Sometimes, I tried to get American experts to work for us. I also tried to stop Soviet experts from being recruited by your CIA. Occasionally, I got Soviet experts to pretend they were working for the Americans when they were still working for us. A big game, really."

Until we caught one of our own people working for the other side. Then the consequences were deadly. I didn't want to go into that now.

"What if you got caught?"

"It was my business not to. Besides, we all operated under diplomatic immunity. When I was stationed here, I was officially with the Soviet Consulate—cultural attaché, the last time. CIA does the same thing. There's an unwritten agreement among the professionals—no physical harm. Catch 'em, throw 'em out, don't hurt 'em. We all knew that if shooting started, it would be hard to stop. Basic self-interest."

"How'd you do this recruiting?"

"You become a good student of human nature. Figure out what makes people tick, all the psychological buttons you can push. It also helps to get lucky. Believe it or not, your two most famous double agents, Aldrich Ames and Robert Hanssen, were volunteers, walk-ins. You had another one, Harold Nicholson, who was still trying to make a buck after he got caught, passing secrets from jail through his son. We used all the techniques you'd expect—bribery, blackmail, sex, appeals to ideology, although those were mainly for show. People have a remarkable propensity to get into trouble, as you know. We'd offer a helping hand."

"You preyed on weakness."

"It was business. Your side did the same thing. *You* do the same thing today."

"That's different. I'm dealing with criminals."

"If you say so."

We paused for more pasta. It almost put the salad and wine to shame.

"So what happened then?"

"Some bad luck. A decision that didn't work out. My career dead-ended. I moved here."

"That's not very specific."

"Let's just say it was 1992, the Cold War was over, a bunch of things came together, I needed a change of scene. I'd done four tours in the States, two in New York. I liked it. It's Moscow with rules—self-imposed, voluntary rules."

"Okay, I won't push it. Married?"

She wouldn't ask that unless . . .

"A long time ago."

She waited to see if I would say more. When I didn't, she said, "You seem—how shall I put this?—very at home here."

I smiled. I don't know whether she meant it, but that was quite a compliment for someone in my line.

"Iakov taught me a valuable lesson. He talked about his days in Beirut and Istanbul and how much better prepared the Americans were for operating there because they came from a more open, more diverse culture. They obviously weren't local, but they knew how to adapt. I had an advantage my fellow officers did not. I'd grown up surrounded by kids from all over—Germans, Poles, Romanians, you name it—in the orphanage and the camps. I was a chameleon. I could fit in with everybody. When I spoke Polish, I sounded like a Pole. When I spoke Hungarian, people thought I came from Budapest. When I was assigned here the first time, I watched TV—cop shows, sitcoms, even soaps. I read all the newspapers and newsmagazines. Also *Rolling Stone* and *Popular Mechanics* and the *Village Voice*. A lot of it I had to do in secret. Most of my fellow Chekists wore Soviet blinders—everything Western was suspect. They wouldn't have understood. I was careful, and I got away with it. I learned to fit in. Your turn. I want to finish my dinner."

"Okay. So happens you're not the only ex-con at the table. Something *I* don't tell everyone every day."

"Things are looking up."

"Don't get excited. One of us rehabilitated herself."

"See, once a *zek* . . ."

"I'm not Russian. You're just another ex-socialist ex-con to me. Anyway, I grew up in a town called Thibodaux, in bayou country. My father left, like I told you. Mother married again—her third. Then she got banged up bad in a car accident. He was driving, smashed. After that she spent most of her time zoned out on painkillers. He tried to put the moves on me, but he was usually too drunk, and I stayed out of his way.

One night, though, when I was seventeen, he spiked my soda with something—maybe my mom's drugs—and I came to on the floor, him on top of me. I was stoned, but he was blotto, and I was able to wriggle away. I laid him out cold with a frying pan, stole his wallet and his car. I slept off the drugs and used his credit card to fill the tank and took off. Didn't stop until I reached Miami.

"I moved in with my half sister, from my mom's first marriage. Pretty soon her boyfriend was hitting on me. He was Cuban-Bolivian, so he took 'no' as an affront to his manhood. One night he caught me. My sister came home just in time and called the cops. They arrested him—and me, too, for stealing that bastard's car. The Cuban got probation. I spent a year in a juvenile detention center."

Based on the Soviet justice system, I'm in no position to pass judgment on America's—but in addition to the innocent, it does favor people with money. The boyfriend could afford a lawyer. No one was interested in extenuating circumstances from a seventeen-year-old with a Bardot pout and an empty bank account.

"It was a good lesson," she went on. "I met girls who'd been in there two, three times, they're not even eighteen. I didn't want that. I finished high school, worked my way through community college, and got to the University of Miami on ROTC. Degree in psychology. Did four years in the air force and got my law degree on Uncle Sam."

"What led you to white-collar crime?"

"My first job after law school, at a Miami firm, one of the partners takes me to dinner, then to a motel. I refuse to go inside. He tells me my job depends on it. I say no. I get fired the next day, professional delinquencies, they said. They refused to give me my back pay.

"The money part was bad enough, but the allegation that I wasn't up to the job really tore it for me. Who'd these bastards think they were? I had my sister take some pictures of me in my underwear. Wrote 'Can't wait till next time' on one and mailed it to his home. Three days later, he appeared at the door screaming about his wife and marriage. I still had my service sidearm. It wasn't loaded, but he didn't know that."

"Still play with guns?"

"Only when provoked."

She returned to her pasta.

"What happened next?"

"One of my professors knew the DA, and he set me up there. Everyone else was doing drug cases, but I went after crooked businessmen. Why should they get a free ride? Ninety percent conviction rate over three years. I liked prosecuting, but I needed to make some money, so I joined another firm. I let it be known at the outset I didn't want to be messed with, and I built up enough of a caseload that people left me alone. They merged with an Atlanta firm, then it merged with Hayes & Franklin. I was ready for a change of scene, too, so I asked to move to New York. My timing was good. A lot of big securities fraud cases were breaking, and all the white-shoe lawyers had long forgotten the little bit of criminal law they'd had to study in school. Pretty soon I was running the whole department. Billed eighty million last year, before I left."

I let out a whistle. I couldn't help it.

"*Now* you're impressed. What is it about men? Sex and money always get your attention. You're like all the rest—only interested in the same things."

"The one thing I'm interested in is why Rislyakov phished Mulholland."

The waiter cleared. We declined the offer of dessert. She ordered coffee.

"There is one thing you could do, if you're so inclined. Kind of make up for all that spying on me."

I wasn't convinced I had anything to make up for, but I had no chance of winning that argument. "What's that?"

"What you said about identity theft. It's a world I know very little about. I need to know a lot more, and I prefer not to ask for an in-house tutorial."

"Don't want to demonstrate lack of knowledge?"

"Were you this obnoxious when you were a *zek*?"

"That's what they tell me."

"Some men I work with would feel right at home in your Soviet system. They resent a woman in my position. So, yes, I prefer not to advertise any gaps in my expertise."

"Good a reason as any. Would you like to come up and see my databases?"

"When will you get it through your bald head that you are not funny?"

"Don't you Americans have a saying about old dogs?"

"I don't mind old. Presumptuous pisses me off."

"And you carry a gun."

"How about first thing Monday?"

"Fine. My office is at 88 Pine. Eight thirty?"

"Great. Thank you. I do appreciate it." She looked around. "Hey, we're going to close the place."

I signaled Giancarlo for the check. I hope I kept a straight face when he brought it—$680, before tip. The wine was $475. Victoria was smiling.

"You're right," I said, handing over my credit card.

"About what? Men?"

"No. The wine. I won't be having that again."

A phone rang faintly. She reached for her bag and pulled it out. She didn't say much, but I watched her face change as she watched me watching her. She was angry—not her temper flaring like earlier. It was more substantive than that. I hoped it wasn't aimed at me, but I had the feeling I was in the line of fire, at least tangentially. Her only questions to the phone were "Where?" "When?" and "You're sure?" After a few minutes, she said, "I'll be there," and put the phone back in her bag.

"Y'all are gonna tell me, goddammit, everything you know about Rad Rislyakov. Tonight."

"What happened?"

"You already know. He was found in a marsh off Flatbush Avenue. Body was dumped there. He's been dead since midweek."

I kept a straight face. "There's not much I can tell you." Sounded stupid, but at least it was mostly truthful.

"Bullshit." She wasn't trying to cover the anger. "I'm not sayin' you had anything to do with Rislyakov's killing, but if you did, I'm sure as hell gonna find out."

"I understand."

"Good. Let's go downtown. You can come up and see my corpse."

I chuckled, I couldn't help it. I think she did, too, just a little.

I followed her outside. A black Town Car idled by the curb.

"It's gonna be straight business from here on, so I want to tell you I had a nice time tonight, most of it anyway. But if you want to see me again, socially I mean, assuming you're not in jail, stay the hell out of my private life."

"Suppose it's your private life I'm trying to get into."

"I don't mind a full frontal assault. Backdoor tactics are different."

"I'm just trying whatever door you leave open."

"Just because you can pick the lock doesn't mean it's open."

"I'll remember that."

"You'd be wise to. Otherwise I'll slam it in your face. There's a cab."

I'd assumed the Town Car was hers, but I was wrong on that count, too. The door opened, and Sergei and another man climbed out. Sergei showed us his gun.

"Get in the car," he said.

"Let me put my friend in a—"

"Both of you, *govnosos*—shit-sucker. Get in."

"No. She's not—"

"In the fucking car!"

It was futile to resist, but I was going to try. Call it chivalry, pride, macho, or just not wanting to be railroaded by a couple of *urki* in front of Victoria. I took a step toward Sergei, who grinned. The other guy moved in to my right.

Victoria said, "Unless I miss my guess, that's a Beretta Tomcat, just like the one I own. Don't be stupid." She turned to Sergei. "Let's go."

She walked to the car, opened the door, and climbed in. Sergei looked disappointed he wasn't going to get to slug me, but he followed her to the car, and the other guy shoved me in after them. The Lincoln took off down Second Avenue and again turned east toward Brighton Beach.

★ CHAPTER 26 ★

Traffic was light, so we made the Badger's palace in thirty minutes. Victoria sat silently through the ride, seemingly cool as ice. No way to gauge the temperature under the skin. Neither Sergei nor the driver said anything. I wondered if Lachko was aware of the identity of his other guest. If so, he was playing an aggressive hand, even for him.

The car went through the security check at the gate and pulled into the courtyard. I was yanked out, pressed against the steel, and patted down. Across the car, Sergei was getting ready to search Victoria.

"Hands off, Sergei," I said. "Lachko won't like it."

"Fuck off."

"She's a U.S. attorney, Sergei. Top Fed, to you. She can bring every cop in New York to Brighton Beach. Boss want that?"

Sergei didn't respond, but he didn't search Victoria either.

I said to her, "You carrying your Beretta?"

"No."

"Anything at all?"

"Pepper spray."

"Hand it over and let him see your bag."

She did as I said.

Sergei took the spray canister and looked inside the bag. "Okay."

Victoria smiled at him and looked back at me. "Thank you."

"My pleasure."

Sergei told me to fuck my mother in Russian and led us into the palace, down the marble hall, through the Beidermeir reception room, and into Lachko's office.

"Well, Electrifikady Turbanevich, you poisonous parasite, what is it I have to do to flush you from my system?" Lachko sat in a wheelchair tonight, wearing a gray tracksuit, *papirosa* smoking in one hand, cashews in a bowl next to him.

212

"Barsukov, Miss Victoria, Lachko Iakovlev Barsukov. A pleasure to make your acquaintance. I apologize for interfering in your evening, but you were clearly in need of an improvement in company."

"Turbo told me y'all were kinda insistent. He wasn't joking." She was laying the twang on thick and heavy.

"Ahhh. What else did my old friend tell you?"

"Y'all don't get on so well anymore. And you're a mean-ass son of a bitch."

Lachko smiled as broadly as his cancer-stretched skin would allow, then laughed.

"What can I offer you, Miss Victoria?" Lachko asked. "Vodka, coffee?"

"Glass of wine, please. Red, if you have it."

Lachko nodded at Sergei. "Turbo? Vodka?"

"Nothing for me."

"Vodka, Sergei. That's twice you've declined my hospitality, Turbo. We have our differences, sure, but that's no reason to be uncivilized."

I shrugged. Lachko scooped up some cashews. Sergei went off to get the drinks.

Lachko said, "I gather you two had a very relaxed meal. Almost three hours. I hope you didn't spend all that time talking about me."

Victoria had disbelief written all over her. "Y'all got an inflated opinion, you don't mind my saying so."

"You are a good actress, Miss Victoria. Better than many I've seen on your Broadway stage. You also have a battalion stationed across the street from my home, men with cameras, telescopes, microphones, and who knows what else. My opinion is my opinion, but it is not far-fetched." He bit hard on a nut as if to emphasize his point.

Sergei returned with a tray. Victoria took her wine. I decided to have the vodka after all. Lachko thought he could intimidate Victoria. It would be fun watching him try.

Victoria gave him a long stare and shook her head. "My predecessor put these men there. Not unreasonable, given that you're a mobster. I haven't had time to think about them myself. Although I can't imagine they're earning the taxpayers' keep watching a bunch of second-rate crooks in a dump like this, dolled up like a Vegas cathouse."

The taunts registered. The black eyes turned blacker. I hoped she knew what she was doing—spearing Lachko's vanity was playing with fire.

She took a sip of wine, wrinkled her nose, and set the glass aside.

"The wine not to your liking?"

"You get points for consistency, if nothing else."

"Why'd you haul us out here, Lachko?" I said.

"A chance to talk, Turbo. And to meet the most attractive Miss Victoria, of course."

"Hold the sugar, sugar," she said. "You missed the opportunity for that."

That got her another black-eyed stare.

"You want to talk, Lachko, that's fine. Tell Sergei to take Victoria back to Manhattan."

"In good time, Turbo. The matters I wish to discuss may involve her, too."

"I'm all ears," she said.

"Rad Rislyakov," Lachko said. "I know you have an interest in him, Miss Victoria. You've had men not busy watching my home watching his." He held up a hairy hand full of nuts. "Spare my patience, I don't need to hear more about your predecessor."

"What about Rislyakov?" I asked.

"Wednesday, when we picked you up on Greene Street, you were outside a building where he did business. You didn't tell me."

Victoria swung toward me.

"I see Turbo hasn't told you about Greene Street either, Miss Victoria. Maybe you are in a similar position—you think someone is a better friend than he turns out to be."

"Who said we're friends?"

"You hear that, Turbo? Even Miss Victoria here questions your friendship. Perhaps you know something about Rislyakov's death. How he became dead, for example."

"What about it?" Victoria asked me.

"Rislyakov rented a loft at 32 Greene, 6A, under another name—Goncharov. Lachko didn't know about it, which raises two questions."

I turned back to face him. "How'd you let that happen? You must be slipping. And what was Ratko hiding from you?" That got me the dark look and the sense that I'd pay a price in the not-too-distant future. "On the other hand, there are rare occasions when Lachko knows more than he lets on."

"Rislyakov worked for me. No secret there. I'm the one who recognized the boy's talent, saw his potential. I nurtured him. He was worth a lot of money to me."

"You're avoiding Turbo's questions," Victoria said.

"Turbo and his questions mean nothing to me. A raccoon has sharp claws, sharp teeth, a pea-sized brain, and a nasty disposition. It also carries rabies. If one crosses the road in front of your car, you either swerve around it or, better, run it over. You certainly don't stop to talk. Miss Victoria, what do you think of Russia?"

"Don't have much of an opinion. Y'all aren't very funny, I know that much."

"An assessment based on your acquaintance with our mutual friend here, no doubt. I mean Russia today, the country, Moscow, the capital."

She shrugged. "What I read in the paper. What Turbo's told me. I'm no expert, if that's what you're asking."

Lachko chewed on a cashew while he watched her. "You do yourself a disservice. That's your prerogative, of course. But you do me a disservice as well, which is stupid." He spat into his bucket.

"You are—"

The right hand came up, smoking Belomorkanal between the fingers.

"You visited Moscow last month. You arrived at Domodedovo at ten o'clock on May fourth, BA flight eight seven four. You stayed three nights at the Marriott Tverskaya. You spent eight and a half hours at CPS headquarters in Ulica Otradnaja. You walked around Red Square, toured St. Basil's Cathedral, and visited the old GUM department store. You did not pay your respects at Lenin's Tomb. You did not visit Lubyanka. Pity. Would you like to know where you ate?"

"You're well informed." She was working hard to keep her temper under control.

"What did you discuss with the CPS piss-drinkers?"

She shook her head slowly, her eyes not budging from his. "As we say down where I come from, ain't none of your beeswax."

Lachko spat again and fired another *papirosa*. "Did Turbo tell you about the Cheka?"

"They arrest people for no good reason. You used to work for it."

"The *zek's*-eye view. I assume he told you where he came from."

"For once, you assume right."

That stopped him, for a moment. Not the implied insult, but that I'd told her. He hadn't expected that.

"Things have changed since Turbo left Russia. He's out of date. Nowadays we always have a reason."

"If you say so."

He chewed a cashew. "Russia is an international power—politically, strategically, economically, in all spheres. The Cheka watches out for Russia's interests."

"You left out criminally," I said. "And the Cheka watches out first for itself."

"I thought y'all were retired," Victoria said.

"Didn't Turbo tell you? No such thing as an ex-Chekist."

"I'm the first," I said.

"You're a *zek*, Turbo. You've never rid yourself of the stench."

Victoria picked up the wineglass, reconsidered, and put it down. "I hate to interrupt this stimulating cultural conversation, but you still haven't told us why you brought us out here."

Lachko nodded slowly. "Turbo and I have business to discuss. I wanted to make your acquaintance—since you take such an interest in my affairs. Also I wanted to offer a piece of advice. You appear to be an intelligent woman, despite your choice of dinner companions."

"Like I said earlier, I'm all ears."

"The pederasts at the CPS—don't put too much faith in them. They get excited at the sight of naked buttocks, but they are as impotent as eunuchs."

"I take it you don't get along."

"They exist because we have allowed them to exist. They are shit-chewing maggots, feeding on the waste of others. Soon they will be squashed like maggots. There is only one power in Russia today, and Turbo is right, we do take care of ourselves. Those who interfere . . ." He spat in his bucket.

"I'll be sure to bear that in mind—but this ain't Moscow. You're just another two-bit hood here."

She was pushing too hard. Color climbed up his pale neck.

"Our reach is as long as it needs to be. London, Zurich, New York . . ." He spat again.

"Y'all threatening me?"

"Sergei! We have no reason to detain Miss Victoria further. Have Dmitri take her back to Manhattan."

"I'm in no hurry. I'll wait and go back with Turbo."

"Turbo could be here quite a while."

"That's okay. I'm trying to learn to enjoy your company. It's a slow process."

I was watching Victoria and Lachko. I didn't see it coming and didn't hear it until too late. The thunderclouds twitched. Sergei moved behind the stool I was sitting on and hit me full force in the left kidney. Sledgehammer fist, freight-train arm. The vodka glass went flying; the force knocked me to the floor. Pain shot through my torso, one searing explosion after another. I fought the overriding urge to vomit mushroom pasta on Lachko's white carpet, although in a fleeting lucid moment, I wondered why I bothered. The white room spun. I thought I heard Victoria shout and Lachko laugh.

I have no idea how long it lasted, but after a while the pain started to recede, in both intensity and frequency. The room turned more slowly. I could feel the bile in my throat. I was covered with sweat.

"Pick him up," Lachko said.

Strong hands lifted me back onto the stool. That set off more explosions. I held my head between sweaty palms until they passed.

Victoria said from somewhere, "Are you all right?" A stupid question if there ever was one, but I suppose she needed to say something. I tried to smile, but I'm not sure I managed. My voice came out as a croak.

"Cheka . . . entertainment."

Victoria went over to Lachko, who was lighting another Belomork-

217

anal. "Those men across the street. I can have them over here anytime I want."

"Turbo, you are a lucky man. I think she likes you, although I can't imagine why. They will find nothing, Miss Victoria, except a sick old man looking after an injured friend. Tell her we're old friends, Turbo."

"We're . . . old . . . friends," I repeated. I had no idea what he intended for me, but the first thing was to get Victoria out of here.

"I think you're full of shit. Both of you."

"I hear you've been creeping around Polina, Turbo. You didn't mention that either."

Uh-oh. How . . .

"Did Turbo tell you about his ex-wife, Miss Victoria? He was a big disappointment to her. She used to get sick to her stomach if I mentioned his name. You humiliated her, Turbo, rubbed her nose in the human waste of life. But you couldn't tell her the truth, could you? Too cowardly, too scared."

"What are y'all talking about?" Victoria said.

"*Zek,*" I managed to spit out. Even the one word hurt.

"She despised him so much she married me," Lachko said. "That should tell you something, Miss Victoria."

What the hell was he doing? Victoria was hanging on every word.

"Vengeance is a poor basis for a lasting union. We had a few good years and went our separate ways. Now I understand Polina's living here, Turbo. On Fifth Avenue, no less. Why didn't you tell me?"

"Assumed you—"

"Bullshit," he said. "You could easily have said something Wednesday. You chose not to."

"Sounds to me like something else you didn't know," Victoria said to him.

"There's very little I don't know, Miss Victoria, when it concerns me. Even less I can't find out if I care to. Would you like to know who you called from your hotel on Tverskaya? Or what you said? For such an attractive woman, you don't seem to have much of a social life. All business, twenty-four/seven, as they say. Too bad. You should have a husband— or at least someone better suited than our retching friend here."

I was listening to him but watching her. She kept a straight face, but he'd found a soft spot in the tough veneer she wore.

"Sergei, tell Dmitri to take Miss Victoria home," Lachko said.

"Goddammit, you can't make me leave."

The thunderclouds twitched. Sergei maneuvered Victoria to the door. She objected loudly the entire way.

"Wait!" Lachko called. "I almost forgot. Did Turbo tell you where our mutual ex-wife fetched up?"

"Lachko, I . . ." I croaked.

"She goes by the name Felicity now, Felix for short, I understand. Married to a rich banker. Man named Mulholland."

Victoria shouted and Lachko laughed as Sergei all but pushed her out the door. Again I tried to figure out what game he was playing. At least Victoria was on her way home. That was something.

Sergei came back and nodded at his boss. The thunderclouds twitched again. This time there was only one explosion as the hammer slammed into the left side of my face. A blast of pain, a burst of light as I fell through the air.

I don't remember hitting the rug.

When I came back to wherever I was, I was lying on the floor staring at the chrome leg of a desk. Lachko's desk. The finish was marred by a big scratch, which made me feel a tiny bit better. I stayed there a while, trying to find some part of me that didn't hurt, hoping to collect whatever wits Sergei hadn't knocked to Vladivostok. Didn't feel like I had any. It dawned on me there was no sound in the room. That's right—Victoria was gone. Where was Lachko?

I pushed myself to a sitting position, which got everything spinning. I waited until the room righted. A sponge-sized splotch of red on the white carpet. Good. I made a stab at standing up. Big mistake. I coughed and spat brownish green bile on top of the blood.

A clock chimed. One o'clock. Maybe everybody had gone to bed. Definitely time to go. I tried standing again and this time got to my knees.

Motion to my left. A wheeze, air sucked through a tube.

"Feel better now that you've had some rest?"

Sergei wheeled Lachko toward the desk. He fired a *papirosa* and blew smoke in my direction.

"You lied to me, Turbo. Multiple times." He shook his head. "You should know better."

"No," I croaked.

"Don't make it worse. You didn't tell me about Polina."

"Like I said . . ."

"Like I said—bullshit. You were going to stay away from Rislyakov, but you went straight back there. You told me this was about kidnapping. Bullshit. What the fuck ever made you dream I wouldn't find out about your childish games? Do you think I'm senile as well as sick? You've always been enamored of your brain, but honestly, it's your most feeble organ. More useless than your dick. I'm tempted to do you a favor and have Sergei sever both, but I need information first. Don't even think about not telling me what I want to know."

Lying—or telling the truth, for that matter—when you're mentally impaired and have no idea what's going on is just plain stupid. I wasn't too enfeebled to recognize that. The sight of Sergei clenching and unclenching his fist made the logic irrelevant. First thing was to buy time, get some wits back. That meant telling Lachko at least some of what he thought he wanted to hear.

"I told you . . . truth as I knew it," I said. Each word felt like a knife slicing into my guts. "Polina's husband hired me. He got a ransom note. Turns out, Polina herself sent it. She . . . needed money to pay off Ratko. He blackmailed her."

"Turbo, what is this fucking fairy tale? You are more moronic than even I thought possible. What the fuck? Polina was fleecing her husband because Ratko was blackmailing her?"

"That's . . . right. I don't know why."

"Suppose I believe you—and I'm more likely to kiss your balls. What did Ratko have?"

"Her new identity."

"Who was she hiding from?"

I just looked at him.

"Me? You pile absurdity on top of stupidity. Polina and I were finished years ago, long before she disappeared. We were separated. We'd made a deal. She was going to start divorce proceedings. She wasn't going to try to clean me out, I wasn't going to contest it. I couldn't have cared less."

He sounded sincere. If Lachko can ever be considered sincere.

"Iakov said she and Kosokov . . ."

"Yes, I know. They deserved each other."

"He said Kosokov stole six hundred million . . ."

"Kosokov? Steal? Hah! This gets more fucked up with every word. A minute ago, Polina's broke, she needs money. Now she has six hundred million. I do think my father's finally losing his mind. Kosokov was so fucking thick he had to be led around by his member just to avoid walking in front of a bus. And you—you're just trying to keep your shriveled skin from being peeled off its useless frame. Don't bother. I intend to take care of that myself."

I ignored the threat. He and Iakov told different stories. That was worth pursuing, if I had the chance.

"What did you find at Greene Street?" Lachko said.

"Iakov, Ratko's body, suitcase, computer, Eva."

"What about bullet holes in the bedroom door, two slugs in one wall, one in another, one in Ratko? Where's the gun?"

"I took it."

"What kind?"

"Glock, nine millimeter."

"I want it. What else did you find on the computer?"

I grabbed hold of the desk leg with both hands and somehow pulled myself to my feet. I leaned on the red lacquer, out of breath, ready to throw up.

"Your laundry," I gagged. We were going to get there sooner or later.

He thought for a moment, no expression on his withered face.

"How much does your friend Victoria know?"

No good answer to this question. "She knows. Don't know how. She knew before I told her."

"Bullshit. You were at the Slavic Center this morning."

"Looking for Eva. Ratko had the home page on his computer. She ran from the hospital. You sent your men there." A guess, but a good one.

I missed the eyebrows twitching, not that it would have made any difference. Sergei came across the room and hit me in the stomach. Another explosion and I was sucking rug shag again, looking for oxygen. I couldn't take too much more of this. No one could.

Lachko and Sergei backed off. I spat again on the brown-red stain and tried to focus. Lachko kept his eyes on me as he chewed some cashews from his pocket. I was almost able to breathe at a normal rate when he said, "Someone copied a large database from Rislyakov's computer, then erased it from the hard drive. That you?"

Were we finally getting to the point? "Not me."

"You took the computer with you. You have a partner well known in technology circles. I want what was taken returned."

I started through the motions of standing again.

"I don't have it. I found the ransom note and Ratko's blackmail note, like I told you. I removed them. You can confirm that. I didn't touch anything else."

"Turbo, you forget I've had the misfortune to know you from the time you crawled out of the Gulag. You learned to lie before you could walk."

I might have pointed out we all did. He turned the wheelchair away. Leaning hard on the desk, I made it back to my feet. The exertion had me gulping air like I'd just sprinted two miles.

I saw eyebrows twitch this time. Sergei lifted me off the floor with one muscled arm, grinned, and hit me in the gut with the other. He let go, and I crumpled back at the base of the desk. The scratch was still there.

Lachko said, "I'm going to give you one more chance, although I have no idea why. *Zeks* can only be dealt with as *zeks*. They deserve no respect. They deserve nothing."

He took a cordless phone from the pocket of his tracksuit and punched in a number. Lot of digits—overseas call.

"Good morning, Vasily. How are you today? How's the weather? . . . Fine, fine. No, no change. There's an old friend here with me. He wants to talk to you."

Lachko pushed the speaker button.

"*Ya sru na tvayu mat*—I shit on your mother," Lachko's brother said.

"Hello, Vasily," I replied, as evenly as I could.

"I understand you are feeling some pain. I thought news from home might brighten you up. I'm in a car with one of the Cheka's best marksmen, in Ulica Otradnaja. You know it?"

CPS headquarters. Panic replaced pain. What time was it in Moscow? Pushing 2:00 A.M. here . . . 10:00 A.M. I pulled myself to my feet again, still leaning on the desk. Sergei backed off, about a foot.

"My friend and I are parked across from your son's building. He's on the second floor. I can see him through the window."

I didn't answer.

"We've been watching for an hour. Right now he's talking on the phone. Wearing a faggy blue sweater, by the way. You should've taught him to be more observant, Turbo. But, of course, you weren't there, were you? Never have been. He hasn't noticed us at all, parked right across the street. Those CPS *pediks* are all piss-stupid."

The unmistakable sound of a shell being loaded into a firing chamber ricocheted across nine thousand miles.

"Dragunov SVDS with a scope, in case you were wondering," Vasily said. "Let's see if your dumb-fuck kid puts in another appearance."

Lachko said, "One more time, Turbo, where's that database?"

"No! I don't have it. I told you the truth!" I threw myself toward his wheelchair. Sergei knocked me sideways with his hip. Lachko shrugged.

Crack!

"NO! ALEKSEI!"

Time stopped.

Then the sound of a car engine starting and Vasily's voice, low and quiet. "A warning, Turbo. Maybe your son needs a new window. Maybe he needs a new head. Understand, you prick. Doesn't matter who they are—or where. We find them when we're ready. Listen to Lachko. With luck, someday I'll eat your blood over ice cream."

Lachko pocketed the phone. "I want that database, Turbo. If you don't have it, find it. You understand the consequences?"

"Yes." Like a Cheka confession—meaningless, but what they want to hear.

"One more thing. Stay the fuck away from my family. Your business with Polina, whatever the fuck it was, is finished. Same goes for Eva. I will take care of them now. Understand?"

No point in arguing. I nodded assent.

"Good. Maybe you're not as stupid as you always seem to be. This is from Vasily."

Sergei hit me once more, this time in the gut. I collapsed to my knees, heaving, then vomited, finally, without control. I couldn't breathe—but I could puke. Sometime during my seizure, Lachko left. Sergei waited until I was heaving dry, then grabbed the collar of my coat and dragged me down the hall and the stairs out into the courtyard. He and another guy dumped me into the open trunk of a car.

I hit my head and passed out again.

★ CHAPTER 27 ★

I'll never know how I got home.

I came to next to some trash cans, reeking of vomit. The thick night air held the stench. That made me want to throw up again, but there was nothing left. I managed to sit up and, after a while, take off my jacket and pull off my sticky, stinking T-shirt. I threw it as far as I could. I rolled on the grass like a wounded animal—precisely what I was. That helped, at least with the smell.

I was lying in a block of neat brick houses. A few lights. Parked cars, both sides of the street. I pulled my jacket back on and tried standing. To my surprise, I could. More lights a hundred yards behind me, so I stumbled that way. I came to a wide boulevard. The sign above me read OCEAN AVENUE. The other read AVENUE K. I had the vague notion that a subway line ran under Ocean Avenue, so I turned right and stumbled in the direction of Manhattan. I came to a station after a long block. I still had my wallet and my MetroCard.

One of the great features of the New York subway, unlike the Moscow Metro or just about any other system—it runs all night. The city that never sleeps. Get beat up and still get home, whatever the hour. The platform was empty, good thing for me. A train came, and I fell into the car. I had to change at Atlantic Avenue, where I figured I'd certainly be stopped by the cops, but another thing about New York, whatever the hour—if you're moving under your own steam, however erratically, however smelly, and you don't look like a Middle Eastern terrorist, everyone, including the police, leaves you alone. I caught a 3 train to Wall Street and had just enough strength to stagger the last few blocks to my building.

Lots of things I should have done. Check messages. Call Victoria. Go to the emergency room. No strength for any of that. I managed to strip and park myself under the shower, sitting on the tile floor, rubbing my skin with soap when I worked up enough strength to do so. After a while I stopped stinking. Toothpaste and mouthwash got the bile out of my mouth. I fell onto my bed and passed out one more time before I was fully horizontal.

The phone pulled me from a netherworld of vixens and violence. Victoria and Polina cavorted half-clothed and just out of reach as Lachko and Vasily chased me with clubs. Iakov floated above it all, thin and ghostly, laughing. I was the one in the wheelchair, in Lachko's replica palace, looking for something I wanted to steal, floating somehow from room to room, the women staying just ahead, the men behind but sometimes getting close enough to hit me or the chair, either one sending a jolt of pain through my body.

The phone was still ringing when I regained enough consciousness to realize where I was. I reached for it and froze as the agony shot through every muscle. My eyes watered and everything started to sweat. The events of last night came into hazy focus. The phone stopped, then started again. Ever so slowly, all the nerve endings screeching, I rolled toward the sound, grasping for the receiver. I couldn't get there.

The ringing stopped. The silence felt good—as did the need not to move. I drifted off into another netherworld, this one an amalgam of Moscow Metro stations, all empty, devoid of life, no trains, no people, just Stalin's silent sculptures honoring the peasants, the soldiers, and the proletariat. The phone pulled me out of that world, too.

I looked at the blurred black object and imagined it was Victoria. She purred over my pain and offered to come right over and soothe my

228

wounds. I floated in the luxury of that until the ringing stopped again.

I awoke, on my own this time, at 10:30 P.M. I was thirsty and hungry and could move a little if I did so slowly. I turned on the light and made it to the bathroom to survey the damage, but one glance in the mirror told me I'd be better off waiting. Getting to the kitchen took time. Anything more than a step or two required support. My reward when I made it was a glass of chilled vodka, which burned beautifully on the way down and washed around my empty, bruised stomach like liquid fire. I took another swallow, and the alcohol began to prevail on the nerve endings to calm down. A third swallow, and I was able to make some toast. Not good to drink on an empty stomach. I sipped more vodka and felt moderately better until I stood and the room spun and the sweat returned. Not ready for prime time. Not ready for anything.

I left everything where it was and weaved back to the bedroom, thankful for the numbing effect of the vodka even if it complicated trying to walk. I found the bed and rolled back in, wondering what netherworld I would encounter on this visit and if it could be any worse than the one I was in.

I emerged from the next netherworld at noon on Sunday. A prison this time—an underground labyrinth of rusty iron doors set in damp stone walls. The jailer was Ratko Risly. He led me down long halls, skipping from side to side to dodge the streams of dirty water dripping from the ceiling. Seemingly leading the way, or perhaps just along for the tour, far ahead of us and almost out of sight, was Eva Mulholland. Voices called from behind the doors, pleading. I recognized them from my childhood. I tried to answer, but I couldn't speak. Ratko carried a big ring of old-fashioned keys that jingled as we walked. I wanted to ask him where we were going, but no words came. I had the idea that until they did, we'd keep walking, perhaps forever. This maze had no center, no destination.

After a time, I realized I was in my own bed, surrounded by Sheetrock and sunlight. Was Ratko sending me a message from the underworld? What was he trying to say? The fact that I was thinking presaged a return to normalcy, or so I assumed until I tried to move. The pain was now a perpetual ache rather than searing jabs, a big improvement, but pain, like everything else, is relative. I made it to the bathroom, no stopping for support, took a deep breath, and looked in the mirror. A victim of serial train wrecks stared back. My face looked like Quasimodo—after fifteen rounds with Joe Frazier. Black eye, blue cheek, yellow nose, yellow neck, puffed purplish lips. A carpet of dried blood over my left eye. Probably should have had stitches. The colors would ripen more before they started to fade. My body was a mass of yellow-blue-purple skin, darkest where Sergei had hit me, but discolored and tender to the touch everywhere. I should have been lying in a tub full of ice, a prospect painful just to think about. Yesterday was a blur, and Friday night seemed like the distant past, but not so far distant that it wasn't real. I'd lost twenty-four hours plus to unconsciousness.

First things first. Terror and the need to know equally balanced. I found the paper with Petrovin's number. I hobbled back to the phone, punched in the digits, and got voice mail.

"Turbo. Something I need to know. Call anytime."

I made it back to the kitchen. The dishes were where I had left them, as was the vodka bottle. Too early for a drink—medicinal? I put the bottle back in the freezer. The answering machine blinked. Four messages. I hit PLAY.

Three from Victoria, early and less early Saturday morning, then one later in the day. The essence was the same, panic level rising. Wishful thinking?

"Turbo, are you there? What the hell was that all about? You okay? Call me."

"Turbo, where are you? Call me, dammit."

"Turbo, if you don't call me, I'm goin' back to Brighton Beach with a legion of FBI. Call me."

The last message was Foos, Saturday night.

"That attorney dame called here looking for you. Sounded worried.

Thought you'd want to know." Typical Foos—note the concern, pass along the message, but think to do something about it? That was one connection his circuitry didn't make.

Maybe it wasn't too early. I retrieved the vodka from the freezer and poured two fingers. Lukewarm still, but the fire felt good.

I tried to bring Friday night back into focus. Lachko must've worked his way through the list of New York hospitals until he found Eva. He sent his men to get her, but somehow she escaped. Having found her, it was a short step to Polina.

The beating Friday night wasn't about them though. He told me to stay away—sure—but that was hatred talking, his perpetual knee-jerk response to me and my past. He didn't care about them—he as much as admitted he had written Polina off in 1999 back in Moscow—but she was still terrified of him. Why? Lachko cared about his laundry. He was convinced I had the missing piece. That was what the beating was about. Or was it? Iakov's lesson about a million shades of gray floated into my consciousness.

The last time I made a list of things that didn't make sense, it had led me back to Greene Street and eventually to getting thumped within an inch of my life. That had been a mental list. This time, I'd be smarter—I'd write the list down so I didn't make another stupid mistake. I got some paper.

1. Lachko didn't have the T.J. Maxx database. Who removed it—Ratko?
2. Neither Lachko nor Iakov had known about Polina/Felix, but Ratko did. He also knew to phish the Mulhollands four months ago.
3. Ratko dropped out of sight around that time.
4. Ratko needed money.
5. Iakov said Kosokov stole from his bank. Lachko said Kosokov was too incompetent to steal.
6. Iakov came to New York to see Ratko—without telling Lachko.
7. Ratko had just been in Moscow.
8. Eva Mulholland was terrified of her father and grandfather.

9. Polina wouldn't/couldn't tell Mulholland about being blackmailed.
10. Polina wouldn't/couldn't tell me about Ratko.

A neat list of ten facts. I drew a line under the bottom and tried to add them up. That didn't work, so I poured another drink. Less burn this time. Something else was bothering me—something that needed to be added. I couldn't quite grab it. The vodka wasn't helping.

Petrovin hadn't called back. How long had it been? I called again. No answer.

I reread the list, considered eating something, and drank some more vodka instead. I thought about calling Victoria.

The glass was empty. I refilled it, staring at the page, waiting for things to clarify. They didn't. Eventually I decided to try getting dressed. The room spun when I stood. I waited, and the spinning slowed. I could make it to the bedroom. Wrong. Three steps, and dizziness swept down my body, starting at the top. I remember the nausea and hitting my face on the corner of the coffee table as I fell, the same side Sergei worked over. I don't remember throwing up again or passing out on the rug.

That's where they said they found me.

★ CHAPTER 28 ★

Americans put a high value on efficiency, and the medical industry, with dubious justification, prides itself on leading the way.

The first thing the youngish lady doctor said was "You've been thoroughly examined and treated. Two cracked ribs, concussion, six stitches on your face, twelve more along the jaw. Various contusions and lacerations. You can go home as soon as you feel ready."

To that I could add a nasty hangover that was fighting a war of supremacy with some powerful painkillers. Hard to tell which was winning. I wasn't even in a position to process her diagnosis.

I lay in a curtained-off space in a room that smelled like a hospital. Noises all around, bad sounds. People in pain, groans, cries, the occasional scream. I felt just like they did. The lady doctor asked how I'd acquired my injuries. I told her I'd fallen, twice. She asked how much I drank on a regular basis. I shrugged and replied not too much, for a Russian. She looked skeptical and repeated I could go home anytime. I think she was using the word "could" in the sense of "free to" rather than "able to," because I could barely move. My left side felt paralyzed. My head pounded as the battle raged. The rest of me just ached, until I tried to reposition something—then whatever it was shrieked with pain. On the other hand, I had no desire to stay here any longer than necessary, so I gave her my best smile and hoped she'd go away so I'd have time to think.

She did. Not long after, the curtain parted, and Foos and Victoria stared at me with a mixture of concern, annoyance, and—on Foos's part—bemusement.

"You are some kind of mess," Victoria said.

Foos held up a foam cup. "Coffee. They say it's okay to drink if you feel like it."

It took me a minute to grasp that they were there.

"What . . ."

"Don't try to talk too much, sugar," Victoria said. "Doctor says it's bad for the stitches."

Foos just grinned his lopsided grin and held out the cup. I took it, gingerly, after he peeled back the opening in the plastic top. The coffee was hot and tasted remarkably good.

"Where am I?"

"NYU Hospital," Victoria said. "You remember the ambulance or the emergency room?"

I shook my head. The painkillers were winning the war, for now.

"You remember our date? You stood me up."

I shook my head, more slowly this time.

"This morning, eight thirty, at your office. Identity theft tutorial."

"What time . . ."

"Coming up on 4:00 P.M. Monday."

Shit. I tried sitting up but didn't get very far. I tried again with the same result. Sweat broke out on my forehead.

"You sure you're up to this?" Foos said.

I had the hazy memory of a country song. A rabbit's being chased by a dog, and the singer asks him if he's going to make it. The rabbit states the obvious—"Got to."

"Got to," I said. There was a reason, too, if I could only remember what it was.

Aleksei. Petrovin.

"Phone," I said to Foos.

He handed his over, and I called my machine. Sure enough, Petrovin had called back that morning. "I will be delighted to assist if I

236

can. You can reach me at this number, as you know." He didn't leave the number, because I already had it. At my apartment.

I pushed my legs over the side of the bed and let gravity pull them toward the floor. The rest of me had no choice but to follow, although my ribs howled in protest. My entire upper body felt drenched. Foos no longer looked bemused, and Victoria looked frightened.

"I'm okay," I lied. "Doctor said go home. Where are my clothes?"

"You weren't wearing any when we found you. I brought these. You oughtta add some color to your wardrobe." She put a shopping bag on the bed.

"You mean . . ."

"I've seen it all, shug. I'll wait outside."

It took time, sweat, and a lot of help from Foos to thread two legs into some trousers and two arms into a T-shirt. When Foos opened the curtains, Victoria was gone. I was happy to rest against the bed while we waited for her return. She came back scowling. "You'd think a goddamned hospital would have a goddamned wheelchair you could borrow."

"Maybe you should launch an investigation into outpatient practices," I said.

"Don't think I ain't gonna look into it. You sure you can make it?"

"Feel better already," I lied again.

I took a step to prove it. Foos caught me before I fell.

"This is silly," Victoria said.

"Let's go," I said to Foos. "I'll explain later."

Somehow they managed to carry me out of the hospital and pack me into a cab, Victoria issuing orders the entire way. The painkillers helped. Foos squeezed into the front, and Victoria sat beside me. The driver took off like the rabbit chased by the dog. I yelped when he hit the first bump, and Victoria shouted at him to slow down. He used his lack of English to ignore her. The name on his license was Slovakian. I said in his native tongue, "My friend here is with Immigration. You don't take it easy, I'll make sure she has you on the first boat back to Bratislava."

He dropped his speed by half. Victoria looked at me.

"What'd you tell him?"

"Used one of your lines. Slovaks scare easier than Russians."

They got me upstairs to my apartment and tried to park me on the sofa, but I excused myself and hobbled to the bedroom to call Petrovin. This time he answered. I did my best to keep my voice low and level and pain-free.

"I need to track down a rumor. I'm told someone took a shot at CPS headquarters Saturday morning. The intended target was an officer named Tiron, Aleksei Tiron."

A pause. "Why call me?"

"You're CPS."

"How—"

"Your cell phone. Calls to your office. Here in America, the land of the free can be an overstatement."

"I'll bear that in mind. You have access to some significant capabilities."

"Will you check on Tiron?"

Another pause. "I know Tiron. I'm sure I would've heard if something happened to him."

"That's a relief. I'd still like to confirm he's okay. I'd also appreciate knowing whether there was a shooting or the whole story is somebody's idea of a bad joke."

"A strange request, if you don't mind my saying so."

"I'll explain when I see you next. It has to do with our friend Barsukov."

"I see. How do you know Tiron? Shall I give him a message?"

"He's . . . the son of a friend. No message."

Victoria was on the sofa, and Foos was in the kitchen. The culprit vodka bottle was standing on the counter amid the dirty dishes. I swore I would lay off the sauce for a while, but I knew I was lying as I did so. Foos held it in my direction. I shook my head. He put it in the freezer and moved the dishes to the sink. I sat next to Victoria. Petrovin's news had alleviated the worst of the pain, but I still hurt all over.

Victoria said, "I feel terrible about Saturday night. I didn't want to leave. That man, he practically carried me out of there."

"I know. Thanks. It's better that you did. Lachko was trying to intimidate both of us, for different reasons. As you saw, he's not subtle, and sometimes he gets carried away."

"Tell me what happened."

"We had a one-sided conversation, Lachko, Sergei, and I. When they got bored, they dumped me somewhere off Ocean Avenue. I took the subway home."

"You took the subway?"

"I told you before, Russians are stubborn. That was before I slipped and hit my head on the coffee table. I did that all by myself."

"With a little help from the vodka bottle, I think."

"Drinking beer without vodka is just a way to spend money."

"What the hell does that mean?"

"What it says. Russian proverb."

"Russian horseshit. You probably already had a concussion, so a couple of shots is just what you needed."

"I realize the visual evidence doesn't support me, but I do an okay job of taking care of myself."

"You sure know how to pick your friends, too."

"Careful," Foos said from the kitchen.

"Present company excepted, of course," Victoria added quickly. "Did Barsukov say anything about Risly?"

"Ahhh, that's why you're so attentive. The depth of your concern is touching."

"Hey! That's not fair. I called you three times. Who do you think got you to the hospital?"

"She's telling it straight, Turbo," Foos said. "You'd still be out cold on the rug."

"Sorry. Meant it as a joke. Barsukov didn't kill Risly, if that's what you're asking. Risly was his protégé, or that's the way he looks at it. He was also a golden-egg-laying goose."

"We reckoned he was the point man on the money laundry."

"You were right. How'd you get onto that, if it's not a state secret?"

"We've been running a joint investigation with your CPS for more than a year now. They've been able to track large sums of money moving in and out of Russian banks. Some of it originates in Russia, some moves in from Asia and the Middle East. It moves out again to the kind of places you'd expect—Switzerland, Liechtenstein, Cayman Islands. We got a break when things in Liechtenstein loosened up, and we could see that money moving into the U.S. in thousands of small chunks. We also found funds headed the other way. But we lost the trail here. Then we got lucky about six months ago. Two of your countrymen got in a fight at an East Village bar. They were drunk. Big surprise."

I let that pass.

"One of them pulls a knife and cuts the other across the chest. Not so bad that it kills him, but enough to require a couple yards of stitches. So one gets taken to the hospital, the other to the precinct house, and miracle number one, the cops at each compare notes on what they found. Both men carrying BlackBerrys, and both BlackBerrys have identical long lists of messages, and the messages are tables filled with some kind of code. The cops didn't know what to make of it, but they sent it up the line, where, miracle number two, a lieutenant figures this might be bigger than a bar fight and orders the BlackBerrys returned to their owners, after they've been bugged. He also orders the owners released, which was easy because when they sobered up, nobody pressed charges. He also ordered them followed. Miracle number three, he calls us."

"You used up your quota," I said.

"You got that right. These two Russians ain't the swiftest bears in the forest, and they go blithely about their business over the following days and weeks like nothing has happened. So we know they spend most of their day at banks and ATM machines, depositing and withdrawing money. We know the money ain't theirs, but we don't know who the accounts belong to and how they can move around as much dough as they do, in such small increments. Nobody can have that many bank accounts. And we can't subpoena every transaction of every bank, every branch, every day."

"Not even under the Patriot Act?" Foos said, making no effort to hide the sarcasm in his voice.

"What's wrong with the Patriot Act?" she said.

"Perhaps you haven't been properly introduced," I said. "Victoria de Millenuits, this is Foster Helix. Foos, Victoria."

"The Foster Helix?" Her head swung back and forth between the two of us. Foos tried to look innocent, something he's not good at. I'm sure I just looked frightful.

"The Foster Helix," I said. "Privacy advocate, STOP founder and CEO, thorn in the side of government agencies everywhere."

"God damn it! You should've warned me. I could lose my job telling him what I just told him. I mean, Jesus, I work with guys who want to bring back the electric chair, just for him."

"Music to my ears," Foos said. He gave her a mischievous grin. "But you don't need to worry. We're all friends here. Right, Turbo? Mind if I sample your vodka?"

"Help yourself."

"Victoria?"

She looked at me. "Don't suppose you have any wine?"

"Sorry."

"I'll have mine on the rocks, then."

"Turbo?"

"None for him," she said.

I looked back at Victoria. "Maybe I can do without your concern."

Foos brought her a glass. It looked good.

"Do you know that goddamned foundation of his has filed a half-dozen amicus briefs in cases we've got under appeal?" she said.

"I thought it was more," I said. "Did I mention I'm on STOP's board? Foos, Pig Pen, and me. You'll like Pig Pen. He's the secretary."

"Shit. It's a good thing for you y'all are in the kinda shape you're in."

Foos arched an eyebrow at her logic. "I'm outta here. Gotta meet someone. Need anything before I split? Can you make it to the bedroom?"

"Think so."

"I'll take care of him," Victoria said. Things were looking up. Not that I had strength to do anything about it.

"Okay," he said, putting the vodka bottle away. I felt a small regret, but that was the last thing I needed.

Foos said good night and was gone. Victoria sat watching me.

"Y'all don't look bad in black and blue and yellow, but I think I prefer the plain shaved head."

"Thanks for everything you did. I'm sorry you got caught up in this."

"Wouldn't have missed it for all the music in New Orleans—except for what happened to you, of course. People in my position, especially people like me who get to my position, we rarely get to see the bad guys face-to-face, and never in their own lair. I'm sorry about what happened, and I do mean that, but I wouldn't trade that visit for ten trips home."

"Glad it worked out for someone."

"I still have to ask you about Rislyakov."

I had the same thought I had at Lachko's about lying and telling the truth. Might as well get some benefit from my injuries. "I know. Tomorrow. I'm not good for much more today."

She gave me a long look. "Okay. You think if you lean on me you can make it to your room?"

"Leaning on you . . ."

"Don't start."

"Let's try."

She came over, and I pushed myself up. The painkillers were still doing their thing. I tried not to put too much weight on her. She took what I had with ease and guided me across the floor. We got to my room, and she let me down easily on the bed.

"Can you get undressed or you need help?"

"Help."

She took a step back. "Sugar, remember I've already seen it all, and I'm excited, but we both know for a fact excitement ain't gonna rule tonight or anytime soon. You really need help?"

"No, but I'm not happy about it."

"Neither am I. Although the why of it mystifies me."

She put her arms around the back of my neck and kissed me gently on the forehead. I felt good for the first time in two days.

"We'll discuss it in the morning."

She left, and I managed to shed my clothes before I fell asleep.

★ CHAPTER 29 ★

The Chekist lighted a cigarette and put the computer aside, his mind still back in the Valdai barn. He'd made Kosokov drink until he polished off the vodka bottle. The man was drunk when he got there; he had to be borderline blotto now, but he wouldn't talk. The Chekist asked again and again about the CDs. Kosokov kept lying—they don't exist.

"I have you on tape, Anatoly Andreivich. You made copies. Tell me where they are and you live."

Kosokov laughed and threw up on the floor. The Chekist hit him with the gun, and he fell in his own vomit. The Chekist kicked him in the face.

The banker was a weak man, but he'd decided to make a stand. Why?

He left Kosokov unconscious and made a survey of the barn, looking for something he could use to break his will. It couldn't be that hard, but time wasn't on his side.

He was passing through the horse stalls when he sensed movement again. The stall to his left. He stopped by the gate and listened motionless. Breathing? A scratching sound. He raised his pistol, kicked the gate open, and fired. The bullet sank itself in old timber. The stall was empty. Had to be rats.

In the garage he found several gas cans. He'd give Kosokov one more chance to talk or burn in the hell he deserved.

The driver helped him bind the banker's hands and feet to a post. The Chekist poured gasoline in his hands and threw it in Kosokov's face.

"Whaaaa?"

"Wake up, Anatoly. This is your last chance. CDs—where?"

"Fuck you."

The Chekist gave him another splash and carried the can around the perimeter, pouring as he went. When it was empty, he went back to the garage and got another to finish the job. There was more than enough to run a liquid fuse out the door through the snow. Kosokov watched from his stake, still in a stupor, with rising terror. He tugged at his knots.

"You wouldn't," he croaked. *"Even the Cheka . . ."*

"I would and I will. CDs—where?"

Something passed through Kosokov's eyes—realization, resignation, defiance, he couldn't tell, but he knew he'd lost the battle.

"One more chance, Anatoly Andreivich. Where are the copies and you live."

Kosokov spat. *"For what? To be shot later. The Cheka's its own worst enemy. Someday you'll understand that."*

"There'll be no someday, Anatoly, unless you tell me what I want to know."

Kosokov spat again—in his face. He could smell the alcohol and gasoline as it ran down his cheek.

"I'm going to light a match. I estimate you'll have five minutes. Shout if you change your mind."

He walked through the open door, waiting for the banker to call his bluff, but he didn't.

Fuck him. Maybe they were still in the house. Maybe Polina had them. He'd deal with it. He fired the match and dropped it in the snow.

The fire snake slithered into the barn. It took a matter of seconds before the walls leapt into flame. The old timber burned fast. He hadn't even needed the gas. He waited for Kosokov's call, but it didn't come. The fire spread across the doorway, shutting off his view. The flames climbed the walls to the roof and kept leaping upward. A few minutes later, sections of the roof began to fall. A few more minutes, and it was over. The whole structure collapsed in on itself, a bonfire of heat and orange flame.

Damned fool.

He had to move fast now. The fire would attract attention, even out here.

There was still Polina to be dealt with.

★ CHAPTER 30 ★

I awoke at six, having slept almost ten hours, to find that I felt semi-human, I could move, with difficulty, and Victoria was still with me. She was in the kitchen, making coffee and looking fresh and rested even though she wore the same clothes as yesterday.

"Look who's back among the living," she said. "Sort of."

"Thanks to you."

"You're welcome. How do you feel?"

"Better than yesterday."

"Better than you look?"

"I haven't checked the mirror yet."

"Don't." She handed me a steaming cup. "Why do you do this to yourself?"

Me? "I don't remember beating myself up."

"You know what I mean."

"You think I go looking for trouble."

"Yes. Not intentionally, maybe, but you don't care if you find it—or it finds you. That's not normal."

"A pig will always find mud."

"Another goddamned proverb?"

"We've got one for just about everything."

"Everyone you know is either dead, has one foot in jail, or is trying to do you harm. Like I said, that ain't normal."

Didn't seem unusual to me, but my brain was probably still addled.

"You think you can manage for yourself today?"

"I do most days."

"Most days aren't the day after you were in the hospital. You want my advice, you stay right here, try to get some more sleep, get your strength back."

"Your concern is still touching. I'll try to take it easy."

"You want to tell me about your friend Rislyakov?"

"Don't you Americans have an amendment that protects against self-incrimination?"

"We do. It works in a courtroom. I've got a rule against fooling around with felons. That applies right here in your kitchen. So you can tell me what you know or I'm outta here—and not coming back."

"Talk about rock and hard place."

"Don't worry." The green eyes smiled. "I won't use anything you say against you—unless, of course, it should be. Besides, I've been reading your notes. You can start there. This Iakov the same guy you told me about at dinner?"

She pushed across the piece of paper with the list I'd written out during my brief window of semi-lucidity.

"One of the first things they teach you in spy school is never write down anything."

"You failed that class. C'mon, give. What were you doing at the Greene Street loft? What happened there? I'm bettin' you found a dead Rislyakov. What else?"

I don't know whether it was the fallout from the pain and painkillers, accumulated stress and exhaustion, or just the green pools staring across the counter, but no chance I could dance around her questions in any way that would satisfy her—or me. I didn't even want to try. So I told my Cheka training to take a rest while I told her what she wanted to hear—all of it. Or at least the all of it that I knew.

We drank two cups of coffee each while I talked. She took it all in, without question or interruption. Along the way, I realized I'd forgotten something important. I gave myself a mental kick. Even that hurt.

I wrote "Blue Impala" on the paper and kept on with the story. When I finished she said, "Why didn't you call the cops?"

"Same question Bernie asked. Short answer, I needed that computer for leverage to get Sasha out of Lubyanka. Long answer, I was determined to figure out what's going on. Still am. We're stubborn, remember?"

"Stubborn ain't the half of it. Did you have to give the computer to Barsukov?"

"That's what Foos asked. I traded it for Sasha. I owed him."

She shook her head. "I'm trying to count up how many laws you broke."

"Didn't Dylan say something about honesty and living outside the law?"

"Give me Hank Williams any day."

"Dylan might agree. I'm just trying to say, what you see is what you get."

"That's what frightens me. Listen, serious now. You and I are gonna have an understanding. I'm willing to let bygones be bygones, I think, mainly because they happened when I wasn't around so I can almost convince myself you weren't trying to hide anything from me. But I meant what I said about fooling with felons. I've worked too damned hard to get where I am. My job and career are too important to me. They gotta be important to you, too, if we're gonna have anything— together, I mean. That means you gotta be a law-abiding citizen going forward, an *American* law-abiding citizen. Those are the ground rules. No exceptions. Understand?"

I nodded slowly, mainly to buy time. Even though my brain was operating at about seventy percent, I knew I couldn't live by those conditions—not in the current circumstances—but the last thing I wanted was to drive her away.

"That a nod of agreement?"

I wasn't going to lie. "It's a nod of agreement to think about what you've said. I'm still not at my best—as you can see."

"Fair enough," she said, to my relief. Perhaps she was worried about driving me away, too. I could only hope. "I wouldn't say what I said unless I cared. You know that, right?"

Hope validated, for once. "It's the one thing that makes me feel semi-okay."

She laughed, and the green eyes pulled my heartstrings like a puppeteer. "Okay, then. I've got to run. Thanks to you, I lost all of yesterday, and now I'm behind a big damned eight ball. I'll stop in on my way uptown this afternoon, see how you're faring."

"Something to look forward to."

The phone rang. Foos said, "Victoria still there?"

"That any of your business?"

"Speaker."

I pushed the button. His baritone rumbled out of the phone.

"Good morning, boys and girls. Thought I'd check in, see how everyone's doing. Big Dick tells me Victoria hasn't gone to work yet. Didn't go home last night either."

"Big Dick? What?! You just say what I think you said?"

"You're playing into his hand."

His laugh filled the room.

"Patriot Act's the best thing that ever happened to the Dick. That's D-I-C—Data Intelligence Complex. It collects information, on you, me, Turbo, everybody. I just ask for little pieces of it."

She said, "Christ. A privacy junkie with an adolescent sense of humor."

"Only making a small point about liberty. Your client's called twice, Turbo. Wants to see you ASAP."

"You're not going anywhere," she said.

"Just relaying the message," Foos said.

"I need some help from the Dick," I said. Victoria shot me a look. "Somebody followed Track and Field from Jersey City to Greene Street Wednesday morning. Blue Chevy Impala. No plate number, sorry."

Victoria said, "Who the hell are Track and Field?"

Foos said, "Turbo, do you have any idea how many Chevy Impalas—"

"Could be a rental."

"Do you have any idea how many rental cars—"

"Look at it as a challenge for the Basilisk?"

"What's the Basilisk?" Victoria said.

"The beast that keeps track of you—whenever I ask it to," Foos said. "Have a nice day, Victoria. I'll be watching."

"Listen, goddammit—"

A click and the dial tone as he hung up.

"I don't know which of you is the bigger pain in the ass. If you take my advice, you'll stay right where you are—all day. But I might as well tell your friend to act like . . . oh, never mind. Why bother?"

"Foos would tell you that you've reached the inevitable logical conclusion."

She didn't respond as she took the cups to the sink and rinsed them.

"Why didn't you tell me your first wife is married to Mulholland?"

"Didn't seem relevant."

"Hiding out, living under a different name?"

"That doesn't have anything to do with Mulholland. He doesn't know who she used to be. He thinks she's a real estate broker from Queens."

"What's she hiding from?"

"Don't know. Lachko, maybe. That's what she says. I'm not sure I believe her, but that means I have to believe Lachko. She had a lover, while she was married to Lachko. They were all in business together. Iakov claims she and the lover stole six hundred million dollars from the lover's bank—and maybe Lachko. Lachko says that never happened. That could be pride talking, but I doubt that, too. Besides, if she had all that money, why did she try that silly fake kidnap scheme on her husband? So I think it's something else, which I intend to ask her."

"Not today, though, right?"

I didn't respond.

"How long were you married?"

"How about I tell you the whole sordid tale over dinner—right here? I'll cook something. We ex-socialist small businessmen can't afford a steady Trastevere diet."

She smiled a big smile. "Deal."

She came around the counter and gave me a kiss on the lips that was much more than a peck. Then she was out the door without looking back.

I sat for a moment sipping coffee and thinking about how good it felt, for the first time in a long time, to have someone who cared what happened to me. Even if she was threatening to toss my ass in jail if I didn't change my ways. Maybe that was part of what made it fun.

I could have—and should have—followed her advice and spent a quiet day in bed, mentally replaying her kiss. She was giving me every incentive to get well soon. However, patience was not among Lachko's virtues, and I'd already blown more than two days. That was his fault, of course, but he wouldn't see it that way.

Using the counter for support (I could tell Victoria I was trying to take it easy), I made it back to the living room, where I'd left my computer, and logged on to Ibansk.com. I wasn't surprised to see Ivanov had been busy. Three new postings, Saturday, Monday, and this morning. The first focused on the Barsukovs' growing anxiety over setbacks to their money laundry and speculated about whether Ratko had disappeared with "the detergent that makes the washing machines run." The second reported the surprise demise of Risly. The third detailed the shooting at CPS headquarters.

OUT OF CONTROL

The Cheka has never been known for restraint. But not since the days of Beria has it felt so emboldened. Ibanskians happening to pass the building housing the CPS in Ulica Otradnaja will see a shattered window on the second floor. The result, Ivanov is reliably informed, of a bungled assassination attempt Saturday morning.

Hard to believe? Not for Ivanov. There's not much the Cheka is afraid to try in its Ibanskian playground these days. The only difference from Beria's era is that now there's nothing—or no one—to rein in their instincts. What intrigues Ivanov more than the brazenness of the act is that the Cheka found it necessary. What would cause them to put an assassin's bullet through the window of a junior CPS officer?

Ivanov has been making inquiries. The answer appears to lie in the murky swamp of Cheka history, where one wades with great caution. Snakes, eels, crocodiles, and a host of other sharp-toothed reptiles all guard their secrets with deathly closeness. Two other CPS officers have died this year—one poisoned, the other gunned down in the street. Ivanov isn't ready to tell yet, but it's clear the Cheka is hiding a mortal secret—deadly to those who own it, deadly to those who find out about it. It's prepared to go to any length to make sure it's never dredged up. That's the message of a shattered window in Ulica Otradnaja.

Three things were clear to me.
Petrovin was spoon-feeding Ivanov.
Ivanov was baiting the Badgers.
Both of them were chasing a lot more than Lachko's laundry.

★ CHAPTER 31 ★

I made two Politburo-level decisions. At least they felt that way. The first was not to call ahead. The second, forgo the subway for a cab. That way, I could tell Victoria I was taking care of myself.

I returned to the bedroom, removed my robe, and, ignoring her advice, checked myself over in the full-length mirror. A Francis Bacon nightmare stared back, a hunched, stretched, distorted mass of colors—reds, blacks, blues, purples, and yellows—none of which looked natural, much less healthy. The stitches on my face and jaw gave a certain Frankenstein's monster appearance—if the good doctor had been drinking while he worked. I wondered idly what Victoria could possibly see in me and concluded there's no accounting for taste. The only possible benefit was maybe Polina would be so shocked that she'd take pity and explain what was really going on.

Right.

I showered gingerly and dressed with equal care. That took twice as long as usual, but I was pleased to feel no sudden shots of pain. Quick healer. I walked the two blocks to the office, which took almost ten minutes, and I felt wiped when I got there. Maybe not so quick. Then again, the temperature hadn't dropped a degree while I'd been out of commission.

Pig Pen took one look and winced. I didn't know parrots could wince.

"Russky. Ouch. Three car pile-up."

"That's right, Pig Pen. Three cars, they all hit me."

"L-I-E?"

"No, not L-I-E."

"Cross Bronx?"

"Not there either. Brighton Beach." That caused him to lose interest. Brighton Beach isn't mentioned often—if at all—on traffic reports, so he had no context. Not that he knows where the Long Island or Cross Bronx expressway is either, but I might be selling him short. The sight upset him sufficiently that he didn't even ask about pizza.

Foos looked up at me leaning against his doorjamb, breathing harder than I should and sweating.

"You up and around already?"

"Don't start. One minder is plenty."

"So, how many Chevy Impalas are there in metro New York?"

I shook my head.

"Two hundred thirty-eight thousand three hundred twelve. None registered to anyone we know, best as I can tell."

"Rentals?"

"Sixteen thousand five hundred sixty-one."

"Okay—lots of data. Rental Impalas?"

"Varies. Right now, five hundred four."

"And?" He wouldn't have started this if he didn't have the answer.

"Three of those belong to an independent outfit on East Eighty-eighth Street—Yorkville Car Rental. One of *those* three was rented last Tuesday afternoon at 3:52 P.M. and returned Wednesday at 12:36 P.M."

"By?"

"Gentleman named Lachlan Malloy."

Five-by-Five. He was limping on Thursday. "Remember when you pointed out I'd been taken for a ride?"

"Uh-huh."

"You didn't know the half of it."

I dialed Victoria's office. She got on right away.

"Are you all right?"

"Fine. Just wanted to hear your voice."

"Bullshit. Where are you?"

"Telecommuting," I lied.

"More bullshit. You're at your office."

"Doctor said get exercise. I'm taking it easy."

"Are all Russians really this pigheaded?"

"National trait. I need a favor."

"What?"

"Hospitals have to report gunshot wounds. I'm looking for a guy named Malloy, Lachlan Malloy, with a bullet in the right leg, late last Wednesday night or early Thursday morning. You must have contacts with NYPD."

"Who's Malloy?"

"Nasty SOB, built like a panel truck, with bad intentions toward me. Also Mulholland's driver."

"Where'd he get the bullet wound?"

"Rislyakov's loft. Wednesday night. After he shot Ratko."

"He killed Rislyakov?"

"Looks that way. Felix Mulholland put him on me, I put him onto Ratko's associates, and he followed them to Greene Street. Ratko wasn't there, but Malloy went back when he was. Shot him and Iakov. Was probably trying to get to Eva Mulholland, maybe to get her home, I don't know, when she shot him through the door."

"Tell me you're not going to see her."

"Good a time as any to get reacquainted."

"Turbo . . ."

"I'm not looking forward to it."

"I'm not either. Watch out for Malloy."

"He's not half as dangerous as she is."

★　★　★

I limped into the lobby of 998 Fifth to the usual impassive greeting. If Christ himself descended from on high, mother in tow, and levitated through those doors, he'd receive the same bland response. We went through the routine of name asking and calling upstairs, and the elevator man drove me to the ninth floor.

The man in the silver tie opened the door. When I told him who I wanted to see, he took me to the library. The room was cool and dark, lighted by the same lamps as last week. I stopped by the desk to glance at the computer screen. Mostly red. FTB was trading in single digits.

I sat in a chair by the giant fireplace and took out my cell phone.

"This is Gina."

"How soon can you get uptown, Fifth and Eighty-second?"

"Half an hour."

"Good. Park yourself on the steps of the Met. You'll have a clear view of this building, nine-nine-eight Fifth. I'm expecting a woman, blond, forty-something version of Greene Street Girl, to come out later today. I want to know where she goes and what she does."

"You got it."

"You're the best."

"Put that sentiment into cash."

"The best mercenary, that is."

Victoria called as soon as we disconnected. "Where are you?"

"Lion's den."

"You mean lioness."

"You're becoming very protective."

"You're getting no less obnoxious. Lachlan Malloy was treated and released by Beth Israel late Wednesday night. Superficial gunshot wound, right thigh."

"I owe you."

"Then get out of there."

"As soon as I've tamed the lioness."

"Turbo . . ."

"Gotta run."

256

Raised voices, one male, one female, outside. I was about to move closer to the door when it opened and Mulholland came in, dressed in one of his Savile Row suits. It was hard to tell in dim light, but he looked as though he'd aged several years since our last meeting. I wondered what he'd make of my appearance.

He came across the big carpet without stopping at the desk or looking toward the computer. His shoulders slumped forward, and his legs moved without purpose, as if they were directing themselves, unsure of where their owner wanted to go. I stood, and as he grew close, he raised his eyes to meet mine.

"Good morning, Mr. Vlost. It seems you were in an accident of some kind."

"That's one way of putting it. I look worse than I feel." Not true, but it sounded good.

He nodded. "Do you have news of Eva?"

"I actually came to see your wife."

He nodded. "Hicks told me. She's . . . she's not well. The accumulated stress—my difficulties, Eva—it's taking a toll."

"Is she here?"

"She's resting. She . . . she had a bad night."

"I'm afraid you'll have to wake her."

"Why? What for?"

"I need to talk to her."

"I hardly think—"

"She can talk to me or talk to the cops. The topic is murder. She despises me, but I'm still likely to be more understanding than they are."

He was tough, or tired, or both. He didn't flinch. He didn't show much reaction of any kind. "Murder? Whose murder? I don't understand. What about Eva?"

"Get your wife and I'll answer your questions."

"Does this have anything to do with your . . . accident?"

"Tangentially."

"Tell me this much. Is Eva all right?"

"She was when I saw her."

"You saw her? When?"

"Friday."

"Friday? Why haven't you—"

"Get your wife."

Thirty seconds or more passed before he stood. His legs seemed to find more intent as they traversed back across the rug.

He was gone almost twenty minutes. I spent most of the time debating whether to beat it while I had the chance, but I'd come with a purpose in mind. When he returned, Felix/Polina—I hadn't worked out which way to think of her—was with him. She was dressed in a rose top and black slacks, no makeup or jewelry. She'd been crying. Sorrow—or anger—turned to surprise as she came close.

"You . . . What happened?"

"Lachko and I agreed to disagree. But it took some time to get to that point."

"My God. Lachko did that?"

"He had help." And I still had some pride.

She didn't express sorrow for my pains. On the other hand, she didn't say I deserved them. She and Mulholland sat across from me. He looked at her. She looked at me. I let them look until Mulholland started visibly losing patience.

I nodded toward him but kept my eyes on Polina. "How much have you told him about me?"

She shook her head.

"And Lachko?"

Another shake.

"You're a piece of work, Polya."

"Polya?" Mulholland said.

"Say what you came to say and get out," Polina said.

"Felix, I—"

"I know you hired him to find Eva, but this man is not our friend," she said. "He's a born liar."

"What about Eva, Mr. Vlost?" Mulholland asked. "You said you saw her. Where was she?"

"The W Hotel on Union Square. She had a room under a borrowed name. She'd borrowed the cash to pay for it, too."

"Borrowed?"

"I was being polite. Stolen. The last time I checked, she'd removed almost eight thousand dollars from various people's bank accounts, using information she bought on the Internet. She used her boyfriend's account for that, but he won't mind. He's the one who was murdered."

I was watching Polina. She didn't flinch. She didn't say a word. She didn't move her eyes from my stitched-up visage. I still remembered all too well what her cold shoulder felt like, and she'd added more than a few layers of ice since then. Mulholland just looked lost. I felt sorry for him, but it was Polina's armor I was trying to find a chink in.

Nobody spoke for a minute. Then Polina said, "Why didn't you bring her home? That's what we're paying you to do."

"She didn't want to come, for one thing. She ran before I could change her mind, for another. She took off when I told her Rislyakov—that's her late boyfriend—worked for Lachko. Why's she so afraid of him?"

"Look in a mirror and ask that question again."

"I'm not his daughter."

"Who's Lachko?" Mulholland asked. "You said that name before."

"Your move," I said to Polina.

"You should have died in the camps." She spoke Russian. "They're the only place you ever fit in."

"You and Lachko agree on that much," I replied in our native tongue, "but I think you just blew your cover with Hubby Number Three."

"*Eb tvoju mat'!*" She stepped forward and slapped me once with the flat of her hand and again with the back side, setting my face afire. Her insult, a form of "fuck you" that translates literally as "I fucked your mother," is one of the worst in the Russian language.

"Felix!" Mulholland shouted.

"Get him out of here. He makes me sick to my stomach," she said, in English.

"If I leave here now, I go straight to the police." I was watching her again. Despite the show of temper, the ice was still in place.

Mulholland spoke. "You said murder. Who's this Rislyakov? What's he have to do with Eva? What's he have to do with us?"

"You want to tell him?" I said to Polina.

She stared back silently as she sat, sparks of hatred shooting through the indigo. I tried to feel some regret for what I was doing, but not very hard, and none came.

"Rad Rislyakov is—was—a computer whiz. He worked for a man named Lachko Barsukov, big-time mobster. I've known Lachko half my life, and there's nothing good I can say about him. Maybe your wife has a kind word—she's known him nearly as long as I have. I'll let her fill in the details, or you can try Google. He probably has a Wikipedia entry. Rislyakov is the guy who phished you with that fake letter back in March.

"What? How do you—"

"For now, just accept that I know and what I know is fact. If anything I say is conjecture, I'll flag it."

"He lies," Polina said. "His whole life is one big lie. Don't believe a word."

"I deceived Polina years ago—about myself, an act of omission, not commission, born of love mixed with fear. I've been paying for my sin ever since, and my transgressions will never be erased in her mind. I can't do anything about that. She can tell you that story, too, or I will, but right now we're talking about Rislyakov."

"Bastard," Polina hissed.

"Go on," Mulholland said.

"Rislyakov learned a great deal from his phishing expedition— he had access to all your computers for weeks. One of the things he picked up was Eva's drug use and stay in rehab. Rislyakov had a gambling problem—he used that to get himself checked into the same place, where he struck up a relationship. Eva claims he loved her. Little doubt she loved him. My money says he was using her for other purposes."

"You'd know," Polina said.

"Rislyakov stole a large file from one of your computers. It belonged to your wife, I'm almost certain of that. Polina doesn't panic often. She did then."

"What's this Polina business?"

"Sorry. That's how I know her. Something else she can explain. You might want to start a list."

She was up again, hand flying. This time I caught it in midair. "Lachko already did enough damage."

She said, "I don't have to put up with this." She tried to pull away, but I held her wrist.

"We're just getting to the good part."

"Sit down, Felix," Mulholland said in a voice that more ordinarily gave orders to subordinates. She heard it, too, and she hadn't heard it before. She tensed for a moment, then relaxed. I let go of her arm, and she took her seat, perched on the edge.

"This is going to be embarrassing," I said to Mulholland. "I'm sorry. But that ransom note and photograph you received were both created right here in this apartment on your computer."

"WHAT?" Mulholland jumped out of his chair. Polina sat ice-sculpture still.

"No question about it. The picture was created on Photoshop. I have the components."

"But how . . ."

"Rislyakov had access to your computers, like I said. I had access to his, I could see where everything came from."

I turned toward Polina. For the first time I saw fear behind the ice.

"Rislyakov was blackmailing you. Somehow he knew about your income stream, probably because the money was moving through the laundry he'd designed for Lachko. So he proposed a partnership, clipping you for fifty percent, and you accepted. Don't object. I have his notes, the instructions, the account numbers, the whole deal. He knew who you were, who you'd become. But my question is this—how did he find you in the first place?"

"I have nothing to say to you—*EVER!*"

"You'll find that a hard position to stick to. Back to the story. This is conjecture, now—Rislyakov needed money, faster than your partnership could provide it. His gambling debts were mounting. He hit on you again. Hundred thousand, cash, small bills, instructions to be issued in a week."

The ice started to melt. I pulled myself up in my chair.

"You didn't have it. Not enough in the accounts yet, or you didn't want to risk accessing them, for whatever reason. You were desperate.

We'll come back to why. You had the idea of the kidnap scheme, and the even better idea that whoever delivered the payoff could also lead you to the blackmailer. Kill two birds with one stone, maybe literally. That whoever turned out to be me. Bad luck."

Mulholland said, "That means the men you paid off were expecting . . ."

"They were expecting someone with a hundred thousand dollars in a red backpack. That's what Rislyakov told them. That's all they knew."

"Then how . . ."

"I tracked the pickup men back to Rislyakov's place. That's where I found Eva, drugged. I also found Rislyakov—dead."

"My God! Why didn't you call the police?"

"The question everyone asks—and I'm still asking myself."

Polina shifted in her chair. I sat forward in mine. Everything felt sore.

"Too many unanswered questions, I guess. I had no idea what was going on then. I have a better idea now, but not a complete one. For example, what did Rislyakov lift from your computer, Polya?"

The ice was melting faster.

"The other question is, again, Polina had done such a good job of hiding herself, not the least part of which was marrying you. How did Rislyakov find her?"

Her hand darted under the cushion. I dove for the floor as she leapt forward. I heard the knife puncture the leather.

I rolled, trying to ignore screaming ribs, until I hit a table leg. I found my knees and came up to see Mulholland behind Polina, his arms wrapped around her. She was pulling and kicking, but he held on. The knife had cut a four-inch slice in the back of my chair.

I got to my feet, setting off more pain, and pulled out the blade. Steak knife, but long enough to do damage. I tossed it into the oversized fireplace. Steel rattled against stone, echoing around the bookshelves. I pulled up the cushion of the chair I'd been sitting in, then the others around us. There was a matching knife under each one. Set of six.

"Looks like you were expecting trouble from someone, sooner or later," I said.

"You evil fucking bastard. You want to destroy me, that's all you've ever wanted to do."

"I think you should leave," Mulholland said.

"I intend to, while I can. But we still have the murder issue. Someone else was at Rislyakov's place Wednesday night. Polina had your driver follow me when I went to pay off the supposed kidnappers. I led him to Rislyakov's, without knowing it."

"Lachlan?"

Polina spat at me. It fell short.

"Conjecture, I'll admit—but I can place him in a rental car at Rislyakov's Wednesday morning. He was treated for a gunshot wound at Beth Israel Wednesday night. Ask him where he got his limp. Eva shot him, in her stupor, through the door. I have the gun. But I'm still more interested in the two questions I asked before the hostilities started. What did Rislyakov phish from your computer, Polya, and how did he know to phish you in the first place?"

Mulholland loosened his hold. Polina lunged, but he pulled her back.

"You warned me about the past catching up," he said. "I didn't believe you."

He had the look of a man who was breaking under the accumulated weight.

"I'm sorry. I'm afraid this is only the beginning."

★ CHAPTER 32 ★

Hazy sun baked the sidewalk outside. A scattered crowd soaked it up on the Metropolitan's steps. I could just make out Gina among them. My phone buzzed.

"You look like hell," she said. "What happened?"

"Everybody has a nice word to say. Lost weekend."

"Lost weekend? Turbo, you need someone to take care of you."

"That seems to be a growing opinion. Listen, I don't know how long this is going to take. I'm going to send Mo up here to spell you with the *Valdez*. That'll be your post. We're going twenty-four/seven. Sheila will take over from her. You're back on in the morning. Okay?"

"Got it. But . . ."

"What?"

"Do we have to use the *Valdez*? That thing's embarrassing."

"Nobody's supposed to see you in it, remember?"

I should have caught a cab. Instead, I walked to Eighty-sixth Street and took the train. The walk aggravated the pain, but moving under my own steam felt good, despite the heat.

The subway ride made everything hurt more, but it was the quickest way to pull myself out of Polina's world and back into reality. I scanned the faces on the train. No one paid attention to my stitched-up face. Subway etiquette—see everything, acknowledge nothing. Ordinary people, going about ordinary lives. No violence. No intrigue. No black pasts and mysterious presents all caught up with each other. Bullshit.

"Eight million stories in the naked city," Lawrence Dobkin told American TV audiences every week for five years. We know better. There are only eight. They just keep getting told over and over again.

I hadn't gotten an answer to my questions. Whatever/whoever Polina was scared of, she was more frightened of it/him than a murder rap. One more question burned—why had Ratko gone underground? He'd stiffed Lachko. He'd stiffed Iakov. Gambling debts were too simple an explanation. A hundred impassive faces on the subway car. None of them had an answer either.

The front door buzzer roused me from another netherworld, this one involving Pig Pen and Polina leering from opposite sides over my battered body. I was on the couch in my apartment, where I'd dozed off after lunch. My watch read 5:14. I'd slept almost three hours. Everything had stiffened. I almost needed a block and tackle to pull myself up. The buzzer buzzed again. Victoria, her patience intact. I hobbled to the intercom, pushed the button, opened my door, and waited. When the elevator arrived, Petrovin walked down the hall in his linen suit, grinning his relaxed grin—until he saw me.

"Someone with your appearance might want to ask his visitors to identify themselves," he said as he extended his hand.

"My brain got rattled along with the rest of me."

"Are you all right? You look . . ."

"I know. I feel just as bad, but I've had medical attention, and they tell me I'll live. Lachko and I had an argument. He won."

"Perhaps you will achieve ex-Chekist status. You certainly appear to be trying."

"Thank you for the vote of confidence. Come in. Drink?"

"I'll join you, if you're having."

"The first one's purely medicinal."

He followed me inside, leaving his messenger bag by the door. "I have the information you requested. I thought I'd come by. I don't like phones."

"You and every other Russian."

"Another Cheka legacy."

"Can't argue." I got the bottle from the freezer and poured two glasses. We took stools on opposite sides of the counter.

"Your health," he said. "Looks like you need it."

"Can't argue that either. What did you find?"

"Your information was good, in part. Someone did shoot out a window at CPS headquarters Saturday morning. It was Tiron's office. But, as I told you, Tiron wasn't there. No one was hurt."

"That's good news. Thank you."

He looked at me over the glass. "Good news—to a point. Whoever fired the shot almost certainly knew the window he was shooting at."

"One more point beyond dispute."

"There's more. The slug was from a Dragunov SVDS. An assassin's weapon. Cheka assassin."

"I know. They were sending a message. I've read Ibansk."

He gave me a sheepish look as he put down his cup. "We all do what we have to do. The light of day—maybe I should say dusk—is one of the few defenses we have left in Russia."

"I'm not questioning motives, but I'll be more careful what I tell you from here on. You'd better be careful, too. The Cheka will be looking into who's feeding Ivanov, if it's not already."

"Of course. Ivanov goes to great lengths . . . well, you can imagine."

"He—I'm assuming he—lives a lot more dangerously than most."

"I won't comment on your assumption. As to living dangerously, it's no more risky now than it was in Soviet times."

"One more thing I can't disagree with. How well do you know him, Tiron, I mean?"

"We came into the CPS in the same class, and we've worked together closely on some things. A good man. When did you last see him?"

"Many years ago. But . . . his father and I were close, so when I heard the news . . ."

"Of course. I'd still be happy to give him a message."

I thought about that a moment. Trust may be the most difficult thing a spy comes to grips with. Iakov taught me that. The working premise, of course, is trust no one, but the need to get things done chips away at that. You make judgments, recognize some will be mistakes, hope you don't make too many. The man looking at me from his one good eye seemed like a good bet. At the same time, he was holding back. Then again, in his shoes, wouldn't I do the same? Circles within circles. At some point you make a call.

"You and Ivanov are correct. The man with the gun was indeed a Cheka marksman. He was operating under orders from Vasily Barsukov. He was in the car with the shooter."

Petrovin put down the glass, and his eye narrowed. "Jesus, that's bold, even for the Cheka."

"To state the obvious, it would be smart for Tiron to lie low for a while."

"I'll tell him, most certainly. But . . . May I ask how this involves you?"

"The Barsukovs are applying pressure. Not just to Tiron."

He nodded and smiled. "We all know that. I must ask again— why does this involve you?"

"Lachko looks for whomever he can squeeze. Any connection is enough for him. I'm sorry to say, he knows me very well." I hoped that would get him off the subject.

"What's he want?"

"The database and code that run Ratko's laundry. He thinks I know how to find them."

"Do you?"

"Maybe."

"You going to give them to him?"

"I don't have them yet. If I get them, I'll try to make a deal. That's what he'd expect me to do."

The eye narrowed again. "What kind of deal?"

"Depends on the cards I'm holding. Lots of interests to be taken into account."

"Including Tiron's?"

"Including Tiron's."

He smiled again. I returned it, which made my jaw ache. "Perhaps you'd like to play a card or two."

"What do you have in mind?"

"Rad Rislyakov."

He watched me while he sipped his vodka. I sat still. If I didn't move anything, most of the pain receded to a low-level throb.

"Vodka's excellent," Petrovin said after a while. "Tastes like home."

"Help yourself."

I slid over the bottle, and he poured.

"What caused you to join the Cheka?"

How much did I want to tell him? I thought—very briefly—about the truth, but as so often I pulled back to the sanitized version of my life story. No sense of liberation with a fellow Russian, even one who would barely remember the Soviet years. "I had a difficult childhood, no parents, lived in orphanages. My only skill was languages. That got the Cheka's attention, and I didn't think twice. They offered a way out . . . a way forward, something better even if I didn't know what it was. Don't put too much weight on the hard luck story, though. I also said there's honor in serving one's country. I meant that, too."

"If you had it to do over, would you do different?"

I reflected on that. I knew the answer, but the question still demanded consideration. "I've never met anyone who's been offered that chance, so I don't spend much time thinking about it. Regret, remorse—sugar-coated poisons. You get dealt five cards in life, maybe seven, depending on the game. Sometimes you get to draw three more. You play them the best you can. I realized a long time ago, the goal is not so much to win but to avoid having to fold unnecessarily. Stay in the game. Make the other guy go out first. The only honest answer I can give you is, no, I wouldn't make changes. No guarantee that whatever changes I made would lead to a better set of cards."

"You might not look like you do this afternoon," he said with a smile.

"I look like hell, true, but I haven't folded yet."

"You're making me rethink my lifelong Chekist stereotype. Do you have family?"

I thought again for a while before I said, "No. Not anymore."

"I'm sorry. I hope I didn't step over a line. I couldn't help thinking you'd make a good father."

"That's quite a compliment, especially for a would-be ex-Chekist."

He nodded and went silent again. He was trying to make up his mind about something, and it wasn't easy for him. Best thing I could do was stay out of the way. I poured a little more vodka and sipped slowly.

"Suppose I dealt your life-hand a wild card, the kind that could change everything you believe, every assumption you've made?"

"That would be some card. Guess I'd have to see it."

"It will also make you immediately and desirably expendable, in the eyes of your former colleagues."

"At least one of them already feels that way. Will I have to fold my hand?"

"Based on what you've told me, I don't think so. Although it could well cause you to play differently from here on."

"All right, I'm game. But tell me something first. How did you lose your eye?"

"You remember Andrei Kozlov?"

"Of the Central Bank?"

"That's right. I was with him when he was assassinated in 2006. I was collateral damage—or maybe they just missed, in my case. We were working together at the time."

"And you believe the Cheka was responsible?"

"Who else?"

"The jury said it was the former chairman of VIP Bank, if I remember correctly. Kozlov had suspended his license."

His voice took on a hard edge, bordering on bitter. "We both know two things. There is no rule of law in Russia, and nothing has happened since the fall of the Yeltsin government that wasn't cleared in Lubyanka."

"I haven't signed on to that platform yet, and I didn't mean to start an argument. I was asking . . . You take a lot of chances. You've already paid a big price. What are you in this for? Love, honor, duty, revenge, money—what?"

He picked up his glass, saw it was empty, looked at the bottle, and put the glass back on the counter. "Not money. This suit is the most expensive thing I own. The rest—maybe some of all of the above. If we both live long enough to get to know each other better, I'll tell you the story. That might explain things. I'd like to hear yours, too. That could explain more."

The bitterness was gone and the relaxed grin back.

"Play the card," I said, "if you're still game."

He paused, considering one more time, but not for long. "What I'm about to tell you only four people know. Used to be a few more, but the Cheka has been chipping away at our ranks, two so far this year. You'll be on the list."

"You're repeating yourself. Tell the story."

★ CHAPTER 33 ★

"Fact number one—there was another corpse in the Valdai shelter with Anatoly Kosokov. Boris Gorbenko, an FSB colonel who was the point man on the 1999 apartment bombings. Fact number two—the bombings were an FSB operation from start to finish. Fact number three—Kosokov and Rosnobank financed them."

Petrovin paused to pour some more vodka while I processed what he was telling me. Kosokov's bank was a Cheka financing vehicle. The Cheka staged multiple bombings that killed three hundred people and pinned them on Chechen terrorists. There had been allegations at the time, but there almost always were, and I hadn't paid them much attention. Now Petrovin was telling me the allegations were true. Kosokov financed the operation, and the Cheka started the second Chechen war. It should've sounded fantastic. Except it didn't.

"You say these are facts. You have proof?" I said.

"We have Gorbenko—on videotape and a signed affidavit. You'd call it a confession. He was a weak man. We'd had our eye on him—he was one of the Cheka's go-betweens with the Chechens. We wondered which side of the street he was playing. After the Moscow bombings we brought him in and sweated him, told him we'd let both the Cheka and the Chechens know he'd sold the other out. He turned, laid out everything, how he'd arranged for Gochiyaev to rent the storage spaces in the buildings, acquired the RDX explosive from Perm, how he directed Kosokov where and when to move money. He knew every supplier, every warehouse."

"He could've told you what he thought you wanted to hear."

Petrovin shook his head. "Remember the bomb that didn't go off, in Ryazan? Putin was busy praising everyone involved for their vigilance, then two FSB agents were arrested for setting the explosives, and Patrushev tried to make that ridiculous claim about a training exercise?"

I nodded. Not the Cheka's finest moment.

"Gorbenko tipped us to Ryazan, and we called the local police. He not only knew the location of the explosives and the time of detonation, he knew the names of the FSB operatives. We held those back. The local cops nailed them on their own, and they were exactly who Gorbenko said they'd be."

"Why didn't this come out at the time?"

"You know part of the answer. The Cheka slammed the lid on. Every attempt at the truth was corrupted. They wanted their war with Chechnya, they got it. They wanted Putin to replace Yeltsin. They got that, too." His voice grew bitter again.

"And the other part?"

"We overreached. We believed Gorbenko, but we also knew he'd say anything to save his sorry skin, as you just observed. The Cheka was moving fast. If we were going to take them down, we needed everything ironclad. We sent Gorbenko to bring in Kosokov and the Rosnobank records."

"Hold on a minute. This was 1999. If you don't mind my saying so, you must have been a teenager."

"True. I joined the CPS in 2004. Worked closely with a man named Chmil. He ran Gorbenko. He was murdered last year. Gunned down in his car at a stoplight. That's why I said what I said earlier."

"And Chmil told you all this, about Gorbenko?"

"He was still trying to build a case. I helped. And I've read the file. It's closely guarded, even within CPS."

I believed him. I also had the feeling their security wasn't as good as they needed it to be, and Petrovin knew it, too. He wasn't just playing with dynamite. He was tiptoeing through the entire Russian nuclear arsenal. His story was a conspiracy theorist's dream come true. It went all the way to the top of the Kremlin. The apartment bombings and the second Chechen war put Putin in power. But if that was the case . . .

"Why hasn't Ivanov run with it?"

"Patience. You'll see."

"All right. Go on."

"Gorbenko arranged a meeting with Kosokov at his dacha in the

Valdai Hills. This was about two weeks after Ryazan, October sixth, rumors were flying all over. Also turned out to be the day that Rosnobank burned. Chmil figured Kosokov wouldn't show, but he did. Gorbenko was wearing a wire, connected to a recording chip taped to his back. We didn't want to risk any of our people in the neighborhood. Gorbenko was supposed to convince Kosokov to cooperate with us, or at least get him to own up that he'd been the Cheka's banker for years and specifically for this operation. We promised what we could—money, a new identity in a new country. Chmil didn't believe it would be enough. He was right. Would you like to hear what happened?"

"You have the recording?"

"We got lucky. It doesn't happen often, but it does happen."

Petrovin retrieved a laptop from his bag. He clicked some keys. Faint voices emerged from the little speakers, talking in Russian.

"That's Gorbenko, speaking first," he said.

"You'll never make it, you know. They'll have men at every border crossing."

"Let me worry about making it. If the Cheka's as smart as everyone says it is, we'd all still be working for the Party."

"Don't be a fool, Anatoly Andreivich. Look what they did to your bank. They're shutting everything down, erasing all the tracks, eliminating all the links. You're a very big link. You and I, we're the only two who could expose everything."

"I'm counting on that fact to keep me alive. You made your deal, Boris. You're on your own with it. I'll take my chances by myself."

"You're crazy! The CPS can provide protection. We can bring the Cheka down. Yeltsin will have no choice but to purge the entire organization when people see what they've done. It's their one big weakness. No one will have difficulty believing they murdered innocent Russians to pursue their own ends. Especially once you and I lay out the evidence. Like the Katyn massacre. There'll be national outrage."

"National outrage? Russia today? Hah! Don't make me laugh. Neither of us will live to see it, in any event. Like I said, you made your deal. Good luck to you. I'm taking my evidence with me. My life insurance policy."

The crash of a door. A new, female voice. *"Tolik, I came as soon as I could. What the hell is going on? What are you doing here? Oh . . . Who the hell are you?"*

Gorbenko said, *"No names. Better that way. Call me Leo. I'll be in the kitchen."*

I recognized her voice, but I still asked, "Who's that?"

He stopped the recording. "Kosokov's mistress. Your friend Barsukov's wife, Polina Barsukova. There's more. Remember, Gorbenko—Leo—is in the kitchen now. We think some time has passed. But here she comes." He tapped a key.

Polina's voice again. *"Leo?"*

"What the . . ."

"Move, out the door."

"Kosokov, what the fuck is this? I have no time for . . ."

The shotgun roared.

Polina spoke again. *"One barrel left. Move!"*

A couple of minutes of indistinguishable sounds.

Petrovin stopped the tape. "We're pretty sure Kosokov and Polina are taking Gorbenko from the house to the barn."

"Over there," Polina said when he started it again.

"What do you want?" Gorbenko said.

"We'll get to that. Open that trapdoor."

Silence, punctuated by a couple of grunts before Gorbenko spoke again.

"Look, Kosokov, I can . . ."

The blast from the shotgun cut him off. The sound of a bang, a thump, and another. Then silence. The speakers died. Petrovin looked at me with a grim expression. "She shot him in the chest. The thumps are the body falling down the stairs. Bomb shelter underneath the barn. Concrete construction, stocked with all the staples—food, water, even vodka. Must've dated from Soviet times."

I'd been luckier than I realized a few hours earlier. "The recording survived all these years?"

"Amazingly, yes. The chip wasn't damaged by the blast, and no one searched the body. Gorbenko was supposed to call that night—one way or the other. When Chmil didn't hear from him, he went to the dacha the next morning. Nothing there, except the ransacked house, some blood, and the burned-down barn. We didn't know about the shelter, of course. It had snowed all night. No way to tell who or what had come or gone. He made a decision to leave everything as it was. Remember, no one knew we'd turned Gorbenko. Maybe he was right, I don't know. The investigation died, with the Cheka's help.

"Then two weeks ago, some kids discover a trapdoor in the foundation of the barn. Under the trapdoor they find the shelter, and in the shelter, what's left of two ten-year-old corpses, one shot, one burned at the stake. The amazing thing is, the local police notified us—not the Cheka. We were able to secure the site."

"And make sure Ivanov announced the news to the world."

He grinned sheepishly. "As I said before . . ."

I wasn't listening. "When did you say the kids found the bodies?"

"Mid-May."

That couldn't be it. Ratko had phished Mulholland months earlier. "If Polina shot Gorbenko, then who killed Kosokov?"

"We still don't know."

"And that's one reason Ivanov hasn't run with the rest of the story."

He nodded.

"The fact that Polina's alive makes her a leading suspect, doesn't it?"

He was lifting his glass, but he stopped midair and returned it to the counter. "You know she's alive?"

I grinned, partly to cover my carelessness. I'd assumed he knew about Polina. All the wits Sergei had knocked out hadn't returned to the roost. No harm done, that I could see, but I told myself to watch my step.

"You're late to the party. Yes, she's living here. I'm surprised you didn't know."

He looked down at his glass. Perhaps I'd nicked his pride. "Where is she?"

"Could be I'm holding the bargaining chip now. Tell me about Rad Rislyakov."

He shook his head.

"You know he's dead? You can't say anything that'll hurt him now."

He nodded.

"You were right the other day, your guesswork about Greene Street. I'd gone there looking for Ratko. I found the body. Iakov was there, too. He'd been shot, he said by the same guy who shot Ratko. I think the killer works for Polina's current husband. I think she had him kill Ratko."

I might have slapped him. He drew back, jumped up, froze for a moment, then walked around the room. When he came back, he said, "Why'd she do that?"

"Multiple reasons. Rislyakov was blackmailing her. He knew who she was, who she'd become. He horned in on a scheme she was running and was taking fifty percent not to tell Lachko. Then he got greedy and wanted a hundred thousand dollars, cash. I delivered the money to his people, and they led me to him. She had her husband's driver follow me. I led him to Greene Street."

He sat down again and rubbed his face. "What kind of scheme?"

"I don't know, but I'm betting it's connected to your two corpses. Rislyakov hacked his way into her computer several months ago. He removed a big file, without her knowing. He also learned enough to get close to her daughter—another way to keep tabs on Polina."

"The auburn-haired girl?"

"That's right. Her name's Eva."

That brought his head around, a funny look in his eye. "But you don't know what he stole?"

"No. Only that she panicked when she found out."

"How do you come to have all this information, if you don't mind my asking?"

"I had twenty-four hours with Rislyakov's laptop, remember?"

"The one you gave Barsukov?"

"Yes. After I copied its hard drive and made a few programming modifications. Rislyakov put a keyboarding bug on Polina's computer. I put one on his."

He grinned. "You can see everything he does."

"Cheka habits die hard."

I poured a little more vodka and offered him the bottle. He shook his head. "Listen to this again," he said. He pushed some keys on his computer, and the tape started.

Kosokov's voice. *"National outrage? Russia today? Hah! Don't make me laugh. Neither of us will live to see it, in any event. Like I said, you made your deal. Good luck to you. I'm taking my evidence with me. My life insurance policy."*

The door crashing open. Polina saying, *"Tolik, I came as soon as I could. What the hell is going on? What are you doing here?"*

Petrovin stopped the computer. "Kosokov says he's taking his evidence with him—his life insurance policy. Suppose that's the records of his bank, all the Cheka's transactions."

"Okay, I'll suppose. But he's dead."

"She's not. Suppose *that's* what she had on her computer. Suppose *that's* what Rislyakov stole."

"Dammit!" It made perfect sense. I did my own revolution of the living room. Polina was scared about Mulholland's bank crashing. She was looking at being cut adrift again—bringing back every fear she ever had since she was a kid. She'd be terrified, desperate, just like that day at Kosokov's dacha. She needed money. She used Kosokov's file to put the bite on Lachko. He still had Cheka connections. They moved the payoff money through Ratko's laundry—and Lachko assigned Ratko to figure out who was hitting on him. Ratko did just that and . . . No, he didn't. He didn't report back. Lachko was ignorant of Polina the day he hauled me out to Brighton Beach. Ratko had kept his discovery to himself and gone underground. Less than perfect sense. I returned to the kitchen.

"If you're right, and that's what Rislyakov stole, why didn't he turn it over to his masters?"

Petrovin held out his glass. "Rislyakov was working for us. He was our man inside the Badger organization."

I laughed. "I may be an ex-Chekist, Alexander Petrovich, but that doesn't make me newly gullible."

He shook his head. "Blood's thicker than money, even in Russia."

"Meaning?"

"Rislyakov had a conflicted relationship with his parents. They were dissidents during the Soviet years. His father spent time in the Gulag. Ratko competed with politics for his mother's attention. He went through a rebellious phase, fell in with a bad crowd, but a couple of teachers recognized his technical brilliance and helped him get back on a straight path. He reconciled with his folks in the midnineties. He was living with them, while he was going to university, in an apartment on Guryanova Street."

"Uh-oh."

"Right. They were all supposed to go to their dacha that night, but he had an exam coming up and decided to study late at school. They stayed home—and perished in the bombing."

"He blamed himself, of course."

"Of course. He started hanging out with his old friends and caught the attention of Barsukov. Chmil was a friend of his mother. He spent years trying to convince Ratko that the bombings that killed his parents were a Cheka operation. Three months ago, something happened, and Rislyakov told him he believed him—and he wanted to get even. He offered to open up the Badger empire. Chmil was murdered before he could do anything about it."

"Cause and effect?"

"I'm afraid so. We have a leak. That's one reason no one knows I'm here."

Not surprising. But that was a hard admission for him. I went around the counter behind him and moved some stuff in the sink, giving him time.

A couple of minutes passed before Petrovin said, "I think Ratko stole that file from Polina's computer. It proved what Chmil had been telling him about the Cheka and the apartment bombings. After Chmil died, I tried to build a relationship with Rislyakov. Slow going—he was cagey, suspicious, as you'd expect. I didn't push too hard. We were making progress; I saw him when he was in Moscow last month. He told me to come to New York, he had something to show me. I recognized Iakov Barsukov on the plane. I followed him to Greene Street. I was supposed to meet Ratko there the next day."

Lots of reasons not to like where this was going. I needed time, alone, to work through that. "If Ratko was going to be your mole in the Badger den, why did he go into hiding? Lachko hadn't seen him in months—that had him worried, suspicious."

"I don't know. We were concerned about that, too, of course. We asked him. He said he needed to do things his way. We didn't have a lot of choice but to go along."

"I think he was using you, just as you were trying to use him. Ratko had expensive tastes, in addition to the gambling. He was blackmailing Polina, remember? I think he was going to keep the laundry running. He was going to operate it himself and use the Rosnobank file to keep the Barsukovs at bay. Iakov didn't follow Ratko to Greene Street. He had an appointment. Eva told me Ratko was expecting him. He wanted Iakov alone—and out of Moscow—when he told him what he had and how he planned to use it."

Petrovin shook his head. "Ratko wanted revenge. I got to know him well enough to see that."

"Don't take this the wrong way. Ratko spent the last several years being tutored by Chekists. He was smart. He would have learned some things. Maybe you saw what he wanted you to see. And maybe, like Kosokov, he wasn't convinced the CPS could close the deal—especially in today's Russia. On the other hand, from his point of view, with the laundry, he'd keep his income stream and he'd hit the Barsukovs—Lachko in particular—where it hurts most, in the wallet."

Petrovin started to object but stopped. He sat for a moment, then did another circumnavigation of the apartment. He didn't like my theory, for lots of reasons, but he could see it fit the facts better than his own.

"Tell me something," I said when he returned to the counter. "Suppose you had Kosokov's bank records. Suppose you could tie the bombings to the FSB. It's explosive information, to be sure, but realistically, a decade later, in today's Russia, what do you expect to accomplish?"

"You gauging my ambition—or my naivete?"

"Only asking if you're trying to change the world."

He smiled once again. "There was a time, not too long ago, I would have said yes. Now . . . I'm just trying hard to hold on to truth as a concept. Not something we, as a people, are familiar with, except perhaps in our humor. It may take us somewhere, it may get pushed into a ditch, but if we don't at least put it on the road . . . You're probably right about Rislyakov. Still, we had to try."

"You might still get what you want. That file's out there somewhere."

"I'd like to talk to Polina Barsukova."

"Her name is Mulholland now. Felicity Mulholland. Married to another banker, Rory Mulholland. Nine nine eight Fifth Avenue. Be careful. She doesn't like talking about the past. Even if there's no history."

He gave me a funny look.

I said, "In your investigation of Kosokov and Gorbenko—their bodies, I mean—did you come across anything related to someone named Lena?"

"Why do you ask?"

"Eva keeps throwing this line at her mother—'You should have left me with Lena.' "

"Lena . . . Yelena . . . there's something in the file. I've got it all on this." He tapped the laptop keyboard. "Here we go. A doll—in the shelter. Under the stairs, female, plastic, forty-five centimeters long, blond hair, remnants of a peasant costume. Also a plastic doll's suitcase, nine by six by three, with three dresses inside, mostly intact. Name handwritten on the inside of each one—Yelena."

"Huh. If the doll was in that shelter, odds are she was, too. Maybe with two corpses. Can you get the doll sent here?"

"I don't know. I suppose so. It's a risk—no one knows I'm here, remember?"

"Have it sent to Victoria, or to me. That'll give you some cover."

"You believe it's that important?"

"She's a screwed-up kid. Mulholland told me she suffered some kind of childhood trauma. He doesn't know what. She was at the dacha with Kosokov and Gorbenko. She might have seen what happened. I know she's terrified of something. The doll could be the key—if I can find her, that is."

He nodded. "I'll call tonight."

The buzzer sounded, and I shuffled over to the intercom. Vodka was definitely having a medicinal effect on movement. "Yes?"

"Your guardian angel. Who else were you expecting?"

"I've been advised to screen my guests." I pushed the door release button and turned to find Petrovin next to me, putting his laptop back in the messenger bag.

"I'll be going," he said, taking my hand. "Three's company, as they say. We'll be in touch." Haste in his voice, bordering on urgency. I had the feeling he didn't want Victoria to know he was here, but when she stepped out of the elevator, he bowed in his formal Russian way and spoke a few words in her ear. She nodded in response before coming down the hall, smiling, briefcase in one hand, shopping bag in the other. She was wearing a sleeveless blue blouse over a knee-length black skirt. All the curves in place. I wasn't ready for a guardian, but the angel set my heart racing.

She gave me a kiss on the cheek and pushed past me to the kitchen. "I gotta warn you, I'm not much of a cook, but I figured in your condition, you'll take what you get."

"I'm cooking, remember? What's in the bag?"

"Chicken. I'm going to call Giancarlo. He'll tell me what to do."

"I'll take care of it."

"You just go lie down. Dinner in an hour, I hope. You get any wine?"

"Still vodka and beer, sorry."

"That's got to change if I'm gonna keep comin' around. Where's the vodka?"

"On the counter. I'll roast the chicken. You like lemon or onions?"

She turned, the vodka bottle in midair. "This about the chicken or control?"

"Probably both. It's my kitchen."

"In that case, you're on your own. I'll be right back. You got a wine shop in the neighborhood?"

"Liquor store, corner of Fulton, across from the Seaport."

She was gone before I could say more. I melted some butter, chopped some garlic, parsley, and rosemary, grated some zest, squeezed some juice, mixed it all together with salt and pepper. I splayed the chicken, painted it all over with the butter-herb mixture, and put it in the oven, reflecting on the fact that none of this felt like it had taken any effort or caused any pain—but that could've been the vodka. I had just poured a small glass in celebration when the buzzer sounded Victoria's return. She came down the hall carrying a bottle of something red, frowning. "Y'all need a new wine shop or a new neighborhood. Hope this stands up to your chicken. Corkscrew?"

I found one in the drawer and went looking for some mood music. *Sketches of Spain* was still on the CD player. I pushed PLAY and went back to the kitchen. She started around the room, wineglass in hand, too-small nose wrinkled in distaste, the rest of her smiling in fun.

"Wine not up to your standards?" I said.

"Passable, barely. Music sounds like a hermit's funeral. Stoned hermit."

"Not a Miles fan?"

"Ain't no Bob Wills, that's for sure."

I switched to Bach cantatas. Her frown moderated a little. Bach wasn't her thing either, but she didn't complain. I left it on, hoping he'd grow on her. Bach usually does.

"What's this?" She held up a small glass case with a medal inside.

"Order of Lenin."

"Hey! That's a big deal, isn't it?"

"Used to be."

"How'd you get it?"

"Recruited some useful agents."

"So, you not only worked for the government that jailed your mother for no reason, you did such a good job they gave you a medal?"

"That's right."

"You weren't kidding about Russian irony. How'd you make out with the ex-wife?"

"I survived."

"Tell me about her."

"That outfit is very becoming."

"Your eyes are taking it off. Don't change the subject."

"It's only fair. You undressed me."

"Not out of choice. Come on, I'm curious."

"I'm crushed."

"Don't be. We might get to what your dirty mind is thinking, but you're not up to it yet. What about your wife?"

★ CHAPTER 34 ★

"She was the daughter of a general in the GRU—military intelligence. Lithuanian mother. Her father distrusted me because I was KGB. He was a drunk, a bad drunk, so bad, he got run out of the army. Then he did some really stupid things and got sent to the Gulag. Family went from privilege to periphery to poverty. Polina was crushed; she doted on him. I don't think she ever recovered, but I didn't see it at the time.

"We were married in 1980, had a son in 1983. Partly because of her old man, and partly because of my own fears, I never told her about my past, my Gulag past. Iakov had buried that, or so I thought. We had our ups and downs, perhaps more than most. By 1989 it was all over. I hadn't seen any of them since—until a week ago."

"Okay, I'm hooked. What happened?"

"Nineteen eighty-eight, I was posted in the New York *rezidentura* for the second time. The *rezident*—chief of station—was one Lachko Barsukov, who was fast climbing a ladder many thought would end as chief of the entire KGB. But Lachko's always been greedy. He and another guy were running a side business, ordering everything from champagne to truffles to designer dresses on the consulate's tab, shipping it all home, where his brother sold it on the black market."

"What's that have to do with you?"

"One of my agents ratted him. Lachko screwed him on a deal, not knowing he was working for us. I turned Lachko in."

"This is better than a soap opera."

"Iakov leaned on me hard not to testify. I made the worst decision of my life—and I didn't even know how bad it would turn out to be. Honor versus loyalty. I opted for loyalty."

"Lots of people would have made the same choice."

"True enough. It's still the dumbest thing I've ever done. At the same time, I couldn't deny Iakov—I still believe that today—so I was screwed no matter what I did."

"You're being too hard."

"The story's not finished. I'd already set certain processes in motion. Stopping them wasn't so easy in the KGB. I recanted, prevaricated, tied myself in knots to back off. Lachko and Iakov had plenty of enemies—you don't get to where they were without them. They thought they had Lachko in their sights. Ultimately, without me, there wasn't enough of a case. Lachko got a slap on the wrist, but the damage was done. He was tainted. His climb to the top of the Cheka was over. He still blames me for that."

"That explains his attitude the other night. But what's this got to do with your wife?"

"Lachko wanted revenge. He mounted a campaign of innuendo, based on my *zek* past. He knew how to use that kind of information, especially in a closed system where everyone talks to the same people every day. Once started, a good rumor could spend weeks going round and round the circuit."

"Wait a minute! Iakov didn't do anything to help? He couldn't get Lachko to stop?"

"Maybe he tried, I don't know. We weren't speaking much by then. But it's also one of life's lessons—don't expect father to turn against son."

"He hung you out?"

"He did what he thought was right."

"Jesus fucking Christ. And you still stick up for this prick?"

"I still owe him. The whispers got around to Polina. She was horrified—at the idea of being married to a *zek* and at the prospect of her life crumbling again. I realize now how much I underestimated the dept of her insecurity. She married me as much for stability as for love. I was a Chekist on the way up, *Nomenklatura*, privileged class—important factors for someone who'd seen her family fall as far as she had. Then all that unravels—all at once. My KGB career is effectively over—and I'm a *zek*, beneath the lowest of the low, right down there with her disgraced old man. I can almost sympathize with her."

"She didn't sympathize with you."

"No. She blamed me for the whole disaster. She took our son and left. I'd counted on something like that, but I didn't appreciate how far she'd go. I found out when she started carrying on affairs with my fellow officers—three of them—in ways that were bound to bring notice. That sounds harsh, but I don't believe there was any love involved on her part, only hatred and vengeance. She was out to ruin my career and make sure I couldn't challenge over custody. She knew the Cheka had no room for indiscretion and her recklessness would mean my dismissal—or worse."

"No wonder you're the pain in the ass you are. What did you do?"

"I put an end to it. I found out before she got too far. Iakov tipped me off."

"And?"

"I was drinking a lot—Russian response to everything, especially crisis, but one day I woke up and realized I had to take control. Life presents an endless series of choices, some bigger than others. Whatever Polina and I had was shattered, I understood that. I could've fought her for custody. Might've won, but I'd be out of a job and in no shape to take care of my son. Or I could make a deal with the devil—in this case, one of his earthly representatives. Polina could raise Aleksei, with my support. I wouldn't interfere, I wouldn't even be a known factor. As if I never existed, a *zek*'s destiny. In return she had to cease the campaign to ruin me, for the sake of the three of us. She took the bargain and so far as I know stuck to it. I didn't reckon on her marrying Lachko, but I'm not omniscient. In retrospect, she was grasping for security and still trying to get even. He'd always had a thing for her, and he wanted to get even, too."

"Perfect fit."

"Yeah. Iakov pulled some strings and I was given an assignment in San Francisco. That was a time-buyer. I was back in Moscow in two years, behind a desk, which I hated. When the opportunity presented itself to call it quits, I did, and moved here. Started over."

"That's some story."

I'd told it straight, as it seemed today, a couple of decades later. Memory simplifies, but it plays tricks, too, and the more time it has, the more mischief it gets up to. I tell myself I did what I did for the love of my son, and most of the time I believe it. Once in a while, though, I ask myself which is stronger—love or the instinct for survival? Then I'm not so sure.

The timer chimed. I took out the chicken and sprinkled some chopped parsley over the top. No fresh vegetables, so I resorted to frozen peas.

Victoria said, "What was . . . Petrovin doing here, if I'm not being nosy?"

So that was the exchange at the elevator—he was reminding her of his assumed name. "He had information for me. Something I asked about. Also, I think he wanted to tell me a story. He's looking for help."

"You going to give it to him?"

"Maybe. Turns out I have an interest in the same matter."

"What's that?"

"Do U.S. attorneys ever take time off, quit for the day?"

"Not this one. I've got a lot riding on the thing we're working on—Barsukov's money laundering operation. It'll be my first big case if I can bring it, and it's not white collar—it's big-time organized crime. Petrovin . . . well, for one thing he's Russian. Y'all are hard to read, if you don't mind my saying so. For another, he plays his cards close to the vest. I'm not always sure what he's up to. That makes an insecure country girl like me nervous. There—I've said it."

I could have taken issue with every adjective—insecure, country, nervous—but I didn't bother. She was trying to fool herself, trying to fool me, trying to charm, and succeeding, as she well knew, on the one out of three that mattered most.

"Your new friend Barsukov is applying heavy pressure to some of his old friends—including me—to keep his laundry running. That's what Friday night was all about."

"That's why he beat you up?"

"That and the old scores I just told you about. Rislyakov had a database—the identity info he hacked from T.J. Maxx and the code that makes all the transactions make sense. Lachko thinks I know where they are."

"Do you?"

"Maybe."

"No bull."

"I have an idea."

"If you're withholding evidence . . ."

"I'm not, at least not yet. If I find it, you'll be among the first to know. Dinner's ready."

I quartered the chicken and put out two plates on the counter. We ate mostly in silence. I had a glass of her wine, which was nothing like Giancarlo's Barolo. Something else to study up on.

"That was an excellent chicken," she said, pushing the plate away. "You're a good cook, among your other talents."

"You haven't begun to explore my talents."

"I've learned humility ain't one of them."

"I have others."

"Sugar, I'll be honest. I've liked you from the first time I saw you—I have no goddamned idea why—and I'm hotter than the Texas Playboys to do something about it. But, like I already said, no hanky-panky with criminals. Deep down I really am a cautious country girl, and I still have no idea where you stand or what game you're playing. If I end up having to come after you in a professional capacity, make no mistake, I'll do that as hard as I know how. I don't want my heart broken at the same time."

I reached across and took her hand. "Vika . . ."

"Vika?"

"Sorry. Russian nickname. Just slipped out."

"That's okay. I never had a nickname. Didn't like the obvious candidates."

"We give everyone nicknames. I won't break your heart. You can trust me because I know how it feels. I just told you the story. I wouldn't wish that on anyone."

★ CHAPTER 35 ★

The Chekist replayed the tape one more time. Just a fragment of sound, less than a minute, before the fire consumed the microphones. The flames whooshed and roared and popped. He could hear Kosokov shouting, the words impossible to make out. Then that other noise—squealing, high-pitched, rising in volume.

Now he realized after all these years, it was the girl. She must have been there the whole time. It was her in the horse stalls, not rats. He'd almost shot her. How the hell had he missed?

How had she survived the inferno? The only answer was the old shelter. Somehow she'd had the sense to seek protection there. Maybe that's what Kosokov was yelling. He'd never know for sure. One more thing that didn't matter.

She was alive, she was here, she knew who he was. That did matter. She would have to be dealt with.

Before anything else went wrong.

★ CHAPTER 36 ★

I woke feeling born again, just like they sing about in those gospel songs, although my particular form of rebirth probably wasn't what they had in mind. A little after six o'clock, and I lay there watching her chest rise and fall under the sheet.

I don't know whether it was the nickname or what I said about heartbreak, but I'd led her to bed without resistance. It was far from my best night, which she more than made up for with her own intensity and tenderness, a combination that took us places where I could leave the pain of my injuries far behind. She'd undressed herself, then me, then used her breasts, eyes, thighs, lips, hands, and teeth to work both of us into a white-hot heat, on the edge of ecstasy, before we wrapped ourselves together and plunged. Sometime later, we broke the surface of reality, panting and sweating, partly sated, knowing there was more to come. We lay quietly, her head on my chest, holding each other close, saying nothing. I dozed until I felt her restless hands start to work, and I responded with mine, and without a word we carried each other a second time to the door of oblivion. I slept through the night, visiting no netherworlds for the first time since Saturday.

"Okay, give." She was looking at me from her pillow, smiling.

"What?"

"How'd you get the funny name?"

I laughed. *"That's* why I finally got you into bed."

"You think it's your shaved head and hairy chest? I've been wondering about this ever since I read your immigration file."

"Talk about privacy."

"Don't change the subject." She doubled the pillow under her head and waited. Her big eyes were green pools I wanted to jump into.

I caressed her cheek. She knocked my hand away. "Get on with it."

"My grandfather, Turba Petrovich, he's the culprit. One of the original Chekists. Ardent Bolshevik. Knew Lenin, Stalin, Trotsky, Bukharin, the whole gang. He worked with Dzerzhinsky, founder of the Cheka."

"But that means he helped create the Gulag!"

"Yes. Grandpa Turba was one of the officers who oversaw the construction of the camps—and became an early victim of his creation. He was caught in one of Stalin's purges, when Comrade Yezhov took over the NKVD from Comrade Yagoda in 1937. Grandpa was taken away on Christmas night, although it was no longer called that, and sent to Norilsk, where he died four years later. But what goes around comes around, as you Americans are fond of pointing out. Yezhov was arrested in 1938 and shot in 1940, after Lavrenty Beria took over the Cheka. I hope my grandfather at least knew he outlived the man who caused his downfall."

She was looking at me, dark eyes wide with interest. I reached for her cheek again, but she pushed my hand away. "None of that. Keep going."

"While he was still on the rise, Grandpa Turba and Grandma Svetlana gave birth to their only son. Nineteen twenty-six; revolutionary fervor was morphing into Stalinist zeal. Turba believed Stalin was a great man doing great things for his country, including pulling it into the modern age. Industrialization was the big thing—railroads, factories, dams, electricity—Stalin was building the new Russia. A lot of people were caught up in the excitement, and they demonstrated their enthusiasm with names for their children. Some kids got lucky—Len, for Lenin, is a perfectly serviceable name. Or Ninel, Lenin spelled backward, for a girl. Even Engelina or Melor, shorthand for Marx, Engels, Lenin, and October Revolution.

"Grandpa had different ideas. Remember, we like wordplay. The family name was Vlost, as you know, which dates from the thirteenth century and is a variation of Vlast, which can be traced to the twelfth. Means 'power.' Seemed perfectly reasonable to him—highly desirable, in fact—to call his firstborn Electrifikady. Full name Electrifikady Turbanevich Vlost. Means Electrifikady, son of Turba, and electric turbine power. Apparently Grandpa was quite a card."

"You know, every story you tell gets more absurd."

"All true. I swear on the graves of Marx, Lenin, and Ronald Reagan."

"But you never knew him, right, the guy with the power name?"

"Right. I think my mother feared they would never be together again and giving me his name was a way to make sure we were part of something that had a history, that had lasted. Technically, I should have been called Electrifikady Electrifikadyvich—Electrifikady, son of Electrifikady. We don't do 'junior.' But she gave me exactly the same name he had. I shortened it all to Turbo as soon as I was old enough to know how."

"I like Electrifikady. Can I call you that?"

"Not if you want to continue whatever it is we've started."

"Don't be so defensive. It's cute."

"So's Vicky."

That brought out the pout. She sat up and the sheet fell away. I reached for her, but she pushed me back.

"I've gotta get to the office."

"I usually run in the mornings. Want to go with me?"

"In this heat? Are you crazy? Never mind, I know the answer to that. What illegal activities do you have planned for today?"

"Going looking for Rislyakov's database."

"What if you find it?"

"Probably go out to Brighton Beach, see Lachko, try to make a deal."

That got a worried frown. "I won't ask if that's wise. We both know the answer. Am I going to approve of this deal?"

"I hope so. You could be the primary beneficiary."

"You want to tell me what you're thinking?"

"At dinner. If we're still talking."

"I'm beginning to have some sympathy for your ex-wife. Since you're such a good cook, you can make me breakfast before you go running or whatever. I like it when a man does that. I prefer my eggs scrambled, with a little Tabasco."

The bare behind sashayed to the bathroom. I waited a few minutes before I got up to follow her instructions, enjoying a long-gone feeling. I hadn't really expected to encounter it again.

Victoria left for the office, declaring my eggs delicious, my health still doubtful, and my plan for the day borderline crazy. This time, she was three for three. I logged in to the Basilisk and retrieved the information it had generated on Ratko and his alter ego, Alexander Goncharov. I found the charge three weeks earlier on a Rislyakov Visa for $862 from a Moscow undertaker. I reached for the phone.

In a ten-minute conversation with a helpful mortician's assistant, during which I posed as the late Rad Rislyakov, I learned that he had arranged for the disinterment of his parents on his last trip to Moscow and the shipment of the cremated remains to New York. That made my first stop of the day Chelsea.

I logged on to Ibansk.com. Petrovin was still feeding Ivanov.

WHITHER POLINA BARSUKOVA?

And how soon, Ivanov wants to know. Whispers from New York are that the once (and still?) wife of Lachko Barsukov and (con?)-current wife of American banker—and potential jailbird—Rory Mulholland is getting ready to repeat the vanishing act she perfected in Moscow back in 1999.

Mulholland might want to take heed from his predecessor (concessor?). Polina saw the writing in the early October snow and left Barsukov—along with her late lover, Anatoly Kosokov, among the smoldering remnants of Rosnobank. Is she getting ready to do it again? Where can she run this time? A few things are evident to Ivanov—and he is only too happy to make them apparent to all Ibansk. One is, Polina

Barsukova sheds identities like a viper sheds skins, and she takes on new ones as easily as any chameleon changes protective colors. Another is, husbands and lovers are no anchor for her. Ivanov is also told that a noose is tightening. Russian and American authorities have Polina in their sights. And there's still Lachko. Hard to believe Badger pride will let her leave him grasping empty air again.

The race is on! Ivanov isn't prepared to take bets on the winner.

My cell phone buzzed. Gina said, "She's on the move. Quite a looker."

"So was Pandora, I'm told. Anyone else following?"

Pause. "Can't tell yet."

"You see anyone else, you think you see anyone else, break it off and get out of there. Okay?"

"Okay. She just came out. I'm watching. We're headed for Madison. I'll call back."

Had Polina been reading Ibansk.com this morning? Had Petrovin counted on that?

Eva could have gone anywhere, but I bet on her clinging to Ratko's orbit. She'd fallen hard. It would take time to shake him, especially since his end was so abrupt. I took a cab to Sixth and Twenty-first, which was showing more activity than my previous visit, though the heat on the sidewalk was no less punishing.

The lobby was cool and empty, other than the doorman behind his sleek blond desk. I was marginally worried about Lachko's thugs, but he has always lacked imagination—or he was counting on me to do his dirty work. No Russian beef in sight.

The doorman looked up helpfully before he recognized me and frowned. I put the photo of Eva on the counter.

"She's upstairs, isn't she? Rislyakov's place."

He stammered for a moment, then looked away.

"How much she give you?"

"What?"

"How much she give you not to say she's here?"

"Nothing! She didn't—"

"Don't lie to me. You're in enough trouble already."

"Trouble?"

"Patriot Act, remember? Give me the key."

He looked around again. No help appeared. "She's not there. I mean . . . she was, but she left."

"When?"

"This morning. Couple hours ago."

Maybe Eva followed Ibansk, too. "Coming back?"

"Didn't say."

"Anyone else asking for her?"

He looked around once more. "Those guys that were here before. They came yesterday."

"You get rid of them?"

"Yeah. They didn't press it."

"You tell her about them?"

If there had been a hole under his countertop, he would have gladly dropped in. "This morning."

"She say anything?"

"Uh-uh. Went back upstairs for a few minutes, came back down and left."

"She won't be back."

"How do you know that?"

"My job. Key."

"Yes, sir."

I took the elevator to seven, inserted the key, rang the bell, waited, rang again, waited, turned the knob, and shoved the door open.

Everything was as it had been. A few articles of women's clothing dropped on the furniture. Ratko wouldn't have approved. It took a short twenty minutes to make sure there was nothing to find, except for the heavily taped box on the kitchen counter with the return address of the Moscow undertaker in the Cyrillic alphabet.

Violating the dead is a difficult thing to do, but neither Ratko nor his parents were going to haunt me. Still, it took a few minutes to cut open the box and a few more to fish through the two containers of coarse, hard ashes inside. Cremains, they're called in the trade. I stuck my arm into Mom until I felt something solid. I did the same with Dad. Buried in each box was a portable hard drive, smaller than a paperback book, tightly wrapped in plastic. I undid one—five hundred gigabytes, more than enough to hold the database and the key to Ratko's laundry. The other, Kosokov's bank records?

I found some tape and resealed the box. Maybe Eva wouldn't notice—if she did come back. No one else would care. I stopped long enough to say a silent prayer for the dead. They wouldn't hear it. They'd never know how they'd been used either. On the way out, I grabbed Ratko's copy of *Travels with My Aunt*. A long time since I read it, and he didn't need it anymore.

★ CHAPTER 37 ★

"Jackpot!" Foos said.

"Whattaya got?"

"Ratko's database. Forty-two million potential bank accounts—along with the code for the laundry. We could go into business tomorrow."

"Victoria wouldn't like that. Neither would Lachko. How much money are they moving? Can you tell?"

"More than fifty mil a month, but they're still ramping up, adding accounts, increasing the flow. May was twenty-two percent higher than April, which was up twenty-one percent over March. Classic early growth curve. Sky's the limit, with that many names to work with."

"Let's see."

He spun the computer screen around. The columns were all the same as the ones that had given me a headache last Thursday. Now they showed bank names and branch locations, account names and numbers and dollar amounts moving in and out. Overseas deposits and withdrawals were shown in local currencies. The sheer volume of transactions made it complicated, but the underlying program was decidedly simple.

"Gotta hand it to him. Helluva operation," Foos said.

"No wonder Lachko wants it back so bad."

"You already gave him half of it. You gonna give him the other?"

"I'm thinking to sell it. About time the Barsukovs started to spread the wealth."

Foos raised a bushy eyebrow. "What's Victoria going to say about that?"

"She's not my minder."

"That's not what you said yesterday. And the lipstick on your neck suggests different."

I put a finger to my skin, where she'd snuggled when we'd said good-bye. It came away purplish red. "I'm doing this partly for her. Can you bug the database the way you did Ratko's computer?"

"I'll attribute the stupidity of that question to your impaired mental condition."

"Okay. What about the other hard drive?"

"That one's your department."

"Why?"

"It's in Russian."

My ribs had started to ache, but I did my best to ignore them as I took a cab to Second and Eighth. The street was much as I'd found it before. All kinds of people going about their lives. I stopped at a bank to buy a roll of nickels before watching Slav House from the opposite sidewalk for about ten minutes. Nobody came or went. That was good for my purposes. The mattress salesman emerged from his store, smoked a cigarette, and went back inside without noticing me.

I crossed the street and pulled open the metal door. The same big guard sat on a stool in front of the turnstile.

"Yeah?" he said.

I put my hands in my pockets and moved toward him.

"You've been in a fight," he said, rising off his stool. "Looking for another?"

I hit him across the face with my right hand wrapped around the nickels. He fell over the stool with a crash. He pulled himself halfway up, and I hit him again. This time he stayed down.

I stood back against the wall under the one-way window until the steel door opened and a hand holding a gun poked out. Colt .45. I hit the door with my shoulder, which made everything hurt, but not as much as the other guy's wrist. Bones cracked as he shrieked in pain. The gun clattered to the floor. I kicked it away and pulled open the door. The short, greasy-haired guy Gina had described held his damaged wrist, the hand hanging as if no longer connected, his face twisted in agony. I grabbed his shirt and yanked him into two hard jabs with the nickels. Teeth dropped to the floor. I let go of the shirt and the rest of him fell on top. He didn't move.

Ten minutes later, I blinked as I stepped into the sunlight, holding Eva by the hand. Slav House consisted of a large meeting room, three smaller classrooms, and a couple of conference rooms and some offices. I found her in one of the latter, asleep on a cot. There were three large safes against the wall, all locked, presumably where they kept the cash. I gave the place a quick once-over before waking her, but it yielded nothing. She didn't seem surprised or resist when I asked her to come with me. She wasn't stoned, as far as I could tell, just exhausted.

"Please," she said, "not h . . . h . . . home."

"My office."

"Okay."

The cab was crossing Delancey Street when the cell phone buzzed.

Lachko said, "You have a fucking death wish, shit-sucker. You'd be a dead man, if you were a man at all. As it is, you'll be a dead non-event no one will remember. By midnight."

"I have the database. I have the code."

A long silence. I pictured him in his all-white office, struggling to bring his temper under control. "Bring them to me. You and your faggot-fucking son can live."

"We're both going to live, Lachko—on my terms. That's where we start the negotiation. I can see how this works now. You moved fifty-two million in May. Not bad. June's on track for over sixty. You going to throw all that away?"

Another silence. "What the fuck do you want?"

"I'll call when I'm ready to talk."

I closed the phone before he could respond. I expected him to call back, if only to throw more insults, but the phone stayed strangely silent. Eva was looking at me, blue eyes wide.

"Your father can be a very angry man," I said.

She closed her eyes and scrunched up her face, shaking her head. The eyes opened again, just as wide. "He's n . . . n . . . not my f . . . father," she whispered.

I tried to get Eva to explain that confession, but she didn't speak another word for the rest of the cab ride, despite my questions and coaxing. She stared straight ahead, as if she'd retreated into her own world where no one could follow. She kept the same stare as I paid the driver and led her through the lobby, into the elevator, and through the server farm. It took Pig Pen to break the spell.

"Hello, Russky. Hello, cutie. Hot number!"

Eva's head spun. "Wh . . . wha . . ."

"Eva, meet Pig Pen. Pig Pen, this is Eva. Be polite."

"Cutie. Hot number!"

Eva looked at Pig Pen, back at me, then back at the parrot. "He t . . . talks?"

"A lot more than he should." Foos taught him the "Cutie, hot number" routine to impress his dates, which, to my surprise, it never fails to do.

Eva approached the door of his office-cage. "Hello, P . . . P . . . Pig P . . . Pen."

"Hello, cutie. Pizza?"

She looked back at me, unsure.

"Don't pay attention to his pizza pleas. He hits on everyone."

"I'll get you pizza," she said.

"Hot number! Hot number!"

Foos was banging on his keyboard. "Who's that?"

"The Mulholland girl."

He hauled his bulk to the door. Eva was still outside Pig Pen's cage. The parrot was hanging on the mesh, talking up close and personal.

"Looks like he's got a new friend," he said. "She staying?"

"Not sure. She's used up Ratko's hideaways and doesn't want to go home."

The phone rang, and Foos answered. He listened a minute and held the receiver out to me, mouthpiece covered. "Victoria. Not a happy camper."

"Y'all told me your business with Mulholland has nothing to do with my case."

"That's true."

"Then what the hell is he doing in Brighton Beach?"

"Are you sure?"

"He got out of a car at Barsukov's place a few minutes ago."

"What kind of car? His or Barsukov's?"

"Hold on."

A click on the line, silence, then another click.

"Lincoln Town Car. Mulholland and two other guys, probably Barsukov's."

"I'll call you back."

"Call me back? Call me back when, dammit?"

"When I get to Brighton Beach."

I phoned Gina while piloting the *Potemkin* out Ocean Avenue. I didn't want to take it—Lachko might try to add it to his collection—but the *Valdez* was still uptown at its observation post.

"We're doing another bank tour," Gina said.

"ATMs?"

"Real branches. She's going in and talking to tellers."

"Keep a record. Branches and times."

"Turbo, what do you pay me for?"

"You see anyone else watching you—or her?"

"No, and I've been looking, but . . ."

"But what?"

"I've got a sense I'm not the only one on this tour."

"How many banks have you hit?"

"Four."

"Get lost. I mean now, right now. E-mail me the bank information."

"Okay, but—"

"*NOW!*"

"Hey, you're scared."

"Down to my shoes. You saw what I look like. Beat it."

★ CHAPTER 38 ★

I pulled up at the pink palace at three ten. A guard pointed a shotgun through the iron bars as I got out of the car.

"Tell Lachko Turbo's here," I said in Russian.

The guard called to someone else while he kept the barrel pointed squarely at my midsection. After a few minutes, the someone yelled back and the gate swung open. The guard didn't move. Two others came out, checked inside and under the *Potemkin,* then signaled me into the courtyard. I parked next to the ZiL limo. Auto détente. I was searched and escorted along a different set of hallways to an open courtyard in the center of the complex. At one end was a chapel in the Greek Revival style. Lachko wasn't remotely religious, probably keeping the bases covered. A large swimming pool took up most of the middle, lounge chairs spaced evenly around. A bar with a fake thatched roof faced the chapel across the pool. Waikiki meets Delphi. Lachko was in his wheelchair on the far side in the shade, oxygen tubes in the nose, *papirosa* in hand. Another muscled thug, could have been Sergei's brother, stood beside him.

First things first, my first thing being self-preservation. "Lachko, let's you and I be clear from the outset," I called across the pool. "That guy or anyone else lays a hand on me, your laundry is out of business."

"You're in no position to dictate anything, Turbo."

"In that case, I drove out here for nothing."

I turned back toward the house.

"Wait. You're not going anywhere."

"That's exactly my point, Lachko. I come and go as I please, unmolested. Your word on that, for what it's worth. Otherwise, we won't even get started."

"Fucking *zek*." He spat on the tile.

"You can drop the *zek* bullshit, too. I'm tired of it."

He let the cigarette fall to the ground. "That's what you are, Turbo."

"I'm here to make a deal. We can talk about that or we can wallow in old insults that don't mean anything anymore."

"So you have come to think. I'm not sure everyone would agree."

"I'll take that chance. Where's Mulholland?"

He ground the cigarette under his foot and lighted another. I could smell the cardboard forty feet away. "I have no idea."

"Come on, Lachko. You brought him out here. Why?"

"What the fuck are you talking about?"

"You know full well."

"I know you're a useless—"

"Where is he now?"

"How should I know?"

My phone buzzed. Victoria said, "Mulholland left that cotton-candy cabin fifteen minutes ago."

"What'd he look like?"

"Look like?"

"Normal or like me?"

"Appeared to be unharmed. Does that go for you as well?"

"So far. But I just got here."

"Turbo! Get out of there."

"I'll call when I do."

She started to say something, but I cut her off. Lachko was watching from across the pool. None of this made sense. Some kind of game—he'd used Mulholland as a lure—but games were never his style. When he wanted something, he sent muscle, as he'd done before.

"I did drive out here for nothing," I said as I pocketed the phone. "See you."

"What's your rush? Company not to your liking?"

"Too much of a good thing."

I started for the house. I hadn't taken half a dozen steps before I felt a hand on my shoulder, spinning me around.

"Handle with care. Boss doesn't have what he wants yet."

The big man took a step toward me but veered away and went inside.

"Come over here, Turbo. I'm tired of yelling," Lachko said.

It might have been the bright sun, or the disease, but up close Lachko looked like he'd aged ten years in the last few days. I didn't feel sorry.

"Tell me about Eva," I said.

"Why should I tell you one fucking thing about anything?"

"It's part of the deal we're going to make—for the code and the database."

"What deal?"

"We'll get to that. Eva. She's not your daughter, is she?"

He threw the smoking cigarette in the pool. "She's Kosokov's."

That admission must have hurt. I still didn't feel sorry.

"I fell hard for Polina, that's true," he said, lighting another. "She was screwing him, but I thought I could pull her away. She told me they were never serious, but that was before I learned she lies as easily as I smoke Belomorkanals. She married me, but I think she was still trying to get even with you. Or she was trading one protector for another—or keeping two on the leash. Kosokov was so fucking venal, he didn't give a damn. The man was a whore."

He was angry. Maybe I could provoke him. "That's why you killed him?"

"What?"

"You heard me."

He threw his cigarette into the water, next to the other one, and held up two tobacco-stained fingers, a half inch apart. "You are this close to choking on that butt underwater." He wheeled his chair a few feet, following the shade. "You've always considered me slow-witted, and perhaps in this instance I was. It took me too long to discover she'll eat your balls for breakfast and throw them back up to make room for lunch."

"She said the same about you."

"I can imagine the lies she told. I didn't kill Kosokov. I would have, gladly, but fate didn't put that in my path."

I kept at it. "He lost your fortune—one of them—or did he just steal it?"

He laughed out loud, long and hard, until he started to hack. He bent over double, body shaking so hard I thought he'd fall out of his chair. I was about to go in search of help when he gave a final, choke-filled cough, spat a cupful of yellow-brown bile on the bluestone, and pulled himself upright.

"Turbo, you are without a doubt the dumbest fucking Russian in all of Russian history. You swallowed Polina's lies so deep, the hook buried itself in your bowels. I ask myself, whenever I'm unfortunate enough to think of you, how the fuck did you ever make it into the Cheka? I told you before—Kosokov was a fool, a big-mouthed moron. He was the tool of our mutual friend, Polya. She suckered me, I admit, but not so much I didn't make sure every kopek of my profit left his fucking bank the moment it was booked. Kosokov made some bad bets at the end, or so I'm told, but he made them with his money—and Polina's—or the bank's, not mine."

That sounded like the Lachko I knew—but it wasn't Polina's hook buried in my bowels. "So who killed him?"

"Who the fuck cares? If I wasted any time thinking about it, I'd assume she did."

"Why was Ratko operating behind your back?"

"What the fuck are you talking about?"

"You hadn't seen him in months. You had your men out looking for some sign of him. You had no idea about the Greene Street loft. He took everything necessary to run the laundry and went underground. He was shutting you out."

"Turbo, you and I have coexisted on the same planet for the last twenty years only because our paths did not cross. Now they have, and it remains to be seen whether we will continue to coexist at all. If we do not, you can be assured your soul will be resting back in the zek-filled sewer it crawled out of in 1953. I practically raised Ratko from the time he was a teenager. When I find out who killed him, I'll make sure he pays. It could well have been you, in which case I'll be doubly happy to even the score. Rurik is watching from the window. He was a guard in the Gulag. He hates *zeks* almost more than I do."

He grunted and moved his chair again. Didn't appear to take a lot of effort. I wondered how sick he really was. Ivanov wasn't infallible.

"Still no answer."

"You despise me, Turbo. I despise you. Part history, part jealousy, part fate. You're still healthy. I sit here in a wheelchair with fucking tubes up my nose."

He sucked the *papirosa* down to the nub. The late-afternoon sun burned as hot as noon.

"You destroyed my career. For what? Score points with my father? Claw your way over my back? You always hated me because I was born with the Cheka in my blood and you were just a shitty *zek*."

He spat so hard the bile landed in the pool with a dull plop. While he fished for another smoke, I walked around the water. The sun bounced off the palace roof, rays splintering off the tiles, solar blades baked in reflected heat. I could see Rurik through the glare, behind a picture window, watching my every step. I stopped in front of the chapel doors. Prayer wasn't going to help. I continued my circumnavigation of the Barsukov world I'd left—been thrown out of— long ago and been sucked back into. The old world had been twisted but something I could comprehend. I understood how it worked. This one, I wasn't sure I could wrap my head around. Bigger question was, why did I want to?

I arrived back at the wheelchair. Lachko was staring at the pool in a haze of cardboard smoke.

"You still haven't answered the question. Ratko was running out on you. Why?"

He bent forward in the wheelchair, hands at his sides, cigarette hanging just above the ground. "I don't know."

I almost believed him, but it could've all been an act. He could lie as easily as Polina—or the Politburo bosses he used to work for.

"What the fuck do you want, Turbo?"

"What was that ruse with Mulholland all about?"

Lachko looked up, eyes as empty as a beggar's soup bowl. "I told you before, I have no fucking idea what you're talking about."

In a strange way, I sensed he was telling the truth.

"Why'd you bring him out here?"

He shrugged and turned the wheelchair away. I'd learned as much—or as little—as I was going to. I said, "Okay, let's talk business. Twenty percent."

He spun back. "What the fuck?"

"You heard me. The database and the code. They're yours for twenty percent of the profits."

"You're out of your fucking mind."

"Business, Lachko. And maybe a little bit of payback. I've got it, you need it. That's the deal."

"Have you forgotten Friday night?"

"Do I look like I have? I've put all the necessary protections in place. Anything happens to me, Aleksei, Victoria, anyone, you're shut down."

"Ten."

"Fifteen."

"Fucking *zek*."

"You'll be a richer Chekist. I'll be a rich *zek*. We'll still hate each other."

I dropped the portable hard drive in his lap.

He spat once more into the pool. "Don't come back."

The *Potemkin* was where I'd left it. The cell phone buzzed again as I crossed the courtyard.

Foos said, "She's gone."

"What happened?"

"Don't know. We went to Lombardi's with Pig Pen, came back, she said she was tired, wanted a nap, and stretched out on the couch. I thought I heard a cell phone ring a little later, and when I came out to check, she was gone."

"Dammit."

"She's a sweet kid, but a real head case. Ratko screwed her over pretty good. Probably best for her he croaked. He would've broken her heart otherwise. It's pretty damned fragile as it is. She's still too hung up on him to see what was happening."

"Sounds like she told you a fair amount."

"I just bought the pizza and listened. Been a long time since any-one took an interest in what she thinks."

"She say anything about her mother?"

"Uh-uh. Only that she and Ratko talked about family a lot. His parents were dead. He was always asking about hers."

No surprise there.

"Can you tell who called her?"

"On it right now."

The *Potemkin*'s tires squealed as I accelerated through Lachko's gate. I knew why I'd been tricked into visiting Brighton Beach. The trickster wanted Eva. I didn't know why, but I had a good idea who. The list of potential tricksters was growing short.

★ CHAPTER 39 ★

"Disposable cell phone," Foos said. "The one that called her."

"Fuck your mother."

He ignored me. He'd heard it before. "Call came in a few blocks from here. Dover Street."

My head whipped around. I yelped as my neck sent a shot of pain down my right side.

"You okay?" Foos said.

"Yeah. Where on Dover?"

"Dover and Front. Right under the bridge."

The pain vanished as I ran for the door.

Spies are a paranoid bunch. For good reason. There usually is someone out to get us. That doesn't mean we lack humor.

One of the trickiest challenges I faced in a foreign city was finding secure venues to meet agents. America's most crowded metropolis, New York, offers wonderful anonymity. Everyone consciously ignores everyone else around them. But it's still difficult to find places where one is truly alone—and out of the reach of prying eyes, ears, cameras, microphones, and binoculars, should there be any interested, which, of course, we constantly assume there are.

I found a few good venues in my time—the bar at the Village Vanguard, any number of undervisited rooms at the Metropolitan Museum (ditto for the Cloisters), the Brooklyn Botanical Gardens (less crowded than its Bronx brethren), windswept piers on either river, especially in winter, and, one of the very best, a well-traveled, thoroughly anonymous gay men's pickup spot in the parking lot of a Queens park. I appreciated the irony of that one more than my agents. By far my favorite was the old Civil Defense shelter in one of the stone piers supporting the Brooklyn Bridge. I happened on it completely by accident, in the mid-1980s. The lock had rusted to the point of breaking, or maybe someone had broken in and run away, leaving the iron door banging in the wind on a sleeting winter night, the noise echoing around the chamber of the bridge's understructure. I was walking to the subway after meeting an agent on one of the East River piers. There was nobody on the street, so in I went.

I found a forgotten Cold War fallout shelter. Big, damp, dirty room, stocked to the ceiling with cases of high-protein crackers (date-stamped 1962), drums of water, crates of medicines, and boxes of blankets. There were some wooden chairs and tables, two dozen folding canvas cots, some kerosene lanterns and multiple cans of fuel. Iron rungs climbed to a second exit in the bridge ramp. Whether the stone of the superstructure was enough to protect the inhabitants from the feared nuclear winter was anybody's guess, but the early 1960s—the months of the Cuban Missile Crisis (we knew it as the Caribbean Crisis)—were hardly a rational time in America. Everyone was scared, for good reason.

I wedged the door shut that night and returned the next day with a heavy-duty combination lock. I spent a good hour kicking it around the street to make it look old. I checked the place periodically over the next three months. So far as I could tell, no one ever got near it. I used the shelter more than a dozen times over the next two years. I never saw evidence that anyone else even knew of its existence. My agents were evenly divided. Half found it fascinating. The rest disdained the dirt and damp. I took pleasure in the irony every time I visited.

Another summer thunderstorm tonight. I ran through seven blocks of rain to Dover Street, clothes glued to my body when I got there. Early evening, sunset still hours away, but it might as well have been midnight. No lights from the buildings. No one on the street. Dim pools of reflection on the asphalt from a few streetlights. The hulk of the bridge weighed heavy above. An urban no-man's-land, bereft of life, except for the rumble of traffic on the ramp.

Lightning flashed off the door to the old shelter. No way to tell if anyone had been there since my last visit in 1988. I took refuge in the entrance of an unlit building and waited. No motion, no people, nothing. The rain slackened some but still fell hard. I didn't have a good idea—I didn't have any idea except to hope the lock was still my own and take my chances. The exertion of running made everything ache. I hadn't brought a gun. A good hand to fold.

I waited another few minutes on the grounds that summer storms pass. The rain kept falling.

Muttering under my breath, I started across the street at a trot. I could see the old iron door more clearly as I got closer, the pockmarks of rust and age brightening in the lightning flashes. I could almost see there was no padlock on the latch when a strong arm grabbed my shoulder and pulled me around. My feet gave way on the asphalt, slick with rain, and my butt hit the pavement, setting off a chain of pain through every bruised muscle I had.

Damned fool! Of course he'd have someone watching.

I looked up, expecting to see the bullet that would split my skull, thinking about Victoria and Aleksei and Eva and my own stupidity.

An eye patch. Then a hand grabbed mine. "This way. Move!"

Petrovin pulled me to my feet and shoved me to the refuge of another pier. Eva Mulholland was huddled in the shadows, hair matted around her head, soaked shirt clinging to her frame.

Petrovin had traded his white suit for black jeans and a black T-shirt. He hadn't lost any of his presence.

"I was following Polina," he said. "I think you had someone on her, too."

I nodded.

"She brought me here and went inside. That was four o'clock. Eva came at five. I waylaid her."

I looked at Eva. "Why'd you leave the office?"

"She c . . . called." Her voice was between a squeak and a whisper.

"And?"

"She n . . . needed m . . . m . . . me. Said I had to c . . . come. Then . . ."

"Then what?" Pretrovin said, with a gentleness I doubt I could've managed.

Tears welled. "She screamed. It w . . . w . . . was aw . . . aw . . . awful."

"I know this place," I said to Petrovin. "I'll go."

"You armed?"

"No. Are you?"

He shook his head. "Are you sure you're in shape . . ."

"I'll be fine. It's an old fallout shelter, one big room. If I'm not back out in two minutes, get her out of here and find a cop."

Nobody came or went while we talked. The rain picked up a little, then slowed. It was falling harder again when I took a breath and started for the rusted door a second time.

The padlock lay on the pavement, cut open, off to the side. Same one I'd bought two decades before, looked like.

I put my back to the wall beside the door, reached around, pushed it open a few inches. If anyone made any noise, it was drowned by the traffic rumble above. I peered into the dark. Couldn't see a thing. There was a light switch to the right of the door. I'd been amazed years ago when it worked. Who was paying the bill? Where was the bill sent? I was just as amazed now.

I flicked the switch and gave the door a hard shove. It struck something. Glass broke. A trail of fire skittered across the floor around a stack of water drums—a whoosh and a flash and flames and shadows danced on all four walls. I could feel the heat and smell the oil.

Behind the drums a circle of fire raged, fed by kerosene-soaked blankets, flames leaping six to eight feet. In the center I could just make out Polina, tied to a chair, head falling forward. A funeral pyre of blankets burned under the chair.

No time. She'd be dead in a minute and the whole place an inferno a minute after that. Holding a dry blanket in front of me—an ineffective shield if there ever was one—I made my way around the fire circle to the back. No room between the fire and the wall. The designer of this execution chamber had done his work well. The heat scorched everything. The fire burned all around—no spaces, no breaks. My clothes would be alight in a second.

I held the blanket out in front and jumped through the fire. I screamed as the flames seared my skin, the smell of burning flesh mixing with kerosene. I wrapped the blanket around Polina, lifted the burning chair off the pyre, and ran through the other side, giving her a final shove as I fell to the floor and rolled, trying to extinguish burning linen and skin.

"STAY STILL!" Petrovin barked. I stopped, and he covered me with blankets. The burning eased. The smell remained. He took more blankets to Polina and covered her. As I sat up, I saw Eva by the door, her whole body shaking. She let out a wail—the sound of a lifetime of fear, pain, and sorrow reverberating around the stone walls before she collapsed to the floor.

"Get the fire out," Petrovin yelled.

"Water drums," I said. "Soak the blankets."

He went to work on one of the metal cans. It took forever—probably just a few seconds—to get one open. We suffocated the kerosene-soaked blankets. The space filled with black smoke. The stench of fuel, wool, and flesh made me gag.

Polina's clothes were badly charred, her skin black and red. The burns could be the least of her problems. She'd been worked over with a blade—disfigurement by a thousand cuts. The wounds puffed and oozed. I put my nose next to one; it reeked of kerosene. I fought the urge to throw up.

Her hands were bound to the back of the chair, and her feet to the legs, with duct tape wrapped thick. Tape covered her mouth. I looked for something to cut her free. A box cutter lay in a corner, blood on the blade. The torture weapon. I slashed the tape on her arms and legs and the chair fell away. I pulled the piece off her face as gently as I could. She was unconscious and barely breathing. I pulled out my cell phone. No way not to get my hands dirty this time.

Victoria got on the phone immediately. "Are you all right?"

"I'm okay," I lied. "Ambulance. ASAP. Front and Dover. In the bridge support. Felix Mulholland. Severe burns and lacerations. Loss of blood. Blood poisoning. She doesn't have long. Cops, too. I'll wait."

She hesitated half a second, a hundred questions running through her mind. She didn't ask one. "I'll call back."

Mulholland next. "Your wife's badly hurt." I repeated the essentials. "Ambulance on the way. New York Hospital?"

"Yes. I'll meet her there. Tell me—"

"Time for that later."

He understood urgency, too. "Thank you," he said. "For everything."

Petrovin sat on the floor, Polina's head in his lap. He stroked her hair. I thought I saw tears in his good eye, but that could have been the smoke. When he saw me looking, he put his finger to her neck.

"Pulse very faint," he said.

"Odds aren't good. Bastard worked her over with that box cutter and put kerosene in her wounds."

"Jesus! What kind of . . ."

He didn't finish. He didn't need to. His shoulders started shaking, and a new look came over his face, one of barely controlled fury. He was close to explosion. Time to get him and Eva out of here.

"Take the girl and go somewhere safe, before the entire New York City police establishment arrives. She's the target now. That fire was set; the door was booby-trapped. She was supposed to set it off—burn her mother to death before her eyes, herself, too, maybe. I'll deal with the cops."

313

He kept his eye on me as he stood, cool returning. "I don't disagree with your assessment, but why are you doing this?"

"Why are you?"

Hard to make out in the dim light, but I think he smiled. "Perhaps we're on the same side after all."

"You're the only one who ever doubted that. Does anyone know where you're staying, anyone at all?"

He hesitated.

"I'll take that as a yes. Don't go back there. Someone knew about Chmil, remember?"

I dialed the office. Foos was still there. "Emergency. I need hotels with vacancies, fast."

"Give me five."

"Call this number." I gave him Petrovin's cell phone.

Eva didn't want to leave. She started screaming and dove at her mother. I put myself between them. Polina's back was to her—Eva couldn't see the extent of her wounds. Petrovin talked quietly in her ear from behind. I couldn't hear what he said, but his calming influence took hold.

"Polina'll be at New York Hospital," I said. "Don't answer your phone after my friend calls back. If I want to talk, I'll call twice. I'll hang up after the third ring the first time. Answer the second call on the second ring. You'd better move."

Petrovin nodded and took Eva's hand. He pulled her to the door. He turned back when he got there, looking at Polina on the ground.

"You know as well as I do there's only one—"

"I know," I said.

★ CHAPTER 40 ★

The police got there first, the ambulance second.

I called Bernie as soon as Petrovin left. "I need a lawyer. Someone who can keep me out of jail." I told him where I was.

"I heard about that place, back at Langley. We never touched it, waiting for someone to return. How bad is it?"

So much for my irony. "Bad." I gave him the details. "I've called Mulholland. Ambulance and cops are on the way. But your former partner's going to have my ass."

"Word is, she already has."

"I've got newfound respect for the CIA. I still need help."

"I'll send Franklin to hold the fort while I arrange more heavy-weight assistance."

Victoria called just before the police arrived. "I've done what you asked. I've got a ton of questions, but I'm gonna let Coyle ask them on my behalf, at least to start. Remember what we talked about this morning—be straight with him. He's gonna repeat everything you say word for word."

The cops moved me outside, searched me, and asked a lot of questions of their own, which I refused to answer.

The paramedics wasted no time in taking Polina away.

"New York Hospital," I said. "Her husband's—"

"We know."

An SUV carrying Coyle and Sawicki and the taxi with young Malcolm Franklin raced each other down the block and skidded to the curb in unison. Coyle headed straight for me. Sawicki tried to cut off Franklin, but he ducked under his arm and sprinted in my direction.

Coyle walked on by and went inside. Franklin slid to a stop by my side. "Don't admit anything. I'll do the talking."

"Good advice," I said.

Sawicki caught up and pushed himself in our faces. "I own your ass tonight."

I did my best to smile. Franklin did his to look stern. We stood there until Coyle came back out.

"How much did you touch?"

"Don't answer that," Franklin said.

"That's okay," I said. "Pretty much everything. The door was rigged to knock over a kerosene lantern, which ignited a fire, which was going to burn the woman—Felix Mulholland—at the stake. She'd already been cut up bad. I got her out of the fire. I put out the fire. I called for help. Beyond that, talk to my lawyer." I looked at Franklin, who didn't look happy.

"What were you doing here to begin with?" Coyle asked.

I looked at Franklin.

"My client will answer all questions in due course."

"Your client's full of shit."

"C'mon, Coyle, look at me. I'm cooked better than a backyard steak. I told you what I found and what I did about it."

"I'm still asking what you were doing here to begin with. Taking a walk in the rain under the Brooklyn Bridge?"

I thought about trying to bluff. I might pull it off. I thought about my conversation that morning with Victoria and her admonition about playing it straight. I thought about the fact that I'd likely need her help—and Coyle's—before this was finished. I weighed all that against the fact that this was Cheka business, family business—none of hers, none of his. I decided to tell the truth. Up to a point.

"Eva Mulholland—the daughter—got a call from her mother, telling her to come here. I followed her."

"So you must have seen the guy who set the fire."

"Uh-uh. I was late. I was in Brighton Beach—you can confirm that—and I had to trace the call through her cell phone. By the time I got here . . ."

"Where's the girl?"

"You know the Russian working with Victoria? Eye patch, curly hair. Calls himself Petrovin, at least to me?"

Coyle nodded.

"He was following Felix Mulholland. She led him here. He didn't like the setup, waylaid the girl."

"Bull. He would've seen the guy come out."

"There's another exit, ladder to the bridge ramp."

"So where are they?"

"The girl was in shock. He took her to get help."

"You're full of shit."

"Think about it, Coyle. Guy brings Felix Mulholland here. Works her over. Makes her call her daughter. Daughter doesn't show. He sets the trap and splits. I trigger it."

"Okay, so who's the guy? What's he want with the Mulholland babe or her daughter? And how'd he know about this place?"

I'd gone as far as I was prepared to. I looked at Franklin. "Your move."

He stepped forward. "My client will answer no further questions."

He was trying to sound important, but he came across as silly. Not his fault—he was being trained to argue the finer points of securities regulation with the SEC. Coyle got that, too, and did his best not to laugh.

"All right, counselor. You and your client can accompany me and my partner back to the office. We'll continue our conversation there."

We continued until sometime after 2:00 A.M. Franklin was spelled at eleven by a criminal lawyer named Lieb who wasn't any more effective in cutting off the questions, but when he said I wouldn't answer, he sounded like he meant it. Coyle made me call Petrovin a couple of times, but he didn't answer, as agreed. Sawicki wanted to lock me up overnight, but Coyle let me go—after I promised not to leave town and to produce Petrovin and Eva the next day, and Lieb promised that my promise was one they could bank on.

We rode a slow elevator to the street and walked out into the hot, damp night. Lieb flagged a lonely cab and offered me a lift. I said I'd walk. I wanted time to think.

The streets were empty. I should have gone home—I was tired and aching and scorched. I was also too keyed up for sleep and keenly aware that a clock hanging over the head of Eva Mulholland—maybe others, too—was close to running out. I thought about calling Victoria, but she was probably debriefing Coyle. The office was quiet, but I woke up Pig Pen when I turned on the lights.

"Russky. Burned crust."

"Not crust, Pig Pen, me. Burned Russky." I reeked of smoke and kerosene. He gave me the same stare I get from his owner when I utter a logical improbability and closed his eyes. His mention of crust reminded me I hadn't eaten anything since breakfast. I found some bread, cheese, and vodka in the kitchen. I was chewing and sipping when the phone rang.

"Coyle says your story's too fucked up not to be on the level. He also says you know damned well who set that fire and why it was set there."

I was right about the debriefing. "And?"

"Between you and him, shug, I'm going with him."

"Thank you for your support."

"Seriously, are you all right? Coyle said you looked pretty messed up."

"Your concern is touching. His, too. I'm self-medicating."

"Uh-oh. Remember what happened last time you went on the vodka cure."

She had a point. "I will. Where are you?"

"Office—but I can be at your place in ten minutes if you want to hold hands and tell me what's going on."

"That's all I have to look forward to?"

"You're a suspect, shug, and I'm beat. You gotta be, too. It's 3:00 A.M."

She was right—and I should have stayed where I was and started working through the Russian file on Ratko's hard drive, my purpose in coming here in the first place.

"I'll wait for you at the front door."

★ CHAPTER 41 ★

I overslept. I would've overslept more if Victoria hadn't shaken me at eight, already fully dressed. We'd gone to bed and fallen asleep immediately, holding hands. Her only words had been "You look worse every time I see you."

I'd taken a shower to wash off the kerosene smoke, and she'd made me ice the worst of my burns. I went along with that until she fell asleep, then tossed the ice in the sink and joined her in happy unconsciousness. The accumulating punishment was taking its toll.

She said, "You're on your own again, which scares the hell out of me, but I figure you'll find more trouble no matter what I do."

I couldn't argue.

"You know what's good for you, you'll get your pal Petrovin and that girl in to talk to Coyle."

"My pal? I thought he was working with you."

"He's off the reservation. Just another ex-socialist to me now."

"We do stick together."

"That's one thing, among many, I'm afraid of. You know who set that fire, don't you?"

A question I could dodge, given the hour and everything that had happened. Given everything I feared could happen, a question I should avoid entirely.

I didn't want to. Life's not as easy as crossing a field, I'd told Bernie. "I have an idea."

She sat on the edge of the bed. "You gonna do anything about it—other than tell Coyle, which is what you should do?"

"I'm thinking about that."

"Sugar, I said it before and I'll say it again, 'cause we both know you're thickheaded. You gotta choose. You decide to pursue this on your own, you're on your own. You can kiss me good-bye, only there won't be no kiss. I won't have any part of it—and no part of you. It's gonna hurt both of us, but that's the way it is."

She stood and straightened her skirt, the simple motion of her hands pulling my heart harder than anything in years.

"Let me know what you decide."

She was gone before I could respond—if I'd had anything to say.

I lay there awhile, the aches, pains, and stings picking up strength with gathering consciousness. I started an argument with myself, even though I already knew the outcome, and kept it up while I dressed. I hit the steaming street and ran three miles at half my normal pace, then stopped at the cool gym and worked the weights until everything in my body said enough. I kept arguing while I went home, showered, made some eggs, drank some coffee, and sat at the counter alone debating whether I wanted to spend the foreseeable—and quite likely my entire—future sitting at the counter alone. Physically I felt better for my exertions. Emotionally I might as well have been marooned in a Siberian blizzard.

The office was empty. Foos had taken Pig Pen on one of his periodic outings. The parrot seems to enjoy them, but he's always glad to get home to the traffic reports. The quiet was fine by me. I pulled up the file from Ratko's database on the computer.

Whatever else Kosokov had been—arrogant, venal, stupid, depending on who you asked and who you believed—he was also meticulous. Ratko's hard drive did indeed include the records of Rosnobank, at least those relating to the Cheka, annotated in painstaking detail by the banker himself. Every Cheka operation financed through Rosnobank from 1992 through 1999 was there—assassinations, at home and abroad (I recognized many of the names), funds channeled to pro-

Russian political parties, insurgents and militias in the former Soviet Republics, money for pro-Cheka entrepreneurs buying up government assets in the early transition years. Thousands of transactions aggregating hundreds of millions of dollars, maybe more. The only thing Kosokov hadn't provided was a total. Every transaction carried the approval of one of a half-dozen Cheka officers identified in code, although they must have felt increasingly imperious over time—in very un-Cheka fashion, they hadn't tried hard to obfuscate. The approval that appeared most often was ChK22. I knew that designation.

The final entries were labeled—in chilling Soviet fashion—Chechen Freedom Security Undertaking, CFSU. The list of transactions showed how the Cheka had moved money to purchase the explosive RDX, rent the rooms where the bombs were placed, compensate the bombers, and bribe landlords, janitors, superintendents, police, and others who might interfere. There was a parallel network of payments, with the money emanating from banks in Grozny—obviously to implicate Chechen separatists once the damage was done. No question, no question beyond a reasonable doubt, no question beyond any doubt, that the Cheka organized, financed, and executed the September 1999 bombings of four apartment buildings that killed three hundred people, started a bloody war, and propelled Putin to the presidency. Gorbenko, Chmil, Petrovin—they were all right, and so far, two of them had died as a result. Petrovin said he was marked. I would be, too. The evidence was all there in bits and bytes. The approvals all came from ChK22. The pain in my gut was worse than anything Sergei could have inflicted.

The door horn sounded, and I jumped eight feet. Foos and Pig Pen. I settled back to earth, my heart still pounding. It went off again. I sprinted to the kitchen and got the SIG Pro from the safe. Carrying it behind my back, safety off, I crept through the last server aisle, where I wouldn't be spotted. The horn blew twice more. I got to the reception area to see a black guy in a FedEx uniform holding a large box. Feeling only a little bit foolish, I tucked the gun in the small of my back and opened the door. The package had a Moscow return address—Ulica Otradnaja. I signed and carried it back to my office. Inside were the old, dirty, burned remnants of a Russian peasant doll and her travel case of extra clothes. Eva's Lena.

I dialed Petrovin's cell phone, hung up after the third ring, and dialed again.

He answered on the second ring. "I was wondering when we'd hear from you."

"Long night with the FBI. They want to talk to the girl, which I think we should do, if only to get me off the hook. First, though, your package arrived. We should show her the contents."

"She's been asking about her mother. Any news?"

"No."

"She wants to go to the hospital."

"Bad idea. My Cheka friends are almost certainly watching."

"Agreed. The same could be true of your place."

"I'll come to you. I'll be sure I'm alone."

"Holiday Inn, West Fifty-seventh."

"Big spender."

"It was that or the Pierre. I'm a poor Russian policeman."

"Give me an hour."

A call to Bernie confirmed Felix Mulholland was still in a coma at New York Hospital. The doctors weren't optimistic. The Basilisk verified I had indeed been talking to a cell phone on West Fifty-seventh between Tenth and Eleventh avenues. This was a time to be doubly careful.

Which is one reason I made it at all.

★ CHAPTER 42 ★

If Five-by-Five had been Russian—or halfway competent—he would have walked up from behind as I left my building, put his gun to the base of my neck, pulled the trigger, and sent my soul to meet its maker, wherever such meetings take place, my SIG Pro still tucked securely in the back of my belt.

As it was, he tried to run me down from a hundred yards away. Then he tried to follow me back inside. While he was still in his car.

I was crossing Water Street when I heard the racing engine, accelerating fast, getting louder as it closed. A green Range Rover coming straight at me from the south. Some piece of memory reminded me Mulholland owned one of those. I ran back to my building. The Range Rover skidded and squealed into the crosswalk, turning in my direction. The engine raced again. I made it through the door just before the car jumped the curb and crashed into the steel and stone of the facade.

The front of the SUV collapsed like an accordion. The windshield shattered. The rest of the cab remained remarkably intact. Five-by-Five was conscious, if dazed, in the driver's seat, cocooned in multiple air bags, which now hung deflated around him.

I was able to open the driver's door. A small crowd gathered behind. Five-by-Five reached for his armpit, but he was much too slow. I yanked out his Colt automatic and tossed it to the back of the car.

"I didn't kill no one," he said.

"Can you get to your seat belt?"

"I didn't kill no one. You fooking lied."

"Okay. Seat belt."

"I didn't kill no one. You lied." He was shouting.

"That's why you tried to run me down?"

"Told you, don't like fookin' snoops. Don't like fookin' snoops who lie."

I reached for the latch. Jammed. I pulled and twisted to no avail. His breath said he'd been drinking beer. A lot of it.

"I didn't lie," I said.

"He fired me. You did that."

That stopped me. "Mulholland? Fired you?"

"I didn't kill no one."

"When? When did he fire you?"

"Yesterday. Said you said I killed that kid. I didn't shoot him. He was dead."

I gave up struggling with the seat belt. A voice behind me yelled, "We called nine-one-one. Ambulance on the way. Is he all right?"

"He's okay," I called back. I said quietly to Five-by-Five, "Tell me quick, what happened at that loft?"

"Don't like fookin' snoops."

"I can get your job back. He'll listen to me."

He looked at me with blurred eyes, half hateful, half desperate. The beer, the impact, and the air bags slowed his processing ability, never swift, to a crawl. I wanted out of there before the cops arrived. They'd have me back in front of Sawicki and Coyle in no time.

"Lachlan, if I made a mistake, I'll make good on it. I mean that. Tell me what happened last Wednesday. I'll talk to your boss, tell him I was wrong."

He looked me over one more time before blurting out his account of events at Greene Street. A few more pieces fell into place.

"I'll take care of it," I said when he finished. "Help's coming. They'll get you out of here."

I backed away into the crowd. "He'll be all right," I announced to anyone and everyone. "More shock than anything else."

"What'd he say?" somebody asked.

"Trying to explain what happened," I replied, continuing to back up until I found myself at the rear of the group, which was collectively pushing forward to get closer to the carnage. I heard sirens as I walked a block south, crossed Water (looking both ways), and trotted up Wall Street. I didn't stop until I reached the subway platform.

★ CHAPTER 43 ★

I used the entire New York transportation system, excluding only ferries, to make sure I arrived at the Holiday Inn free of tails. The hotel looked out of place in Manhattan, as do almost all chains, but the white brick, balconied, utilitarian architecture appeared true to its brand. The frayed carpet in the lobby and the smell of institutional cleanser in the hallways may have been more true than the brand wanted. Petrovin had rented two adjoining rooms on the fourth floor, the door between them open. He greeted me with a handshake, Eva with a hug and tears. "I kn . . . know you're trying to h . . . h . . . help, m . . . me, but it's all m . . . m . . . m . . . my f . . . fault."

I said, "Your mom's still in a coma. The doctors aren't sure what will happen. She was badly hurt last night—which wasn't your fault at all. Someone else did that to her. You have any idea who?"

She shook her head. She was dressed in clean jeans and a T-shirt. Petrovin had bought her some new clothes.

"We can't take you to see her until we figure out who wants to hurt you. You understand that?"

She nodded slowly.

"You're going to have to talk to the police, tell them what happened last night. Okay?"

She nodded again.

"I brought you something. I'll put it in the other room."

I went next door and laid out Lena and her case on the bed. Petrovin followed me. I held my breath and called her.

She saw the doll and collapsed in the doorway. Petrovin and I moved to help, but she pushed herself up and fell again across the bed, holding what was left of Lena in her fingers. She started to cry. Petrovin sat on the bed, moving ever so slowly, and put an arm around her shoulders. "We know about you and Lena and that day in the barn. But we want to hear your story. Will you tell us what happened?"

She looked up at him and then at me.

"He's right, Eva. I want to hear it, too."

She looked back and forth between the two of us, her eyes heavy with tears. "I t . . . t . . . tried to do s . . . something! I d . . . did! I tried so h . . . h . . . hard. But the ropes . . . The fire was too h . . . hot. I t . . . tried . . . ."

She collapsed again, crying without control. Petrovin cradled her.

"This was your father, right, your real father?" I asked as gently as I could. "You tried to free him. He died in the fire at the barn."

She stopped crying just long enough to nod. Then she returned to the Gulag of memory.

★ ★ ★

Eva cried herself out and fell asleep. Petrovin and I let her rest. We ordered sandwiches from room service and ate next door, not saying much, each of us working through his own thoughts. I wondered if his were that much different from mine.

She slept for more than an hour before she appeared at the doorway. I said, "Hungry?"

Half a sandwich disappeared in a flash. She was working on the second when Petrovin said, "Feel like talking?"

She nodded slowly and sat on the corner of the bed. It took a couple of false starts, but once she got going, the story came tumbling out. Having decided to tell it, she wanted to get through it as quickly as possible. The sandwich was forgotten. Only her stutter slowed her down.

I had pieced most of it together in my own mind—I assumed Petrovin had, too—and her account contained no surprises. As she told the story, Petrovin paced the room. At first I thought he was just antsy. He'd been holed up here for hours. In fact, it was anger. The cool customer was losing his composure, like he had last night. Or perhaps he hadn't pieced it together after all.

As Eva wound down, I could sense him glancing in my direction, eager for action. I was forming a plan. It would require his help. But when the time came, he wasn't going to have any part of it.

Cheka business, family business. My business to take care of.

Eva stopped talking and looked at the sandwich in her hand, as if she'd forgotten how it got there. She took a bite and chewed, took another and chewed that, but I doubt she tasted a thing. She'd kept her story bottled up for half her life, her secret—I wondered whether even Polina knew the whole tale. Now that she'd told it, she'd cut herself adrift. Disoriented, disconnected, she'd lost track of where she was. Petrovin sensed the same thing and went to the bed and put his arm around her again. She looked up at him, unsure at first—of him, of herself—then she buried her face in his chest and cried. He waited until the sobbing slowed, then disengaged himself. A few minutes later, she was asleep. He and I went next door.

"Murdering bastard," Petrovin said, not bothering to hide his anger.

I couldn't argue. I felt the dull ache of loss, as I had the previous night, mixed up with the pains of my other wounds. Friendship masks, loyalty blinds, and I was guilty of both.

"I have one question," I said as calmly as I could. "He set that fire last night to mirror the fire in the barn. Eva was going to watch her mother burned alive, just like her father. If she didn't die, the trauma would drive her over the edge."

"The one person who can place him at the dacha that day. She knows he murdered Kosokov."

"How did he know she was in the barn? How did he know to stage that fire?"

"Easy," Petrovin said. "The Cheka had the whole place wired. We found the bugs in the house. I bet they did the barn, too. If he didn't know at the time, he did when he listened to the tape."

That sounded right. Suddenly I felt my own rage rising, as much at the calculated premeditation—against a child—as at the heinousness of the crimes themselves.

"I need a favor, some help from your pal Ivanov."

He arched an eyebrow. "I don't know. I can't—"

"You can try. For Eva as well as for me. Tell him Polina's dead. Eva, too. The papers reported one victim, in critical condition. Ivanov can break the story that there were two—and they didn't make it. Tell him that fallout shelter was an old KGB meeting place in the 1980s."

He gave me a long look. "I'll try. But what are you hoping to achieve?"

"I would have thought that was obvious—flush a badger from his lair."

"And then?"

"Haven't got that far yet," I lied. "Right now, we need to take Eva to talk to Coyle. She has to sooner or later, and I need her to support my story and get them off my back. Meet me downtown and we'll figure out how to get into the hospital to see her mother, assuming she's still alive."

Or he could. I'd be doing something else entirely.

329

Bernie had yet another lawyer meet Eva and me at the FBI's offices. Coyle was mildly surprised I'd delivered on my promise and was almost friendly until Bernie's lawyer arrived and started making demands on behalf of his client. Coyle threw me out. I didn't blame him.

"Russky! Where's cutie?" Pig Pen squawked as soon as he saw me.

"Busy right now, Pig Pen. Maybe she'll be by later."

"Hot number!"

Petrovin had moved quickly and Ivanov even faster. A new post on Ibansk.com couldn't have been more than a few minutes old. I took in the substance. They'd done their work well. The recipient would feel one step from liberation. He didn't know I was that step. Not for sure—yet.

MURDER MOST FIERY

Anyone who had any doubt of the Cheka's long reach (Ivanov's not one), read on. The Sword and the Shield and the flamethrower claimed two more victims last night—in a former Cheka safe haven in New York City.

Ivanov's network reports this particular inferno took place in a Cold War fallout shelter under one of New York's most famous bridges—named after borough Brooklyn—that was once used by enterprising Chekist spies as a secret meeting hall. Polina Barsukova—long known to followers of Ibanskian intrigue—was one victim. Roasted on a kerosene-soaked funeral pyre. But wait! The Cheka's cruelty knows no borders. Polina's daughter, Eva, was lured into igniting the blaze. It roasted her mother—she made it through the night but died this morning—and snuffed her young life as well. New York authorities have clamped on a tight lid, but Ivanov's sources know no borders either.

What does the Cheka want? Why take such chances? Murder in Moscow is an organizational right—at least in the eyes of its perpetrators—but American authorities won't necessarily see it that way.

Then again, maybe the re-emboldened Sword and Shield is so confident that the flamethrower doesn't care.

I had to admire Ivanov's editorializing—"Murder in Moscow is an organizational right"—but it wouldn't register where it counted. Ivanov spoke truth to the powers that couldn't see it anymore. In a society where murder had long been an organizational right, that was one reason Ibansk.com had achieved the status it had among the rest of us.

On the other hand, the facts, the details, they would register—at least where I wanted them to. The shelter, the kerosene, the fire, the booby-trapped door—they comprised the message I was sending. He'd have to assume I was the source. Time to make sure my message was received.

I went down to the street and walked a few blocks north until I found a pay phone. I dialed Brighton Beach and put a folded paper towel over the mouthpiece.

"Read Ibansk."

★ CHAPTER 44 ★

The empty construction site at John F. Kennedy International Airport wasn't as cool or pretty as Central Park had been ten days before—but it was as good a place as any again to contemplate irony and fate. The roar of aircraft above the *Valdez,* parked in a rain-rutted access road, provided a backdrop of white noise. The airport hummed with early-evening activity, but my spot was empty and lifeless—the reason I'd chosen it. Whatever happened later, I didn't want any witnesses.

Play the cards you're dealt, I'd told Petrovin. Here's one that'll change your hand, he told me. Play it straight, Victoria said, and play according to Coyle. Sometimes the straight fills or you draw that fourth queen. This wasn't one of them. However the hand played out tonight, nobody was going to be happy with the outcome, except perhaps to still be alive.

Ivanov turned out to be prescient in one respect—Polina hadn't made it. She'd slipped off into her own netherworld, without regaining consciousness. Probably just as well. The pain would have been unbearable, and the sight of her mutilated face would have sent her screaming into lunacy. I felt more anger than sorrow. She'd done her best to ruin my life and done an excellent job, but no one deserved the fate she got, and neither God nor predetermination had a damned thing to do with it.

I'd called Petrovin with the news. There was a long pause before he said in a quiet voice that he'd tell Eva, if that was okay with me. I told him to go ahead and felt even worse when I lied about meeting them back at the Holiday Inn.

It was still light when I got to the airport. I drove around the loop road twice before I found what I wanted—a construction site for a new terminal, I didn't care whose, locked up for the night. I pulled into the access road, cluttered with building materials and debris, parked to one side, and put a Homeland Security card—the companion to my forged ID—on the dashboard, just in case. The Basilisk had told me what I needed to know. Air France flight 9, departing JFK at 11:00 P.M., connecting at Charles de Gaulle with AF 2244 to Moscow, had a new passenger. I'd joined the evening rush hour into Queens.

I keep the trunk of the *Valdez* stocked with tools likely to come in handy, such as wire cutters. As dusk lowered, I used a pair to open a hole in the chain-link fence behind a construction trailer and took a stroll around. Hot, muggy, muddy. The steel frame of the new terminal was silhouetted against the hazy orange-gray sky. Looked as though the building would follow the curve of an airplane wing, rising from maybe two stories in the back to four or five in the front. A concrete floor had been poured at ground level, covering half the space; the rest was still open to the gaping foundation below. The site itself was mud and earth, mounded and rutted by rain and trucks.

I needed a place to wait and watch, out of sight, and I found what I wanted in a row of giant concrete pipe sections, easily eight feet in diameter, not far from the building. I could stand inside any one, invisible in shadows and the darkening night, with a clear view to the fence. With luck, the pipes would echo, too, and he might not be able to tell where I was. We'd get to that in due course—or so I hoped.

My watch read 8:02. Time to make the call, before he got here. I punched in the number. He answered on the third ring.

"We need to talk," I said.

"About what? I'm on my way home. I'm sick of this place."

"I know. I'm at JFK. You've got plenty of time."

"How did you know . . . Where are you?"

"Construction site between Terminals Seven and Eight. There's a little access road on your right as you come along. You'll see my car, black Ford Crown Victoria."

"We can't meet in the terminal, like normal people?"

"I have people looking for me, official people, thanks to you and last night." The best kind of lie—plausible and uncheckable.

"What is it we need to discuss—in such clandestine fashion?"

"I have what you want."

That stopped him cold. I think he muted the phone—the silence was complete, no background noise, just ether hum, for a good thirty seconds, maybe more. When he spoke again, his voice had changed, hardened.

"What makes you think so?"

"Gorbenko, Kosokov, Polina, Eva. They all died for it." The hook set, I could feel it. "Three hundred other Russians died, too, for what? Putin? A war? The Cheka? They included Rislyakov's parents, by the way. At Guryanova Street. You missed that. Not like you."

He bit. Hard. "Stay where you are. I'm half an hour away."

"There's a hole in the fence behind the construction trailer. I'll be inside."

He hung up. I walked back to the *Valdez,* retrieved an aluminum baseball bat from the trunk, leaned against the back side of the trailer, and waited.

Thirty-two minutes later, a car pulled into the access road, headlights off. It rolled up behind the *Valdez,* and the driver cut the engine. The noise of traffic and planes hadn't lessened. The doors stayed closed, no one moved, nothing happened for five more minutes. Then two of Lachko's men climbed out. The driver came in my direction, and the other went behind the car. I moved deeper into the shadows.

The driver passed by me and went through the fence. His colleague lifted a flat canister out of his trunk, the size of a small trash can lid, and approached the *Valdez*. He put the canister on the ground and knelt over it. I covered the distance between us in half a dozen steps. He heard me when I was six feet away and got out a yelp before the aluminum bat caught the side of his face. He fell forward into a muddy puddle. I pulled him to one side so he wouldn't drown and examined the bomb he was about to attach to the underside of the *Valdez*. They'd come prepared. I searched the man until I found a small radio detonation device. I put that in my pocket, took the Glock automatic he was carrying, and crouched behind the car. The other man returned a few minutes later. When he saw his partner, he ran forward, adding force when I stood and swung the bat into his gut. He doubled over and collapsed. I grabbed duct tape from my trunk and bound his ankles and wrists. I did the same to his unconscious colleague and dragged him to the back of their car. It was open. The utility light reflected off two ugly machine pistols with big silencers. I removed the clips, tossed the guns aside, and lifted the comatose weight into the trunk. I returned to the driver, who was trying to relearn how to breathe. A search of his pockets yielded another Glock and a cell phone. I hefted the car bomb and dropped it on his chest, dealing his lesson a setback. Yards of duct tape later, it was strapped securely to his midsection. He could almost breathe again, but he was shaking with terror.

I held out his cell phone. "Here's what's going to happen," I said in Russian. "We're going to make a call. To your boss. You're going to talk. Then I'm putting you in the car and going inside with this." I held up the detonator. The eyes told me all I needed to know. "Say the right words, and he shows up here, you live, maybe. Say the wrong ones, he doesn't show, in ten minutes I push the button. Ten minutes. That's all you get."

He nodded hard.

"Number?"

He reeled off ten digits in Russian. I punched them into the phone and held it to the side of his head. He spoke fast. "The cinema's open, the movie starts soon," he said.

I had to assume that was code for all clear. He was too scared to lie. I put one more piece of tape over his mouth and shoved him toward the back of his car. A judicious tap with the bat, and he fell over into the trunk. I lifted in his legs and slammed the lid.

I used his phone to call Brighton Beach. One more check, to be sure. Lachko came on immediately. "What the fuck now?"

"Your men fucked up. You should have sent competent people, not useless old cunts." I used *urki* slang.

"What the fuck are you talking about? I didn't send anyone anywhere."

"Just checking."

I cut the connection and got my vest out of the *Valdez*. I put it on under my jacket. It added to the heat of the night, but I ignored that. With a quick look around, I returned to the row of outsized pipe sections to wait, Eva's story running around in my mind.

★ CHAPTER 45 ★

She and her mother had moved out of the apartment they shared with Lachko a few months before the fire. Eva wasn't sorry—Polina and Lachko had been fighting continuously for half a year. They were staying at their dacha in the Valdai Hills, which Eva didn't like because there was little to do compared with Moscow. She was having trouble fitting into her new school, both educationally (she was at least a year ahead of everyone else) and socially. They were also spending a lot of time with Uncle Tolik, as she knew him, and she wasn't sure how she felt about that. She had picked up on his signals. Most of the time, he didn't want her around, and he was sending those signals that day, even before the stranger arrived.

She went out to the barn with the doll she called Lena, despite the cold and snow. She was still exploring all the rooms and spaces of the old structure, which had horse stalls and haylofts, a workshop, garage bays and a warren of under-rooms that smelled like pigs. She was upstairs in the hayloft when Mom and Uncle Tolik and the stranger came in. The man came in first, then her mother carrying the shotgun. Uncle Tolik trailed behind as if he wanted to be somewhere else. Her mother made the man open the trapdoor—something Eva hadn't discovered yet.

The blast from the gun was so loud she thought the whole barn had exploded. She hadn't seen it, since she'd ducked behind the hayloft wall. When she peeked over, the stranger was gone. Her mother still held the gun. Had she fired? Where was the other man? Her mother and Uncle Tolik argued. She was too shocked and scared to remember the specifics. She heard her name—they didn't know where she was. No way she could come out now, they'd both be mad at her. Her mother said she was going back to their dacha to pick up some things. Then she'd come back here and they'd all leave. Eva didn't know where they were going—or why. She decided to wait right where she was until her mother got back. She was scared of Uncle Tolik and what he might do if he found out where she'd been.

She was watching for her mother's return, out the hayloft window, when she saw another car pull in, a big limousine. She saw the driver shoot the caretaker as he came out to greet them. Now she was really scared. Then he got out of the car. The man her mother had taught her to fear above all others. "He hates you, as he hates me," she told her whenever she mentioned his name. "Never trust him. Never trust any Chekist. He wants to see you boiled alive."

She went looking for a better hiding place.

She was near the horse stalls on the main floor when the door opened and the light came on. The Chekist came in with Uncle Tolik. She saw the gun in his hand and ducked into a stall. She was afraid she'd been spotted, but he didn't come to look.

The Chekist had a bottle, and he made Uncle Tolik drink. Again and again. He kept asking the same questions—"Where are the CDs? Where are the copies you made?"—over and over. Uncle Tolik wouldn't answer. The Chekist got madder and madder. Uncle Tolik threw up. She could remember the smell. The Chekist hit him with the gun and kicked him on the floor. Then he came toward her.

She thought she'd been discovered. She climbed through a loose board into the stall next door. The gun fired. She heard the *crack* and the thud of the bullet as it sank into the wood—right where she'd been. He must have seen her. No. He walked on, into the garage. Terrified, she wanted to run, but even if she made it out of the barn without getting caught—a big if in her nine-year-old mind—where would she go? She huddled in a dark corner, behind an old hay trough. She couldn't see what happened next. She heard the Chekist doing something, then smelled the petrol. He went back to the garage—she heard him go past a second time—and the petrol smell got stronger.

Finally, he spoke again, still asking about the CDs. Uncle Tolik's voice was faint, but somehow she knew he wasn't telling. After a minute, the Chekist said, "I'm going to light a match. I estimate you'll have five minutes. Shout if you change your mind."

She heard Tolik's answer this time.

"Fuck off. You're just another Cheka killer."

She came out of her hiding place and saw the fire encircling the barn. She remembered that clearly—it was like a train, the fiery engine racing along an invisible track. Behind it flames climbed the old wooden walls. In seconds, she was surrounded.

She ran to Uncle Tolik, who was tied to one of the wooden columns supporting the barn's roof.

"Eva! What the hell? Get out of here! Quick!"

She ignored him and pulled at the ropes. The heavy knots were too much for her little fingers.

"Eva! Find a knife or saw. Something sharp!"

She ran around the barn, but there was nothing she could use. The fire had already blocked off the workshop.

She went back to Kosokov and pulled at the knots again.

"Eva! Listen to me, you can't do it. Run, while you still have time. Run!"

She ignored him. The fire had enveloped the walls. She remembered the searing heat as it started to spread across the roof. Kosokov must have used his hip to push her away as burning wood and shingle fell where she had stood. It exploded as it hit the ground, and a chunk landed in her lap. Her skirt was aflame in an instant. Panicked, she ran in circles, only serving to fan the flames.

"In the hay! Jump in the hay!" Kosokov called. She did as he said. The pain was like nothing she'd ever felt. When she stopped rolling around, she wasn't burning anymore, but the hay was. There was nowhere that wasn't aflame. She had no idea anything could be this hot.

"Eva! Do this for me. Please. For your mother. The shelter. Over there. The trapdoor. Go down there and close the door. It's your only chance. Now, child! Please!"

Another piece of roof fell, this one striking Uncle Tolik on the head. He slumped sideways, the ropes holding him up as his clothes started to burn. Another load of burning wood and shingle fell next to her. The hay pile was a bonfire.

She did as Uncle Tolik said. She heard the roar of the roof giving way just after she pulled the door closed.

It was hot, but nothing like aboveground. Her legs felt like they were still aflame. She slipped on the stairs and fell, landing on the stranger's body. His dead eyes stared at her. She screamed and screamed and screamed. There was no one to hear her but him.

She had no idea how long she was down there. All she remembered was her burning legs. She found some water and poured that on, which helped a little, but the pain wouldn't let up. Eventually, she thought, she just passed out. She didn't remember anything until the trapdoor opened and she screamed again, certain the Chekist had come back for her.

"Eva! Oh my God! Eva!"

It was her mother. Polina carried her up to the smoldering ruin, the snow, and the dark night above. Eva's memory was of a full moon, dark gray and hostile behind the black clouds blowing across the sky.

Her mother took her to the house and tried to treat her with snow and creams, but the skin was already twisted and discolored, and it stank. Eva threw up.

The rest was a blur. Her mother gave her something to drink—doubtless laced—and they drove for hours. She didn't get medical attention until two days later, the first of several attempts to deal with what must have been second- or third-degree burns to her thighs. Somewhere along their journey, Polina informed Eva that Lachko wasn't her real father, that it was the man she hadn't been able to save from the inferno. I don't often give Polina credit for kindness, but I do believe she was trying to help. The main thing she accomplished, of course, was to pile an unbearable failure onto the already hopeless guilt of a nine-year-old child. She started stuttering a few months later.

★ CHAPTER 46 ★

He arrived at nine twenty-four. I heard the car pull in and stop, the engine cut off. One door opened and closed. A minute later, he stooped through the hole in the fence. He was wearing a suit and tie. His hands were empty. He stopped a few feet inside and tried to scan the building site. His eyes weren't as well adjusted to the dark as mine. I let him look for a minute before I called from inside one of the pipe sections.

"Hello, Iakov."

He turned and moved toward the noise, stumbling once or twice on the uneven ground. He couldn't see me. When he was about twenty feet away, I said, "That's far enough."

He stopped. "Where are you? Show yourself."

"Maybe in time."

"What do you want?"

"An accounting, to begin with."

"Accounting? Of what?"

"Apartment bombings, Kosokov, Polina, Eva, Rislyakov, last night. You choose where to start."

"You're talking rubbish. You said you have something."

"That's right. The file Rislyakov lifted from Polina's computer. Kosokov's Rosnobank file."

Even twenty feet away in the dark, I could see him stiffen.

"You've examined this file?" he said.

"Yes. I also know about Gorbenko. He was wearing a wire that day, a CPS wire. You missed that, too. Sloppy."

He swore under his breath. I moved two pipes away, staying in the shadows. I'd been right about the echo. My voice bounced all around.

"What do you want, Turbo? What's the point?"

"An accounting, like I said. I want to hear what happened. In your words. You're the only one who knows the whole story."

"You mean, you want a confession?"

"The Cheka has always excelled at those. Why not? You and I both know there isn't going to be any trial. The Cheka would never allow it. *You'd* never allow it."

"Then I repeat—what's the point?"

"I lied for you twenty years ago, because you gave me a chance. I lied for the Cheka, because I took an oath. I'm prepared to hand over Kosokov's file, and you can bury it along with him and Gorbenko. But I want to hear what happened. That's my price."

"There are things about you I've never understood, Turbo. Probably never will. Come out here where we can talk face-to-face."

"I'll stay where I am."

"I mean you no harm."

"And the two *urki* with their machine pistols and car bomb?"

"Shit! Those were Lachko's men. I told him—"

"The blinders have been removed, Iakov. You took them off yourself, last night, with the box cutter, the kerosene, and the fire. Tell the story." I changed pipes again.

He looked at the ground and shook his head. He spoke without raising it.

"It was a fuckup, a giant fuckup, from the start. Patrushev's operation—he said he had Putin's blessing. I never found out for sure. A number of us opposed it—if the goal was war with the Chechens, there were other ways. If the goal was to make Putin president, that would happen in due course. But some of my colleagues were impatient—he was one—and they had to have their way.

"Patrushev actually got the idea from the Chechens. They planted a bomb in July in Krasnodar. Didn't go off, faulty timer. We caught the bombers, they confessed, they named names, and they were dealt with. We took out the whole hierarchy, almost got to Maskhadov himself. Patrushev realized what would have happened if it had exploded, the public outcry, the demand for revenge—it was a way to achieve a goal he'd been after a long time. He took over where the Chechens left off. Gorbenko was his choice to run the operation. We already knew he was a problem for us, but he had the expertise and he was a known go-between with the Chechens. When it was over, we could expose him as a Chechen agent and toss him to the wolves."

I listened in my pipe section, glad he could not see my face. I probably could have covered my surprise, but any little tic, he would have spotted it. It wasn't the lie that shocked. I was prepared for that. It was the indifference with which he told it—and the realization that he'd been doing so for as long as I'd known him. I should have spotted that years ago, had I been looking.

"You know the rest," he said. "Bombs in that mall, Buynaksk, Pechatniki, the Kashirskoye Highway. Then Gorbenko got cold feet. He bungled the job in Kapotnya. It didn't matter by that point. The outcry was everything Patrushev wanted. Even the fuckup in Ryazan—and his foolish statements—couldn't undermine it."

I had a minor epiphany as I switched pipes again. Iakov—the ultimate Cheka puppetmaster—had sent Patrushev out to try to deflect accusations against the Cheka, and he'd done it with a claim of innocence he knew full well would meet with disbelief bordering on incredulity.

Iakov was still talking. "There were factions within the organization, as always, but we came together, as we do when we're under attack. No one could prove anything. I thought we were out of the woods. Then Kosokov's problems started.

"We'd done business with that bastard for years, since '92. He was stupid and greedy—easy to manipulate. I never trusted him, though, so we kept watch. Office, apartment, dacha, all wired. That's how I knew about Polina. We thought he'd weathered the financial storm in '98, but he'd been adept at hiding his losses. He made the same stupid bets as everyone else. The bank's balance sheet was in tatters. Only a matter of time until it failed—which would bring in auditors, the Ministry of Finance, that bastard Churnin, and who knows what they'd find?"

"That's not true—you knew exactly."

"Fair enough. So, yes, we set the fire at Rosnobank Tower. We took care the backup data center. I figured Kosokov would make a run for it, and we'd get him at the border, which would look good at the trial. I knew Gorbenko would turn anywhere to save his worthless skin, but the one place I didn't count on was the CPS. They were impotent—not a factor, not even a consideration."

Cheka arrogance.

"I heard Gorbenko at the dacha that day—on the tape. I heard him and Kosokov discussing another set of records. I listened to Polina kill him. She shot him in cold blood, if you don't know. Kosokov didn't have the balls to do it himself."

"You set the fire?"

"What?"

"The fire in the barn. The fire that killed Kosokov. The fire that almost killed Eva."

He took a step forward and peered through the night in my direction. His eyes would be adjusting. He was also buying time to think. I moved deeper into the pipe.

"Why don't you just tell me what you want me to confess to, Turbo? Then I can catch my plane."

That's the way it worked in the old days. The interrogator dictated the confession. The only thing the confessor caught was a bullet—in the back of the skull. "The fire, the barn—you burned Kosokov alive."

I couldn't make out his face, but I sensed worry, maybe even fear, for the first time.

"I set the fire, yes. I needed the CDs, the bank records he copied. For the Cheka. It never occurred to me he'd die before he talked. I always thought he was a weak man."

"And Eva?"

"I had no idea she was there."

"And if you had?"

"Turbo! What the fuck is the point? Shall I just confess to every supposed crime of every Chekist right now? Will that satisfy you?"

"Keep going. What happened next?"

"I followed Polina to her dacha. Just missed her. Maybe we passed on the road. It was snowing hard by then. I went back to Kosokov's, but travel was slow. She'd come and gone. She slipped through our fingers.

"She'd put what was left of Kosokov in the shelter with Gorbenko. I left them. Better to have everyone asking what happened to the crooked banker than how the crooked banker got burned to death. Once we had Polina, we could discover the bodies and hang both murders around her neck. I never stopped looking, like I told you, but she covered her tracks well. In my mind, it was still unfinished business, and it looked more and more like it would remain unfinished. I'd almost written it off until one day she called—out of the blue."

"She called you? When?"

"December, just before Christmas."

Shit! I was the one who was sloppy. I'd missed that. The Basilisk had served it up, and I'd ignored it. The trips to Hammersmith. She'd gone expressly to make untraceable calls to Iakov. She'd gone straight to the source with her blackmail threat. The one man who had everything to lose from exposure. That's why she'd been so scared. Lachko she could handle. Iakov—she knew better.

He said, "She had the file. Kosokov had hidden the CDs in Eva's stuff. She demanded a hundred million! Polina was never shy."

"So the six hundred million you told me she stole, that was another lie."

"Polina could never get enough. She was the most venal—"

"I've heard that speech, Iakov. I was married to her for eight years, remember?"

"If you know so much, why are you asking?"

"Keep talking."

"Rislyakov set up the payment system. He was supposed to find out who and where she was."

"Wait a minute. How'd you know about Rislyakov? I thought you and Lachko weren't talking."

"As I asked the other day, what kind of jackass do you take me for?"

Of course. He had his own man—or men—inside Lachko's organization.

"You're right about Rislyakov's parents. I didn't check that, until later, after he disappeared. He was another one—he thought he could outwit the Cheka. Sooner or later, they all learn—you take on the Cheka, you take on the whole organization. Something you might want to bear in mind."

"Keep going."

"He was clever. Took a couple of months to catch up. We pegged him in Moscow last month, right before he came back here. I took the next flight and went to the place on Greene Street. That's where you came in."

I checked my vest and came out of the pipe. "You shot him, didn't you?" I said as I came close. "He was going to put the bite on you. You didn't follow him. He invited you. You gambled that the file was on his computer, or if it wasn't, no one would find it with him dead. So you killed him as soon as he opened the door."

"If I did, where was the gun? And who shot me?"

"Polina's husband's driver. He arrived at just the wrong time. You'd pulled Ratko into the back hall. Left the door open. He came in after, saw the blood, just like I did. He surprised you, you shot at him, missed, he shot you. He was taking your gun when Eva fired through the door and hit him. They exchanged blind fire, and he left while he still could. You passed out until, as you say, I came in."

"That's a fanciful story."

I was a few feet away. He looked old. He looked tired. The blue eyes still burned defiant.

"You shot Ratko, yes or no?"

"If it makes you happy, yes. Cheka honor was at stake. The only person who will truly miss him is Lachko. *That* should make you happy."

Lachko and Eva. "Move to last night."

"What about it?"

"The scene at the fallout shelter—why? You tortured her, you destroyed her life, then you set it up for her daughter to finish her off—and burn to death herself, too. You hated her, I understand that. She crossed the Cheka, I understand that, too. But why go to all that trouble?"

"I believe this interrogation is over. I have nothing more to say, and I do have a plane to catch. I'll take the records now. How did you find them, by the way?"

"Not quite yet." I took the SIG Pro from my vest pocket. "Raise your hands."

He laughed. "Turbo, such melodrama. You've been in this decadent country too long. You think you're Clint Eastwood."

"No drama, Iakov. Hands up."

He raised them slowly, still smiling. I ran my free hand over his suit. A Beretta in the waistband, which I tossed aside. The cell phone was in his breast pocket.

"Hands down now," I said as I dialed the office. Foos answered right away. "This the phone that called Eva last night?"

"Give me thirty seconds." He came back on in twenty-five. "That's it."

"From Front and Dover?" I said, eyes on Iakov. The smile narrowed.

"That's right," Foos said.

"Can you testify to that, under oath?"

"If that's what you need, sure. He used a carrier that's easy to track."

"That's exactly what I need."

I pocketed the phone. "There'll never be a trial in Moscow, that's true—but there will be one here, maybe two. One for the murder of Ratko Risly. You've confessed to that. And one for the murder of Polina."

The grin was back. "You left out Eva."

"Eva didn't die. I was with her. I opened the door and triggered the booby trap. I tried to save Polina, but she was already too far gone."

"You'll have to do better than that, Turbo. You were in Brighton Beach."

"That was a good trick you pulled, with Mulholland. But I got back early, and I had help. Eva would have opened that door. Someone stopped her."

"Help? Who?"

Iakov didn't know about Petrovin. That was good for Petrovin. "A friend, a Russian friend. He's close to Ivanov."

The smile disappeared.

"That piece today . . ."

"I can play tricks, too."

"This is pointless, Turbo. Like a Politburo debate. We all knew the outcome before we started. A phone call is nothing. Give me those records. I want to catch my plane."

"You shouldn't have come here, Iakov. You should have stayed at home, where you're untouchable—but there was too much at stake, wasn't there?"

"I told you, Cheka honor."

"No. That's not it. Never was. This is about the Cheka, but it's more about you. The apartment bombings were never Patrushev's operation—they were yours. Gorbenko didn't report to him, he reported to you. You didn't have Putin's okay—you were too wily to ask for it, he was too cautious to give it. All went well until Gorbenko realized he was on a one-way trip to his grave. Somebody must've made a mistake. Could even have been you. Doesn't matter now. It all began to come apart with Ryazan. You had to fix it—to save your own skin. You went back to cover your tracks. You got most of them—Kosokov, the bank, Gorbenko, you probably doctored the files to make Patrushev appear responsible—but you missed two. Kosokov copied the records. And Eva. She was in the barn. She saw you. She watched you set the fire that killed Kosokov and almost killed her. That night at Greene Street was the first time she'd seen you since she was nine years old. No wonder she was terrified. Even doped up silly, she knew you'd come back for her."

"You can't prove—"

"It's the reason you worked over Polina the way you did. You needed the girl. You needed Polina to make that call. From what I could see, she held out as long as she could—longer. Whatever else you say about her, she loved Eva."

"You still can't prove anything."

"You forget. I have Kosokov's records. The one unmolested set. The ones he hid, you couldn't find, and Polina took with her. The ones that made her go to you in December when she needed money. She saw what I saw. Kosokov covered his ass. He made sure every transaction was client-approved. The client doing the approving is you, Iakov. ChK22—that's your Cheka designation. She knew enough to recognize it. So did I."

He took a step back. It might have been the darkness, or my imagination, but the blue eyes turned color, closer to Lachko's gray. "What do you want? Money? Position? Rehabilitation?"

I shook my head. "I'm not a Chekist anymore, Iakov. I'm just an old *zek* trying to make my way. I was reminded recently about the light of day. I want this whole affair to be seen in the light of day. That's why there's going to be a trial. Here. A jury may well decide there's not enough evidence to convict, but the world—including Russia—will get to see what happened, in 1999, in those apartment buildings, at Rosnobank, in that barn, at Greene Street, last night under the Brooklyn Bridge. Russians will gain a little better idea who runs their country and how they came to be there. I'm not naive, I don't expect much to change—but we've spent too long hiding under a cloak of secrecy and deceit. Tsarist cloak, Bolshevik, Stalinist, Chekist, doesn't matter. They're all the same. I'm pulling this one off so everyone can see. That's what I want."

"SERGEI!"

"I'm right here," a new voice said from behind. "Drop the gun, shit-for-brains. Only thing pulled gonna be this trigger."

Sergei stepped out of the same pipe section I'd been standing in a few minutes before, his big frame just visible against the wall of darkness behind. He held a silenced machine pistol at his hip, like the ones in the car. I let the SIG fall from my hand.

"Move away from him," Sergei said. "Over there."

"No."

"Turbo, don't be stupid," Iakov said. "There's no point now. You played out your hand. You lost. Game over."

He ran his hands over me and pulled out the hard drive, the

recording device in my vest, the detonator, and his cell phone and mine. He picked up my gun and moved away.

"Clint Eastwood," he said. "Nobility is a fool's pursuit. If you're lucky, you end up a dead hero. Usually you just end up dead. Especially when you're stubborn.

"Just so we're clear, not that it will matter. Lachko knows nothing of this. Sergei has worked for me for years. Long before Lachko. I recruited him into the Cheka, like you. I flattered you at the hospital, when I said you were the best. Loyalty's the ultimate test, Turbo. I thought you'd learned that back in 1988."

I wasn't ready to fold. Not yet. "I'm not stupid, Iakov. You trained me, remember. I copied that hard drive. It's in a safe place. Anything happens . . ."

"You're bluffing. I don't blame you, it's all you have left. Even if you're not, I'll take that chance. I'll be back in Moscow. Sergei will be in Brighton Beach. The girl . . . things happen, as we know. But no one will be able to put together the story you have, however fanciful. A nick to the Cheka's pride, perhaps. We've endured worse."

He was right, of course. There would never be a trial in Moscow. Mulholland might try to protect Eva, but he didn't begin to understand what he was up against. Polina was right to be paranoid. I, on the other hand, had been stupid and, worse than that, arrogant, thinking I could do this myself.

"I'm sorry it worked out like this, Turbo. You always had this streak, you know, I saw it way back when you started with the Cheka. I thought you were smart, you'd learn how the world works, you'd adapt. After all, you'd survived all those years in the camps—you must have learned something. I was wrong. You didn't learn. You had a chance in '88. You made the right decision then. It was difficult, I know, but you overcame your misguided instincts and did what was best for yourself, your friends, the organization. I see now that was an aberration. You did what you did for whatever reason, but you hadn't changed at all."

There it was. For me anyway, the final Russian irony. Absolution on my execution ground—from my executioner. I'd die, if not happy, without sin.

"I have to get my plane," he said. "Good-bye, Turbo. I wish it had been different, I mean that."

He started for the hole in the fence.

"Not yet," a new voice said.

"WATCH OUT—IN THE PIPES!" I dove at Iakov. Sergei's machine pistol flashed, and the fire was returned from in front. No noise, just deadly muzzle flame. Iakov sidestepped my lunge and turned toward the intruder, bringing up my SIG. Sergei's muzzle fire arced upward and disappeared. Iakov was lining up a shot in the dark.

"NO!" I dove again, from my knees, knowing I was too late.

More fire. The force of the slugs threw him back into me. I caught the body and we fell backward into the mud. He was dead before we got there.

I sat in the muck holding his corpse. I felt motion to my right and heard running feet. A minute or two passed before Petrovin walked out of the darkness, dressed in black, head to toe. He held up his own machine gun. "Would have intervened sooner, but it took a while to find the clips for this thing. Next time leave them in one place. Dead?" he said.

"You hit him square."

"Big guy, too."

My head was spinning. "How'd you find me?"

"Victoria—and your friend with the hair. She got him to trace your cell phone. He pegged the call you made to Iakov. I convinced them to let me handle it, but I suspect the police aren't far behind. Victoria—well, you know how patient she is. I heard that speech, by the way, the one about the trial and the cloak, while I was looking for the clip. You'd better watch that idealistic streak. Might cause you to fold prematurely."

He was smiling. I couldn't respond. My mind was still on the dead man in my lap. All the emotions fought with each other—sorrow, anger, resentment, doubt—mostly aimed at myself.

"He was going to kill you," Petrovin said.

"I know. I could have stopped—"

"No. You did what you had to. And you didn't change a thing. Not as far as he's concerned."

"I don't follow."

"If I hadn't killed him tonight, I would have sometime soon, back in Moscow."

A bell rang in my head. It pointed to something I should see but couldn't quite make out.

"That doesn't sound like you," I said. "Why?"

"You don't know? Polina was my mother."

★ CHAPTER 47 ★

Too much to process, and no time.

One imperative—get Petrovin on a plane. If the Cheka got wind of his presence on this killing ground, he'd be a dead man the moment he set foot on a Moscow street, maybe sooner. No one could know he'd been here—ever.

I pulled Iakov's airline ticket from his pocket—miraculously, it hadn't been shredded. He was still traveling as Andropov. He had a passport in the same name. I held both out to Petrovin. "Exchange the ticket, take a ride home on the Cheka. Dump the passport in Paris. I'll take care of things here."

He looked skeptical. "How are you going to do that?"

"I'll think of something. If you don't go now, you won't anytime soon. We both know what that means. Leave the machine gun. Dump this cell phone, too—with the passport. It doesn't mean anything now. There's a Beretta over there. Iakov's."

He found the pistol while I laid Iakov on the ground. We moved outside the fence.

I tossed the detonator and pistol in the backseat of the Lincoln. "There are two of Lachko's men and a bomb in the trunk."

"You've been busy."

"But not smart. Thanks for saving my skin."

"The first ex-Chekist should live long enough to learn what it feels like."

I gave him the hard drive. "Take this. Kosokov's bank records—but you know as well as I do, the Cheka will never allow a trial, not a real one."

He nodded. "They squelched the official investigation back then."

"Your friend Ivanov won't feel so constrained."

He smiled. "I can almost guarantee that."

I got some rags out of the back of the *Valdez.* "You'd better move. I've got some rearranging to do, before the police arrive."

"Do you . . . do you ever visit Moscow?"

"Had a trip planned a couple weeks ago, before events intervened." That seemed like a different era.

"Look me up next time. You'll find me—"

"I know," I said. "I know everything I need to. Get going. I hear sirens, and I've got work to do before they get here."

That was a lie, but certainly a short-lived one. He had to realize the truth, too—neither of us wanted to broach the subject. There'd be time enough later—if he got on the plane and I stayed out of jail.

He held out his hand, and I took it. I wanted more than anything to pull him to me, but I gave him a firm grip, avoiding his eye, looking past his shoulder to the main road.

"Go."

He went. I watched him trot out to the service road and disappear into darkness. I ran back with the rags to wipe down the machine gun he'd used, work Iakov's prints over it, and help the lifeless hands fire a quick burst into the mud. I laid the body down again. The sirens came into range shortly after.

★ CHAPTER 48 ★

I stayed out of jail—but it was close.

I used one of the eight stories the naked city keeps retelling—this one, the falling-out among thieves over a girl, specifically Iakov and Sergei, who, in my version of the tale, was sweet on Polina and intent on revenge. Iakov foresaw that and lured him to JFK with two of Lachko's thugs waiting. Sergei anticipated the trap and disposed of the thugs, and he and Iakov fought a Cheka-*urki* duel to the death. I had phoned Iakov to say good-bye, and he had called me to Kennedy. I arrived too late to stop the bloodshed.

I needed one supporting fact. Just before the cops arrived, I got Foos and the Basilisk to tap into the Big Dick and adjust the location of my cell phone call to Iakov. Dzerzhinsky would have killed for that capability.

Tell a lie, but stick to the plot—one more proverb. I made up the plot and held on, all the way through the weekend. I doubt they believed me, but they didn't care much about a couple of dead Russians either. It helped that I was able to give them a front row ticket, as Foos put it, to Lachko's laundry. They'd be able to watch every dollar moving through Ratko's washing machines. It also helped that there was no one left to contradict me.

Except Victoria, who wasn't buying any of it. "Where's Petrovin?"

355

she asked, after Coyle and Sawicki finally let me go. "He said he was going to JFK. Where is he? Don't tell me you didn't see him. Don't tell me you don't know. I don't believe it."

We were sitting across from each other at the counter in my apartment. I was sipping vodka, my first in four days. She had a glass of wine.

Coyle and Sawicki hadn't asked about Petrovin, which meant they hadn't known to ask, which meant Victoria hadn't told them to ask, which meant that maybe she wasn't going to throw my ass in jail after all. Maybe. Once again, I found the idea of lying to her impossible. But I couldn't tell her what had happened either.

"I can't tell you," I said. "I can't tell anyone. Ever."

"Why not?"

"I just can't."

"You covering your ass or his or both?"

"It's complicated. Goes all the way back to the Gulag."

The glass was halfway to her mouth when the green eyes froze. She returned the wine to the counter. "Jesus Christ, he's your son, isn't he? The one you left with your wife."

I nodded.

"You told me his name once . . ." She pulled at memory. "Aleksei."

I nodded again.

"That's Petrovin's name, his real name—Aleksei. Aleksei Tiron. Wait . . . Polina was his mother!"

I could only sit there silently, filled with sadness and pain.

"Christ! How long have you known?"

"Since Thursday."

"Does he know—about you, I mean?"

"I think he's known longer than I have." I remembered his words almost a week ago—right here at this counter.

I couldn't help thinking you'd make a good father.

If we both live long enough to get to know each other better, I'll tell you the story. That might explain things. I'd like to hear yours, too. That could explain more.

"He did go to the airport, didn't he?" Victoria said. "He was at JFK."

"Don't ask me that."

356

I watched her work it out—she knew enough to put the story together and come out somewhere close to the truth. I sipped my vodka as I wondered what she'd do.

"I warned you—twice."

"I know."

"Remember that promise about not breaking my heart?"

"Yes."

"You're awfully damned close."

She went back to her thoughts.

I made a silent bet on her leaving.

I won.

"I might call tomorrow. More likely, I won't." She put down the empty glass, collected her stuff, and went. No kiss, just as she'd said. I didn't try to stop her.

The door closed, and I heard the elevator chime in the distance when it arrived to carry her off. I stayed right where I was, drinking alone at the counter where I'd told myself I didn't want to end up drinking alone. I didn't bother to question or rethink or look for options. There wasn't a damned thing I could do.

I poured another two fingers and put the bottle away.

Love's a bitch. But it's got nothing on that pig fate.

★ ACKNOWLEDGMENTS ★

Anyone interested in the history of the Gulag should read Anne Applebaum's absorbing and heartbreaking account, *Gulag: A History* (New York: Random House, 2003). The impact of the Gulag on the Russian psyche is movingly explored in *The Whisperers: Private Life in Stalin's Russia* by Orlando Figes (New York: Metropolitan Books, 2007). David Remnick's *Lenin's Tomb: The Last Days of the Soviet Empire* (New York: Random House, 1993) is a page-turning account of the fall of the Communist Party and the Soviet Union. *Spy Handler: Memoir of a KGB Officer* by Victor Cherkashin with Gregory Feifer describes the daily dealings, activities, and thoughts of a senior KGB officer stationed in the United States. Robert O'Harrow Jr. tells in quietly chilling fashion how everything we do these days is watched, recorded, and manipulated in *No Place to Hide* (New York: Free Press, 2005).

I am very fortunate to have had two terrific editors at Thomas Dunne Books: (in chronological order) John Schoenfelder and Brendan Deneen. I am grateful to both for their ideas, insights, assistance, and good cheer. My gratitude also to Tom Dunne.

Numerous people read and commented on various drafts of assorted stories that resulted in this one. I am grateful to all for their time and suggestions: Richard Bradley, Charles and Sandi Ellis, Sheila Geoghegan, Bill and Carmen Haberman, Cindy and Steve

Heymann, Bill Hicks, Bruce and Turi MacCombie, Myra Manning, Colin Nettelbeck, Dan Paladino, Jonathan Rinehart, John Sanchez, Elena Sansalone and Jan Van Meter, David Stack, Curt Swenson, Peter Standish, and Albert Zuckerman.

I must also thank a marvelous copy editor, India Cooper, who saved me from a multitude of mistakes.

Special thanks to Sarah Haberman. Extra-special thanks to Polly Paladino, whom I will never be able to thank enough.

Last in mention, but first in my heart, is my wife, Marcelline Thomson, who urged me to write this story and then had to put up with me while I did.